Praise for Elizabeth Boyce

Honor Among Thieves

"Intriguing and unique, with likable, human characters ... mixed with competition, sexually charged scenes, and danger, this latest from Boyce is highly recommended for historical romance lovers." —*Library Journal*

"... a romantic version of a very grim (or Grimm) fairytale where the danger and horror of the journey is balanced by the exquisite and hard-fought peace of the ending." —*Heroes and Heartbreakers*

"...an unflinching look at the violent part of the Regency rarely seen. Boyce's prose is magnificently gritty and heartfelt, imbuing this romantic suspense with the perfect mix of light to calm the darkness ... " —Erica Monroe, *USA Today* Bestselling Author

Truth Within Dreams

"If you enjoy an historical romp, or a little madcap short story, *Truth Within Dreams* will fit the bill." —*Long and Short Reviews*

Once a Duchess

"Sparkling characters, a fast-paced plot, and beautiful descriptions of Regency England made this moving story of love lost and found once again, a book I couldn't put down. A delicious debut by an author to watch!" —Danelle Harmon, author of *The Wild One*

Once an Heiress

"*Once an Heiress* combines everything readers love about historical romance with a twisting, suspenseful story that will have you on the edge of your seat ... I loved every second of *Once an Heiress*—it had the intrigue I love about historical romance combined with an excellent storyline that kept me on my toes."—*The Romance Reviews*

"If you like historical romances with a strong heroine that doesn't stick to society rules and a scarred hero with a wonderful hidden heart then you will like *Once an Heiress* by Elizabeth Boyce." —*Harlequin Junkie*

Once an Innocent

"*Once an Innocent* by Elizabeth Boyce is a fantastic espionage romance that has some surprising action and gripping drama. If you are a 007 fan, you will be entertained by this novel."—*The Romance Reviews*

For Angel, from your farang *auntie*

CRIMSON

Crimson Romance
An Imprint of Simon & Schuster, Inc.
1230 Avenue of the Americas
New York, NY 10020

ISBN 978-1-4405-8508-1
ISBN 978-1-4405-8509-8 (ebook)

The HONORABLES

BOOK 4

LOVE

BEYOND
Measure

Elizabeth
Boyce

Adams Media

New York   London   Toronto   Sydney   New Delhi

Chapter One

Somewhere in The Gulf of Siam, June 1818

In the end, Harrison mused, it figured that a woman would end his life. For more than half of his twenty-nine years, he'd had a nagging suspicion that a female would be the death of him. There was surprise in the lady's identity, for he'd assumed it would be a woman of a human persuasion that would do him in.

But then, blindness had always been his downfall. He should have known, should have at least given credence to the possibility of danger. She'd killed so many of her lovers before him, the sea had, and she'd kill countless more after he was gone.

"*Mea culpa*," he whispered hoarsely through lips parched and peeling.

Eyes half-blinded by the relentless glare of the sun roved the clearest blue water he'd ever beheld. Tender puffs of cloud lazed their way across the sky. A steady, fine wind ruffled his hair and bobbed his lifeboat up and down. Too bad he'd no means of steering the fifteen-foot craft. No sign lingered of the typhoon that had overtaken *Brizo's Woe* and dallied with the merchant vessel for days as if it were no more than a toy in a tub. A field of debris surrounded his rowboat, ragged lengths of plank dark with pitch, a grim honor guard that had escorted him since the accident.

Harrison scratched his bristled cheek; his sun-scorched skin smarted, tight and hot. Rocked by the sea, his lids slid closed against the merciless sun. One arm draped over the rail, his fingers trailing through the water. It was invitingly cool. How simple it would be to slip into the sea, to disappear beneath the surface with barely a ripple. Drowning was not an easy death—that knowledge won by witnessing it dozens of times in a single, harrowing day—but it would be quicker than this slow death by heat and starvation. He'd lingered on two weeks. The days had blurred into a singular episode of mundane terror.

Evaporating salt water caused his wrist to itch. Harrison pulled his arm back and rubbed idly, his dirty nails following the linear paths of scars carved into his skin. The nine months he'd spent aboard *Brizo's Woe* as it voyaged eastward had finally freed him from the periods of despair that had plagued him since adolescence. Now that he'd come to value his life, he found it was abruptly over. The old habit of picturing—and planning—his exit from the mortal realm returned with ease, though he did so now with a sense of regret.

He would've liked to have completed the trade expedition, to have returned to England in triumph with a cargo of riches that would be the making of him and Henry De Vere, the friend who had employed him. He could've bought the land and breeding stock needed to begin the horse stable he used to imagine when his spirits were brighter. Or he could have returned to sea, helped De Vere and Sons Shipping Company become a force to rival the East India Company.

The nanny goat bleated. Begrudgingly, Harrison opened his eyes and turned to regard his companion. Tilda the goat picked her way through an assortment of tin cups and a cooking pot set out to capture rainwater. He set the cooking pot at her feet. "Here now, have a drink."

Collecting a little water daily had been no hardship; it had rained every afternoon since the storm. Even now, nonthreatening clouds gathered on the horizon, heavy with the day's allotment of moisture. Harrison wondered, not for the first time, whether or not this ready supply of water was a mercy. Perhaps it only delayed the inevitable, but he could not stop himself from swallowing the life-sustaining fluid, even as he questioned the wisdom of it.

Pivoting, he made his unsteady way on hands and knees to mid-ship, to the chest his friend, Lord Sheridan Zouche, had gifted him upon Harrison's departure from England. He'd spotted it bobbing in the water when the rowboat was lowered into the frothing chop and dragged it into the little vessel, rescuing it from the watery grave from which he could not save so many men.

Lifting the lid, he took stock of his possessions. Sheri had packed the chest, measuring about three feet by two, with all manner of objects he thought Harrison would need or enjoy, entertainments such as books and playing cards, as well as a volume of dirty illustrations with which a man might wish to pass a private interlude. There had been some foodstuffs, but those had been consumed during Harrison's first months at sea.

Harrison drew out a slim wooden box and flipped it open. Resting on a bed of blue velvet, the silver-handled razor was pristine, unused. Throughout the voyage, when he'd bothered to shave at all, he'd employed his own, familiar razor with its simple walnut handle and soap-spotted blade.

He took the razor from its nest, his rough, sun-darkened fingers too crude for the elegant bauble. He tested the weight of it in his palm, fitted his fourth finger onto the tang, admired the scrollwork adorning the piece. It was an item of no small value— more jewel than tool; except, when he flicked it open, the edge gleamed, wicked and sharp.

Longing tugged at his gut. His gaze flicked from the razor to the water then back again. Experience had taught him that the initial slice of a well-honed blade would be painless. After would follow a bite, and the warm gush, the pain of his lifeblood leaving his veins still less than the pain that had driven him to such an act.

But he'd never been good at it, had he? Never cut deep enough, or long enough. The cross-hatching of scars on his wrists ran both across and up, but no matter the orientation, he'd never managed to inflict worse harm than a swoon. With a deft gesture, he twisted the blade, held it to his own throat, a variation he'd never tried.

The ocean turned a steelier shade of blue as the shadow of the afternoon deluge marched across its surface. Drops pelted the sea, transforming in an instant from good, sweet water to noxious brine. A breeze slipped through the tunnel of sea and sky to whip his hair about his ears. The clouds lumbered onward, dumbly wasting fresh water upon creatures who had no liking for it. No reason, no rhyme, just chaos and suffering. He swallowed, felt a bead of blood well at the razor's edge. His forearm tensed.

Something hard hit him square in the back, between his shoulders. Harrison's arm jostled, the blade skidded across his skin, no worse than a shaving nick.

"*Baaah*," Tilda groused in his ear. Her warm, goat smell filled his nostrils and her beard tickled his bare shoulder.

Carefully, Harrison lowered his arm. Then the sun was blotted out and the rain was upon him. Harrison jerked his shirt back over his head. It quickly soaked through and plastered to his skin. Despite the heat, he shivered as he reset the cups and pot to catch water. His heart raced, working too hard to power his meager exertions.

The goat folded her legs beneath her lean body and watched Harrison, brown eyes blinking dully. Tilda had given her milk to sailors for nine months, and to Harrison their first few days as castaways, until lack of food had dried her teats. Harrison had given her nothing in return. It would be a kindness to end the animal's torment, he thought, even if he lacked the courage to end his own. But if he did, he really would be alone. Utterly isolated in these alien, blue waters.

He scrubbed a fist across his eye, rubbing away the dreary ruminations. Tilda was asleep, her head bowed, untroubled by nightmarish memories. Not conflicted about the future.

Taking a cue from the beast, Harrison curled up beneath a bench. Later would be soon enough to wrangle with decisions about life and death. For now, the patter of rain inside the pot and cups sounded almost like drops falling on a tin roof, and he could pretend for a few moments that he was elsewhere, sheltered and safe.

Harrison awoke to a pain in his neck. Not in the muscle or bone, but on the skin. Was it—? "Ow!" A stinging sensation suddenly tingled on his arm. "Damned mosquitoes."

Mosquitoes? Under their own power, mosquitoes ventured only a few miles from shore. They could—and did—stow away on ships, but the little devils were one torment that had not survived the sinking of the merchant vessel. He'd not seen a single one for weeks, and now—

A dry laugh barked in his throat. After all this time, the idea that he might actually survive this ordeal was nearly unbelievable.

He crawled to the rail, astonished to see he'd slept through the afternoon and night, and now fingers of golden light touched the eastern horizon. They'd been aiming for Brunei, but the typhoon had driven *Brizo's Woe* into the Gulf of Siam. Land should be there, to the west. Harrison could make out nothing in that direction. Perhaps to the north?

"Land!" he croaked, his head ringing with shock. And then, a hoarse whisper, "Land."

A glorious ribbon of green lay that in that direction, and not too far away, either. Harrison faintly discerned the trunks of individual trees, and the expanse of pale sand that swept from the tree line to the sea. Never before had he felt gratitude for the existence of a forest, but now his heart was full to bursting with it. And there was a shack of some sort, too—no, several of them!—huddled about a dock on the beach.

And there—*there!*—oh, there, in the water, halfway between himself and the shore were boats. Six little fishing vessels in a long string. Even as he watched, a net, heavy and distended with glistening fish, was hoisted into one of the boats. The sail swiveled to catch the breeze and the boat started homeward. Five remained to gather the day's catch.

He would be rescued.

Tears blurred Harrison's vision. He swiped them with the back of his wrist, unwilling to relinquish the sight of the first human activity he'd witnessed in weeks. Now, how to get there? He opened his mouth to shout, but only a strangled yelp emerged. Weakened from hunger and exposure, Harrison was in no shape to swim the third-mile or so to the boats. Too, there was Tilda to consider.

As if sensing his thoughts, the goat let out a plaintive bleat. Reluctantly, Harrison turned from the sight of his salvation to his fellow survivor. When he saw the goat's sorry state, he groaned. Tilda lay on her side, panting hard. Every inhalation pulled her skin tight around protruding ribs. Like the mosquitoes, gnats had found their way from land. The insects swarmed Tilda's head and strolled along the rim of her eye as if it were a boulevard.

Harrison crawled to the animal, cramped limbs protesting every inch. By the time he reached her, he was shaking and sweating, his heart fluttering weakly. He pulled Tilda's head into his lap and shooed away the flies. He brought the cooking pot to her mouth, but she made no move to drink.

"Come now, Tilda," he whispered, his throat tight, "we're almost there. Just a little longer, and you'll have lov—" His voice gave out then, and so he mouthed the words. *—lovely oats and herbs to eat. There's sure to be a barn, and a pasture to cool your hooves.* He stroked one long, velvet ear over and over. Tilda made a sound that was like a hiccup. One foreleg juddered, and went still.

The weight of the last weeks came crashing down. Hot tears scalded his eyes and burned his abused cheeks. He hugged Tilda's head to his chest and wept as he'd not done since he was a child, when, sick with scarlet fever, he'd felt so dreadful that he had cried in response to his own suffering, calling for his mother through a swollen throat. Fearful of contracting the disease herself, she had not come. He was left to the ministrations of Nurse and the new governess, Miss Meyler. He had not wanted them, he'd wanted his mother, and he'd cried. A similar feeling of helplessness had him in such a grip now; he could not control himself. Chill and hot flashed through him in turns, and his poor heart pounded in his ears. It was beating wrong, weak and irregular despite its racing exertion. Every breath dragged like razors down his throat, the air struggling to inflate unwilling lungs.

He almost wished he'd not found rescue. Almost, he wished for another day alone at sea. It would need only that for Harrison's own strength to fail. Of all the worthy men aboard *Brizo's Woe*, how had it happened that Harrison alone had lived? Where was the justice? Why could not one of those stalwart sailors have taken Harrison's place? Or, of the two lives remaining from that ill-fated ship, how could it be that the gentle, harmless creature in his lap should succumb to their shared ordeal while Harrison was once more spared?

The boat shifted as someone stepped aboard. A hand took his arm, tried to pry it away from the goat. Harrison fought to maintain his hold. His bare heels drummed harmlessly against the planks. The hand took his chin, forced up his face.

Through bleary eyes, Harrison looked upon his rescuer, crouched in front of him. Deep lines crinkled dark eyes as the fisherman peered from beneath a shallow, conical straw hat. Grooves creased his mahogany skin as he frowned at Harrison.

The man said something. He had no front teeth, and the ones he did have were brown. He tilted his head expectantly. It took Harrison several seconds to puzzle out that the fellow wanted a response.

Harrison shook his head, mumbled, "I don't understand."

The man stood, looked to his left, and began speaking to someone Harrison could not see. The chap was small, barely more than five feet tall.

After a moment, another man clambered over the side of the boat. He glanced around at the cups and trunk, took one look at Harrison and Tilda and shook his head while clucking his tongue. The men exchanged a few more words in their tongue then went to work tying Harrison's boat to their own.

Feeling his part in this production had ended, Harrison allowed his eyes to close. Tilda was uncomfortably warm. He'd expected the dead goat to cool, but the sun, now fully above the horizon and making itself thermally known, kept her toasty. Or perhaps it was just that the furred beast acted as a blanket.

He opened his eyes again when something slapped upon his head and glimpsed the brim of a straw hat. His rescuer, the first man, had placed his own hat upon Harrison, leaving himself exposed to harsh rays. His scalp was shaved bald, except for a knot of glossy black hair at the crown of his head. He gripped a long pole now and took position at the rear of the boat.

The fisherman called out to the man on the other boat, and soon the two were in motion, slowly maneuvering toward the dock Harrison had glimpsed in the dawn. How long ago that now seemed, though it couldn't have been more than an hour. He closed his eyes once more, perfectly willing to allow someone else to take charge for once.

When he roused again, Tilda was gone. As was the boat. Harrison lay upon a pallet and was being carried, head first, by four fishermen. They did not bring him into any of the dockside shacks, but further, into a village. Children playing in the dirt street in front of one humble structure stopped to stare at the little procession.

More villagers halted their labors to gape at Harrison. A woman standing beneath an awning, behind a table laden with produce, tracked their progress. Harrison's eyes riveted upon her wares. *FOOD* went his brain. *FOOD*. Breathing rapidly, he lifted an arm toward the grocer. There was no hope of reaching the booth; it was twenty feet away. A whimper rose in his throat.

One of the men carrying him glanced down and spoke rapidly. Whether to him or the other men, he didn't know, but Harrison forced himself to be quiet. If his rescuers thought him mad or threatening, they wouldn't help him. They might toss him back into the sea, rather than give him anything to eat.

Some of the children fell in with their elders. One small person—boy or girl, Harrison could not say, as all the youngsters had shaved heads except for a tuft on the top, and sported only sarongs about their waists—leaned over the side of the pallet to examine Harrison's face. Small, brown fingers prodded his nose and sank into his beard. The child squealed with delight and rattled off something to which one of the elders replied, *"Farang."*

Farang. The word passed through the children in an awed hush. Idly, he wondered what it meant. Something like "idiot Englishman who is about to die," he presumed. The procession passed through an ornamental gate. At once, the children ceased their chattering.

Harrison craned his neck, but made out nothing but a high, peaked roof. As he settled back, movement overhead caught his eye. A trio of vultures circled lazily above the trees a short distance away. His mind went to Tilda. Was it his ruminant comrade the carrion birds sought, or did his own impending demise draw the scavengers?

At a word from an adult, a child ran ahead while the men carried Harrison down a graveled walkway. There was grass beyond it, lush and green. Splotches of bright color danced at the edge of his vision. Flowers? It all began melding together then darkness crept into the periphery. His breath was loud in his ears, muffling the sounds of anxious speech.

Then he was in a dimmer place—not dark, not *the* darkness, not yet—and movement ceased. For the first time in many months, his body was still. It was a blessed relief, but a short-lived one, for soon enough he was pulled upright and something was pressed to his lips while a male voice spoke in gentle, soothing tones.

He parted his lips. Cool liquid washed his tongue, a little sweet, slightly thicker than water. Delicious. He swallowed greedily. After several mouthfuls, the beverage was taken away. "More," Harrison protested, blindly reaching for the cup. Again, the man's voice. Again the kind hands, this time pushing him back onto a cushion. Accustomed to the damp, hard planks of the boat, Harrison's bones ached as he relaxed into the soft embrace of the bed.

Behind voices carrying on a hushed conversation, he heard a cry. His scattered thoughts first went to Tilda, but then he remembered: Tilda was dead. It was a child, frightened or hurt, calling out in need. How strange, that nature should make a child and a goat sound so very much alike in their distress. The cry once more sounded, working upon his nerves, compelling him to go, to help, to intercede. Protect the little ones. Why wasn't anyone tending the child? Didn't they know what happened to children when no one was looking?

Hands upon him again, restraining his weak, fretful thrashing. Blessedly, the child's cry stopped, and the knots of panic in his muscles eased. The hand stroked his hair. Oddly, Harrison didn't mind the contact. Soon, he exhaled a sigh of contentment as his mind slipped into a blissful stupor. If he was yet to expire from his ordeal at sea, this was an ending he'd not anticipated, but one for which he was heartily glad: thirst slaked, in the comfort of a bed, and—most importantly—not alone. Harrison wasn't going to die alone.

Chapter Two

The two men reclined in their cushioned chairs like princes upon their thrones, indolent, confident in their mastery over all they surveyed. *Khun* Gaspar was proud, his expression satisfied as he considered the four females kneeling in a neat row, while his guest's dark eyes gleamed, drunk on power. When the guest's eyes moved to Lamai, she dropped her gaze to her lap, forcing her hands to soften upon her knees. Compliant. Nonthreatening.

"Are they really all your slaves, D'Cruz?" asked the guest, another Portuguese trader whose name Lamai had not heard.

"Given me by the king himself," Khun Gaspar boasted. An untruth. Two of the women, Mi and Nan, were Burmese, taken captive in battle and gifted as slaves to Khun Gaspar by the minister of the treasury in thanks for the *farang's* contributions. Khun Gaspar had never had an audience with the king, much less received a gift from the king's own hand. He might own a splendid mansion not far from the palace, filled with treasures from Europe and Asia, but he was as far from invitation to court as Lamai herself—a fact that rankled the proud Portuguese man to no end.

The third slave woman—or girl, rather—was Thai, like Lamai. Kulap had caught Gaspar's eye at the market one day last month, and Lamai had been ordered to negotiate with the girl's parents on his behalf. He didn't know how little the peasants had asked in exchange for their child's servitude. Lamai tripled the price, and Gaspar, made stupid by his lust for the fifteen-year-old, had not

16

hesitated to pay. The girl had sulked since her arrival, complaining that her exorbitant purchase price made her freedom impossible to redeem. She didn't seem to understand that she would never be free again, that this was the only time her parents would be able to pawn their child.

Slaves in Mueang Thai could sell and buy their own freedom as often as they liked, but Gaspar did not always behave according to the rules, especially with his bed slaves. These he kept until they no longer interested him, then he passed them along to his European friends, without any by-your-leave from the women themselves. Unfortunately for Kulap and the others, where *farangs* were involved, the law was limp as old celery.

And then there was Lamai herself, who inhabited a limbo world of unbelonging. Neither family member, nor slave; neither fully Thai, nor fully white. Less than a ward, but more than a servant, she was simply … other.

"How utterly decadent," said the guest, swallowing Gaspar's lie. "You're a veritable sultan. And I may enjoy one tonight?"

"Whichever you'd like. Such an arrangement is possible for you, too, you know. You needn't be as well connected as myself to enjoy such luxuries, but we can discuss that later. For now, take your pick."

Boots scuffed on the tile, little particles of dirt and dung and refuse ground into the floor of their home, their sanctuary; Lamai shuddered. *Farangs* had repulsive habits.

The man crossed the room and examined each of their bowed figures in turn, beginning with Lamai and ending with Nan. At the end of the line he pivoted, grinding more filth into the floor, then retraced his dirty steps.

"Her," he said, stopping in front of Lamai. "I'll take this one."

Lamai blinked in surprise. *What?* He didn't want the fresh little beauty, or one of the delicate Burmese women, each as alluring as a mali blossom?

"She is not beautiful," Khun Gaspar warned. "And she's old. Take one of the others."

Scowling, Lamai almost lifted her head to glare at the master of the house, but stopped herself short, remembering just in time that she was not supposed to let Khun Gaspar's visitors know she understood their language. Besides, the merchant had spoken true this time. Lamai was twenty-three, far older than the youthful Kulap. Nor was she beautiful, and when the *farang* saw her face, he would turn his attention to one of the others.

The man chuckled. "I don't mind a plain girl." Cupping Lamai's chin, he tilted her face for his examination. Lamai arched her neck, flagrantly inviting the lamplight to show her ruined face to its worst advantage.

The *farang* recoiled, but quickly recovered himself. His eyes met Lamai's and she stared back defiantly, refusing to be ashamed of her ugliness. It had protected her when she had no other protector. It would protect her now. She curled her lip in a sneer, making herself even less desirable. *Farang* men expected docility from Thai women. They sought it, paid handsomely for it. Lamai was not that. He would choose another.

He smiled. "I'll have her," he said, straightening. "Send her to my room."

Lamai's eyes flew to Khun Gaspar. Still sitting at his ease, legs splayed wide like a Chinese pirate king, his graying head tilted as he looked at Lamai, assessing. He was taking too long to refuse his guest.

A lump rose in her throat. Lamai worked in multiple capacities, but never like this. Gaspar had utilized her in this charade before, liking the boast of owning more bed slaves than he actually possessed, but had always promised her safety. Lamai, he'd said, was too valuable in other ways to be used as a bed toy. No guest had ever chosen her. Now that one had ... He wouldn't. Would he?

Her keeper lifted a brow. Lamai shook her head, frantic now. Khun Gaspar lowered his eyes to his glass of golden liquor, hiding his thoughts. He swirled the liquid, took a long sip, let Lamai stew in an agony of uncertainty.

Had he discovered her duplicity in his purchase of the new slave, Kulap? Would he rescind his promise to her as punishment for costing him so much money?

"Choose one of the others." He tossed back the remainder of his drink. "Hell, choose two."

The *farang* huffed. "You said I could have whichever I like, D'Cruz. I want the ugly girl."

Khun Gaspar's mouth tightened in a false smile. "Sorry, friend, you can't have her."

Snorting like a grumpy monkey, the man snatched the new girl and one of the Burmese women by their arms, hauled them to their feet, and marched them out of the room.

With a word, Khun Gaspar dismissed the other woman. She scurried out on small, bare feet.

Rising, Lamai shook out her skirt and moved to find her way to her own bed.

"You were not given leave to go." Khun Gaspar's voice cracked behind her.

Slowly, she turned to meet the cold gaze of her tormentor. "I am not your slave."

He smirked. "More's the pity for you. If I held your paper, I would be bound to keep you. As it is, if you are no longer useful to me, I may cast you off." Standing, he sauntered to a lacquered table to refill his glass from a fine porcelain bottle. Another example of the special treatment of *farangs*: strong drinks were forbidden in in this country, but this law, too, was not enforced for foreign merchants and dignitaries. Khun Gaspar brought his glass to his nose, breathed the fumes. *Brandy*, he called the drink. Vile, Lamai named it.

"I do not serve you in bed—not yours, nor any other man's."

His eyes moved over her right temple and cheek. *"Hmm."*

Beneath the scars, her face burned. Always it had been this way with Khun Gaspar. With each language he'd taught her, he'd bound her more tightly to his service. For every *farang* he dangled before her, each presenting the tantalizing hope of a long-ago promise fulfilled, he reminded Lamai that she was flawed, unwanted, unwantable.

She turned again and fled from his mocking eyes, not stopping even when he called behind her, "You'll want to lock your door, Lamai. I don't think he'll be satisfied at two."

Through the darkened house she ran until she burst into the back garden. Pausing to slide her feet into slippers, she jogged to the stable, cursing the heavy European dress Khun Gaspar made his females wear when he entertained other *farangs*.

Inviting light shone from the broad door, which stood slightly ajar. Lamai slipped inside and spotted her friend, Panit, at work feeding the animals and getting them settled for the night. The older man's bare torso was slender, his arms rangy with lean muscle. He wore loose, yellow trousers tied about the waist. His bare feet, beyond rough, beyond calloused, looked as though they'd never been touched by shoes in their life—they probably hadn't—and had grown their own boot soles in self defense.

Panit tossed a smile over his shoulder. "I was just wishing a girl in a pretty gown would come muck out the stalls." As Lamai approached, his smile slipped. "You should go. He'll be angry if you spoil your dress."

Stubbornly ignoring his advice, Lamai hefted a large basket of fruit from the floor. "I'm staying here tonight. If my dress is ruined, all the better. Maybe I'll shave my head, too."

Setting down her burden in front of a stall door, Lamai selected a section of melon and reached into the enclosure. A pink-mottled gray trunk snatched the treat from Lamai's hand and carried it to the young elephant's mouth.

"Greedy girl!" Lamai teasingly scolded. "Not even a kiss first?"

Wan Pen snorted, all the while chomping on her treat. Her trunk snaked around Lamai's shoulders and pulled her to the door in a playful embrace.

"Better." Lamai fondly patted the animal's nose. Wan Pen lowered her head, inviting Lamai to scratch her brow. At five-and-a-half feet, the elephant was several inches taller than Lamai, far taller than any human child of the same five years would be. While she petted Wan Pen, Lamai sensed movement near her leg. "Oh no, you don't!" Lamai pulled the fruit basket out of reach of the questing trunk. Wan Pen trumpeted plaintively. With a sigh of exasperation, Lamai fished in the basket until she found a pineapple, Wan Pen's preferred sweet, and gave it to the elephant child.

"You spoil her," Panit scolded.

"She's my favorite girl," Lamai returned. "I'll spoil her if I wish. Besides, she wasn't naughty in her lessons today, was she?"

Chuckling, Panit shook his head. "No, she always learns her lessons quickly. I'll give her that." As a *mahout*, Panit was charged with the instruction and care of elephants. Dusting his hands on his pant legs, he came to Wan Pen's stall and gave the end of her trunk a waggle. "She's smart, like you." His eyes flicked to the twisted rope of hair slung across Lamai's shoulder. "Will you really cut it?"

Lamai sniffed. "It would be more comfortable, and stay out of my eyes."

"*Mmmm*, sensible." Panit returned to the other side of the stable and resumed forking hay into the stall of Goui, Wan Pen's nanny. The old elephant cow munched her grass while keeping an eye on her young charge.

"It's very hot, and it falls into my face." She demonstratively swiped back an errant strand of black hair near her temple.

"Then surely, you must shave," Panit said, nodding gravely. He drove the fork into the hay and expertly pitched a bundle across the space to Wan Pen. "Doesn't hurt that it will devil Khun Gaspar."

Lamai grinned. Panit knew her too well. "And I will look properly Thai. Less *farang*."

Panit stilled, the weathered tool gripped in his calloused, capable hands. "You *are farang*, girl. Cutting your hair will not make it untrue."

Her smile slipped. She turned to feed Wan Pen more fruit, giving Panit her back. "Only half-*farang*, and no white person in the world would accept me as theirs. My skin's too dark and my eyes are too long. But thanks to my father's blood, I'm not entirely Thai looking, either, and with my long hair—" Lamai bit her tongue, cutting off a well-tread path of frustration. Lamai's in-between state had been a bane of her life.

"How many women get to dress up in those fancy clothes, huh?" Panit's tone was too jaunty, as if in apology for upsetting her. "You must be able to style your hair to suit your attire. Imagine how funny you would look in that dress with only a tuft like mine!"

"That would be silly, you're right." She returned the fruit basket to its place in the corner.

When the chores were done, she climbed the ladder to the hayloft. Panit, already making himself cozy on his cot in the corner, had lent her a blanket to spread over a pile of straw. She shimmied out of her dress and lay down in her shift, thin cotton clinging to her sweat-damp body. As she struggled to find a comfortable arrangement for her limbs on the lumpy hay, and tried to ignore the battling snores of man and elephants, Lamai spared a wistful thought for her room with its tall windows and soft bed. Then the warm breeze carried a cry to her ears, and she heard the squeak of the kitchen door's hinge as a woman went looking for Cook's homemade salve. The one that sped the healing of burns and bruises.

Lamai burrowed her head into the straw. Despite the discomforts, there was no bed she'd rather sleep in tonight.

• • •

Two days later, Khun Gaspar summoned her to his study. The footman, a male slave, who escorted Lamai preceded her into the room, bent at the waist to show deference to his master. Gaspar, standing beside a tall bookshelf, looked up from the volume he held and regarded her coolly. Lamai suppressed an urge to bow like the servant.

I am not a slave, she reminded herself, folding her hands at her waist and holding her spine erect. And yet, she could not stop herself from lowering her eyes to Gaspar's desk. The surface was littered with papers, scrolls, and writing sundries. The chair behind the desk was an ornate affair, heavily carved, dark wood, padded with red leather edged with round studs.

"You wished to see me, *senhor*?"

Gaspar made no reply, but must have given a signal to the slave. That fellow withdrew from the room, leaving the door open.

A quiet minute passed, the only sound the slide of paper against paper as Gaspar turned a page in his book. The slave returned, shoulders hunched, and placed a tray of refreshments on a low side table before bowing his way out and closing the door behind him.

"Please serve," Gaspar said.

Lamai poured fruit juice from an enameled jug into two china cups.

Gaspar accepted his beverage and gestured to one of the two teak-and-rattan chairs opposite his own. "Have a seat, Lamai."

She settled herself, crossing her ankles and tucking her bare feet behind the hem of her sarong.

To her surprise, Gaspar did not take his commanding seat, but the twin of her own chair. Her gaze slid sideways, watching as he reclined, extending his bare feet along the floor. When there were no Europeans about, Gaspar dressed in Thai fashion. Today, he wore a loose muslin shirt, light in color, embroidered at the bottom hem, and linen breeches. His calves were sunned and covered with crisp, dark hair at odds with the silver adorning his head.

His nearness made her uneasy. Since he'd nearly given her to his guest the other night, she'd successfully avoided Gaspar, busying herself in the kitchen or doing the shopping for the day's food or other household needs. At night, she slept in the stable. The other man had left yesterday morning, but Lamai could not yet feel entirely safe in her own bed.

She barely tasted a sip of the mango and coconut juice, though it was her favorite combination of flavors.

Gaspar quickly drained his cup and exhaled a satisfied *"Aaah,"* then returned the cup to the tray. "I have a letter here." He reached over to pluck a document from the top of a stack. The square of paper showed creases where it had been folded several times, and ink bled through the back of the weave. He gave her a sly smile. "Guess who it's from."

Lamai's heart leapt; her breath stopped in her throat. "My father," she breathed. Excitement fizzed in her blood; she felt it even in her dead cheek. Gaspar had told her he did not know where his friend Peter Hart had gone after leaving Mueang Thai, much less how to contact him. But Gaspar had lived in the same house for twenty years, and Lamai had lived with him for the past eight. Reaching out to Gaspar would be an obvious early step in Peter reclaiming his lost family.

Gaspar had taken in Lamai when she was fifteen, like Kulap. Unlike Kulap, however, Lamai had not been purchased, but brought on out of a sense of duty to Gaspar's old friend, Lamai's father, the Portuguese man had claimed. Already proficient in multiple languages by the time Gaspar found Lamai living in troubled circumstances with relatives, she'd been given a proper education, in addition to a home. When Gaspar first asked Lamai to translate for him in a business meeting, she'd been happy to oblige. That happy obliging turned to a sense of obligation as her tenure with the Portuguese man stretched into years. Lamai was duty-bound to assist her benefactor until such a time as she reunited with her father, and they made their own home. Over the past few years, however, Lamai had become increasingly uneasy with things Gaspar required of her. But she had no family she could turn to, and Gaspar was the only link she had to her father. When Peter Hart returned to Mueang Thai, Lamai would be here.

At last. *At last.*

Gaspar chuckled. "No, no, not Peter—though I'm certain we'll hear from him soon. Try again."

Her hopes plummeted, leaving her almost giddy as she was suddenly voided ofelation, as quickly emptied as a slop bucket cast out the window. "I don't know," she whispered.

He scanned the page. Cleared his throat. "It's from the office of my country's ambassador."

Lamai shook her head, bewildered. "How could I have known that?"

"You couldn't have!" He playfully chucked her on the shoulder, as he used to do when she was young. "The challenge is what makes it a game."

Her eyes stung. She lowered her gaze to her lap, where her hands were tight around her unfinished beverage. Gaspar had known what she would think. Wasn't he the one who'd encouraged those hopes these past eight years? He was cruel to tease her so, mean to find humor in her despair. The liquid in her cup rippled.

Carefully, she placed the dish on his desk and willed herself to calm, forbidding herself to show any more of her hurt.

"Have you a summons from the ambassador? Do you require my assistance?" Her voice was once more placid, even if her emotions weren't quite.

"No and yes." Gaspar scrubbed a hand through his short hair. "One of my countrymen has washed ashore in some godforsaken village several days' east of the city. There are no scheduled Portuguese ships unaccounted for, so he was either sailing under another country's flag, or he's a smuggler. Until the facts are known, the ambassador won't instigate any official action. He's asked me to ascertain the man's identity and business."

The left side of Lamai's mouth twitched downward; the right remained immobile. "His identity? Didn't the ambassador give you the man's name?"

"No, the poor devil was nearly dead when he was fished out of the water. Insensible at the time the notification was written to the ambassador."

"Then how is it known that he is Portuguese?"

Gaspar's palm slapped the arm of his chair. "Confound it, girl, I only know what I've been told."

"*Sim, senhor,*" Lamai murmured, her tone conciliatory. The mystery of this new European intrigued her. Despite the cruel trick Gaspar had just played, she couldn't stop a stirring of hope in her bruised heart. It was the same whenever she encountered a new *farang*. There was always the chance that it might be her father. And if it wasn't this man, then it could be the next. Or the next. So had she lived the past eight years in a state of heightened expectation. There was never enough time following a disappointment to be entirely let down before the anticipation of another new arrival buoyed her spirits.

"When do we go?"

"First light tomorrow. A shipment from Chiang Mai is expected any day, so I need this business concluded quickly." One heavy, black-and-gray brow lifted. "Did this trip not involve unschooled peasants, I wouldn't inconvenience you with accompanying me."

Lamai heard his unspoken meaning. She was useful only because she could translate for him. He did not wish for her company otherwise. On another occasion, his increasing coldness toward her might have stung, but not this time. She ducked her head so he wouldn't see her ghost of a smile. Wouldn't it be amazing if this man who'd washed ashore was her father? A hundred times, a thousand, she'd imagined their reunion. *"Here I am, Father,"* she would say in his language, *"your own dutiful daughter."* He would be crushed to learn of his wife's death, but he would have Lamai, and she would be a comfort to him in his grief. That spark of hope, continually damped and rekindled, began to glow brighter.

"I'm pleased to assist you in this task, Khun Gaspar." Her fingers tightly threaded together, she pressed her combined fist to her belly. She must not allow herself *too* much hope. In all likelihood, this was just another *farang*, not her father, at all.

"Knew I could depend on you."

"Once we know the man's identity and business, what shall we do? Bring him to the city?"

The white man snorted. "If he's someone of interest to the ambassador, then by all means, we'll collect him. Otherwise—if he's competition—I intend to leave him where he is. He can find his own way."

It seemed to Lamai there were many other possibilities. The man might be a world traveler. A visiting scholar. One of the missionaries the Christians were so fond of sending. Her father. But she held her peace as she took her leave, pressed her hands together, and bowed.

"It shall be as you say, *Khun* Gaspar."

• • •

The following morning, just as the sun painted the sky in streaks of pink and gold before showing itself above the horizon, Lamai met Panit in the paddock outside the stable. Goui was harnessed and ready for travel, a canopied *yaeng* secured to her back over a large blanket. The carriage was large enough to carry four passengers if both cushioned seats were in place, but the back seat had been removed and Panit was busily arranging luggage in the empty space. The old lady calmly chomped grass while her *mahout* worked.

Lamai went to Wan Pen, who stood beside her nanny, anxiously swaying side-to-side. Her trunk, curled in a tight coil, stroked Goui's side.

"Are you sure you want to take her?" Panit asked. "We'll make better time if we only take Goui."

"We must take her! The poor baby is afraid of Goui leaving without her. If Wan Pen stays home, she'll cry the whole time we're gone." With hearts as gentle as their bodies were large, elephants formed close bonds with one another. The separation of a young elephant from her mother or nanny would be as upsetting for both parties as ripping a human child from her mother's arms.

Panit bobbed his head in acknowledgment as Lamai stroked Wan Pen's face, assuring the girl she'd not be left behind.

Lamai's soothing and the additional enticement of a banana cheered Wan Pen. Lamai went into the stable to retrieve her tack. When she returned, Gaspar had made an appearance and was stepping up to his seat in the *yaeng*. Once again, he wore simple, loose-fitting clothes in the Thai style, though once the curtains were drawn around him, there would be no mistaking him for anything but a prosperous and important man.

At a word of command, Wan Pen knelt, allowing Lamai to toss up a pad before she scrambled up and settled herself just behind Wan Pen's ears.

"Sure you know what you're doing?" Panit scurried over. "Maybe it would be best if Wan Pen wore reins."

"She's had more training with this," Lamai said, waggling the bamboo rod she held in her right hand.

"This morning, if you please." Khun Gaspar was half-turned in his seat. "You and Panit can gossip on your own time."

The *mahout* looked from Gaspar to Lamai and cocked his head in question, awaiting translation.

Lamai smiled. "He's ready to go. Don't worry about us," she said, giving Wan Pen's head a pat. "We'll be fine."

Panit made a sound that could have been interpreted as either agreement or doubt, then climbed onto Goui. At the click of his tongue, the huge animal rose, pressing one foot at a time into the soft earth. Wan Pen followed suit. Lamai gripped firm with her thighs, the elephant's muscles rolling as she stood.

"*Pai dai,*" Lamai encouraged Wan Pen when Goui exited the paddock. *Go ahead.* The little girl fell into step behind her nanny.

Rain set in as they left Bangkok behind, and continued unabated for two days. The third day of travel offered a reprieve from the inundation, but the hot sun only lifted billowing clouds of steam from the saturated ground, with no hope of drying it out. In the late afternoon, they reached the village where the mystery *farang* was said to be found. It was a small fishing community, and the arrival of an august personage in the form of Khun Gaspar stirred excitement.

At a dried-fish stand, Lamai learned the European was being tended by the monks of the community's *wat*. She purchased a sack of fish and made *wai*, bowing her thanks. Along with the mosquitoes, the rain had suppressed thoughts of finding her father, but hope surged during the final stretch of their journey.

They reached the *wat* in a quarter of an hour. It was a small compound, with a modest temple situated in a central pavilion, and other buildings scattered haphazardly across the grounds.

All was neat and well tended, but by Bangkok standards, the provincial *wat* was decidedly unimpressive.

As they dismounted, a pair of monks scurried across the lawn, saffron robes flapping about their ankles. Panit and the monks took the elephants away.

Now dressed in European clothes, Gaspar's torso was swathed in layers of shirt, waistcoat, and coat, all of it cut close to show his broad shoulders and thick waist. His collar was tied with a neck cloth knotted just below the chin. The costume must have been stifling, but he allowed no sign of discomfort, striding confidently in his long trousers to the temple. Lamai's breath hitched when he started up the steps in shod feet, but just before reaching the top, he paused to slip out of his shoes. She exhaled a little sigh of relief.

Clutching the sack of dried fish, Lamai followed behind him. "Khun Gaspar," she said sotto voce before he could cross the red threshold of the sanctuary. "Take this." She thrust the parcel into his hands. "For making merit to the *Jao Ar-wart*, the head of the monastery."

He drew back, dark eyes flashing. "I certainly will not!" he exclaimed, thrusting the fish back into her hands. "Respecting the decorum of your religious institutions is as far as I can bring myself to go. I'll do nothing that could be misconstrued as participating in a faith ritual. Bowing to your priest would be an insult to God."

"Please," she begged. "We must make an offering. The monks won't take it from me."

His affronted expression melted into an amused smile. "Lest contact with your female person throws them into a lustful frenzy? I think they're safe from your wiles, but very well, give me the food. Eve's sin is a universal truth, I suppose. Who says we aren't building bridges of understanding?" He snickered as he turned and entered the temple.

Inside the large, central chamber, Lamai only had time to bow three times to Lord Buddha, as the Jao Ar-wart, his office denoted by the crimson sash around his waist, was crossing the crimson rug to meet them. Lamai knelt respectfully. Gaspar only inclined his head, as though greeting a peer. Lamai was suffused with shame for his impudence.

"*Bem vinda, senhor.*" The old monk's Portuguese was thickly accented, but he was obviously proud to greet Gaspar in the *farang's* language. It would have stretched Gaspar's limited grasp of Thai to return the greeting in kind. "My name is Thawichat. You've come from Bangkok to see our guest? You made excellent time."

"How does he fare?" Gaspar asked.

"Better, but he still spends most of his day sleeping. He is taking food now. I think he will not perish."

"Splendid. For your trouble." Gaspar presented the bag of fish with a flourish, as though making a grand gift. Lamai could have combusted, her face was so hot with embarrassment. Thankfully, the men did not look in her direction.

"Oooh, *obrigado, senhor.*" The head monk politely made much of the humble contribution, gushing over Gaspar's generosity instead of offering a blessing. Merit had not been made. Lamai sighed inwardly.

"You are most welcome to stay here," Jao Ar-wart Thawichat said, "though your female servant must find accommodation in the village. We've no matron here."

"No. She must stay with me."

At that point, Lamai wished a mouth of hell would open beneath her and swallow her up. She was heartily glad Thawichat did not realize she understood the Portuguese conversation, else the shame she felt for Gaspar's disregard of custom would have been too much to bear. Of course she must stay in the village if there was no woman to supervise! She'd never have supposed otherwise.

"Well … all right." The Jao Ar-wart smiled warmly, only tension around his eyes betraying his displeasure. "If you'll come with me, *senhor*, we can have tea while your servant sees to your things."

Gaspar accompanied their host into a back room. When they were gone, Lamai touched her head to the floor, murmuring prayers and apologies to Buddha for the *farang's* disrespect.

When she lifted herself, a monk was standing off to the side, quietly awaiting the completion of her prayers. Outside the sanctuary, he nodded to a group of quaint huts that lay beyond a narrow stream, arranged in a semicircle around a bed of flowers and statuary. "The guest quarters. The sick man is there." The monk pointed to the far end of the arc. "Your master can have the closest—it's the best. You must have your own, of course," he said stiffly.

Lamai's hands trembled, her gaze riveted on the unassuming structure on the far end of the row. Her father might be there. She might be mere moments from reuniting with her long-lost parent.

"And Panit, our *mahout*?" she asked, struggling to control herself. She wanted to sprint across the bridge, throw open the door of the hut, and put an end to the years of dreaming. She was ready to be a daughter. She was ready to have a family again.

"He wishes to stay with the elephants. Our livestock are there," the monk gestured toward the rear of the property. They walked the rest of the way in silence, the monk keeping careful distance between himself and Lamai. He even waited for her to cross the narrow bridge before doing so himself, lest he inadvertently touch her, which would breach his vow of celibacy. "Your belongings will be brought shortly."

Lamai thanked him for his hospitality and watched him return towards the stream. Gripping the end of her braid in a white-knuckled fist, she stepped away from the door. She couldn't wait any longer.

The monk glanced over his shoulder at her. Lamai smiled and waved, then pointed at the flowers, as though she was captivated by the horticulture. The monk frowned, then continued on his way.

When she was sure it was safe, she darted between huts and circled around the back side to the one at the far end—the one that held her father.

Her heart pounded in her ears as she pressed herself to the western wall, the low-hanging sun drenching the wooden slats in yellow light. In the center of the wall was an open window. Lamai crept to it, slowly rising to peek over the ledge. She could scarcely breathe.

The interior of the hut was dim, though she detected a man's recumbent form on the futon. She squinted, willing her sight to adjust.

His back was turned to the window. Sun-browned white skin slid over a lean frame as he inhaled and exhaled regularly in slumber, as Jao Ar-wart Thawichat had said. The skin was smooth, young.

Her heart teetered, but she refused to give up hope just yet. Her father *would* be young beyond his years, healthy and robust to make such a perilous journey.

As she struggled to make out the color of his hair, the man turned onto his back, and the sun washed over his head, illuminating a head of shaggy, middling brown locks.

Lamai's father was fair. Golden-fair and English, her mother used to say. Beautiful and pale.

This man was not her father, she thought, choking on a wave of bitterness. This man was nobody. He was just another stupid *farang*.

Chapter Three

There came a time when Harrison awakened himself, rather than at the prodding of his caretaker. He lay on his stomach, arms flung wide. Sunlight streamed through unglazed windows in the whitewashed wall. He was not, he found, in a bed, as such, but rather on a cushioned pallet on the floor. From his position, Harrison saw a low, wooden table upon which rested a bowl filled with flowers. A green lizard, about four inches in length, scuttled across the wall. On the wooden floor close to his pallet was a trunk—his trunk. The sight of it caused emotion to swell in his chest. Perhaps because it was something familiar in this unfamiliar place, but too, its presence was evidence of kindness. The trunk may have been emptied of valuables, but Harrison didn't think so. Here—wherever *here* was—he was safe.

His gaze came to his right arm. It was, he noted, quite thin and heavily bruised. His skin was an odd color, reddish-bronze from sunburn, but yellowish, too. Besides myriad bruises, he sported several purple splotches, as if blood had simply oozed from his veins to pool beneath the skin. His hand was knobby and gnarled, knucklebones prominent beneath wasted flesh. He was little more than a skeleton.

He closed his eyes.

• • •

Later—hours, days maybe—he opened his eyes to see a man with skin the color of butterscotch crouched at the table. His head was clean-shaven, and he was swathed in a saffron robe that exposed his right shoulder and arm. On the table sat a tray, and on the tray were two bowls. Steam rose from one. Into the other, the man poured liquid from *something* that had come from nature. It was green and oblong and about the size of a child's head.

Harrison must have made a noise, for the man glanced over his shoulder to the bed. When he spotted Harrison watching him, the man smiled and rose to his bare feet. He brought his hands together at his chest, bent his head, and bowed.

"*Sa wad dee krap.*"

Bewildered, Harrison nodded in return. Should he stand and bow as the man had done? He wasn't certain he could. A little jolt of anxiety went through his middle. After all this person had done for him, Harrison had no wish to offend.

The man, however, seemed satisfied with Harrison's weak greeting, for he returned to the tray to finish his task. Bowls in hand, he knelt at Harrison's bedside and handed over the dish containing the liquid from the large pod, which turned out to be the same thin, sweetish substance he'd been drinking all this time. When Harrison had finished the … juice, he supposed it was, the bowl was lifted from his hands.

Crouching at the bedside, the man tapped his own chest. "Wirat," he said, then nodded expectantly.

"Harrison Dyer."

Harrison's caretaker exclaimed, *"Aaaaaah,"* as if a great mystery had finally been solved. "*Khun* Harrisondah."

Harrison smiled weakly. Close enough.

Wirat gave Harrison the steaming bowl. It contained pale broth, a few scant pieces of green and yellow vegetables, and a single, glistening curl of fish.

At the sight of meat, Harrison's stomach growled ravenously. Wirat said something; his language was full of elongated vowels and soft consonants. Harrison plucked the fish from the soup and popped it into his mouth. Succulent, oily flesh melted against his tongue. He groaned in ecstasy. Had anything ever been so delicious? He brought the bowl to his lips and gulped the contents, ignoring the scald of hot fish broth. The soft vegetables slid down his throat unchewed.

The berobed man spoke again, his words carrying an unmistakable, chiding tone. Chagrined at his poor manners, Harrison lowered the empty dish, wiped his mouth with the back of his hand and met his host's disapproving gaze. "Beg your pardon." He returned the bowl. "Thank you," Harrison ventured. "It was delicious."

Standing, Wirat made a sound and shook his head. Then he returned the dishes to the tray and left.

A few minutes later, Harrison's middle felt squeezed in a vise. Painful cramps assailed him until he scrambled off his pallet and made it to a chamber pot just in time to bring his meal back up.

Realizing too late the caution Wirat had attempted to communicate, Harrison went much slower in consuming his next meal, and it remained where he put it. By the following day, rice and more vegetables were added to his diet, and still more variety the next.

On the fourth day after fully regaining his senses, Harrison was quite alert and feeling restless. He ransacked his trunk for the books Sheri had gifted him, blushing when he came across the erotic illustrations and hiding that volume at the bottom, and spent an hour reading a less lascivious tome. Then his mind refused to focus any longer on the text. His eye wandered to the window, beguiled by sunlight slipping through the wooden slats, his other faculties enticed by scents of rich vegetation and other, unfamiliar aromas, and the sounds of birds and the occasional bleat of a domestic animal. The lizard he'd spotted days ago crept up the wall and slipped over the windowsill, vanishing into freedom.

Harrison stared after it wistfully, then chuffed a laugh at himself. "Come on, old fellow, if you're envious of a reptile's life, then holiday is over." His voice, though thin like the rest of him, was unmistakably his own.

Pressing his hands into the cushion that had cocooned him in his convalescence, Harrison came to kneeling, the lightweight bed cover falling away to reveal his nude body. Glancing down, he experienced a shock of non-recognition, so great was the alteration in his form. Always lean from a life of activity, Harrison's happy months on *Brizo's Woe* had trained his muscles into sturdy ropes that lashed about his frame, well-suited to the tasks of climbing the rigging, hoisting sails, and hauling casks out of the hold. The shapes of those muscles were all that remained, their substance now sadly depleted. Hip bones jutted beyond his gaunt belly. The skin covering his sunken chest was sallow; even the dark hair on his torso and groin was sparser and paler than it had been. As he rose onto unsteady legs, he saw that his knees and feet were now as bony as his hands.

The clothes he'd arrived in were nowhere to be seen. Glancing about, he found some spare bedding neatly folded on the floor beside his trunk, but no clothes. Pulling the undyed linen from the pallet, he wrapped the sheet about himself in crude imitation of the drape his caretaker wore. A handful of wobbling steps brought him to the door. Harrison's hand rested on the twisted iron handle. What would he find on the other side, beyond the shelter of his little sanctuary?

Brushing aside his trepidation, he pushed open the door and blinked into the early morning sunlight. Stone steps descended from the door onto a paved path. His gaze followed it to the next structure, a small hut like his own, and another—five in all. Vibrant flowers and weathered statues of fantastic creatures adorned the hollow formed by the cluster of huts, while manicured grass and shrubs and a variety of trees dotted the landscape beyond the little enclave.

The path led to a stream, across which stood a building unlike anything Harrison had ever seen. Pristine white walls supported a flamboyantly steep, three-tiered, red tiled roof. Gilded finials placed at the corners and intervals around the perimeter of the roof rose like flames to heaven. Intricately carved woodwork surrounded the windows and gables.

"What is this place?" Harrison whispered, awestruck nearly to silence. Had he been brought to a palace? No, too small for a royal residence, he decided. The manor of a rich lord, perhaps?

His bare feet sank into dew-damp grass, his sheet toga trailing behind him. In a stupor, he strolled across the lawn, pausing to sniff unfamiliar flowers, or to run his hands across the rough bark of a palm tree. As in England, birds greeted the new day, but the songs Harrison heard were not those of the gentle larks to which he was accustomed, but brasher, showier, like the vegetation.

He returned to the path and approached the bridge that arched delicately above the stream. Stone animals—stylized lions, he thought—crouched at the foot of the structure. He stopped to admire the craftsmanship of the railing, bending low to examine the supports. Careful attention had been given to even these lowly beams, carved in a spiral and waxed to smooth perfection.

A sharp hiss just to his right pulled a yelp from his throat. Three feet away, on the bank of the stream, was the largest lizard Harrison had ever seen. Dark-skinned and mean-eyed, it glared balefully at Harrison, mouth open to show pale gums and fangs he wanted no part of. Four stout legs held its belly off the ground, while the tip of its thick tail was lost in the murk of the stream. All told, the monster must have measured five feet long.

It may have been a reptile, such as the little green fellow who supped on the mosquitoes in Harrison's hut, but this behemoth was as dissimilar from Harrison's harmless housemate as a canary was to a falcon. With a growl, the creature took two quick steps in his direction. Scrambling back on hands and feet, Harrison gracelessly pushed upright and staggered across the bridge, quickly putting distance between himself and the animal.

"What the devil was that?" Heart pounding, he swiped sweat from his brow, glancing over his shoulder to make sure the thing wasn't following him. It wasn't, but now that he knew what to look for, he spotted more of the loathsome beasts along the shoreline. Green, brown, and black mottled skin camouflaged them with their grassy, muddy surroundings. As he watched, another slipped into the water and glided silently beneath the bridge—undoubtedly to lie in wait for hapless pedestrians, like a Norse troll.

Something brushed his arm. Harrison screamed and jumped, turning mid air to confront the new terror.

His friend in the saffron robe startled back at Harrison's unmanful display.

Clasping the sheet to his chest, Harrison panted as his heart returned to a more moderate pulse. "I beg your pardon," he said, bowing to communicate his apology. Wirat's deep brown eyes crinkled in a smile. Harrison thought he was forgiven.

"Careful of them." Harrison pointed to the behemoth lizards guarding the creek. "I nearly became breakfast for one of those chaps." Pulling back his lips, he hissed demonstratively. The other man chuckled and said something in reply.

Wirat touched Harrison's arm again—no resulting conniption this time—and gestured for Harrison to accompany him.

A bell tolled from somewhere on the other side of the large, ornate building. Within seconds, more men shrouded in identical orange robes emerged from the doors of the large building, streaming around Harrison and his escort. Many stopped to greet Harrison, pressing their hands together and bowing before returning to their business. More men came from elsewhere on the grounds, while others entered through the compound's front gate, carrying urns and sacks to another building. Some of the robed figures were little more than boys, while others were wizened old fellows.

All of these identically robed fellows put Harrison in mind of some sort of religious order, like paintings he'd seen of the appropriately-named cardinals of Rome, or a gathering of more sedately dressed Anglican bishops. But as several set to work with knives and spades to tend the grounds, Harrison realized these were not cardinals or bishops, more like—

"Monks," he concluded, plain folk dedicated to the service of their faith.

A lone monk, an older man, wrapped in saffron like the others but set apart by a vermilion sash, met them at the bottom of the stairs in front of the magnificent … church? Sanctuary? Harrison didn't know what to term the building.

The monks conversed briefly, with much gesturing to Harrison. Then the old monk turned his attention to the Englishman and bowed. Harrison returned the greeting.

The old man said, "*Bem vindo,* Khun Harrisondah. *Meu nome é* Thawichat. *Eu sou o abade do templo.*"

Harrison blinked in surprise. Portuguese? He'd not expected to hear any European tongue in this place. Hearing it now—even one he'd not mastered—was greatly cheering.

Thawichat gestured for Harrison and Wirat to precede him up the stairs. Harrison's supposition of being sheltered by a holy order was borne out when he followed his guide across the threshold of the ornate building and into a large chamber. His breath caught at the sight of a magnificent, golden Buddha—ten feet in height—seated upon a raised platform occupying the far end. The Buddha's right hand draped across one knee, while the left rested, palm up, in his lap. Serenity emanated from the Buddha's visage, but Harrison, unaccustomed to such displays, quailed in the presence of the larger-than-life idol.

So commanding was the idol's presence, it was a long moment before Harrison could look elsewhere and observe that the rest of the chamber was lavishly adorned to provide the statue a fitting abode. Stately pillars were lacquered a deep, oxblood red. Banners of red and white hanging from the ceiling were painted with images of animals and figures, all in gold. Pierced dark wood carvings ornamented the base of the shrine and overlaid red walls. Vases and bowls overflowed with fresh flowers, and platters piled high with food and flowers rested in offering. The heady aroma of incense filled the air, emanating from small bowls lined along the base of the altar.

A woman, a worshipper, he supposed, was on her knees near the front of the chamber. When Wirat knelt to bow before the golden figure, Harrison dropped to his knees, too. It seemed impossible to do otherwise. He'd never experienced such overwhelming religiosity. *Here* was holiness. *Here* was a place that compelled awe. Being in this sanctuary was akin to being in a royal presence. Though he did not offer himself in worship, he felt instinctively that kneeling was the proper, respectful thing to do.

After finishing his veneration, Wirat indicated in small, quiet gestures that Harrison should follow to the front of the sanctuary, where Thawichat sat cross-legged on a broad, low chair placed off-center in front of the grand altar.

The woman supplicant was still there, head bowed, a long, black braid nestled in the hollow of her spine. Glancing down as he passed on the woman's left side, Harrison glimpsed a high cheekbone beneath café au lait skin, a lovely slope of cheek, and a hint of full lips.

Then his attention was upon the senior monk. Thawichat bowed from his seat. "*Khun* Harrisondah. *Há alguém aqui que ...*"

Quickly losing the trail of the man's accented Portuguese, Harrison waved his hands. "No, sorry, sorry to interrupt, but I don't understand." Raking a hand through his disheveled hair, a frustrated growl rumbled in his throat. "I'm English. *Inglês,*" he finished lamely. If he couldn't communicate, how would he ever find his way home?

A feminine gasp sounded behind him.

Spinning, he found the female worshipper fully upright. The right side of her face, he saw, was badly scarred. But more arresting were her dark eyes, wide with shock and riveted upon him.

Her gaze searched his features, her shock quickly turning to confusion and, just as quickly, to joy. Lips trembling, she gave him an openmouthed smile like she'd just heard music for the first time in her life. The stiff right corner of her lips detracted nothing from the loveliness of her expression. Though he couldn't imagine why, the young lady was beyond happy to see him. No one had ever been so happy to see his ugly mug. All it took to find such welcome was traveling halfway 'round the world, getting lost at sea, and washing up on some unknown shore. Why hadn't he thought of it sooner?

He couldn't help but return her smile. They might not share a language, but he hoped she understood his wordless gratitude and reciprocation of friendliness.

A breath hitched in her throat. "Have you …" the woman started in accented, but perfectly clear, English. "That is, please, sir, are you here for me?"

• • •

When his warm smile fell to a frown of confusion, Lamai knew she'd made a terrible mistake.

Blinking at a sudden burning at the back of her eyes, she ducked her head, her cheeks burning. How could she have been so foolish? It was only, that feeling she'd had when Gaspar had told her about the shipwrecked *farang*, the sense that she would soon be reunited with her family, had blazed in her heart when he opened his mouth. Hearing him speak her father's language, learning that he was from her father's country … For a brief, beautiful moment, it had been true. Her father hadn't come himself, but had sent someone to find her.

She wished Gaspar was still here to deal with the *farang*. But when it was made clear the castaway's health was still precarious, her Portuguese keeper had returned to Bangkok by junk, leaving Lamai to handle the situation.

"What do you think, girl?" Thawichat said in Thai. Lamai lifted her head to meet the *jao ar-wart's* kind eyes. "He can barely speak and dresses like … that." His gaze slid to take in the *farang's* strange wrap. "Despite Luang Wirat's hard work saving this man, I fear his mind may have shattered at sea."

Perhaps it had, at that. Steeling herself, Lamai forced her eyes to return to the *farang*. His brown hair was long, almost to his shoulders. Unkempt moustache and beard of darker, reddish-brown covered the lower half of his face. He looked like a beast, and would have been frightening, but for being comically swathed in a sheet.

And his smile was not frightening, either, she allowed. When he'd turned and their eyes met—his being also brown, but a peculiarly light, caramel shade of it—something had passed between them. He'd smiled at her and she'd felt a sense of recognition, of kinship. But that had been wishful thinking on her part. She'd been looking for a connection to her lost father where one did not exist.

Probably, he was half-mad.

"I believe I can communicate with him," she told Thawichat. "He does not speak Portuguese, but another language. If you'll permit, I'll see what I can learn."

Permission granted, Lamai rose. The *farang's* attention was an uncomfortable thing, like Wan Pen chafing at her first lesson with reins. Subtly rolling her shoulders, Lamai spoke to the base of the man's throat. "Will you come with me, please, sir?" She spoke slowly, because she had not practiced English in a long time, and because the *farang* might be stupid, as he appeared.

He bowed, but different than the way with which she was familiar. "My pleasure, ma'am." He stepped close, closer, and poked his arm out at her, elbow bent. And he stood there, so strange and tall, expectant in his silence. His nearness was even more distressing than his attention. She could feel him there, the aura surrounding him. It crawled under her scalp, into her pores, carried his scent into her nose. A sort of animal funk, an undeniably male aroma.

The younger monk, Luang Wirat, clucked his tongue, shaking his head sadly. *Mad,* he seemed to say. *Definitely mad.*

Politely ignoring his odd arm gesture, Lamai tilted her head to the door. "This way, please, sir."

When she paused on the temple steps to slip into her shoes, he caught up to her. "In my country, England, a gentleman offers his arm when escorting a lady."

"*Mmmm,*" she replied noncommittally. Did Englishwomen present their arms in return, she wondered. She pictured scores of *farangs* parading about with bent elbows held aloft. What purpose did it serve? Maybe it signaled to others that one was occupied with a companion, while solitary people with arms at their sides were available for conversation. What a strange place England was!

"Do you care to walk the grounds, sir?"

"I would like that very much. And please, my name is Harrison Dyer, not *sir*." His eyes crinkled in a smile. "Might I have the honor of your name, ma'am?"

"My name is Lamai, Khun Harrison."

He reached out and took her hand, quite without invitation. A shock of alarm pulsed through her, but he smiled down, his clear brown eyes crinkling in that kind way. "The honor is mine, Miss Lamai." Then he bowed over her hand, doing her honor, as if she were a venerable person. It was most unsettling.

She heard a low hum and spotted the monk, Wirat, hovering in the temple door, frowning in disapproval. Lamai snatched her hand out of the *farang's*.

Spinning on her heel, she followed the paving stones around the side of the temple. "What have you seen so far?"

The man, Harrison, kept his strides short to remain abreast of her. "Nothing but the bit between the room they've given me and here. Tell me, Miss Lamai, where am I?"

"This is Wat Wihan." At his puzzled expression, she clarified, "A *wat* is a temple to Buddha."

"Thank you. What I meant to ask was, in what nation am I?"

Lamai felt her eyes widen. "You are *that* lost, sir?"

"I'm afraid so."

Sweeping an arm before her, Lamai proclaimed, "This is the Kingdom of Mueang Thai, known to others as Siam."

He let out a low whistle. "Why did those fellows, the monks, assume I was Portuguese?"

"There are more Portuguese in Mueang Thai than citizens of any other western nation," Lamai explained. "Many Thai people—those out in the countryside, like your hosts—are unaware of any European country or language besides that of Portugal." She passed her hand over the white blossom of an orchid. "You are white, so they assume you are Portuguese." Lamai courteously kept to herself the monks' conclusion that their European guest swathed in a bedsheet and gibbering in an unfamiliar tongue was mad.

"What's this creature called?" Harrison asked, stopping at a juncture in the path and indicating a bronze statue with the upper body of a woman, and the legs, tail, and wings of a swan.

"A *Kinnaree*. Such beings are beautiful, graceful, and accomplished in dance and song."

Harrison cocked his head as he studied the statue. "The song part I believe, but she must have a devil of a time dancing on those legs."

Lamai cleared her throat. As delicately as possible, she corrected him. "I assure you, Khun Harrison, the Kinnaree is most adept at dance."

The bird legs and clawed feet of the mythical creature had been a solace to Lamai during her insecure adolescence. Thanks to her *farang* blood, she was larger than most women, with veritable flippers for feet. If the Kinnaree could master graceful movement with her nonhuman limbs, then there was hope for Lamai, too.

The scrub on Harrison's face shifted; she thought his lips twitched. "That remark was intended to be humorous. It was a jest. A poor one, evidently. I beg your pardon."

Mock a revered being? Who would do such a crass thing? This Harrison Dyer did not speak as if he were mad, after all—just *farang*. Good thing Lamai knew her father was a man of honor, else she might judge all Englishmen by the poor example given by this one.

From the corner of her eye, she noticed Wirat ambling in their direction, hands behind his back, as if taking a stroll. Evidently, he was to be their escort, following at a discreet distance to ensure there would be no further immodest displays like the one on the shrine steps. Bad enough Gaspar had made a poor impression on Jao Ar-wart Thawichat; now Harrison, too, was disrespecting their beliefs and customs. Why must she always suffer the humiliation of association with these boorish people?

"Come, *farang*."

Without looking to see if he followed, she took the paved path leading to the rear of the *wat* compound. She wanted to check on the girls.

His bare feet slapped the paving stones as he hurried to catch up; his sheet-wrap *swish-swished* behind him. She cringed in sympathy for the monk who would have to launder the abused linen.

"What does that word mean? *Farang*?"

When she glanced to the side, she saw his chest was rising and falling quickly; perspiration dewed his throat. Recalling he'd recently endured an ordeal at sea, she felt a twinge of sympathy.

"I vaguely recall the villagers calling me *farang* when they brought me ashore," he elaborated.

A group of laughing young novices beat rugs against a wooden post, dust billowing around their shaved heads, dirtying their golden-orange robes. One of them spotted Lamai and Harrison and whispered to the others. Immediately, the boys fell silent and gawked as the woman and white man passed. Elsewhere on the grounds a bell pealed, calling the monks to meditation. Each man they passed greeted Harrison and expressed their gladness at seeing him restored to good health.

Naturally, he did not understand their good wishes. He grinned and nodded like an imbecile, leaving Lamai to thank the monks on his behalf.

These good people had done more than bring him ashore; they had provided him shelter, food, and healing for ten days—but who was counting? Not him, it seemed. Like nearly every *farang* before him, Harrison hadn't bothered to learn their language before coming here, just expected to be accommodated, for others to shoulder the burden of learning a new language and bend to new ways.

She waited until they were once more alone before answering his query. "*Farang* means a European, a white person. Sometimes it is not a courteous term," she told him crisply.

"Oh." He was silent for a few seconds, then: "But I'm sure *you* do not mean it unkindly, Miss Lamai. Not when we've only just met, and you do not know me at all."

"In Thai custom, you should address me as *Khun* Lamai, not *miss*."

"In *my* custom—"

"You are in Mueang Thai," she snapped, lips trembling with indignation and heat flooding her face, "not your England."

Something flashed in his eyes; his brows snapped together. Her breath caught, waiting for him to scold her show of anger. Instead, he pressed a hand to his chest and bent his neck. "You're quite right. Thank you for teaching me, Khun Lamai."

She jerked her head in reply. Gaspar had never given Lamai the courtesy Khun, even when she was full-grown. Why did she expect it from this Englishman?

Harrison held his hands behind his back, echoing their silent shadow, still trailing them at a distance. "Why did you think I had come for you?" he asked, just as she said, "Why have you come to Siam?"

He laughed; she gave an awkward smile. She'd hoped he had forgotten the impetuous words she'd spoken in the shrine. No such luck.

Thankfully, they arrived at the area where the monks kept their few animals, and a happy trumpeting caught Harrison's attention. "My word, are those elephants?"

Goui was having a good wallow in the dirt, while rangy chickens flapped around, keeping out of her way as they scratched for supper. As for the little girl—

Lamai laughed when she saw Wan Pen. Perched on her back, balancing on dainty hooves, was a little fawn goat.

"Is that …?" Harrison whispered. His face had paled. He clutched the rail of the enclosure, staring at the smaller elephant.

"Wan Pen, you made a new friend," Lamai called—in English, for Harrison's benefit; the elephant wouldn't understand anything in that language.

The animal on Wan Pen's back started bleating and prancing in place.

"Tilda?" the *farang* said. "Tilda, you're alive!"

Unlatching the gate, he sprinted across the enclosure to Wan Pen. At the fast approach of a stranger, the young elephant lurched sideways and cried out, eyes rolling to show white. The goat stumbled, barely stopping itself from tumbling to the ground. At the sound of Wan Pen's distress, Goui lifted her head and bellowed. Ears flapping madly, she lumbered to her feet, preparing to charge in defense of the little one. Chickens squawked and scattered, smarter than the white man in the face of an upset elephant.

"Harrison, stop!" Lamai shrieked. The Englishman froze. The sheet slipped from his shoulder; he caught it at his waist. "Don't move," Lamai scolded, panic ringing in her ears. "You're about to be trampled."

"So I gather," he drawled. "What should I do?"

Just then, Panit appeared from a small barn, towing a cart full of straw. When he saw the situation, he dropped the cart and quickly moved to put himself in Goui's line of sight, talking so she could hear her *mahout*. With hands extended, he slowly approached the old lady, speaking soothing words to calm her.

Meanwhile, Lamai went to Wan Pen, stroking her face in comfort. Goat droppings bounced off the elephant's thick skin, reminding Lamai there were three frightened animals at risk. In a gentle tone belying her anger, she said, "Get away from here, *farang*."

"I—I'm sorry," he stammered. "I didn't mean—"

"Get away," Lamai repeated firmly. "Go outside the fence, so the elephants know they are safe." Without another word, he did as she told him, drooping sheet dragging forlornly behind.

When she heard the gate close she glanced at Panit, who was restraining Goui by means of his outstretched arms. If she wanted to, Goui could shove past the man easy as passing through grass. Fortunately, the elephant minded her *mahout* and stayed put. As her heaving breaths subsided, Panit stepped aside, allowing

Goui to come verify Wan Pen's welfare for herself. Lamai found herself shouldered away by the seven-and-a-half-foot tall creature. Rumbling communication passed between nanny and girl.

"That's the *farang* we came for?" Panit's tuft stood out at crazy angles on top of his head, like the hackles of an enraged dog. He snorted derisively at Lamai's affirmative. "Fine thing for us to come all this way and cool our heels while he lazes in bed." Planting his hands on his slim hips, he strode back to the cart, ranting all the while. "Then the minute he's up, he nearly gets himself and the girls killed. The fishermen should have left him in the sea." Rocking back and forth to get the laden cart moving, the *mahout's* eyes narrowed on their visitor. "What is that he's wearing?"

Feeling Harrison's gaze on her as she had in the temple, Lamai glanced over her shoulder. Standing well back from the fence, he still clutched the sheet with one hand, the other hanging at his side. His shoulders were broad, his bare chest lean—but not a healthy leanness, she saw. Collarbones jutted prominently from the base of his throat. The shapes of muscles were visible on his chest and belly, but the skin above them was a bit slack. He'd been quickly depleted.

Their monk-escort, Wirat, stood awkwardly close to, but behind, the Englishman's side, as if wanting to intervene somehow, now that the crisis was over.

Harrison's lips were turned down, like a dejected child's. "I'm sorry," he repeated. "I deserve whatever curses that fellow laid upon my head." He glanced at Panit. "I should've known better. A horse would have spooked, too."

Lamai smacked lips tingling with tart words, but kept them to herself. The Englishman might have some superficial understanding of animals, but clearly not enough to be trusted around them. Lamai had never seen an African hippopotamus in person, but she knew good and well not to charge one.

"It's just, that's my goat, you see, Tilda. I thought she was gone. Dead, I mean. She died in my arms just before I was rescued." He shrugged. Sharp bones threatened to pierce his thin skin. "I was surprised to see her."

All that fuss, all that foolishness, over a goat? Lamai couldn't credit it. The English! Lamai was glad she'd not inherited that peculiarity from her father's people. Or perhaps, she considered, his wits were addled, after all. "Another step, and you'd have had an even bigger surprise, when Goui stomped you into the ground."

He winced. "I know. Thank you, thank you both," he said, nodding to Panit, "for saving my idiot skin."

"Your words, *farang*," she returned, imitating his drawl. His smile flashed a row of white teeth and a hint of pink tongue. Lamai's neck prickled. Turning abruptly, she saw the elephants' reunion was concluded. Goui trundled back to her dust bath. "Kneel," Lamai told Wan Pen, and kept a steadying hand on the goat while the elephant lowered to her foreknees. She lifted the little creature, legs stiff, to the ground.

"Tilda," Harrison called, stooping at the fence. "Come here, girl."

"He treats it like a dog," Panit said. Having dumped the hay in a pile for the girls, he now stood beside Lamai. "Goats are stupid."

To the surprise of them both, the goat trotted to the fence, bleating happily, and thrust her face between the rails to receive Harrison's pats. Lamai's brows rose. "Maybe English goats are smarter than ours." She'd prefer that explanation to having to admit that Harrison might have some expertise with animals, after all.

Panit snorted. "They must have borrowed brains from the people. Now they're equal, man and goat."

The left side of Lamai's mouth lifted. "Is it really his goat?" Sauntering to the gate, she directed this question to Wirat. "He said his goat died."

The monk nodded. "The fishermen thought it dead, too, and brought it here in offering. But when it was dropped in the temple, it opened its eyes and pissed on the floor." Eyes crinkled in smile, he watched the little creature lick the white man's face. "Goats don't like to die if they don't have to," he concluded with a shrug.

Harrison lifted his face, strings of goat slobber clinging to his whiskers. "What was that?" Lamai translated the gist of the monk's words. Bolting to his feet, Harrison extended his hand to Wirat. The monk gamely took it. "Thank you," Harrison exclaimed. "Thank you so much. How do I thank him?" he asked Lamai.

"You make *wai*," she demonstrated, pressing her palms together and bowing, "and you say '*kob khun khap.*'"

Harrison's execution was poor, but Wirat appreciated the attempt, smiling and nodding in return. Reflecting on Gaspar's humiliating refusal to show the monks deference, Lamai, too, grudgingly respected Harrison's effort.

Wirat rattled off a question. She translated, "Khun Harrison, Luang Wirat would like to know how you came to be here. What happened to you in the ocean?"

The smile slipped from Harrison's face; a shadow crossed his golden brown eyes. "I sailed with *Brizo's Woe*," he began. "We embarked from London in September, on a trade expedition to Brunei." Lamai translated at pauses in his speech. Panit perched on the top rail of the fence to listen to the Englishman's harrowing tale of a tsunami that hounded the ill-fated ship for a week, driving it off course and ultimately destroying it and almost everyone aboard. When he spoke of the ship's demise, Wirat gasped and brought a hand to his mouth. Lamai saw Panit discreetly swipe a finger across his eye.

"We never meant to come to Siam at all," he finished, "but I am most grateful for the kind hospitality I have received here." He made *wai* again, more smoothly this time. "*Kob khun khap.*"

Wirat gave a quiet sigh of satisfaction at the conclusion of his guest's story.

Like the great storm he'd described churning up the sea bed, Harrison's tale agitated Lamai's emotions. She pitied his suffering, but knowing with a certainty that he'd sailed from England generated resentment, too. Why couldn't her father have been on that ship? Why couldn't it have been he brought here by fate? Or … a terrible thought pierced her heart: What if he had tried to come for her, any time in the last twenty years? What if he, too, like the men of *Brizo's Woe*, had been lost at sea?

Loss and fear clutched her throat. "*Farang*," Lamai blurted, "why do you wear no clothes?"

His tanned face turned ruddy, and pink spread across his paler chest. "There were none in my room. I don't make a habit of going out in my bedclothes, I assure you."

"He says he has no clothes," she put to Wirat. The shift in conversation took her mind off her wild imaginings. Images of dead men and animals battered by the sea receded before concrete domestic banalities.

The monk waved a hand. "The clothes he arrived in were ruined, but I placed new ones in his chamber myself."

When she relayed this, Harrison's brows drew together in a firm line. "I must have overlooked them. I saw only fresh bedding."

"*Ooohh.*" Lamai thought she understood the matter. "*Panung?*" Wirat nodded. To the untrained eye, the long, flat rectangle of material might appear to be a coverlet. To Panit, she said, "He doesn't know how to use the *panung*. Will you show him?"

They trooped to the guest quarters, and the two men went into Harrison's hut. When they emerged about fifteen minutes later, the Englishman was properly dressed, the blue *panung* having been pleated and tied around the waist, then tucked between the legs to create breeches. A red sash held the garment up. "Ha!" the white man crowed. "I should have figured it out myself. Women do this at home, sometimes, to get their skirts out of the way if they're going wading or what have you. How did I do?" Holding his arms out, he turned a circle.

"I showed him three times, then he made me watch him do it another three, to make sure he got it," Panit reported. "Wan Pen learns her lessons on the first try."

When she chuckled, Harrison's eyes flicked from her to the mahout. "What does he say?"

"That you are a good student," Lamai hedged. "You did a fine job, *farang*."

The sun was slipping low. Wirat took his leave, and Panit loped along after the monk to return to the animals. Lamai wanted to be back in the village before it was full dark.

"It was nice to meet you, Khun Harrison." She made *wai*, bowing lower than he deserved. But she would never see him again, and he *had* done honor to her by bowing over her hand, even if it had been wildly improper. "Good luck in your travels, sir."

His hand shot out, enveloping her arm in a warm grip. Lamai startled, jerked, but he held firm. "Why do you sound like you're taking your leave of me for good?"

"Because I am, sir. In the morning, I must return to my master's home in Bangkok."

A wild look blazed in his eyes, rendering him once more the untamed, feral beast she'd espied in the shrine. "Who the devil is your master? And what am I supposed to do?"

With a solid yank, Lamai succeeded in freeing herself of his hand. Her own clapped over the place where he'd held her, rubbing her skin as if she were bruised, trapping his heat in her flesh. "My master is Gaspar D'Cruz, of Portugal. He received word of you, and so we came."

"But now you're going to leave me?" He swayed where he stood, like an anxious elephant. "Why?" he breathed.

Lamai thought of all the reasons: He was no one who would be of interest to the Portuguese ambassador in Bangkok; he was not a direct competitor of Khun Gaspar, but he was in commerce, and therefore, her master would expect her not to assist him; and finally, he was not her father. In short, he was everything he shouldn't be, and nothing anybody wanted.

When the words formed in her mind, though, she didn't have the heart to say them. She simply shook her head and took a step back.

"Don't leave me here. Please." There was desperation in his voice, naked fear in his eyes. "I don't know how to get home."

His plea tugged at her heart, but Gaspar would not thank her if she went soft on this man. Lamai crossed her arms, hugging herself. "I'm sorry, sir, but I cannot take you with me. Goodbye."

His face, crumpling in despair, was her last sight of the lost *farang*.

Chapter Four

It rained through the night and into the next morning. When the sun should have risen and brought color, the world became lavender-gray, instead. Lamai trekked from the coastal village to the *wat* one last time, a small pack slung across her body, struggling through the slurry the road had become. The break from her life at Khun Gaspar's house should have been a respite; rather, she felt older and wearier now than she had before she'd come to this place.

She had only herself to blame for dashed hopes. Her overwrought imagination had encouraged her to believe her father might await her at the end of her journey. Nebulously *knowing* she'd find her missing family in a backwater *wat* was not the same as true knowledge. The pain she felt was just punishment for manufacturing fantasies.

A gust of wind loosed rivulets of water from overhead branches. Lamai tugged her hat lower and scrunched her shoulders against the cold liquid slipping down the back of her neck.

Her father *would* come, but she was too old for girlish dreams. She hadn't even had such hopes until Gaspar invited her to come live with him eight years ago. Before then, her late mother's steadfast avowals that her English husband would return for her and Lamai had been eroded from Lamai's heart by years of disparaging talk from relatives who claimed Lamai had seen the last of her father when he left Bangkok so many years ago. Gaspar had known her father, knew he was as good as his word, and offered Lamai a place to live while she waited for her parent.

That connection and testimony from Gaspar had taught Lamai to hope again. To dream of a future in which she had a place in the world. Family who wanted and loved her, instead of her late mother's relatives, to whom Lamai had been an unwanted burden. From now on, though, she would look for concrete signs—a letter or a ship from London—and not search for omens in every white face she encountered.

At the *wat's* front gate, she encountered a group of monks armed with urns for collecting alms. Bowing deeply, she waited for them to pass before continuing on to the back of the compound, where Panit would be readying the girls for the trip home.

Her eyes were drawn to the guest quarters. Wary for any sign of the *farang*, nerves scurried through her belly like a mound of busy ants. Harrison's hut was as dark and still as the rest of the shelters in the row. The tension in her middle eased.

Tilting her face so the brim of her hat blocked the guest quarters from view, Lamai hurried to the paddock. She glimpsed Panit concluding preparations with the elephants. The head monk, Thawichat, stood outside the gate, hands at his back, unperturbed by the rain. Two men accompanied the Jao Ar-wart, Wirat and—

"No," she groaned as she went to the trio. Making *wai*, she greeted the holy men, then lifted her gaze to the insolent Englishman. Overnight, Harrison Dyer had transformed. If not for his height and the shade of his skin, she wouldn't have known him at a glance. The scruffy beard was gone, in its place a clean, firm jaw and square chin. Newly-revealed cheeks skimmed the ridge of sharp cheekbones, then sloped smoothly into dells on either side of his mouth. His longish hair was rain-dark and waved around his face, softening the features unearthed by some hardworking razor.

"Khun Harrison." She gave him *wai*, as well. "I did not expect to see you again, sir. What a surprise."

"Good morning, Khun Lamai." Harrison bowed in his English fashion. He wore the blue *panung* and red sash again, with a loose white shirt and red vest. Battered leather boots covered his feet and calves. "By the intonation of your voice, I cannot determine whether the surprise of seeing me is a good one or a poor one."

He paused, subtly lifted a brow. It was another attempt at humor, she deduced. He did not seem to understand that his teasing put her in a predicament. The tips of her ears warmed.

"A good surprise, of course," she answered, as politeness required. She glanced at the monks. Though they could not comprehend the English language exchange, she had a suspicion Thawichat, in particular, would be able to intuit any impropriety on her part.

"Lamai." Panit trotted over to the rail. "Tell the *farang* to give me his trunk."

Swiveling, Lamai looked where the *mahout* indicated and saw a slightly battered container on the ground, partially concealed by an overhanging shrub.

"What ...?"

"Too bad about the weather." Harrison glanced upward before settling his gaze on her. His lips—starkly naked now—quirked, but not in a smile, not anything that touched his hard eyes. "We're in for a soggy day of travel."

Lamai shook her head, bewildered. Yesterday, she'd made it quite clear that he would not accompany her today. "Sir, you're not ..."

He continued, taking no notice of her objections. "Fortunately, we English are practically semiaquatic, thanks to our own incessant rain. A little damp won't bother me in the least."

"Khun Lamai." Wirat sidled as close to her as he dared, his fingers tucked safely away in the folds of his saffron robe. "Please ensure Khun Harrisondah eats regularly to continue building his strength. During your journey, permit him breaks to exercise, so his muscles will not wither further. When it's time for sleep …" The monk continued prattling off instructions like a fretful nursemaid. Lamai's mouth opened and shut, working silently.

Behind her, Panit huffed. "I need that trunk, Lamai."

"There's been a mistake," she said weakly to Wirat. The monk frowned.

"What does your friend say?" Harrison asked. "He seems most insistent."

"Panit wants your trunk," she parroted, "but why?" Her muddy shoes came almost toe-to-toe with his boots. Abstractedly, she noted that her large feet were dainty in comparison to his great flippers. "I told you no, *farang*. I told you, you cannot come."

Thawichat cleared his throat. "Everything all right, *phar?*"

Lamai ducked her head. Thank goodness the Jao Ar-wart could not discern her words, but her tone was testy, impolite.

"Miss Lamai, might I trouble you for a word of advice?" Cupping her elbow, Harrison steered her to his trunk and tugged her arm to make her crouch beside him.

A clever diversion for their confrontation, but it wouldn't change the outcome. "You can't come with me," she hissed.

His fingers worked a metal clasp. He lifted the lid and scanned the contents. "I want to give the monks a gift to thank them for saving my life."

What sorts of things did he own? Not clothes, she presumed, since those had to be provided for him. The fact that his luggage had survived the sinking of his ship made his inability to dress himself even more puzzling. She would not permit herself to be distracted, however, and kept her eyes trained on Harrison's profile. The bridge of his nose was straight, a slope that sheltered his lips—lips, which, from this angle, were not as firm as they looked straight-on. Though by no means plump, they were full, as if they would be soft to the touch.

"How about this?"

Harrison's question snapped Lamai out of her meditation on his mouth. She wouldn't have been studying it so closely if he had been paying attention to her words, instead of his luggage.

He withdrew a smaller wooden cask, held it out to her. "Well?"

"You aren't listening," she grumbled, giving the geometric inlay design on the lid a glance before opening the cask. "You can't travel with me."

The box contained a tea set, a pot and four cups nested on their sides in a cushion specially formed to support the china. The decoration was foreign, lilac sprigs of flowers she didn't recognize and simple lines of gilding along the rims, instead of intricate designs. But the familiarity of the vessel itself touched something inside her. All the way in England, people had teapots. Gaspar had a fine tea set, of course, but something about this one made it seem a precious artifact. Perhaps because it was a clue about her father. If this Englishman valued the consumption of tea highly enough to bring this service with him from across the world, then her father probably drank tea, too.

"I'll beg your forgiveness later, but I *am* coming with you." Blinking her stinging eyes, Lamai met Harrison's grave expression. "Bangkok is where I need to go if I'm to return to England, yes?" She grunted. "As I thought. I've no money and no friends. It doesn't please me to intrude where I'm not wanted, but ..." He shrugged. "That's just how it is. I'm coming with you. And as you see, the monks and your friend over there think I'm going, too." He closed the tea set and took it from her hands.

"You don't need me." Lamai touched the cask, felt the smooth warmth of the wood. The box by itself would fetch a pretty price in the right shop. "You could sell that set for a lot of money."

One of his straight brows rose. "To the fishermen? I suspect the nearest buyer with riches to spare is in Bangkok." Grudgingly, she allowed he was probably correct. "Will this do for a gift?" he pressed.

Lamai hesitated. Monks took vows of poverty and renounced personal property. This tea set was a treasure. Even Thawichat would not be able to accept it. Harrison looked so earnest, though, and it was a kind gesture he wished to make.

She nodded. "It's a wonderful gift, Khun Harrison."

His eyes relaxed and he smiled. He rose, then offered Lamai his hand. His palm was pale pink and calloused. An impulse took her to feel that rough skin against her own. But she must not do such a thing here, before these holy witnesses. Pretending she didn't see his offer of help, she stood.

"Will you translate for me?"

"Yes. Kneel before Thawichat."

Harrison sank to his knees at once, with none of the resistance or pride Gaspar showed in a *wat*. "Thank you for saving my life," he said softly, "and for your generous hospitality. I wish I had more to give, but I hope this will serve as a token of my gratitude and esteem."

Lamai translated, then added, "This gift is intended for the use of all, Jao Ar-wart, to remind the monks of Wat Wihan of their English friend." Thawichat took the box from Harrison, opened it. He and Wirat *ooh'ed* and *aah'ed* over the fine china. The senior monk passed the box to Wirat, then settled a hand on Harrison's head and prayed.

When Harrison stood, he bowed to Thawichat and then to Wirat, offering his thanks, *kob khun khap,* to each. Turning to Lamai, Harrison's face was serene. "What did Thawichat say?" he asked as he hoisted his trunk onto his shoulder.

"Thawichat gave thanks for your gift," Lamai explained. "He blessed you with abundance in your next life, to never know hunger or thirst."

Harrison nodded thoughtfully. Inside the paddock, he passed the trunk to Panit, then called to his goat. Tilda, who had been sharing some fruit with Wan Pen, ambled over and nudged Harrison's thigh.

"Ready, girl?" Harrison patted the goat's head. "How would you like to see a big city?"

"No!" Lamai gestured sharply. "The goat stays here."

"I can't leave her."

"Then maybe you stay, too," she shot. Harrison scowled, and Lamai scowled right back.

"What's the problem?" Panit asked.

"He wants to bring the goat." She cocked her head, knowing the *mahout* would be on her side.

"Of course the goat comes, too. Wan Pen is very attached to her new friend."

The goat gamboled around the young elephant's feet. Wan Pen gave a happy toot. Harrison smiled innocently.

Lamai groaned.

• • •

Ensconced in a chariot atop an elephant, waving goodbye to the monks, nodding at gawping locals as they passed through the village … For the first hour of the trip, Harrison felt like a sultan.

Then the goat threw up on his boot.

While Tilda had never suffered from seasickness during their time as castaways, she seemed to have a sad case of elephant-sickness. The smell of her mess on his boots did nothing for Harrison's own digestion; when his ruminant friend sniffed his feet and began licking up her own sick, he had to squeeze shut his eyes.

Midmorning, the rain finally stopped. The sun emerged, and about thirty seconds later the air was hot. Then bloody hot. Sweat poured from every inch of his skin and pooled in unmentionable crevices. That morning, after his bath, one of the monks had offered to shave Harrison after scraping the stubble from the cheeks and scalp of another priest. After tending his face, the monk had playfully mimed shaving Harrison's head, and they'd all had a good chuckle when Harrison waved his hands in refusal. Now he wished he'd taken the man up on the offer. This was intolerable. He shifted in his seat, the bench's padding losing something of its comfortable luster in its propensity to retain warmth. The awning blocked the sun's direct rays, but it couldn't save him from feeling like a partridge roasting in the oven. He'd be cooked and ready for serving by dinner.

Ahead of him, Panit sat just to the rear of the elephant's ears. His red-brown back was dewed with sweat, but nothing like the rivers forging brave new courses across the landscape of Harrison. The Thai man held the reins in a loose grip and every so often spoke a word or two to the animal.

The elephant's plodding pace was maddening. What Harrison wouldn't give to move at a horse's gallop, to create a cooling wind of his own and devour miles until he reached Bangkok. "So, how fast can one of these go? How's it take curves?" Panit glanced over his shoulder, nose wrinkled against the sun, and smiled.

Twisting in his seat, Harrison looked at Lamai perched atop the little elephant, Wan Pen. She used no reins at all, instead guiding her mount by means of a bamboo stick, which she tapped on the elephant's shoulder when she issued a command.

"How long did it take you to learn to do that?" he called.

Lamai lifted her face. The brim of her hat shaded her eyes, though he felt her watching him. Her lips were a pretty plum, full and round. The scarring on the right side of her face tugged the corner of her mouth slightly downward, resulting in a permanent pout. Harrison had known many a lady in London who practiced long hours to achieve just that air of vague dissatisfaction. He very much doubted Lamai's version was intended to make him rush to appease her with a glass of punch or a strained compliment.

"Not long." Her tone did not invite further questions. It was a cryptic remark. *Not long* by what metric, Harrison wondered.

Was riding an elephant the sort of skill one picked up during term break from school, or did it require dedicated practice over a year or more?

He swiped his sleeve across his brow. "When will we be there?"

"Not long."

"Is that the same 'not long' as learning to command an elephant?"

He thought he saw a ghost of a smile shift her lips. "Your goat is sick, *farang.*"

Indeed, Tilda was once more emptying the contents of one of her stomachs on the floor of the carriage. *Marvelous.*

Late in the afternoon, they stopped at a farmhouse. As the elephants knelt to discharge their passengers, a woman rounded the side of the house, wiping her palms on her skirt. It was a familiar, homey sort of gesture, the action of a goodwife engaged in domestic chores and surprised by company. Less familiar was her bare chest.

In his haste to avert his eyes, Harrison fumbled his descent from the elephant carriage, bumbling his way to the ground. Lamai hopped off of Wan Pen and slid her hat off her head. It dangled onto her back by a red string around her neck. He could see now that her long, inky hair had been tied into a topknot that reminded him of the Buddha idol. Lamai greeted the woman, then gestured to Harrison and Panit as she spoke. The goodwife bowed to them, her eyes alight with curiosity when she saw his pale face. Harrison scarcely knew where to look when he returned the greeting, opting to train his eyes over the lady's shoulder. As no one else seemed the least bit discombobulated by the woman's nudity, he gathered it was not out of place. His discomfort, therefore, was his own to bear.

As the women conversed, two young children emerged from inside the house. The younger, naked, toddled to his mother and latched onto her leg. The other, a child of indeterminate sex of about seven years, skipped toward the elephants until spotting Harrison, at which point, the child's dark eyes flew wide, and he or she joined the baby beside their mother.

Lamai produced a pouch and fished out a few coins. The woman accepted these, bowed again, and gestured towards the farmyard while she herded the little ones back indoors.

"We will stay here tonight," Lamai told him, tucking her purse behind her waistband.

"You paid that woman?" Harrison's index finger indicated the door of the house.

Lamai's broad nostrils flared. "Don't point, *farang*, especially not at a person. It's very rude."

He curled his finger back into his fist. *Pointing, out. Bare breasts, fine. Noted.* "I beg your pardon."

"And yes, I paid that lady. Do you English not pay to spend the night when traveling?"

"We do, it's just …" He shifted his weight. Mud squelched beneath his feet. "Customarily, a gentleman would settle the arrangements, is all."

"What gentleman? You?" A tinkling laugh fell from her lips.

He scowled at her laughter. "If I spoke your language, yes, I'd have done so."

Her left brow lifted in a smooth arch. The right was lashed down, held flat by scars, rendering her expression skeptical. "Have money, *farang*? You can pay tomorrow night."

Harrison's purse lay somewhere at the bottom of the sea. His coins were British, in any event, worthless here. He was as utterly dependent upon her charity as he had been with the monks. All of his adult life, he'd worked towards freedom, striving to find his own place, his own peace. Helplessness was a hair shirt he couldn't wait to shed. "How about Panit?"

Lamai snorted. "Panit has charge of the elephants, not the money." Her tone suggested this should have been obvious to any fool. "Why do you want a man to do the business? Am I not capable?" She extended her hands, palms up. "Tell me, *farang*, are my hands broken?"

Her palms were creamy taupe, crisscrossed with lines made bold by the grime of the day's journey. She'd have made the job easy for a country fair fortune teller. Harrison brought his own hands beneath hers, skated the pads of his thumbs over the ridges of her fingers. Lamai inhaled sharply, quivering imperceptibly like a hare that feels the hawk's gaze, weighing whether prudence required stillness or flight. Harrison stilled, giving her no reason to flee.

This delicate touch was sufficient; any more would disturb him, too. It was enough to feel the faint shiver of warmth passing between them. No Romani seer, he, but the almonds of her nails and thick places on her palms revealed much. Lamai's life was not one of habitual hard labor, else she'd never maintain that neat manicure. But neither was it one of total leisure. He already knew she worked at elephant riding, but she didn't use reins—any callouses she bore from that exercise were elsewhere on her body. Rather, the thickened skin at the base of her fingers indicated she carried things—buckets of water or animal feed, baskets of market goods, maybe ... not heavy labor, but regular.

"These are good, capable hands." Glancing up, he met her wary look. He lowered his arms, freeing her from his featherlight snare. "I apologize if I offended you, Miss Lamai."

"Khun—"

"*Khun* Lamai," he corrected himself, chuckling. He wanted to tell her it wasn't lack of confidence that drove his queries about her role in transacting their accommodations, but concern for her safety. Even now, when a dog's bark and the sound of male voices heralded the arrival of two men, Harrison subtly shifted to place himself between Lamai and the newcomers. Highway robbers, leering innkeepers, village drunks with roaming hands—these were all very real dangers from which honorable English gentlemen shielded women.

He did not think she would welcome yet another lecture on how things were different in his country, though, so he kept silent. And felt rather ashamed of himself, anyway, when the men appeared. The elder of the two was all of five feet tall, scrawny and grizzled like a scrap of dried beef, and didn't have a right hand. He carried buckets of water on a pole across his shoulders. The younger fellow had the look of the first, obviously his son, a lanky youth hauling farming implements in his slender arms. When they spotted the strangers on their land, the farmer and son were all smiles and greetings.

In short order, the gathering had the feeling of an impromptu party. Their hostess and the other children spilled out of the house again, chatting and laughing while the scruffy mongrel that accompanied the men yapped at the elephants and goat.

Soon, another bucket, this one containing milk, was produced, and bowls passed to the visitors first before the family partook. The Thai men squatted in a circle in the muddy yard, while Lamai disappeared with the woman and children behind the house. The dog was quickly accepted by Wan Pen as another playmate, though Tilda seemed less inclined to share her new, enormous friend, going so far as to butt the mongrel when it came near. Harrison stood, stiff and awkward in his English leather boots and Siamese garb, fitting nowhere in this scene.

"*Farang!*" Panit waved him over to join the men. Harrison tried to imitate their stance, but wound up splashing his arse into a puddle. The resulting laugh that mishap elicited from the men— and himself—earned Harrison a friendly slap on the shoulder from the farmer, and just like that, he was one of the fellows. No matter he couldn't understand a word they said, there was an inherent maleness to the cadence of conversation that Harrison found comfortable.

Fragrant cooking aromas drifted on the evening air. Harrison's stomach rumbled in sharp anticipation. After a time, the farmer's wife leaned out of the door and called the men in to supper.

Everyone slipped off their shoes before entering. Harrison was obliged to sit on his rump and perform a hurried wiggle-and-tug to shed his tall boots. Ducking under the low lintel, he blinked in the dim interior. The house was comprised of a single room with a dirt floor. A cross-work of bare beams covered with roofing material were just above Harrison's head. A few wooden toys were jumbled in one corner, beside a stack of mats. A shelf on the wall held a mishmash assortment of bowls and plates, and there was a standing cupboard next to it. That was the entirety of the house's contents. Through an open back door, he spied an outdoor kitchen arrangement. A simple shelter covered a fire pit and a table littered with vegetable scraps. A dented and rusty tin washbasin rested on the ground, several pans soaking inside.

The family arranged themselves in a circle on the floor, surrounding steaming, covered baskets and platters. Lamai glanced over her left shoulder and smiled, patting the empty place between herself and one of the children. It was plenty of room for a Thai person of slender and short stature, but Harrison had to fold his knees tight and hunch his shoulders to fit into the narrow spot. The child stared solemnly up at him with large brown eyes. When Harrison returned the favor with an exaggerated, stern expression, the tyke giggled, then scooted close, pressing a thin brown arm against Harrison's thicker, paler limb.

Their hostess removed the lid from a woven basket, revealing a mound of white rice. A wooden paddle was deployed to heap a serving onto the plates in front of each person. Next, a stew of vegetables and a few lumps of greasy meat was spooned beside each child's rice.

With a flourish, the farmwife lifted the cover from a platter, releasing a billow of steam. When the fog cleared, Harrison found himself staring into the milky, sightless eye of a whole, steamed fish swimming in a fragrant broth and topped with a medley of chopped red, white, and green vegetables. A beautiful presentation impressive in its wholesome simplicity. He was given the honor of first choice. White, flaky flesh lifted clean from the bone as he transferred some fish to his plate.

Of long habit, he reached down for a fork. His fingers closed on nothing. Had the utensils been forgotten? "Umm …"

Lamai's elbow nudged him. "Like this." She demonstrated how to take some rice and roll it into a ball, which was then flattened into a disc. This was pinched over some meat, then the whole parcel was popped into her mouth.

Harrison clumsily imitated her, absurdly proud with his own efforts in creating a little bundle of fish and vegetables. His pleasure lasted only until his teeth punctured the wrapping of rice, and his mouth was suddenly washed in liquid fire.

Choking back a cough, Harrison forced himself to swallow the spicy bite, but that only spread heat down his gullet. Sweat popped out of his pores. His eyes and nose watered. Unable to restrain himself any longer, he coughed and coughed.

The farmer pounded Harrison's back, as if to save him from choking. Harrison waved a hand. "I'm all right," he croaked, then opened his mouth to fan his scalded tongue. The hostess jumped up and scurried around to hand him a cup of water, which he greedily gulped. The fire persisted. He stifled a whimper.

"Too hot?" Lamai's eyes danced with mirth. "Eat rice."

Harrison dutifully pinched off more of the sticky grain and ate it plain. Finally, blessed relief as it sponged up some of the hellfire in his mouth.

"Here." Lamai pressed a scrap of cloth into his hands. Harrison swabbed his face. The flow of tears and snot slowed, but he found himself blinking and sniffing more than was seemly.

Across the circle, Panit shook his head. He and the oldest son murmured and laughed. Harrison's face flushed, but he doubted it could get redder than the spice had already made it.

Lamai exchanged a few words with the wife. Harrison's plate was whisked away and cleared, then returned to him with a fresh serving of rice topped with a scoop of the stew.

He sniffed it cautiously before tasting the smallest bit. No fire, just a pleasant medley of aromatic herbs with a mild touch of heat. He gave an appreciative *"Mmmm,"* and rubbed his stomach, which sent the children into gales of laughter. Their mother hushed them, casting Harrison an apologetic look.

He didn't care if it was pap for children; it was a delicious meal and he enjoyed every morsel.

That evening, after assisting Panit with the elephants' and goat's care, Harrison washed up at an outdoor basin on the side of the house. Mosquitoes made a meal of him, as they did whenever the light was low. Scratching at a new welt on his chest, he sauntered around back, and was startled to see their hostess making beds for the children on the ground beneath the kitchen shelter. His little dining companion eyed his hairy chest and giggled.

Inside, Lamai sat cross-legged on a bamboo mat on the floor, slowly unplaiting her hair. An oil lamp glowed where their dinner had been earlier. Two more mats had been laid out for himself and Panit, the three beds circling the lamp like a campfire.

"Why are they out there?" he inquired, jerking his thumb to the door.

"We paid."

"Yes, but ..." Harrison settled onto a mat, folding his legs to match her posture. "Back home, if I asked a farmer if I could spend the night, he'd probably put me up in the hayloft."

Lamai wrinkled her nose. "Even if you pay?"

"Yes. He wouldn't give up his own bed for a traveler—much less his house."

Her fingers worked into the weave at the bottom of her braid, loosening the strands until they came apart like ropes of black silk. Harrison watched her repeat the process again and again, unhurried. "That is poor ... I don't know the word. Welcoming to others."

"Hospitality, I think you mean."

She made a noncommittal noise.

Panit came in, damp from his own basin bath. He and Lamai exchanged what sounded like 'goodnight' wishes, then he waved at Harrison. The *mahout* stretched out, settling his hands on his belly. Within moments, he was snoring softly.

Lamai's mouth curled in a wry smile. "He's always like that. Goes to sleep with no trouble, then wakes as quick." From her pack, she retrieved a wooden comb with thick, wide teeth. "Me, I hate waking up. You'll see. I'm the laziest thing in the morning."

"You were ready to leave the temple before dawn, without complaint."

"If you could hear my thoughts, *farang*, the complaints would've scorched your ears."

Watching her carefully tend her hair made Harrison acutely aware of his own sorry state. Besides the silver shaving kit in Sheri's chest, he no longer owned grooming implements. He raked his fingers through his damp locks. Lamai's eyes tracked the movement, riveted onto the scars on his wrist. The lamplight caught the slim ridges and cast shadows, rendering them more prominent than they were beneath the sun.

He tensed in anticipation of questions, but they didn't come. She lowered her gaze to her hair and picked at an imaginary knot, allowing the light to wash across her features.

The trick the light played on his wrists was mimicked on the right side of her face. Shiny, unnaturally smooth patches of skin reflected gold and white. They were overlaid by dull webs of thick, ropy scars. The injury must have been sustained some years ago, as the scars' coloration nearly matched the rest of her face, except for a livid patch in front of her ear.

He saw, and wondered what had happened. He saw, and saw beyond; like midnight at a masquerade, mentally removing the disguise to reveal her true face. There was no denying her beauty. The unblemished left side told him plainly. Before her unhappy accident, Lamai would have been stunning, her full lips an invitation to kiss deeply, the golden porcelain of her skin demanding a gentle touch.

His body stirred, and Harrison flinched. He turned his attention to his feet, wiggling his bare toes. The bottoms were dirty, the soles blackened by foreign soil. Getting it off would require dedicated scrubbing.

The heat singing in his blood did not seem inclined to abate. His pulse was attuned to the delicate, beautiful creature facing him, her crossed, bare shins lining a path to ecstasy. Like a caged great cat yearning for liberty, one part of his mind invented images: his clumsy hands in her hair; her mouth sweetly yielding to his; the soft press of her body against his hard frame.

Like the lion tamer, another part of his mind reacted violently to the incipient response of his body, cracking a whip woven not of fantasy, but memory: a palm pressed to the front of his breeches, his young body betraying him, readying to perform acts he wanted no part in; whispered words of desire laced with threats; secrets, secrets, so many secrets. *Our secret, your secret, your dirty, dirty secret, Harrison. What would your mother say if she knew you'd such an eager, greedy prick? No, no, my funny boy mustn't cry. I'll take care of you and keep your tawdry little secret. All I want in return is … You're getting better at it—almost, you don't embarrass yourself. What's this? You don't want …? My funny boy likes to protest, likes to pretend he doesn't like it, but this cockstand tells no lies. Still, if you'd really rather I didn't …* Calculating eyes turned to the nursery door. *I've heard these sorts of filthy compulsions run in families. Shall I find out if that's true?*

A hand, tight on his arm. Harrison yanked out of the grip.

"*Farang?*" Lamai knelt beside him, melted-chocolate eyes clouded with concern. Her hand reached for his brow damp with cold sweat.

He turned his head sharply. "Don't touch me."

"Are you ill? Luang Wirat said you aren't fully strong yet."

"I'm …" Harrison gulped hard, swiped his forehead with the back of his wrist. "Tired is all. The ride was harder than I expected."

Lamai's mouth screwed up at the side. "Men are stupid and stubborn the world over, it seems." She jerked her chin to the sleeping *mahout*. "Wan Pen stepped on his foot a couple years back, and he wouldn't stay in bed. Kept hopping around to give her lessons. It was very slow to heal. He almost became a one-legged beggar."

Harrison's lips carved a hollow smile. "But he didn't. Seems he knew what he needed, after all."

She scowled, then retreated to her own mat. "If you're as smart as you think you are, you won't let yourself get sick between now and home. Khun Gaspar will not take you in like the monks did."

"I don't expect charity."

Her responding voice was flat. "Expect less. Expect nothing."

She lay down, her back facing him. Her long hair broke around her stiff shoulder like a stream parting for a boulder. She must have been vexed, indeed, to abandon the ubiquitous feminine routine of unbraiding, brushing, and rebraiding and go to bed with hair unbound.

Harrison attempted to arrange himself for sleep. The mat was too short by more than half a foot, leaving his feet on the packed earth floor, and there was nothing with which to cover himself. Granted, the air was in no way cool, just a milder sort of hot, but his exposed body felt defenseless. Rolling to his side he drew his knees up, withdrawing from the damp earth, curling around the bruised, vulnerable place inside.

For a long time, he stared at Lamai's back. Gradually, her shoulders softened, her spine melting towards the floor as she sank into sleep. She was a pretty woman, and his body responded to hers. It was the oldest algebra in creation. Simple. The stuff of primers. But for Harrison, it was as arcane as theoretical physics, as unknowable as a long-dead language.

Turning the rust-pocked wheel on the lamp, he extinguished the light.

Some years back, after ages of trying to force himself to be normal like everyone else, Harrison had come to the realization that his life would not be like other men's. The simplicity of man-plus-woman was not the hand he'd been dealt. Dreams of a family of his own had died a slow, agonizing death, their passing recorded on his flesh.

Still, he'd supposed, if he couldn't have happiness, he could at least find peace in the form of meaningful work. Animals had always been easier to get along with than people. A stable would be exactly what he needed. He'd embarked on this journey to make the fortune that would allow him to have it. Naively, after so many months of contentment aboard *Brizo's Woe*, he'd believed his personal troubles had remained on the other side of the world, waiting for his return. Now he found he'd brought them to this distant shore, after all.

Lamai sighed in her sleep, a soft, feminine sound. Harrison's fingers twitched at a pang of longing.

Desire was not so easily left behind as a coat, nor did it sink to the bottom of the sea with the rest of one's belongings. It had been with him all along, lurking in his blood, just waiting to loose hell upon him again.

Chapter Five

The road was little more than a track of mud. Progress was slow, as the elephants had to lift their feet clear of the morass every step of the way. Meanwhile, the falling rain did its best to churn the sticky muck into a slick hazard. Lamai and Wan Pen led the way today. Keeping her eyes sharp for holes or other obstructions concealed by the mud took all of her concentration. There was an elephantine grunt, and Panit's quick "Hey, hey! *Pai dai,* Goui. Go on." Wan Pen's ears flapped, aware of a disturbance behind her.

Twisting around, Lamai saw the larger, older elephant recovering from a minor stumble. Panit kept the reins in a tight grip, steering Goui to safer ground.

Behind the *mahout,* Harrison Dyer was wide-eyed, his left hand clasping the arm of his seat, the other gripped tight onto the scruff of his pet goat.

"If that had been one of your horses, *farang,* its leg would have snapped, and you'd be walking to Bangkok. The elephants may seem slow, but I warrant they make better time than you." She couldn't resist the little tease after his complaints yesterday.

Harrison's bleak eyes met hers through a curtain of rain, unmoved by her bit of humor. His lips were pressed in a grim line, the skin around them white with tension.

Unnerved by his silence, she returned her gaze to the road. Since they met, the Englishman had been pleasant and polite, if obstinate in pressing her to carry him to Bangkok. He'd even been good humored about his experience with the spicy meal. Whereas Gaspar would have been downright angry if he'd been given a supper with such heat, Harrison had simply eaten the children's food with gusto.

Last night, though, something had shifted. She'd watched a pall come over his face, shuttering his smiling, bewildered curiosity. There'd been a haunted look in his eyes—one she suspected to be connected to the scars on his wrists. Lamai had never been driven to such desperate measures, but she knew what it was to feel despair.

Passing through a stretch of thick, dark forest gave some reprieve from the downpour, though mosquitoes also took advantage of the twilit, green world. A chorus of insect life droned while birds cawed. The air was thick with the scent of damp rot. On a low branch, Lamai spotted a langur monkey, silver shoulders hunched against the weather, glaring balefully at the human and elephant intruders. It was on the cusp of Lamai's lips to point the creature out to Harrison, but his own sullen silence stayed her tongue. His mood was an oppressive presence behind her, as close and dark as the trees. Why hadn't she been firmer and left him behind? He would cause her nothing but trouble.

On the far side of the forest was a farm. A little shack—meaner than their abode last night—stood on the side of the road, surrounded by a grain field turned to a lake by standing water. When they approached, a fellow's face popped out of the door, shouting the price of his bundles of straw. "*Yood*," she instructed Wan Pen. *Stop*. Lamai passed the farmer payment. He brought some straw and plopped it into the mud at the elephants' feet, then bellowed at the house. A scrawny youth took off running in front of them. For the next mile, the boy fetched straw from storage bins and left it in the road for Wan Pen and Goui. The elephants ate as they walked, finishing one mouthful just as another appeared at their toes.

At the end of the feeding run, Lamai bent over to press a coin into the mud-caked boy's hand. His palm was hot and rough.

She shouldn't have touched Harrison when the darkness came over him and he seemed to take an ill turn. Their hands had mingled briefly earlier in the evening, and Lamai had thought … Well, it didn't matter what she'd thought. She rolled her shoulders against a tightness in her back. *Farangs* were loose about contact between men and women, but Lamai knew better. She knew, but she'd touched him anyway, sensing phantom familiarity and an urge of tenderness.

She patted Wan Pen's broad head. "It's better just to tend you, isn't it, my favorite girl? That dour man can do for himself."

That dour man did do for himself for the remainder of the day. When they broke in the late afternoon in a town just outside Bangkok, he shook his head when offered a bowl of rice noodles and broth. "It's not spicy," she promised. "Some green onion and bean sprouts, see? No pepper."

He stood outside the shelter of the kitchen where Lamai and Panit sat at a plank table. The rain fell on his bare head. He was like a pathetic, muddy puppy. "Thank you, but I don't have an appetite."

Panit's gaze went from Harrison to Lamai while he slurped noodles through pursed lips. "What's wrong with him?"

"He says he isn't hungry."

"That's stupid. Who turns down good, hot food?"

Lamai shrugged.

"Give it to me if he doesn't want it." The *mahout* held out his hand.

"Are you sure?" Lamai asked Harrison.

The *farang* turned his tortured expression on the woman busily cooking for customers. "What is that?" Ignoring the indignant squawks of protest from the proprietress, Harrison strode into the preparation area and hefted a green, oblong pod in his hands. "This. What is it?"

Lamai spooned hot broth into her mouth while the cook snatched her wares from the white man with a blistering scold it was well he couldn't understand. "A coconut," she said at last.

Harrison frowned. "The few coconuts I've seen were smaller. Brown and hard, too, with stiff bristles all over."

"Hmm." Lamai was mildly surprised an Englishman knew anything of coconuts, at all. "The brown part, that's inside the fruit. They grow on the tree like that." She nodded at the disputed food the cook had returned to the table. "I suppose they keep better if you take away the husk, but we always have them fresh here." When Harrison kept looking at the coconut, Lamai ventured, "Would you like to try? There's water inside, and sweet flesh."

He jerked a nod; Lamai asked the cook to prepare the fruit, then gestured for Harrison to sit. The woman brandished a wicked looking machete, quickly hacking away at the coconut and finally lopping off the top. She brought the fruit to Harrison with a bowl and a spoon.

"Pour the water into the bowl," Lamai instructed. "You'll need the spoon to eat the meat."

Harrison lowered his nose to the bowl, then took a sip. For the first time all day, his lips gave the ghost of a smile, like a shy little boy's. "This is what Wirat gave me when I first arrived. It was all he gave me for days."

Panit asked for a translation. Nodding, he offered his input. "He says coconut water is nourishing like mother's milk," Lamai interpreted. "Very good for you, especially when you're sick, or for the infirm."

Harrison took another swallow of the liquid, but made no move to touch his spoon. Lamai tapped the implement with her own. He blinked at the bright *ting*.

"You're going to undo all of Luang Wirat's hard work, *farang*? Decided to starve to death, after all?"

He lowered his eyes, abashed. "I'm just not hungry. I don't always care to eat."

Lamai's temper spiked. Gaspar was going to make her life difficult enough when she brought home the Englishman; heavens preserve them all if her stray *farang* was also bent on self-annihilation and in need of intense care. She snapped in his face, drawing his startled gaze. "I know what ails you." She glanced meaningfully at his wrist. "If you wish to die, all you have to do is walk into the forest. A viper or a tiger will take down a stupid *farang* like you in under an hour. Don't make me haul you about if you're nothing but a breathing corpse."

Harrison's eyes hardened; his chin jutted mulishly. "I don't wish to die." His words were clipped now, his tone one of affronted pride. His brow lifted. "Thank you for your concern, but my condition is none of your affair." Nevertheless, he took up his spoon and scooped a bite of coconut into his mouth.

Lamai watched him eat with steam curling from her flared nostrils. None of her affair! He'd damned well made his condition her affair when he'd insisted on accompanying her, helpless and ignorant as a babe though he was.

Their meal concluded, Lamai made inquiries regarding the nearest *wat*. They would find accommodation at the temple, but no room for the elephants, so she and Panit set about stabling the girls here in town. While they performed those necessaries, Harrison remained at the kitchen. Lamai crisscrossed town to find someone with space to let for the elephants, while Panit bought fruit to add to their supper of hay. Each time she saw him, Harrison stood, awkward and stiff, at the edge of the kitchen. He'd moved his trunk onto the wooden bench, taking up the space where people should have gone. He probably didn't notice the laborers squatting nearby, bowls cupped in their palms, their place at the table occupied by a white man's luggage. Hands clasped at the small of his back, nose raised, Harrison looked every inch the *farang* who expected his Thai underlings to tend his every need without lifting a finger of his own.

He did hoist his trunk onto his back for the short walk to the *wat*, but by then, Lamai was out of charity with him. The temple complex was larger than Wat Wihan, with separate guest quarters for men and women. Grateful for the excuse to get away from the Englishman, Lamai went to the women's lodge and availed herself of the opportunity to wash and dress in a dry wrap provided by the matron while her own clothes steamed in front of a fire.

A woman about Lamai's age sat on a nearby cot, struggling to wrestle a squirming little girl into a jacket. The child squealed and flopped about like a boneless fish, making the mother's task difficult. When Lamai caught the girl's attention, the child froze, eyes wide.

"Mama, look at her face!"

Lamai flinched, but forced herself to hold the child's gaze and smile. *Young children don't know better,* she reminded herself.

Glancing up, the mother blew a strand of hair out of her eyes, taking advantage of her daughter's distraction to stuff the little arms into sleeves. "That's a punishment for bad karma," the woman said, as if Lamai could not hear her. "She must have been a naughty girl in her last life. Remember that! You have to mind me, or else you could be deformed in your next life."

Lamai's fingers trembled. Her lungs forgot to breathe. It had been a long time since she'd been used as an object lesson in karma. Gaspar's house had not always been a happy home, but she had been largely shielded from the sorts of unkind remarks she'd heard from her mother's relatives and neighbors when she was younger.

The young girl's curious expression turned to apprehension. *Please see me,* Lamai silently implored the child. *I'm a person, not a walking punishment.* The small, round nose wrinkled in distaste.

Swallowing her humiliation, Lamai smoothly rose from her bed, made *wai* to the matron, and serenely walked outside. If she could not find solace in the company of women, then she would find it in prayer.

A covered walkway kept her dry as she strolled towards the central shrine. A long row of stone Buddhas in various postures monitored her progress. What troubled Lamai most about what had just transpired was not the child's bluntness, nor even the mother's words. Most unsettling was that the mother might be right. Illness, injury, bad luck—these were all evidence of sins committed in a previous life. Her fallible human nature stirred her to anger or hurt when her burns were pointed out as divine punishment. She must strive harder to separate herself from such emotions.

There was a market on the *wat* grounds, stalls where vendors peddled everything from fish and vegetables to household goods. At a flower seller's booth, Lamai selected a bunch of purple orchids and several cones of incense. From the corner of her eye, she spotted a figure standing head and shoulders above the milling throng.

Harrison was with a fruit merchant. The vendor, a toothless old woman, beamed at her *farang* customer, her expression positively giddy.

Lamai groaned. "What now?" she grumbled as she made her way through the crowd of shoppers.

The Englishman acknowledged her with a nod. His arms were loaded with a mound of loose lychee fruits.

"What are you doing, Khun Harrison?"

"I bought these for the monks, to pay for my lodging." He hefted his arms to show her his precariously balanced haul. Two bright pink-red orbs tumbled from the pile. Lamai caught them; the rough rinds damaged the petals of her flowers.

Plunking them back onto his load, she huffed her annoyance. "How did you pay for this?"

His brow lifted in aristocratic hauteur. "I struck a bargain with the lady," he answered mysteriously.

Lamai glowered, then turned on the shopkeep. "What did he give you, *phar*?"

The woman's bright smile slipped. She glanced uneasily at Harrison. "What does he say? Does he want something else? My jackfruit is good." She nodded to a bin heaped with yellow, pulpy flesh. "He can have some—free of charge."

"Auntie, what did he give you?" Lamai demanded. "How did he pay?"

Reluctantly, the woman reached an arthritic hand into the pocket of her apron and showed her earnings. A single spoon. A single, *silver* spoon.

With a gasp, Lamai snatched it out of the woman's hand. The shopkeep screeched. "No deal," Lamai snapped. "You should be ashamed of yourself." She set her purchases on the table and began transferring Harrison's lychee back into the vendor's bin.

"I say!" Harrison protested. "Those are mine."

"For the price of a silver spoon, you could have had all her wares, and everything in the next five stalls, besides. That was not a good bargain, *farang*. You must all be princes in England, to spend so freely!"

"It was all I had."

Lamai stopped shoveling fruit and glanced into the man's face. His posture was all stiff, wounded pride, and sadness—that unfathomable sadness—pooling in his golden-brown eyes.

In his gaze, she recognized the same pleading she'd only just delivered to the little girl in the lodge. *Please see me. Please understand.* Something in her grudgingly relented.

"I'll buy these for you," she told him.

"But—"

She lifted her hand. "I know you don't want charity, Khun Harrison. I will give you the opportunity to repay me later, alright? But you must not barter away your belongings in shabby deals."

His forearms were bronzed, and dusted with appealing, masculine hair. She just stopped herself from bringing her palm to one of those limbs. *Don't touch me.*

He nodded stiffly. She saw what it cost him to accept her money, but she thought the better of him for permitting it. She gave the fruit seller twice the value of the lychee. "To compensate you for the spoon," Lamai explained. "But give the man something to carry this in, for goodness' sake. And next time, don't be blinded by the shine of silver."

Together, they went to the temple proper. People gawked at the tall, white man, though Harrison paid no heed to the attention.

"Your dress is pretty." He gestured with his head at the light blue linen she wore.

"It's not mine."

"The color looks very well on you." Lamai ducked her head, uncertain how to respond to such a statement.

"Tell me about your hair."

She glanced up, startled.

"Yours is long," he clarified, "while all the other women"—he cast his gaze over the shoppers—"have shorn theirs like the men, with only a little tuft or topknot left."

Lamai shrugged, uncomfortable with a man's attention to her looks. "Khun Gaspar insists the women of his household keep their hair in European style, for the comfort of his visitors."

"What of your comfort?"

He looked befuddled; in turn, his confusion puzzled her. "Are English servants free to present themselves as they please?"

He did not reply, but his silence was answer enough. "Still," he said, "I can't be sorry you kept yours. It's beautiful hair." One blunt fingertip slipped down a loose tress, skating over her shoulder blade.

Heat bloomed in her cheeks. Compliments from a man were unfamiliar territory. The warmth spread to her chest, a secret kernel of golden light that settled behind her breastbone.

She was grateful for the distraction of shedding shoes at the temple door. Harrison set his basket of fruit on the ground and clumsily hopped on one foot, and then the other, to pull off his boots. If he stayed much longer in Siam, she would have to see he had sensible slippers.

On one side of the worship area, a monk sat on an elevated platform, chanting and praying before about a dozen people kneeling on cool, unglazed tile. Hefting his offering, the Englishman strode off in that direction.

Lamai hissed, catching him back. "Not yet. There will be time to make merit shortly." She nodded toward an out-of-the-way corner. "Why don't you wait there? After my prayers, I'll take you."

Harrison looked at the corner then frowned down at her. "I'd rather stay with you, if it's all right. I'd be interested to learn about Buddhist worship."

Lamai's heart sank. For all his curiosity, Harrison had done little but tell her how things were done in England. She knew the reason behind him questioning her handling the money and negotiating their lodging the previous night. He might have phrased his words as a straightforward comparison, but she'd heard the judgment behind them. Things weren't just different in England, they were *better*, was what he'd really meant. Thanks to Khun Gaspar, Lamai had enough experience with Europeans to know Harrison's attitude wasn't novel. *Farangs* always found Thai ways lacking in comparison to their own. Lamai could allow a lot of it to roll off her back, but her faith was the line in the sand. She would not have her worship disrupted by Harrison droning on about how his Christian customs were superior to her Buddhist ones. He might be more accepting in general than other *farangs* she'd known, but—

"Please," he interrupted her thoughts. That troubled look had returned to his eyes. Lamai recalled her own reasons for prayer—a need for consolation, for peace. How could she begrudge him the same?

"Very well, *farang*. This way." She led him to the large, central shrine occupied by a majestic, golden Buddha. A halo adorned with sapphire enamel radiated behind the awakened one's head, symbolizing enlightenment.

"First, we make offerings to Buddha." He stepped forward with his basket of fruit. "No, here." Splitting her bunch of orchids, she gave him half. They laid the flowers at the statue's base, then she passed him an incense cone. These went into an iron trough of sand. Each lit their incense with candles provided for the purpose.

Backing away to make room for the supplicants behind them, Lamai found a vacant spot and knelt. Harrison lowered beside her. "Now you say a prayer or make a wish," she explained. "Pray to your Christ, if you prefer. Buddha is not jealous."

She did not watch to see what he did. Worship was ultimately a private affair, even in public. Lamai's eyes closed. Her lips moved as she exhaled her prayers in the barest whisper. At the conclusion, she drew a deep breath. Rather than incense, her nostrils were filled with the scent of the man beside her—a warm, earthy contrast to the heady fragrance of smoke.

When she fluttered her eyes open, he was watching her. He raised his brows in question. She nodded.

Wordlessly, they rose and made their way to the small congregation. The monk had finished his chant, and worshipers stepped forward to give alms. Harrison took his turn, placing the basket of lychee fruits at the monk's knee.

"Did I do that properly?" he whispered.

"Yes, yes. Kneel again. Here." From a low table, Lamai fetched them each a small brass bowl and vial of water. Kneeling once more beside the large *farang*, she placed a vial and bowl before him just as the monk lifted a hand and began speaking, his sonorous voice filling the air.

"He gives thanks for the generosity of the people," Lamai murmured, "and he blesses them."

"Your money, your blessing," Harrison returned.

Lamai scowled. What a thing to say! She knew Harrison's intentions would be reflected in his karma, even though she had intervened in his purchase of the fruit.

She kept her thoughts to herself, though, for the monk had moved on to the final prayer of the service. "This is a prayer for the souls of the departed. Slowly pour the water from the bottle into the bowl. Think about a loved one whose soul you want to receive the prayer." The delicate sound of water against thin metal provided a tender backdrop to the monk's prayer.

When everyone stood with their bowls, Harrison frowned. "Now we pour the water onto a tree or plant," she said, "to show that we return the blessing we have been given to the earth. We pass it along to others."

That completed, Harrison gave her a pained little smile. "I'd rather hoped to keep that blessing for myself."

Lamai lifted her face, enjoying the rare touch of coolness in the evening breeze. It could be months before she felt it again. "You do, *farang*." She cut her eyes to him. "A blessing is like love. Once given to you, it's yours to keep, even as you give it to others. You can't ever use it up. This" – she lifted her bowl – "is just a symbol. Blessings, love, they all flow through you. An endless river. You must accept those gifts, so you can bless others with them."

Harrison's lips twisted, and his eyes misted over. He sniffed.

She understood how he felt. Sometimes, after a difficult day dealing with Gaspar and his business associates—or on days she doubted her father would ever come—Lamai went to temple and was overcome by the vastness of Buddha's peace. When she felt so worn down by a dismal world, she was buoyed again by her prayers and the blessings so generously given in return for her humble offerings. Harrison had been through a dreadful ordeal at sea. That he was touched by the service was an admirable thing. If anyone's spirit needed healing, it was certainly his. She should have invited him to join her in worship, Lamai reflected with a bit of chagrin, instead of steeling her heart against him when he invited himself.

Harrison swiped his sleeve across his cheek.

Lamai politely looked the other way.

Chapter Six

Late the next afternoon, Lamai wearily dismounted from Wan Pen in their own familiar paddock at Gaspar's house. The juvenile elephant wasted no time in flopping onto her side and heaving a great sigh. Goui knelt beside the youngster and stroked the little girl with her trunk while her two human passengers disembarked.

Lamai fisted knotted muscles in her back. There was no question of sleeping in the stable tonight: nothing but a hot bath and her own soft bed would do. First, though, she would have to speak to Khun Gaspar and prepare him for meeting Harrison Dyer.

That Englishman stepped unsteadily to Goui's knee, then to the ground, where he listed a bit before righting himself. Tilda, his troublesome pet, skipped behind like a born mountain goat, giving no sign of the travel sickness she had suffered. Prancing over to Wan Pen, velvet ears twitching, Tilda bleated as if demanding her large friend get up and play. Wan Pen responded with a lethargic wave of her nose.

A masculine chuckle drew Lamai's eye to Harrison. The Englishman's smile for the animals warmed her heart, even as she felt a pinch of fear.

During the day's trek, she'd dreaded Gaspar's response. He had ordered Lamai to leave the *farang* at Wat Wihan unless the stranger would be of interest to the Portuguese ambassador, through which Gaspar might increase his standing with the diplomat. In particular, Gaspar had a loathing for merchants competing for coveted royal contracts. Harrison was a merchant; ergo, Gaspar would immediately regard him as a rival. If she could make Gaspar see lending aid to the Englishman as the quickest way to eject him from Mueang Thai, ensuring there would be no—

"Lamai!" From the kitchen outbuilding burst Kulap, her pale, young face streaked with tears and swollen from crying. The thin cotton of her skirt clung to her lithe limbs as she hurried across the yard to the paddock. "One of those Burmese witches took my new parasol and turned it inside out. It's ruined!" she screeched. Her fists pounded the rail of the enclosure. "You must make them tell you which one did it, and have them beaten. Or, if they will not say, beat them both!"

Lamai hissed through her teeth just as Harrison walked around Goui. Kulap gasped. Instantly, she fell to her knees and bowed her head to the ground, making obeisance such as one would give a prince.

"Good God, is the girl all right?" Harrison's startled tone and curled lip created an almost comical expression—a stew of alarm, concern, and distaste. He eyed the kneeling girl as though studying a rare specimen of slug.

Lamai crossed her arms and sighed. Sore and weary from days of hard travel, she had no patience for one of Kulap's tantrums. "She is embarrassed that you saw her outburst, so she's hiding her face. What Kulap doesn't realize," Lamai said, switching to Thai for the girl's hearing, "is that she makes us all look foolish with this bad behavior."

Tilda let loose a bleat that was almost a shriek. Lamai winced at the beginnings of a headache. Wan Pen rolled to her knees and answered with a trumpet, and Goui rumbled, unmistakably warning the others, *Keep it down, children!*

"Tell her to get up, please," Harrison said over the din. "I don't mind—it's already forgotten. On no count should the young lady drown herself in the mud for my sake."

When Lamai attempted to coax the girl, Kulap shook her head into the earth and cried harder. "I won't rise until he leaves." Her voice was muffled by the wet grass in her face. "Why didn't you tell me there was a *farang* with you, Lamai? You're as wicked as the witches!"

A back door of the main house slammed. All of Lamai's hopes for paving a smooth path for this introduction evaporated as Gaspar strode across the waterlogged lawn.

"What the devil is this ruckus about?" he shouted in Portuguese. "Kulap!" He nudged his slave with a foot. "Get up, you ridiculous girl."

The youngest of his bed slaves couldn't comprehend his words, but the toe digging into her ribs conveyed the message well enough. She drew herself upright, then came to her feet, her loose limbs and pouting, dirt-smudged face full of adolescent sulk. She blinked her wide, guileless eyes on their master. "*Me perdoe,* Khun Gaspar," Kulap said in a breathy, childish voice. *Forgive me.* It was one of the few Portuguese phrases every member of the household had learned. They had occasion to use it often.

Gaspar's red lips twitched in the frame of his silver mustache and beard. He slapped a palm to Kulap's rump. The girl squealed. "Off with you, pet," he said, pointing to the house. "*Tiiang.*" Bed.

Lamai's face flushed, burning to her ears. Thank goodness Harrison did not understand where the girl had been ordered to go.

Kulap made *wai,* bowing deeply in the flattering way Gaspar always enjoyed, and minced off to the house.

Gesturing with her head for Harrison to accompany her, Lamai shouldered her pack and led the Englishman through the paddock gate. Gaspar met them on the other side.

"*Bem vindo, senhor.*" Gaspar bowed crisply. "*Eu sou* Gaspar D'Cruz. *Tenho o prazer de vêlo em boa saúde.*"

Harrison gave a smart nod in return, then turned bewildered eyes on Lamai, his brows lifted.

"This is Gaspar D'Cruz. He welcomes you to his home, and says he's happy to see you in good health."

"Ah. Thank you for your kind concern, sir, and for your hospitality. My name is Harrison Dyer. Honored to meet you, *senhor*."

It was Gaspar's turn to make Lamai the target of his confusion. "Who the hell is this?" he demanded in Portuguese.

"Harrison Dyer," she replied.

"I heard that much," Gaspar snapped. "English?" At her nod, his eyes narrowed, but he pasted on a false smile for the benefit of his unexpected visitor. "Do you speak Portuguese?" he directed to Harrison. The Englishman answered in the negative. "Why the devil did you bring him here?" Gaspar asked through his teeth.

Lamai shifted her weight. Her *panung* breeches were beginning to dry stiff around her legs. Her belly itched from the chafing of wet material. She'd known she was defying Gaspar by bringing Harrison here. What had she been thinking? She should have taken the *farang* straight to the docks and sold him to pirates. She licked her lips. "Khun Gaspar, I ... Well, you see ..."

Gaspar rolled a wrist, gesturing with an elegant hand. "Did you suppose, Lamai, that because he's English, you had license to bring him to my home?"

"No, sir."

"What am I supposed to do with him?"

"Miss Lamai?" Harrison looked between her and Gaspar. "Is everything all right? Should I go? I don't want to cause you any trouble."

She shook her head. "Don't worry, Khun Harrison, everything is fine. It's just—"

"What did he say?" Gaspar interrupted. "What are you telling him?" The Portuguese man shot a feral grin at the Englishman.

The rapid-fire bouncing from one language to the next was beginning to muddle Lamai's thoughts. "He, umm, *ele* ..." Tears pricked the backs of her eyes. "He said he will go away if being here is trouble, is all. He only wants to go home, back to England. He isn't here to take business from you."

"Is he a merchant?"

"Yes, but—"

Gaspar inhaled sharply, nostrils flared.

Fighting back the cold lump of fear in her chest, Lamai plowed on. "His cargo ship was lost at sea. He has nothing. He is no threat to you. He only wants to go home." Her master gave no reply. "Do you hear me, sir?"

Finally, Gaspar blinked. Then he laughed. "Fell off his horse, and now he's never going to ride again, eh? Well, what the hell." He slapped Harrison on the back and gestured to the house. "This way, my gutless friend."

Ignorant of the insult, Harrison smiled gamely and followed his host into the house.

"Lamai," Gaspar said, "show him to the guest apartment then go to your room. I do not wish to see you again tonight. Dinner will be sent up. I'll see you both in the morning. But don't think you and I are done, my dear." He spun on a heel, strode down the hall, and slammed the door of his study.

Lamai winced at the sharp sound. She'd known it would be bad. *But it was all bluster and wind,* she told herself. *A night with Kulap will put him in a better humor, and in the morning, Gaspar might be more kindly disposed towards me, too.* She quelched a pang of guilt at hoping the foolish girl would serve her master well in bed. Lamai was powerless to change Kulap's fate. She was desperately grappling to maintain any sort of control over her own.

"This way."

She led Harrison up a stairwell of polished teakwood, then down the hall and around a corner before stopping at an ebony door. "This is your room."

"I take it I'm lucky not to have been tossed out on my ear," Harrison drawled.

A lump rose in Lamai's throat. Gaspar had only been as terrible as she'd known he would be. And she had warned Harrison, she'd told him to expect nothing. Why then, did she feel shamed by how the Englishman had been received?

"A meal will be brought to you. I'll tell the servants to prepare a bath, too." She turned to make her escape. His hand caught her wrist and pulled her back around, drawing her close to his chest. He smelled like a man who needed a bath, but his own, unique scent was strong, too. It filled her nose, and then her mind, addling her thoughts.

"Lamai, is everything all right?" he asked in a low voice. "Are *you* going to be all right?"

His jaw was shadowed with two days' worth of bristle. The hand on her arm exerted a steady, pleasurable pressure.

"I don't know more than a few words in Portuguese," Harrison said, "but I did catch 'English' several times. Why is Mr. D'Cruz so put out by my nationality?" He gave a lopsided smile that made Lamai's blood quicken. "Has he been away so long that he doesn't know we Brits saved his country's hide from Napoleon?"

"No, it's ..." She let out a sound of frustration. "It's my fault. Because I'm half-English, he thinks I brought you home as some sort of pet—"

"You're half-English?"

Lamai sucked her lips back between her teeth. She hadn't meant to tell him that! Damn him for scrambling her wits, when she was already tired and upset from a trying day.

Harrison tilted his head, brought his face closer to hers. Lamai felt the tips of her breasts tingle against the linen of her shirt. "You didn't tell me that before, you sneaky devil." His whisper was conspiratorial, intimate, and gave Lamai a thrill that traveled through her body and settled between her legs. She squirmed against the sensation, wishing it away even as the pressure of her thighs squeezing her mound made a pleasurable ache.

Then she thought again of Kulap, that stupid, petulant girl waiting in Gaspar's bed. She thought of the Burmese witches, as Kulap called Nan and Mi, the other two bed slaves. Who was Lamai to find pleasure in the touch of a *farang*? A single, hot tear slipped down her good cheek. Another left her right eye, but then it vanished from her perception when it reached her ruined flesh.

"Why this?" She shrugged her shoulder, pulling her arm from his grasp. "Why do you touch me whenever you like, but make me feel I've done something wrong when I touch you?"

His expression shuttered at once. "Lamai, I didn't mean to hurt your feelings. That wasn't my intention. It had nothing to do with—"

"*Don't touch me.* That's what you said. Go to your room, *farang.*" She backed away, swiped a hand across her cheek. "Just … go to your room."

• • •

Harrison sat in the window seat of the sumptuously-appointed guest apartments. Hot sunlight streamed through glass—the first window glazing he'd seen in Siam, now that he thought of it—to illuminate gleaming wood floors and a hodgepodge of Eastern and Western decorations. The bed was outfitted with damask, but draped with mosquito netting. Twin nooks in the wall flanked the headboard; one housed a statuette of the Virgin Mary, the other, a Thai female icon in a similar pose of prayer-hands and a beatific smile.

Early this morning, a servant had scratched at the door to deliver clean clothes. They were familiar in their European styling, but ill-fitting, being a bit short in the arm and leg, and a tad loose in the waist. Harrison tugged ineffectually at his shirt cuff. As soon as he let go, it retreated inside the sleeve of a burgundy coat. He wondered that Gaspar would wear such attire in this climate. The lightweight *panung* Harrison had worn the past few days was a far superior garment in which to face the heat and damp of Siam than stiff, stuffy European styles.

A rumble in his middle reminded Harrison he'd not yet broken his fast, but he was loath to leave his chamber. Just as Lamai predicted, Gaspar had not offered a warm reception, only false smiles that failed to mask an undercurrent of fury. Harrison felt now as he often had done as a boy, riddled with anxiety and the unhappy certainty that *something* was wrong. He was not wanted here, just as his party-loving parents had not appreciated the dampening presence of their own children in their home. In his parents' case, they had removed themselves from the premises as frequently as able, jaunting off to London for the season, or to Bath or Brighton, or whatever watering spot was fashionable that year, leaving Harrison and his siblings to the care of servants.

His belly twisted again. Harrison scowled. Supper had been delivered on a tray last night—roast pork served beside thin, almost transparent noodles tossed with sautéed vegetables. He wished he had more of the same. Perhaps someone would soon be along with a breakfast tray? The thought of venturing into the house in search of food sent a trickle of sweat down his temple.

Despite the heat pounding his back, a doughy lump of dread rested in his lungs, forbidding him a proper, full breath. Not that he imagined he'd be set upon by brigands if he stepped into the corridor; but that amorphous, nameless, unpleasant *something* lurked beyond. As long as he stayed here, he wouldn't have to discover whether the reality was less or worse than he feared.

The decision was taken out of his hands by the arrival of a servant—the same chap who'd brought the clothes—bowing and gesturing for Harrison to follow. Wiping clammy palms on his borrowed breeches, he padded barefoot behind the servant.

The sight of Lamai seated at a round table set for three eased his trepidation somewhat, until she stood to greet him. She wore a muslin frock such as any miss in England might have worn. Her hair, which he had only seen loose or in a braid, was curled and twisted into a pile of ringlets atop her crown, with loose strands kissing her jaw. She was lovely—so lovely it made his palms itch, but the sight of her in European attire was jarring.

Lamai fidgeted, clearly uncomfortable in her dress, which only deepened that pervasive sense of wrongness Harrison felt today. He bowed and bid the lady a good morning. "Good morning, Khun Harrison," she returned. "Did you sleep well?"

"Thank you, yes. And you, ma'am?" Dark circles bruising the delicate skin beneath her eyes had not escaped his notice.

"*Bom dia,*" boomed Gaspar as he entered, striding with Iberian swagger undiminished by his bare feet. Besides that one nod to Siamese custom, Gaspar looked every inch the European gentleman in a sateen waistcoat, snug coat, and nankeen breeches. Thick, steel-gray hair and trimmed beard set off a sunned complexion. The lines around his dark eyes were as neat as the crease left in folded paper, as if they daren't do anything as undignified as feather. Gaspar shook Harrison's hand firmly, his genial smile a far cry from the brittle ones he'd delivered the previous evening.

Bewildered by this about-face in his host's temper, Harrison cut an inquisitive glance at Lamai. Her eyes were lowered, shielded by fans of black lashes. No help there.

The Portuguese man followed the track of Harrison's gaze. Releasing his guest's hand, he scooped up Lamai's and delivered a kiss to her unscarred cheek. Then he turned and gestured for everyone to sit. Two servants materialized from a door that opened to the outside to lay the table with numerous dishes of food. So discreetly did they go about their business, Harrison thought any butler in London would've gladly struck a diabolical bargain for the glory of managing such a staff.

Gaspar took up his napkin, snapped it open with a flick of his wrists, and smoothed it over his lap. He sipped his tea, then directed speech to Harrison. Lamai translated. "I trust your room was comfortable?"

"Very much so. I'm sorry to have arrived on your doorstep unannounced. Thank you for your hospitality." He speared a sausage on his fork, mouth watering as juices ran from the crackling casing.

"Not at all!" Gaspar gave a dismissive wave. "We Europeans must stick together. Now that you've had a night's rest, you must tell me how you came to be here. I'm wild with curiosity."

Through the medium of Lamai, Harrison related the task he'd undertaken on behalf of De Vere and Sons, and the sorry history of *Brizo's Woe*. He paused in his narration, allowing Lamai time to catch up. Her plate of food was untouched, oil congealing around her sausages. When she nodded for him to continue, Harrison shook his head. "We men are monopolizing you. Please eat. The remainder of my tale can wait."

But no sooner had she taken a bite of melon, Gaspar spoke to her sharply. "He wishes you to continue."

A muscle in Harrison's jaw ticked. "This is silly. Eat your breakfast, Miss Lamai." To Gaspar, he said, "I'll be glad to tell you all after our meal, sir."

Gaspar slanted a look at Lamai, awaiting her translation. Harrison watched her jaw firm stubbornly. "Please do not treat me as a child, Khun Harrison."

Harrison drew back. "I beg your pardon?" Treat her as a child, indeed. He'd done no such thing.

She leveled a cool gaze on him. "I'm capable of speaking for myself, feeding myself *and* handling the money." At his incredulous expression, she lifted a brow. "Does my competence shock you?"

Harrison threw back his head and laughed. When he dabbed his eye, Lamai had thawed; her rich brown eyes danced with merriment. "Point taken, Miss Lamai. Very well then …"

He continued his story, telling Gaspar of his rescue by fishermen, his recuperation at Wat Wihan, and his meeting of Lamai. "In my desperation, I'm afraid I quite foisted myself upon her traveling party. It speaks well of Miss Lamai's character that she did not toss me into the jungle."

Lamai's lips quirked. He no longer saw her lopsided smile as a physical impediment, but as a delightful, mischievous feature. "If I'd dropped you on the roadside as you'd deserved, Tilda would have followed you, and then Wan Pen would have refused to leave her little friend behind. Really, you must credit your goat for keeping you alive." She did a credible job calmly delivering her withering set-down, but the effect was ruined when laughter gurgled in her throat. Lamai clapped a hand over her mouth and turned her head.

He smiled to see her laughing. Her teasing—or perhaps just her presence—had helped put him at ease, Harrison realized. Apprehension still gripped his guts, but the fist had loosened. And when he was engaged with her, he forgot his unease altogether.

Gaspar spoke then, and Lamai instantly dropped the silliness. Harrison marveled at Lamai's facility with languages. She fluently spoke three languages that he knew of. Harrison's linguistic achievements were limited to his mother tongue and French; the classic Greek and Latin he'd not used since leaving Oxford—a sorry waste of learning. As for ladies, the most accomplished females of Harrison's acquaintance spoke conversational French in addition to English, and perhaps a few phrases in Italian and German for the purpose of ordering about Continental waiters and maids. How had Lamai come by such an excellent education?

The lady disrupted his thoughts with, "Khun Gaspar is satisfied that you are not competition for his business."

Harrison fought a scowl. "How magnanimous."

"He offers you employment with him, so you may earn money for your trip home."

He took a long swallow of tea. "What is the position?" he asked, carefully setting his cup on its bowl.

Lamai opened her mouth, shut it, then spoke to Gaspar. Nodding at his answer, she said to Harrison, "You would be Khun Gaspar's agent, overseeing his warehouse and workers here in the city."

Gaspar stood and came to stand behind Harrison, then clapped a heavy hand onto his shoulder as he declaimed for a moment.

"You might think it misfortune, but it was kind fate that brought you here, my boy," he said through Lamai. "I've long desired a helper in my affairs—and here you are, the answer to my prayers."

Harrison craned his neck to look up at the man. "Surely a successful merchant such as yourself already has a manager." Too well Harrison knew he'd done nothing to earn his place with De Vere and Sons Shipping Company. Henry De Vere had offered him the position out of charity, nothing more. He did not wish for more of the same. "I'd be happy to labor in your warehouse under the supervision of your manager."

Gaspar snorted. "I've a Thai manager, yes, but he's lazy, like his countrymen, and doesn't make the men work. Before you arrived, I'd already decided to replace him. I prefer a trustworthy white man in the position, but there aren't many educated Europeans in Bangkok who aren't already engaged."

Harrison cringed at this speech, but Lamai delivered it without flinching. How often must she have heard such talk to have grown immune to it?

Gaspar D'Cruz may have given Harrison a bed to sleep in and food for his belly, but he was despicable. Harrison had not forgotten the scene with the young servant last night. The sight of the girl flinging herself into the mud had been odd, but the way she'd unmistakably flirted with her employer—and the way Gaspar had touched her—had been downright unsettling. There were mysteries in this house, and Harrison wanted no part of them. He'd grown up in a house sick with secrets, rotten to the core with things left unsaid.

The hand on Harrison's shoulder tightened. Gaspar gave him a little shake as he spoke.

"Khun Gaspar wishes to know your answer. Will you take the position he offers, or no?"

No, he wanted to say. No, and no, and no again. He didn't trust Gaspar, didn't like the familiar way the man's hand rested on Harrison's shoulder, or the current of disrespect that flowed through every word he spoke to Lamai. He wanted to walk away, to return to England, to leave this man and his putrid prejudices to his hemisphere, while Harrison did his level best to forget such an unpleasant being existed.

Something of his thoughts must have shown on his face. "Khun Harrison?" Lamai said softly. "What would you do?"

"There must be a British ambassador or consul in Bangkok. I'll go there. I'm a subject of the Crown, they'd have to …"

His words puttered out as Lamai shook her head. "There is no representative of the British government in Siam, *farang*. Your country is getting too fat on India and China to bother with mine. I have only met a few of your countrymen in my entire life."

"Including your mother?" he snapped.

"My father," she answered calmly. "And he was gone before I was three."

Harrison exhaled, the fight draining out of him. Well and good to have principles, but how long would they last if he walked away now? Having so recently suffered hunger and privation at sea, he'd no wish to experience it again. He knew no one in this city—or in this country, or the entire continent of Asia, for that matter. He had nothing and no one to fall back upon. His nearest friends were in England, thousands of miles away. It would take most of a year for a letter begging their help to reach them.

His hand was a bloodless fist on the table beside his abandoned breakfast.

Tentatively, Lamai extended her hand, covering his with those slim, elegant fingers that could manage money and elephants with equal adroitness. Her lifeblood thrummed through them, vibrating against his skin. Their gazes met, and held. "Please, *farang*," she whispered, "be sensible. You will not find better."

Between Lamai's almost weightless hand and Gaspar's oppressive one, Harrison was trapped. He barked a bitter laugh. "It seems I've no choice, do I?" He pushed back from the table and stood to face his new employer. "I accept your gracious offer, Gaspar D'Cruz," he said with a slight bow. "I shall work for you until I've earned my way home."

… but not a day longer.

Chapter Seven

Charged with seeing Harrison Dyer established as the manager of the menial aspects of Gaspar's trading concern, Lamai spent the next week escorting the Englishman around Bangkok and getting him properly outfitted with new clothes and other essential items.

The morning of their shopping expedition, Lamai and Harrison departed Gaspar's house through the heavily carved front door, which let out onto Soi Sukha. Following the street past more residences—some as grand as Gaspar's, some grander, and some little more than shacks clinging to the fences of the rich—they came to a canal. They stopped on the bridge to watch an elegant barge pass, a golden naga at the helm protecting its wealthy passenger. A simpler boat followed. Lamai called down to the oarsman, who agreed to carry them to the market.

Harrison lent his hand as they descended the steps set into the bank and clambered into the boat. Even once they were seated, he did not loosen his grip. Taking note of his scowl, she couldn't resist teasing.

"Are you restraining my hand so I cannot abandon you? You're safe here. There's no jungle for many miles."

Startled, he looked at their clasped hands as though surprised to find them entwined. "Forgive me," he said, snatching his palm from hers as the boatman pushed off. "I suppose I'm … less than enthused to be in a boat again. My last excursion at sea did not end well, you may recall."

It did, she wanted to protest. *It brought you to Mueang Thai.* Thankfully, she checked herself before speaking glibly. So many men had perished. She must not make light of his experience. Instead, she tried to distract him from his present surroundings. "You will like the tailor we are going to visit. He knows all the styles the *farangs* like to wear."

"European styles, you mean?"

"Yes." Lamai idly twirled the stem of her open parasol. When she turned to face him, the painted silk acted like colored glass, casting red and blue shadows across Harrison's face. "He spent ten years in Lisbon, so he knows how you like the cut of your coat and such. Khun Gaspar sees no one else."

Harrison scrunched his nose. "At the risk of sounding ungrateful, do you suppose we might go elsewhere? I'd rather have clothes more Siamese in style." He listlessly flapped the sides of his borrowed coat. "I'll melt to death if I'm forced to wear clothes like this. They're stifling. Intolerable. I'm dying right now."

He jested, but there was a flush creeping above his cravat to his jaw. Lamai scooted closer, sharing the shade of her parasol. "You came here in the rainy season, the hottest time of year. It isn't always this bad."

"Thank God for His tender mercies."

Harrison angled his shoulders to bring his chest nearer to her side, the better to duck his head under the shelter she offered. The broad expanse of his shoulders served as a masculine wall, entirely blocking the far bank from Lamai's view. His face filled her vision. Their eyes met. A thrill of sensation went through her. Lamai's breath caught in her throat. Harrison's gaze fell to her mouth. She bit her lip against a spark of energy that seemed to arc across it at his attention.

Their oarsman called out a greeting to someone on the bank, startling Lamai. How could she have forgotten herself and made a spectacle in public?

Turning to the water in front of them, she cleared her throat. "Good thinking, to choose Thai clothes. You'll be more comfortable. You are very smart. For a *farang*, that is."

He chuckled at her gibbering. "Doesn't take a needle-wit to recognize the natives of a place know best how to dress for their own climate. If we were in London, I'd be perfectly comfortable, while you'd freeze in that thin skirt." He pointedly cocked a brow at her diaphanous attire. The lilac sarong, covered all over with batik flowers and leaves, was opaque, but clung to her thighs, perfectly revealing their shape and length. She'd worn such garments all her life, never once minding that a man might observe her limbs—who would consider such a thing, as every person had them!—but Harrison's attention set her utterly on end, keenly aware of her own body while her brain retreated, leaving her unable to formulate a sensible response.

"Look, we're nearly there," she trilled, delighted to be rescued from her momentary stupidity by the appearance of the marketplace in the near distance. "We'll still visit the tailor I recommended to you. He can outfit you in Thai style as you like, but you'll need a few pieces in European fashion for meeting Khun Gaspar's friends."

Harrison pulled a hand through his tousled hair; damp with perspiration, it held the furrows created by his fingers. He really ought not to be buttoned up in those stuffy, starched clothes, Lamai fretted, lest he suffer heat stroke. She would be sure to purchase something ready-made for him to change into. If not from the tailor—which occupied a shop bordering the sprawling open-air market—then from the stall of a vendor who sold to Thai people, not foreigners with more money than sense.

"And to pay this paragon of yours, I suppose I'm once more beholden to your charity."

She regarded him from beneath her lashes. "Not mine, but Khun Gaspar's. And it isn't charity. He is advancing you a sum, which will be repaid from your earnings."

The heavy sigh that met this intelligence marked an end to the moments of awareness that had passed between them, and Lamai could only be glad. Even the mildest flirtation carried her far out of her depths.

In the days that followed, flirtation seemed to be the farthest thing from Harrison's mind, though they were much in one another's company. To help him find his bearings (and acclimated just to the climate which still saw him sweating from dawn to dusk), Lamai had Harrison accompany her whenever she left the house. The dark cloud that hung over him during the trek to Bangkok dissipated in the face of so much novelty. Eschewing the European dishes Gaspar provided, Harrison was always game to try any Thai food Lamai put in front of him. She quickly learned to refrain from telling him what it was he'd eaten until after he'd already consumed it, when he balked at the suggestion of tasting putrefied fish. After cottoning on to the trick, she sneaked chicken stomach by him by vaguely offering a "chicken skewer," and he gobbled down a delicious larb redolent of lime and mint before she told him the "mince" the street vendor used in the meal was actually red ants.

His horrified expression sent her into peals of laughter. "I'm not sure whether to throttle you, or return to the cook for seconds." He chomped a cucumber spear, chewing thoughtfully, as if giving the matter due consideration.

Lamai nudged him playfully. "Don't think too hard, *farang*. Your brain is already soft from the heat. Tax it too much, and it'll dribble out of your ear."

"It may have already done so," he rejoined. "I might have dashed it away as rain, or sweat, or God-only-knows what other liquid flowing hereabouts, and never knew the difference." His eyes crinkled in a sly smile. "There wasn't much matter there to begin with, you see."

Rolling her eyes at his silly jest—while secretly admiring the self-deprecating humor so different from Khun Gaspar's stiff ways—Lamai informed him it was time to visit the warehouse.

They wended their way westward through the city, Lamai taking quick, small steps and Harrison loping at her side. His easy stride was belied by the tense lines of his mouth. Was it the gawping attention that the presence of a tall white man drew that made him uneasy, or did his restless eyes always look for danger lurking in every shadow?

She turned the corner of the next *soi*, then another. Eventually, they emerged at the banks of the Chao Phraya. Its summer inundation well underway, the river was swollen in its banks, fat and lumbering like a pregnant buffalo. The water teemed with activity. Junks laden with goods and passengers traveled both north and south, while fishermen returning from the morning's harvest bawled their wares to passersby, selling directly from their boats. At landings dotting both sides of the river, as far as the eye could see, dockhands loaded and unloaded ships, as well as carts bound for warehouses or market stalls.

A cacophony of languages assaulted her ears: Thai, of course, but just as much Cantonese, Mandarin, Burmese, and Malay. There was a fair bit of Japanese and Hindustani, a smattering of Portuguese, Dutch, and one of the Arab dialects. Strolling along the riverside, she spotted faces in a wide range of hues to go with the multitude of tongues. No one looked at her askance or scorned her scarred face. Here, where all of Bangkok was gathered to the bosom of the mother river, Lamai was not out of place. Her half-*farang* blood wasn't readily apparent, and her ugliness was nothing exceptional to sailors, workmen, and peasants whose hard lives accustomed them to injury and deformity.

Struggling to take in the sheer mass of human activity, Harrison's head swiveled back and forth unceasingly, to the point Lamai wondered that it didn't snap off at the neck.

At Khun Gaspar's warehouse, Lamai first took Harrison to the office, to show him his new desk and ledgers. Then they went into the storage facility itself. Harrison let out a low whistle as he took in the three stories of goods. Most of the laborers had gone for the afternoon, except a watchman dozing in a chair and the rat catcher, who popped out from behind a pallet of bagged rice. He waved cheerfully, heedless of the dead rodent in his hand.

Another few came in from a side door. Lamai called them forward and introduced them to Harrison. Cowed by their new *farang* manager, the men made *wai*, bowing deeply and promising their faithful service before backing away.

"This is ... most impressive," Harrison said after the men scurried outside. "I must own to doubting whether I'm up to snuff to manage all this."

Lamai laughed; Harrison frowned. "You're teasing about yourself again." She wagged a finger. "You worked for a London shipping company; this must seem like nothing!"

Scratching idly at his afternoon whiskers, Harrison tilted his head. "As to that, De Vere and Sons is a rather modest concern, and my job there was ..." His eyes touched hers, then darted away. With a toe covered in the black, embroidered silk of his new shoes, he rubbed a circle on the floor. "And my position ..." Clearing his throat, he halted his foot's fidgeting and straightened his spine before meeting her gaze squarely. "I was not fit for the job, in point of fact. My friend gave me a position I didn't deserve, so that I might earn money to start my own horse-breeding stable. Had my ship not been lost at sea, the expedition would have met with disaster and failure when I attempted to conduct business in Brunei."

"This man, your friend, must have believed you capable, or he would not have entrusted you with his business."

Harrison gave an enigmatic smile. "He's a good friend." His teeth flashed white in the dim warehouse. "Why Gaspar D'Cruz would trust me, a stranger, with his affairs is even more of a mystery. He's certainly no friend of mine." This last statement was delivered with a note of doom.

Worried his mood was turning dark, Lamai strove for pragmatic confidence. "You are nervous, as anyone would be in a new position." Gesturing to the stairs, she escorted him once more to the upstairs office. "Now, let's take a look at your ledgers. I will come in with you the first few days, and I shall help you with all the various papers that cross your desk. The last manager was Thai, but I have always translated for Khun Gaspar. It will be easy for me to do the same for you."

Harrison's first official day went smoothly, with the exception of one or two hiccups. Lamai introduced him to the men, then served as interpreter for the Englishman's instructions. With the laborers busy at their jobs, she and Harrison removed to the office to look over orders and invoices. Lamai showed Harrison the safe in the corner of the room, concealed by a false cabinet. Inside was kept a supply of ready cash, as well as the book of blank bank drafts. After showing him once where to write the figures and where to sign his name, Harrison dashed off payments for the invoices in short order.

Slumping back in his chair, he blew a breath up, ruffling the hair fallen across his brow. Lamai's fingers curled against the impulse to brush it back with her fingers. "These numbers test my nerve like nothing else."

Lamai rounded the desk to look over his work. "Why? Everything is entered correctly on the drafts."

He leaned forward, bringing his shoulders alongside the curve of her hip. Her stomach fluttered. "Because I don't know what the confounded things mean!" He jabbed the figure on one draft. "Six hundred twenty-seven. Six hundred twenty-seven *what?*"

"*Baht,*" she evenly replied. "Our currency is called baht."

"But what does that mean?" Thunking his elbow onto the desk, he lowered his brow to his palm. "What's a baht against the British pound? I haven't any sense of how much money this is. How am I to run a man's business when I don't—"

She tugged his ear sharply. His startled face snapped to hers. "Calm down, *farang*. It will be fine. You don't have to know how much a baht is worth to your pound, though if you really want to know we can go to the exchange house and find out."

Rubbing his abused ear, his mouth quirked up on the side in a rueful smile. "No, I don't suppose that will be necessary. You're quite right, Miss—"

"Khun—"

"Lamai," he interloped right back, eyes flashing. "It's simply a matter of keeping the numbers balanced, same as at home—and showing more in the revenues column than expenditures."

"Most wise," she pronounced.

"Very well," he said under his breath. "This won't be so hard, after all. Pluck up, old boy. You can do it."

Lamai quickly turned her head so he wouldn't see her valiant battle to hold back a giggle. His little speech of encouragement to himself was most adorable, but she didn't suppose he would appreciate her opinion.

"Now then," he said in a steadier tone, "these six hundred-odd baht—what have I bought with them?"

Lamai ran a finger down a column in the ledger until she found the entry. "Three piculs of cardamoms. That's a spice," she helpfully provided.

"Three pickles?" he spat. "There is no pickled spice worth six hundred of any currency for three meager pieces, I don't care how rarefied."

This time, she couldn't hold back her laughter. "Not pickles, you ridiculous man! Piculs."

"And what, pray tell, is a picul?"

"A measurement of weight. It's very heavy. Three piculs is quite a lot of cardamoms."

"How much is a picul to the stone?"

Lamai shrugged, powerless against the mirth rising in her chest as she anticipated his inevitable response. "I'm sure I don't know."

"Oh my God!"

The following days brought more of the same, but Harrison adopted a more sanguine attitude to his ignorance—good thing, too, as Lamai did not have the mettle to handle him flying into the boughs over every bill.

About ten days into Harrison's term as manager, Gaspar told Lamai he required her service for a meeting regarding a new contract. The potential partners came to the house in the late morning. There was a long period of formal greeting to be done, as well as the usual pleasantries wishing health and prosperity all around. Gaspar's grasp of Thai was sufficient to see him through these rote exchanges. Lamai sat quietly to the side, hands folded in her lap and eyes lowered. She was supposed to listen for any hint that the Thai men meant to cheat Gaspar, but she found herself unable to concentrate on the mundanities. Instead, she wondered how Harrison was getting on at the warehouse. Nothing about tonnage duties or bills of lading moved her soul, but she very much enjoyed spending time with the Englishman.

Assisting Gaspar always left Lamai feeling somewhat soiled. Used. Even in straightforward interpreting work, such as today's meeting, he expected her to sneak and eavesdrop, to uncover his enemies so he might outmaneuver them. For her pains, he gave no hint that he appreciated her work or respected her as a person. She was merely a tool to utilize as he saw fit.

By contrast, Harrison never made Lamai feel degraded. Though she knew he did not like relying upon her for translating documents and interpreting conversations, his dislike was born of his own bruised pride, not an aversion for Lamai herself. Gaspar relied upon Lamai as an old man would a walking stick—habitually—and with as much feeling for the implement. When Harrison requested Lamai's aid, she sometimes sensed an apology in his asking. He didn't care to importune her, any more than he relished his inability to read or speak for himself.

She could wish he might be less prideful in the matter. Lamai didn't mind helping Harrison. He didn't just ask her to tell him what words said, he asked her advice on all matters of business—and he listened, too, even if he ultimately went a different way. Lamai was unused to being asked her opinion about anything. She quite liked the way Harrison made her feel his equal in intellect and sense.

Thai women were accustomed to running their own little businesses or partnering equally with their menfolk in work. *Farangs*, however, treated their women little better than children who lacked understanding, or as blossoms that must be kept indoors, too delicate to flourish in the dirt and mess of the world. Having lived in Gaspar's house for so long now, she had almost forgotten what it was to be seen by a man as a capable person.

"Lamai!" Gaspar's frown and reddened cheeks told her this wasn't his first attempt at catching her attention. "Get over here, girl. Now," he ground out in Portuguese between grinning teeth. He preceded her into the formal dining room, as he called it, where his guests were seated at the long table. Allusions to business might be made over the meal being carted in by a string of servants, but negotiations would wait until afterward.

Seating himself at the head of the table, Gaspar cut his eyes to a small chair placed to the side of, and slightly behind, his own. There was no place setting for Lamai. She was to be his voice and his ears, but she was not to share the meal. Gaspar would not give either Lamai or his associates the impression that she was, in any way, important.

• • •

After the arduous meeting—the conclusion of which saw Gaspar and his guests sign a contract for the delivery of so many units of products delivered by a date some months hence for an astronomical sum of money—Lamai escaped to the kitchen to scrounge up something to eat. Cook gave her a link of the spicy Portuguese sausage leftover from Gaspar's meeting, sliced up and fried with vegetables, tossed with a green curry sauce, and spooned over a bowl of rice.

No sooner had Lamai tucked into her meal, than Kulap burst into the building, moaning that Lamai just *must* implore Khun Gaspar on her behalf for an ivory hair comb she'd seen at the market.

"You ask him for it!" Lamai shot hotly.

"I can't!" Kulap protested, all wide-eyed innocence. "I don't speak enough Portuguese to do it myself." A blush stained her cheeks. "Though he does like it when I try. When I say, '*Leve-me, mestre,*' he gets so hard and excited, he cannot last long. He goes at me like a beast, growling and pawing like a dog."

Kulap's lascivious words put Lamai off her food. "You talk like you enjoy being treated that way. Your mother would be ashamed," she scolded, pushing her bowl away.

Idly twirling a strand of hair around her finger, the girl shrugged. "I don't mind it so much. It's easier work than farming with my father, or selling in the market all day with my mother." Kulap wrinkled her little button nose. "My mother's face is dark and wrinkled from being outside every day—she's almost as ugly as you."

Lamai's temper flared. "At least your mother isn't a *farang's* whore!"

Kulap gasped just as the cook squawked an indignant, "Watch your mouth!"

Lamai shot to her feet and stomped out the door. Kulap's taunting voice called after her, "You would be, if that handsome young Englishman ever looked your way, but he doesn't! No man will ever be hard and desperate to have you, you jealous old hag."

Seething with hurt and fury, Lamai went to the stable. She could trust Wan Pen and Goui not to fling insults at her. Damn Kulap's mouth! Lamai hated what she and Mi and Nan were forced to do, but it was hard not to think Kulap didn't deserve her fate, at least a little, when she spent every moment fighting with the other two bed-servants and scorning Lamai.

Even worse, her description of copulating with Gaspar affected Lamai. … *he's so hard and excited … he goes at me like a beast* … Lamai had known since forever what men and women did together. The one-room houses she'd shared with various relatives during her childhood left no gaps in her knowledge as to where baby cousins came from.

Lamai had sometimes admired the fine face of a man seen in passing. Once, she'd spent the better part of a morning peeking out the window at the bare-chested laborers making repairs to Gaspar's house. But she'd never felt real desire until she met Harrison.

Now her imagination provided images of the Englishman acting out Kulap's words upon Lamai … his body hard and ready for her, a growl of wanting rumbling in his chest. Much to her consternation, she discovered that her body reacted to those erotic phantoms, just as it did to the man's actual presence. The misbehavior of her flesh only soured her temper further.

As she pushed open the stable door, she endeavored to shove aside the unwelcome thoughts. Her heart stuttered when she discovered Harrison laid out on the straw-covered floor of the stable in front of Wan Pen's stall. Tilda the goat stood on his chest, lipping at a bit of hay tangled in his hair.

"Harrison!" She skidded to a halt and crouched to find him glaring at the rafters far overhead. "Are you injured?"

"Only my pride."

"What are you doing?"

"Brooding."

Lamai sat back on her heels. "Bad day at the warehouse?"

He turned his head to look at her. "It would be hard to imagine how it might have been worse."

Wan Pen, having heard Lamai's voice, appeared at the door of her stall and kicked it, rattling the panel in its frame. "Stop it, brat!" Lamai scolded. She felt the still-sharp edge of her own temper and took a steadying breath. She gave her knees a dusting and fetched the hamper of fruit to offer Wan Pen an apology. "Do you want to talk about it?" she asked Harrison over her shoulder.

Nudging Tilda aside, he sat up with a groan and swiped a hand over his rumpled hair. "Ugh! Goat slobber."

"Som nom naa," she answered, laughing.

"What's that mean?" He swiped a wedge of cabbage out of the basket, broke it, and offered a chunk to Tilda.

Lamai slanted a wry look at him. "It means, 'You get what you deserve.' Lie down with goats, get up with slimy hair."

Harrison scowled at the tattered cabbage he held, as if it had done him ill. Wan Pen's trunk snaked forward, undulated along his arm, then snatched the leafy vegetable. "Someone came to the warehouse today." One hand went to his hip; the other came to his brow. Blunt fingers rubbed hard, creating little ripples of skin, as if to erase a headache. Or a bad memory. "Some Siamese fellow dressed in smart-looking silks. Accompanied by an armed man and a menial toady with a ledger—clerk, or a secretary … something of that nature. He—the toady—handed me a document. Very official," he said, gesturing with a hand, "seals and stamps all over. The writing was all in Thai, of course, so I couldn't make heads nor tails of that. I couldn't understand a word they said." Now Harrison's hands came before him, fingers spread, trying to catch something slipping from his grasp. "All I could do was smile like an imbecile, shake my head, and chirp, 'Sorry, I don't understand. Sorry, I don't understand,' as if they would somehow, magically, comprehend *me*."

What a predicament! Lamai clucked her tongue. "You should have sent for me, *farang*. I would have helped you."

A growl escaped Harrison's throat. Not a passionate one like she'd so recently fantasized, but the frustrated, aggrieved snarl of a beast caught in a trap. The side of his fist crashed against the wall. Wan Pen startled and let out a little cry. From across the stable, Goui vocalized a warning rumble.

"*Farang*!" Lamai snatched his wrist and shook, forcing his fist to loosen. "Remember yourself around the elephants. You put them, yourself, and everyone around you in danger when you behave so badly." She flung his hand away.

His expression changed to one of chagrin. "You're right. I apologize." He ducked his head. "And I know you'd have helped me, Lamai. Believe me, the only thing I wanted at that moment was to have you there to make sense of it for me." The corner of his lips kicked up a rueful smile.

Her mulish, pinched mouth softened. "That must have been upsetting," she allowed.

Sliding his gaze past her shoulder to the yard beyond the stable door, he shrugged. "It was humiliating. How am I meant to be a proper man of business, if I can't interact with the tax collector, or inspector, or whomever the hell that fellow was? I'm tired of being mute and illiterate." He gave a firm jerk of his head, from east to west. "The fact that I can't make it one day without you is insufferable. A grown man shouldn't require a … a governess. I must learn Thai, and that's all there is to it."

Lamai passed him an overripe mango and nodded at Wan Pen's stall. Taking his cue, Harrison gave the young elephant the peace offering. Tilda nosed around the hamper to select her own treat. The goat, Lamai noticed, was getting fat in Panit's care.

"It's not easy to learn a new language, *farang*." Reaching down, Lamai tucked her skirt up between her legs so she could ascend to the hayloft unencumbered.

"I know that." Harrison's voice filled the stable, a soft, silky rumble like gentle thunder. "Believe it or no, I do possess an education. I had a tutor, and I went to university. Ask me anything about classic Greek, and I'll prove to you just how much I've forgotten since my salad days."

Lamai snorted at his jest, the barb once more aimed at himself instead of another. Retrieving a pitchfork, she sent piles of hay sailing to the ground below. "Give the girls fresh bedding, would you? One less chore for Panit to do later."

For a few minutes, they worked in companionable silence. Then his voice filled the space again. "How did you learn English? Did your father teach you before he died?"

Driving the fork into the hay, Lamai swiped her wrist over her brow. "Maybe a little. But he didn't die. He went back to England when I was two years old."

The sounds of rustling straw stopped. The silence was no longer friendly, but tense. Lamai was glad she couldn't see Harrison's face, fearful of finding recrimination in his eyes. Her cheeks burned in remembrance of the insults slung at Lamai's mother, Waan, and her half-breed child. Her family had warned that the white man did not intend to marry Waan. Even as the couple lived together, made a home together, had a child together, many relatives turned their backs on what they saw as a Thai girl's degradation at the hands of a *farang*. When Waan's husband, Lamai's father, left—that was all the proof those relatives needed. Waan had been nothing more than a white man's whore. Used and abandoned, just as they said she'd be. *Som nam naa.*

There was a note of defensiveness when she spoke again. "My mother taught me what English she knew. She spoke pretty well, but didn't read or write. She wanted me to be able to speak to my father when he comes back for us. Me," she corrected. "He will come back for me," she flung into the void beyond the loft, daring Harrison to contradict her. He did not. "She made the acquaintance of English people whenever she could, always putting me forward, forcing me to converse with them." Lamai's gaze drifted to the loft window. The shutters were open, giving her a view of clouds painted raspberry and violet by a sun sinking in the west.

"After my *mèè* died," she went on, pulling herself from her reverie, "I went on practicing whenever I could. Then Khun Gaspar took me in eight years ago. He hired a tutor to teach me Portuguese, but the fellow knew English, too, and I persuaded him to teach me more. I learned to read it a little, but only what my teacher copied out by hand. He didn't have any books in English."

Harrison had been quiet such a long time, Lamai wondered if he'd slipped outside and left her talking to no one but the elephants. Leaning over the edge of the platform, she saw him cast a brooding look out the door in the same direction she had been watching the sunset.

Sensing her attention, he glanced up. Something passed between them, there in the stable, bathed by the day's last golden rays. She was glad she'd told him a bit of her history, she decided. It had been a long time since Lamai had had a friend. Even though, as Kulap said, he didn't look at her with desire, it was a fine thing to have a handsome Englishman take an interest in her life. To need her.

"I will teach you, if you like."

A wince flickered across his face; he quickly recovered it into an unconvincing smile.

Lamai withdrew from the ledge. He didn't want her to tutor him in Thai. Naturally not. Hadn't he just said he didn't wish to be so reliant upon her? The man had his pride.

Why, then, did his reaction sting?

She clambered down the ladder and shook out her skirt. "Actually, it would be best to find you another tutor. Helping Khun Gaspar keeps me very busy."

Harrison nodded gravely. "Of course. I understand. I wouldn't like to be an imposition."

Wan Pen reached her trunk down to pat Tilda. The goat pranced a little circle. Lamai opened the stall door to let the friends enjoy one another's company before Panit came with their evening feed.

A feminine shriek rent the idyllic evening calm. Harrison darted out into the paddock, Lamai close on his heels. Across the back lawn, Lamai could just make out figures through an open upstairs window: Kulap quarreling with one of the Burmese girls, Nan. Kulap's hand was tangled in the other woman's hair, pulling fiercely while she screeched about some offense or other.

"Kulap," Lamai called, cupping her hands around her mouth, "stop that at once! You're yowling like a cat in season. Khun Gaspar hates such racket."

Releasing the other woman's hair, Kulap came to the window, her pretty young face flushed with ire. "She's wearing a new dress, Lamai, and says Khun Gaspar bought it for her."

Lamai planted her hands on her hips. "So? Maybe he did."

"I'm his favorite." Even from below, Lamai could see the girl's lower lip press out in an impressive pout.

"Not for long, if you keep acting like this, you ninny."

"What's the problem?" Harrison inquired after Kulap had slunk away from the window.

Lamai huffed, taking a few seconds to reorient herself to speaking English. "Kulap forgets herself. She acts like she's mistress of the house, and not just a slave." Twitching her skirt, she started forward to the house. Harrison's arm caught her wrist. When she turned around, his face was a mask of confusion.

"Slave?" He shook his head. "What …? D-do you mean 'servant'? Someone paid for her work?"

Lamai snorted. "Paid? Kulap? The only payment was the one Khun Gaspar made to Kulap's parents, when he bought the girl." Harrison's fingers tightened on her wrist, almost to the point of pain. "Ow!" she yelped, snatching her hand back. "What's gotten into you?"

Something dark flashed across his face. "Slavery, Lamai? The … the *owning* of a human being by another person? That's what goes on here?" The sun, easing its way into the warm bath of night, cast a few last rays over the darkening city. One slashed across Harrison's throat and chest, like the vicious slice of a saber. A mosquito whined in Lamai's ear, but she daren't slap it while he pinned her in that fearsome glare. "Slavery is barbaric." He took a step forward, from which she retreated in measure. "I won't be party to it, not in any way. How can you treat the topic so lightly?"

The judgment in his words, the disgust writ large across his face, made Lamai's innards roil. "How dare you?" she snapped. "You, citizen of an empire that engaged in the trade of African slaves, find fault with Mueang Thai?"

"Slavery has been abolished in the West," he retorted. Feet rooted wide and hands planted on hips, he leaned in, crowding her. "It's a shameful, inexcusable part of our past—*our past*—as in, it doesn't happen anymore." Harrison's voice rose in volume to a shout that filled her ears, drowning out even the drone of the mosquito. "I can't answer for the madness still going on in America, but Europe is enlightened enough to have done away with that heinous crime."

Enlightened? Crime? *Crime?* Did he regard all Thai people as criminals? Did he think *she* was a criminal?

It didn't help that she deplored her part in Gaspar's purchase of Kulap. Lamai had negotiated the purchase of numerous slaves over the past eight years and felt no shame for it, for they were all treated honorably and given fair terms to redeem themselves from service. But all of those had been household staff—maids, gardeners, and the like. Kulap had been different. Lamai knew at once that Gaspar wanted her for a bed slave, and those women Gaspar did *not* deal with fairly. She'd felt dirty even as she'd made Gaspar pay three times Kulap's price. Every time Gaspar or one of his friends took the girl to bed, a knife twisted in Lamai's gut. Grateful for the camouflage of darkness, she dashed away hot water before it could spill from her eye.

"At least our slaves are taken honorably in battle, or willingly sell themselves, unlike the poor wretches you *farangs* stole from their homes. Thai slaves can buy their freedom again, once they've repaid their masters what they owe. I can't believe you ..." Lamai pulled her trembling lips back between her teeth. Took a calming breath. Another. "I can't believe you think your ways are superior to ours."

His voice dripped disdain. "Well, perhaps in this instance, mine are." He made a sound of disgust. "I can't get out of here soon enough."

Lamai's face burned as if she'd been slapped. She'd thought Harrison was different from other white men. Open-minded, curious. Just a short time ago, he'd expressed his desire to learn her language, something few *farangs* ever bothered to do. More, he'd seemed interested in *her*. She thought he was her friend. "For such enlightened people, you Europeans are happy enough to come here and own slaves again. More than happy to indulge in our *barbarism*." Her lip curled on the word.

His hand found her arm again, gentler this time. The other came to her scarred cheek. She felt the brush of his small finger against her jaw, but nothing else. "Lamai," – her name was an anguished moan – "... are you a slave? Does Gaspar own you?"

"No!" She recoiled from his touch. She didn't want his tenderness. Not now. "I am ... bound ... to Khun Gaspar, but not like that."

She felt his question in the space between them before he voiced it. "Then how? What holds you to him, Lamai?"

Maybe once—the moments ago that already felt like another lifetime—she could have confided in Harrison, explained the obligation that held her. But it turned out he was just like every other *farang*: quick to condemn and eager to lord over cultures deemed inferior to their own—which was every culture comprised of peoples with complexions darker than yak milk. She already regretted telling him so much of her history; she wouldn't compound her error by exposing her heart's duties and yearnings to one so quick to scorn.

"Do not trouble yourself with my concerns, Khun Harrison." Her voice was sweet and quiet, the perfect, subservient Thai girl that European men preferred. "My affairs are far too small for a man such as your great self." She made *wai* and bid him good night, bowing low, formal and distant.

When he called after her, she glided onward into the house, perfectly composed. No one who saw her would suspect her feelings had been shattered.

Chapter Eight

It was late August, and Harrison wanted to die. Not for any of the old reasons this time, but because the city of Bangkok was a sweltering, dank armpit he couldn't escape. Even now, in the "cool" of the evening, with the windows and door of his apartments open to encourage air circulation, sweat ran freely down his torso, adhering his thin shirt to his skin. He'd utterly abandoned waistcoats six weeks ago. Oddly, he didn't think so much about the heat during the day when it was worse—perhaps because he was too busy with work to dwell on physical discomfort. But at quiet times like this, sitting at the table that doubled as his desk, with paper before him and a quill gripped in his right hand, all he could think of was the infernal swelter. And the mosquitoes, of course. A sharp *thwack* to his neck exterminated one of the little blighters. Always the damned mosquitoes.

Grimacing at the crimson-smeared fingers, he wiped them on the handkerchief he always kept handy for mopping perspiration, then bent to his task. *Dear Henry,* he wrote. A droplet of sweat fell from his nose and plopped onto the words he'd just written, diffusing the ink in swirls and eddies like watercolor paints.

"Buggering bloody ralph spooner!" He crumpled the spoiled sheet into a ball and fobbed it across the table.

Having never been much of one for cursing, Harrison had become something of a connoisseur of British vulgarities of late. Rarely hearing his native tongue anymore had done strange things to his brain. Snips of gutter talk overheard at moments in his distant past swept across the surface of his memory like a lighthouse beacon offering security in a foreign sea awash with a strange new vocabulary. He clung to those words, parroting them with gusto when occasion warranted.

"Several of those terms are unfamiliar; you must teach me."

His head snapped around. The air left his lungs in a *whoosh*.

After not seeing her for nearly two months, Lamai stood in the doorway. Two days after that dreadful quarrel, she and Gaspar had departed for a trip to the north. *Need to check in on some holdings,* the Portuguese man had said. *Won't be long.* That had been eight weeks ago.

Since then, Harrison had had ample time to regret the condescending attitude he'd struck during his last conversation with Lamai. At night, he closed his eyes, heard himself term her culture *barbaric* and winced, wishing he could call back words spoken in anger and haste. Lamai was no more culpable for Thai slavery than Harrison was to blame for British travesties, like pickled onions. No matter his opinion of the institution, he'd no right venting his spleen on her. He'd scripted the eloquent apology he'd offer, edited and revised until it shone.

"You're back."

Not exactly the smooth opening he'd planned. She gave a small, guarded smile, her eyes wary. Over the course of her absence, Harrison had forgotten how Lamai's mouth curled up on the left while the right corner remained locked in place, stern as a schoolmarm. It was an expression as unique as Lamai herself, and he'd missed it. He'd missed her.

"I am." Her eyes flitted around the chamber, taking in the personal touches Harrison had added in the past two months. Her toes, however, did not cross the threshold.

Belatedly, he snapped out of the shock of her sudden reappearance and stood. "Please, won't you come in?" His small sitting room had a pair of plush armchairs, but he pulled out a chair at the table instead. When she stepped into his sitting room and the light of his several lamps, his mouth went dry. Taking in the fall of her loose hair, waved as though she'd only just released it from a braid, his gaze traveled downward. She wore a sarong skirt of dazzling blue-green silk that skimmed her gently rounded hips and swayed against shapely calves. Lamai's top was another sarong, this one a vibrant, deep pink that was wound about her torso like a bandage and tucked across her shoulders to create snug cap sleeves. The garment's effect was similar to a corset, accentuating the slim lines of her body while plumping the pale tops of her breasts just above the material.

The response of his body was as sudden as it was unwelcome. Hot blood thundered through his ears in its race south. His groin tightened as sparks ascended his spine, widening both eyes and nostrils, his every sense homing in on the luscious woman crossing the room.

Clutching the chair to his front, he prayed the rungs of the ladder back were sufficient to conceal his burgeoning erection. When she lowered into the chair, he scooted it snug beneath her rump and right to the table, as if they were about to be served a course of asparagus soup and crimped cod.

For a moment he paused to collect himself, his hands tight on the rails of the chair. He stared at the top of her head, at the vulnerable line of scalp exposed by the parting of her hair. Her tresses fell down her back and covered her shoulders. The gloss of her ebony strands was like the reflection of the moon on a dark, still lake, inviting him to sink into the depths. Discreetly, he ran his fingers across the warm silk of a lock and released an inward sigh.

He'd hoped their time apart would have allowed him to get the better of his attraction, but to no avail. "I'm glad you're home."

"Naturally you are," she chirped, her bright tone forced. "I see you need rescuing. Well, Khun Harrison, I'm here to help. What do you need me to scribe for you?" she inquired, reaching for a fresh sheet of paper.

"No, Lamai …" Harrison took his seat. When he looked into her dark eyes, his nerves abated somewhat. She had come to him, after all. "I wanted to talk to you."

She tilted her head, spilling a curtain of hair across the unscarred portion of her face. *Fearless.* The word came to mind as he took her in, indifferent to the exposure of her extensive scarring. So often in his life, Harrison had checked and double-checked his cuffs, ensuring no part of the injuries on his wrists would be visible to the outside world. But Lamai didn't cover up. Others similarly disfigured might be shamed into reclusiveness, but Lamai just carried on doing what needed to be done. He could do worse than follow her example.

"Lamai, I wish to apologize for the way I spoke to you that night."

Her hands were neatly folded on the table. He reached out and took one. Longing pierced his gut, an empty, lonely wanting that yearned to be filled with companionship and home and, yes, passion. Despite the strides he'd made the last two months in finding his way here in Bangkok, he was yet in need of everything that made a life worth living: friends, family, lovers. He'd never had more than one of those, though. Family he had but nominally, and as for lovers—well. There had been physical interludes, but nothing lasting. Nothing true.

A lump rose in his throat and his fingers tightened on hers.

"Khun Harrison …"

Shaking his head, he pressed a fist to his mouth and cleared his throat. "I'm all right," he assured her. "After you left the city, I thought again about what you told me, Lamai, about slavery here in Siam."

Her features went wooden; her fingers pulled against his.

"What I realized," he hastened to continue, "was that what you described isn't true slavery, but indentured servitude. Had I not completely overreacted at the word 'slave,' I would have realized your translation error. Over in England, why, we used the same sort of system, too, as a way for debtors to repay their creditors. It's not perfect, and there's always a possibility of exploitation, but at least—"

"They are slaves, Khun Harrison." Lamai's voice was assertive, flat. A plank of information. "Some can be redeemed by repayment; others are held for life." Chin ticking back and forth, she lowered her eyes to their connected hands. Her shoulders dropped a fraction. "Our ways are difficult for outsiders to understand, I think." Her words were gentler now. "But at least you have the experience of comparing. I've never been outside the kingdom of Mueang Thai; even though I am half-English, I'm sure I would be bewildered by your country."

"England *still* bewilders me. You've never seen such confusion as a hostess sorting out her guests into an order of precedence before permitting them to file in to supper. God save us if a senior Irish bishop should appear at the same function as a newly-consecrated English bishop. Vapors for all."

He huffed a laugh, and was relieved when she smiled in return.

"Thank you for your apology," Lamai said. "And I apologize, too, for accusing you of being no different from other *farangs*. At least you try to understand. Many foreigners do not." She picked up his quill and twirled it in her fingers. "So, what are you working on?"

Content that peace had been achieved, he leaned back, accepting her change of conversation. "A letter, but I'm not having much success."

"Do you need translation help?"

"Thank you, but no. I know the language, but not the words." At her puzzled expression he continued, "I need to write home. Tell my friends what happened."

Lamai's eyes widened. "You haven't written yet?"

His cheeks flushed. "I don't know what to say. How can I tell my friend—who also happens to be my employer—that he's lost everything?"

Liquid brown eyes creased in a sympathetic smile. "A difficult undertaking, to be sure. Have you written your family, at least? They will want to know that you are safe and well."

The heat in his face intensified. "My parents are deceased and my siblings and I ..." He lowered his eyes to the blank paper that awaited his words to fill it. "We are not on easy terms. My older brother, my younger brother and sister ... I haven't spoken to any of them in years."

"*Mmmmm.*"

In spite of himself, Harrison smiled. Until now, he hadn't realized he'd missed that sound of hers, her hum of understanding.

"Tell me about your friends," she surprised him by saying. He met her gaze; she tilted her head. "If you don't mind, that is."

His smile deepened. "Not at all. There are five of us: Brandon, Sheri, Norman, Henry, and myself. We met at university." Harrison's memory tripped back through time. He could still recall the strange feeling of his black scholar's robe swishing around his legs as he made his way to lectures, the smell of old paper and leather in the libraries, the overwhelming sense of history bearing down from the very rafters of the university campus. "I hadn't gone to school, you see. I'd studied at home, with a tutor."

"Were you a sickly child?"

"No, it was ..." Another memory. Eyes flicking to the nursery door. *Does it run in the family, I wonder?* "I didn't wish to go to school." His voice rasped. "Staying home was my choice."

He told her how overwhelmed he'd been by Oxford, but how the friendships he'd made with the Honorables had been—

"The Honorables?" she interrupted, her plump lips twitching in a frown. "What does that mean?"

"Oh, well, you see ..." Harrison's fingers drummed on the tabletop. "Each of us five belongs to an aristocratic family, though none is heir to a title. Gentlemen in our position are styled 'The Honorable Mr. So-and-So.' It's just a silly name we gave our group," he finished with a shrug.

"Your father is a lord?" Lamai asked, her tone impressed. "Wait until Khun Gaspar hears! He'll go out of his way to assist you, if he thinks it might earn him—"

He cut her off with a wave of his hands. "No, no, no. Please. I've had nothing to do with my family in a long time. They're no more eager to claim me than I am them. That's why I was writing to Henry, and not my elder brother Charles, who is now the Earl of Ingran."

Her brows drew together, her lips parted; he heard the soft intake of breath. After a pause, she released it.

"What is it?" he pressed.

"It's not my place to pry," she said, each word careful, "but I am curious about why you do not speak to your family."

Having opened up this much, her question didn't surprise him, but it still struck Harrison in the chest. A cold *thud* on his heart. Emotion rose in his throat, old fears and sadness he had never been able to express any way other than by punishing his own flesh. He'd never spoken of it to another; he couldn't, not fully.

"Something bad happened." His words were just as careful as hers had been. "To me. I was … hurt. And no one believed me."

Her nose wrinkled. "Didn't you show them your injury?"

He gave a ghost of a smile. "It wasn't that kind of hurt."

Her face cleared as understanding dawned. She said nothing for a time. Harrison felt like he'd suddenly stepped naked onto a stage, entirely exposed for her judgment or condemnation.

Her hand slid across the space between them, and took his. He felt the invitation in the squeeze of her fingers, but he held his peace. This was enough. For now, this was enough.

• • •

The next day, Harrison was at the warehouse, muddling through a conversation with some of the laborers when Gaspar and Lamai came in. After issuing his instructions to the workers, he turned to greet them. The previous night's conversation with Lamai had left Harrison vulnerable, but he awoke this morning with a feeling of calm.

From behind Gaspar's right shoulder, Lamai gave Harrison a wide smile. "Listen to you, Khun Harrison! I'm proud to hear you speaking Thai so well."

Even as her approval warmed his heart, Harrison chuckled at the exaggerated compliment. "Without you here to translate for me, madam, I've been forced to learn through trial and error— mostly error, as you just witnessed."

Over the past two months, Panit and the rest of Gaspar's household had provided Harrison with an intense immersion in their language. Every day, the *mahout* had patiently exchanged simple conversational phrases with Harrison, using hand gestures and sketches to illustrate meaning when it was not obvious. In the kitchen, Cook had pointed out every vegetable and cooking utensil and named them, over and over, then quizzing Harrison by pointing and waiting for him to provide the nouns. The house servants did the same for objects of furniture. At the docks, workers had patiently repeated themselves, sometimes throwing in the odd word of Portuguese or French, until mutual understanding could be reached. The gentle, tonal language did not come easily to a mouth accustomed to guttural consonants and hard stops. The vocabulary of shipping and enterprise was yet beyond him, but if this new language was a pond into which he'd been tossed headfirst, Harrison's flailing splashes were beginning to resolve into a clumsy dog paddle.

Gaspar wanted to see the ledgers. After looking over the books and laughing in delight when he saw the hefty numbers in the revenues column, the merchant put his arm around Harrison's shoulders. "A good friend of mine is coming to supper tonight, Affonso Sales. Make sure you're there, eh? I have to crow about my gift from the sea."

When their Portuguese guest arrived, Harrison was standing at Gaspar's side to greet him.

"Affonso Sales," Gaspar said after giving his guest a friendly slap on the back, "Harrison Dyer."

Harrison and the newcomer exchanged nods and polite—if spotty, on Harrison's part—greeting in Portuguese. The fellow soon retired to his rooms to rest and refresh himself, and Harrison went to his own apartments. While the sultry afternoon passed, he labored over the shipping manifest of goods Gaspar had brought with him from the north, compiling orders for where the items should be stored within the warehouse.

When the sounds of male laughter reached him, Harrison lifted his head from his work to find the sun low in the sky. He changed for the evening, resentfully stuffing himself into a cravat, waistcoat, and jacket.

He stepped into the corridor and heard a heavy thump from Affonso's apartment, which adjoined Harrison's, and a feminine curse.

"What the devil?" Harrison stepped down the hall to investigate. The curves of a familiar bottom bobbed in the air, while Lamai, on hands and knees, crawled beneath a table.

"What are you doing?"

She yelped at the sound of his voice and jerked upright, striking her head on the underside of the table.

Harrison struggled not to laugh as she backed out of her precarious spot, but the glower she leveled on him when at last she emerged, top bun askew, communicated his failure to conceal his amusement.

He offered a hand to help her to her feet. Her palm fit against his, comfortable and neat.

"What were you doing under there?" he asked as she shook out her skirt. The sarong, he noted, was the same drab blue worn by all the household servants. His smile slipped. "Lamai?"

Shooting him a sharp look, she brought a finger to her lips then padded across the floor to hold the door open. "You should go downstairs," she said, her voice hushed.

He returned in a whisper, "Why are you dressed as a maid?"

"Because today I am one." She jerked her head. "Go."

What nonsense was this? Harrison frowned sharply. "What are you about?" Crossing his arms, he made it abundantly apparent he had no intention of budging until she'd given a proper accounting of herself.

Rolling her eyes, Lamai snagged his coat sleeve and towed him deeper into the chamber, their bare feet silent on the soft Turkish rug.

"I dropped some things while I was tidying." She pointed beneath the table. Harrison, ducking, spotted some papers and raked them out. Straightening them, he noted the documents evidenced signs of having been posted: fold-creases, worn edges— one, lying facedown, bore a stamp of franking. He recognized Gaspar's sharp, slanted hand on the page. The Portuguese words *carga* and *gado* jumped out at him—*cargo* and *livestock*, words he'd added to his burgeoning collection of foreign terms related to his work soon after assuming the position.

Lamai snatched them out of his hands before he could read more. Shoulders hunched and eyes resolutely on the papers, she arranged and folded them until they were once more a neat packet. She did not replace it on the table but held it, her face averted from Harrison and eyes sliding to the door.

"You're not a maid, Lamai."

The tips of her delicate ears blushed; pink washed over her high cheekbone on the left and limned the scars on the right.

Her behavior screamed guilt, but she wasn't lying, wasn't making excuses. Instinctively, Harrison knew Lamai trusted him—or wanted to.

Before he could think better of it, his hand came to her back and rubbed circles over taut muscles. "Whatever it is, Lamai, you can tell me." Her wary eyes turned to him. With a wry smile, he added, "It's not as if I could share your secret with another living soul in this country."

He felt some of the tension leave her body. "Khun Gaspar …" she began haltingly. Harrison waited. "He is jealous of competitors. You know this, yes?"

"My first lesson on the man," Harrison drawled. "You were prepared to leave me to the monks and fishermen on his orders, as I recall, because of my work."

She chuffed an anxious laugh. "Right. Well, he is suspicious of all *farang* merchants—even the ones he works with and likes, like Affonso Sales. Khun Gaspar schemes to gain advantage over them, and he's paranoid that they all scheme against him. I …"

Lamai's gaze dropped once more to the letter in her hands, the packet trembling with the hum of her unease.

"I spy for him sometimes," she confessed in a murmur. "Snoop through belongings, read documents, looking for evidence of a plot that never exists. He likes me to—" Lamai's lips closed over her teeth, pulled down at the corners. Her nostrils flared on a sharp inhale. "He expects me to listen, dressed as a maid or … to be invisible like a servant and listen. No one expects a Thai slave woman to know Portuguese, so they are careless with their words." A shudder passed through her, and Harrison instinctively knew she'd heard words that had nothing to do with trade contracts.

Harrison had witnessed the proclivity some men had for casually abusing women. The groping of a barmaid as she delivered a pitcher of ale, pulling a dairy girl into a barn stall, obscenities yelled to a washerwoman as she carried a basket of dirty shirts down the street. Wealth and social standing did not make men inclined to such behavior better, only bolder. How much worse might such a man behave when he thinks he is insulated by a language barrier?

His heart twisted in sympathy. He wrapped his arms around her shoulders and drew her close in an embrace. Lamai exhaled a long sigh, melting against his chest. Harrison's heart pinched again, harder, recognizing in her some of the same loneliness he'd felt for so many long years.

"Why do you do this?" he murmured, dipping his head to speak near her ear and trying to persuade himself that the wave of warmth washing through him had nothing to do with how she felt so good snugged against his chest. "It's clear you don't want to do this. Why do you remain with Gaspar? With your talents, you could work as a translator for any Portuguese merchant or diplomat."

A low, sad moan slipped through her throat. "I must do as he says, Harrison. I have to stay with him."

Frowning, Harrison brought his hands to her arms, pushed her back so he could look into her miserable eyes. "Why? What does he have on you? Whatever it is, Lamai—"

"My father." She slumped in his hands, as if exhausted from carrying a heavy burden. "Gaspar is the last tie I have to him. They were friends, you see, and when he returns, my father will come to Gaspar. My father is the only family I have. I must be here, so he can find me. So we can be together again."

Her words were hopeful, but her tone was so bleak, Harrison wondered if she even believed them anymore. What kind of a man abandoned his wife and child and went to the other side of the world, with only a vague promise of returning "someday?" This was the behavior of a callow youth, a coward, not the actions of a respectable man.

And yet, Harrison knew, too, how people could hold themselves captive in bad situations out of habit or despair. Or—maybe worst of all—out of hope. Hope that enduring hell now would, at last, end in the opening of paradise, the respite of all worry and woe.

That hadn't been his good fortune. He'd endured his hell, and when it was over (was it ever really over?) there was no redemption, no salvation. Instead, he'd emerged gutted, broken. And he'd stayed that way, never been made whole.

But maybe … maybe it didn't have to be that way for Lamai.

"I will help you," he vowed. "What's your father's name, by the way?"

"Peter Hart."

Harrison smiled while something grew inside him, filling him, pressing his ribs outward, stretching his smile into a grin. "My dear Miss Hart," he said, bowing with a flourish, "It's an honor to make your acquaintance."

Lamai blinked, dazed. "Miss Hart?" she murmured. "No one has ever called me that." Her fingers drifted to her face, as if to verify she remained the same person.

He took her hands. "I don't know your father, Lamai, but I can help you. I know people who know people who know people … you're not alone, Lamai, not anymore. With a name and whatever additional information you have, my friends in England will be able to find him."

Lamai brought a hand to her mouth; her eyes welled. "You would do this for me, Harrison?"

"I stand your friend, Lamai. It would be my honor to assist you in this matter."

She threw her arms around his neck. "Thank you! You are too good."

Chuckling, he circled her waist with his arms and brought his cheek to her hair. His nose brushed the knot atop her head, lightly fragranced with coconut and exotic flowers. "I've done nothing yet to earn your praise—and it's my friends back home who will do the work. We'll send them your letter. Hopefully, by the time

I'm back in England, they'll have news for me to pass along to you."

Lamai gave his neck one more good squeeze then stepped back, beaming. "I can't believe after all this time, I'm finally going to find my father."

"It will be a long time yet," he cautioned. "Nine months alone for our letter to reach England, and nine months for the reply—plus however long for the search itself. It could be a matter of weeks, or it might require a year or more."

Pressing her hands to her belly, Lamai nodded. "I understand. I'll try to be patient."

"Meantime," Harrison said, strolling to the door, "you needn't remain with Gaspar. As long as I know where you are, I can get word to you."

The image of her happy face—and the joy she radiated—carried Harrison through supper with Gaspar and Affonso. He understood perhaps half of the men's conversation, but he smiled and laughed when they did, pleased with the knowledge that he had the ability to empower Lamai to choose how and with whom she made her living. Harrison had taken away the one hold Gaspar had on her. She was free to do as she pleased.

After supper, all three men retired to the salon for port and more (from what Harrison gathered) braggadocio and banter. The Portuguese gentlemen occupied a low couch, laughed, and slapped each other on the back. Meanwhile, Harrison, ensconced in a deep armchair, gazed broodingly into his glass, lifting it to his lips intermittently for a taste, the ruby liquid thick with nostalgia for other evenings in other places. A double clap of Gaspar's hands roused him from his thoughts.

The young servant girl, Kulap, carried in a small strongbox that she placed on the side table at Gaspar's elbow then bowed her way out again. Setting his glass aside, Gaspar pulled a key from his pocket, unlocked the box, and threw back the lid. Affonso leaned across Gaspar to peer inside and made a sound of appreciation.

Must be some European luxury, Harrison assumed. Spanish olives were worth their weight in gold here. What he wouldn't do for a kippered herring, he thought wistfully. It was strange, as he'd never cared for kippered herrings before, but exile made him long for the comfort of anything familiar.

Gaspar reached into the box and stirred his fingers. Coins tinkled and slid against one another, the bright, metallic sound like nothing else in the world. He lifted his tanned hand and tipped it. A stream of currency glimmered in the lamplight, bronze and silver and the occasional flash of gold.

Harrison didn't get too excited. The baht, he'd come to learn, was worth little against the British pound and the Portuguese *real.* A mountain of coins might make an impressive sight, and they spent beautifully in the marketplace, but the modest sum Harrison had thus far saved made barely a dent in the sum required to secure passage on a ship bound for Europe.

As if hearing his thoughts, Gaspar shot a cunning look at Harrison. "Affonso's and my profits from our dealings up north. What do you think?"

Harrison raised his glass in salute. "*Impressionante,* Senhor D'Cruz. To your continued good fortune." Tipping his head back, he drained his glass then rose. "If you'll excuse me, senhors, I shall retire now. *Boi noite.*" The cravat and waistcoat were suffocating. He looked forward to shedding them and washing himself with cool water.

Face red with drink and merriment, Gaspar shot to his feet. "Stay, my boy! Stay! This fortune is yours, too. I couldn't have taken care of my business up north without you keeping everything running here in the city." Thrusting both hands into the strongbox, he pulled out a double fistful of bills, spilling coins, scattering them across the floor. Harrison watched one roll beneath an antique Japanese cupboard. Finding it would brighten the day of one of the maids.

The Portuguese merchant thrust money into Harrison's hands. "For you. *Inglaterra!*" he cried.

England.

Harrison's brows lifted. Flipping through the notes, he saw they were each marked at five and ten baht each. This was a Siamese fortune, but would it meet his needs? "England? This is enough? *O suficiente?*"

"*Sim, sim!*" Gaspar affirmed. "Enough. Plenty. You go home now."

Harrison was suddenly lightheaded, as if his skull had abruptly expanded to twice its size and all the contents vanished. Home. Home! It had taken two months of diligent work, muddling his way through a language that had seemed utterly confounding, carefully feeling his way through a very different culture, but he'd done it. He was going home.

Gaspar's friendly punch to his shoulder snapped him out of disbelief. This was real. As soon as he could find a ship sailing west, he could begin the long journey back to England. Kippered herrings and port and cold, rainy days—God, how he missed the cold, rainy days—all of it, waiting right where he'd left it nearly a year ago. He grinned so big, so enthusiastically, his cheeks hurt.

"Tonight we celebrate, *sim*? Affonso, my friend, I offer you the pleasures of my house." He clapped twice. A Thai footman opened the door, took instructions from Gaspar, and bowed. "You, too, Harrison," Gaspar said as the fellow scurried off. "You've earned a little treat, eh?" This he punctuated with a slap to Harrison's midsection.

When the servants appeared, Kulap and the two Burmese women, Harrison looked for platters or bottles, musical instruments, something that fell under his preconceived notion of celebration. Their hands were empty. They weren't dressed in their drab sarongs anymore, either, but now wore gowns of European design, muslins and silks, lace and flounces.

The hair on the back of Harrison's neck rose. "What is this?"

The three women, a triumvirate of elegant swans, glided forward in a line, turned to face Gaspar, and knelt.

Affonso, leaning forward in his seat, rubbed his hands together. Gaspar said something to his compatriot in Portuguese, too rapidly for Harrison to follow. The other man's eyes boldly roved over the women, arrayed before the men like a buffet of sweets.

"I don't understand," Harrison muttered to himself even as, with a sudden, dreadful certainty he *did* understand.

The hair these women had, the full heads of long hair, unlike the shaved, cropped tuft sported by most Thais, even the women—how had that not raised an alarm? They'd been compelled to keep their hair, not because it was familiar in appearance to European visitors as Lamai had once claimed, but because, in its familiarity as a feminine trait, abundant, beautiful hair was sexually desirable to white men.

The room suddenly went askew and he felt as if he was falling. Even as his eyes confirmed that he was still seated in a luxurious armchair, the world slipped away, the wind whipping past his ears (or was it a rush of blood?), hurtling through space, racing backwards through time to strike a brutal point of impact.

"Affonso?" Gaspar's smile was lurid, his bright eyes eager to see which woman his business associate would choose. The guest hummed as he perused the women from his seat. Then he rose, taking no pains to conceal the bulge in his breeches, and inspected the women up close, like a thrifty hausfrau agonizing over the selection of the butcher's wares to ensure acquisition of the best joint for her money.

At last he stopped in front of Nan, his bare feet tipped by thick, yellowed toenails almost touching her satin-covered knees. He snapped his fingers in front of her nose, forcing her to tilt her head back, her face close to his tented pants, to look into his looming face.

The woman rose smoothly, even giving Affonso a small smile. He put an arm around her waist and tugged her to his side.

"*Sua vez!*" Gaspar turned to Harrison, gestured to the remaining women.

"I don't understand," Harrison heard himself repeat. Some part of him was still tumbling. He was cold now, chilled by the gale of an endless plunge. Another, base part kept his body functioning, kept his eyes open to witness, his mouth working to form words, even as his mind both recognized and refused to acknowledge what was happening in front of him.

His employer chuckled. "A treat, *meu garoto*, for all your hard work. Choose! One for you, one for me."

Harrison was on his feet then, clammy and cold, stammering his excuses, making his regrets in English, if in any comprehensible language at all. Staggering from the salon, listing, drunk on the horror of what was happening in this house. Intoxicated on acute psychic trauma.

He was in his room. Had he gone up the stairs? He must've, but he didn't remember. He couldn't remember anything past the smile the Burmese girl had given Affonso: not a smile of seduction or happiness or gratitude, but the smile of a captive reaching out to he who had all the power, a smile that ingratiated with the aim of mitigating the coming carnage.

In the smile of a slave girl, he'd seen himself. His muscles remembered how to make the smile that appeased Miss Eliza Meyler. His face remembered how to be passive and bland, masking the howling cries of his soul.

He was in his room, he remembered. He was in his room and the bed had been turned down—by whom? Not by Kulap or the Burmese girls. No maids, they. No, those creatures were about their own special menial tasks now. Downstairs. Below his feet.

He gasped. Panted. Lungs bellowing to pull air in, in, in. Not enough air in the world to breathe through this bitter, bloody—*I'm a woman of all work,* Miss Meyler had once coquettishly claimed, twirling a fingertip in a circle on Harrison's hairless chest. *I deny none of my master's commands.* Kulap and the rest, they were women of all work, too.

A horrible laugh cracked in his throat; his neck caught, as in a noose, on the tightness of his cravat. Clumsily, he pawed at the knot. His fingers were wooden, useless. "Get off me," he growled, clawing at the snare he'd tied for himself, pulling hard on the loose ends when he gave up on the knot. "Get off!" And then: "Blast it. Where's my knife?" He spun a circle, but nothing was what it was supposed to be. Wrong clothespress, wrong bed; and in the other room, there was a table. It was his table, wasn't it? Those were his things, his inkpot and blotter and the ledger with the stain on the cover, in the bottom right corner. All of this was his, but it wasn't *his.* It wasn't right. None of it was. This wasn't— Where the devil was that knife?

"Harrison?"

There she was, in the doorway. Lamai. Dressed as a maid, but acting the spy. Lamai, with her lovely, utterly lovely, face—one side a mask of concern, the other merely a faint echo of it.

"Harrison, what's wrong?"

A slip in his awareness. She was standing right in front of him, close. Her hands were tugging his, gently prying them from the stranglehold he had on himself.

Lamai. Her mouth a pretty plump plum, pouting at his predicament. "Did this neckcloth attack you?" she teased as her slender fingers picked the knot loose.

Attack. *Attack?* "Dow—downstairs. Gaspar and Affonso, they're …" He was stuttering, stammering, but his thoughts weren't any clearer than his mouth. All he knew was danger—imminent, close to hand. Coming. Not for him, not this time, but it felt like it. It felt the same. Suppressing a surge of panic, he gulped on a dry throat. "Kulap and the other two, the Burmese girls. With their hair—"

Lovely, long, black hair. Like Lamai's.

"Oh God," he rasped, gripping her hair in two fistfuls and stroking her cheekbones with his thumbs. "Lamai, your hair."

A crease between her brows. Dark, soulful eyes narrowing to match the slender outer corners. "My hair?" Her hands were caught between their bodies and fluttered over his chest, unsure where to land. "What's my hair got to do with anything?"

"What has he done to you, Lamai?" Darkness welled inside him, a hot, tarry mess of memory and pain burbling away. These weeks and months, Harrison had not seen what was happening right inside the house where he lived. Hadn't seen what had been done to the woman he had come to admire and long for. Brave, stubborn, lovely Lamai. "Tell me," he demanded, unable to keep a note of panic from creeping into his voice. His emotions were coiling tighter, spiraling lower, threatening to pull him down into the cauldron of despair. "I'll put a stop to it. I'll kill him for what he's done to—"

Her mouth covered his, and he said no more.

• • •

Lamai felt a shock pass through Harrison when their lips came together. She was no less surprised than he. She didn't know why she'd done it, only that he was lost in some labyrinth of fear and pain, and she had to retrieve him back again.

He was still as stone, his hands tangled in her hair, the pads of his thumbs rooted to her face. His mouth that uttered so many words, ones that exasperated and infuriated and beguiled her in turn, was a hard line, a boundary against which she crushed her own lips. His chest was broad, hard as a wall, another barrier. Her palms tested the muscle he'd regained in the last two months, searching for chinks in his defenses. How could she help him if he would not let her in? Bringing one hand to his nape, she squirmed closer. Beneath her other hand, she felt the only sign of life: his strong heart drumming a cadence that her body fell into step with.

A whimper slipped through her lips, a breath of wanting, of need. A masculine hum answered; his hand crashed to the back of her head, pulling her close, desperate and hot. She'd never before kissed a man, but some ancient wisdom in her marrow knew what to do. Instinctively, she tested the seam of his lips with little flicks of her tongue, silently pleading for—and offering—more. Harrison's lips parted on a groan. Exultant, Lamai slanted her mouth, tasted forbidden wine on his breath.

Abruptly, he tore away. Lamai stumbled into the sudden void. Her hand flew out; she caught herself on his chest. Harrison's palm clapped over her hand, snatching it up in a fist. Whereas he'd been like stone when they kissed, now he was all agitated motion: His chest moved up and down rapidly, his nostrils flared, and his left hand twitched on its way to rub the back of his neck.

"I'm sorry. Forgive me. That … that shouldn't have happened." His voice wavered, as unsteady as his gaze that darted around the room.

Lamai's stomach squirmed uncomfortably. "You did nothing wrong, Khun Harrison," she said, just louder than a whisper. "It was I who acted rashly. If there is any blame to be had, it is mine."

"No," he retorted. For the first time since she stepped into the room, she saw something besides panic kindle in his eyes. He brought her hand to his mouth and kissed her fingers, firm and fierce, his eyes steady on hers. Then he kissed the inside of her wrist. "I'm glad you kissed me. I've been dreaming of that for months. If I could, Lamai …" His Adam's apple bobbed. "If I could be with someone, it would be you. But I can't. It isn't possible."

She shrank away from an unexpected ripping sensation in her heart, but forced herself to smile, even though she knew her eyes were bright with gathering moisture. "Of course, Khun Harrison."

She slipped her hand out of his grip and took a step back. "Once more, I beg your pardon. It won't happen again."

Matching her steps, Harrison disallowed a broadening of the distance between them. "Be quiet, damn you," he rasped, "and listen to me. *Listen.*"

As he stalked her, harsh lines of shadow fell across his face. His mouth was a hard slash, his eyes two glittering coals. Lamai had never feared Harrison, but now a tendril of unease twined about her spine. Downstairs, Gaspar barked a word of command. A feminine squeal followed, and then an answering laugh from both men.

Harrison halted; his attention shifted away from Lamai. "*That's* what's wrong." He pointed at the door, then strode over and closed it, tapping the panel with the side of his fist.

"I didn't know," he muttered to the portal. "I didn't know how those girls are used. Are you?" He turned his eyes on her, his gaze desolate. "Are you used like that, Lamai?"

Oh, that explained why he'd raved about her hair. Now Lamai was the one closing the distance to place a comforting hand on his arm. "No, Khun Harrison, I am not used as the others."

"Why am I Khun Harrison again?" he demanded. "What happened to plain Harrison and Lamai? Ought I call you Khun once more, as well? Or perhaps you prefer Miss Hart."

"That's entirely besides the—"

"You still think you did something wrong," he interrupted, grabbing her by the arms.

Lamai drew a deep breath, filling her head with his warm, male aroma. During the two long months of her trip to the north with Gaspar, she had been plagued by the memory of his smell and hounded by the fear that he would be gone when she returned to Bangkok. She'd convinced herself that the quarrel before their parting proved that nothing could come of her attraction to the handsome Englishman. She was disfigured, ugly. And she'd had the audacity to kiss him when she found him in a moment of weakness. Of course she'd done something wrong.

"You did the right thing, Lamai," he said earnestly, answering her unspoken question. "I was caught in an old trap, but you freed me from it."

She hesitated a moment before asking, "Will you tell me, please? Why are you so dismayed by learning what is done with the young, pretty slaves?"

His hands fell away from her arms. She sensed his withdrawal. "Because it is wrong," he said woodenly. "Slavery is wrong. This even more so—using another person's body for physical gratification without their consent …"

Something in his tone prompted Lamai to hold her peace. She waited until the silence stretched into awkwardness.

Harrison drew his arms across his chest. Lamai reached out with her hand, the only physical comfort he seemed comfortable receiving.

Finally, she was unable to bear the silence any longer. "Who hurt you?"

"The governess," he said, his words heavy, dead. "Eliza Meyler. Miss Meyler."

"A servant?"

A smile ghosted across his lips. "Yes, but not in the sense you're thinking. A governess has great latitude when it comes to the children in her care. She was the closest thing to parental authority in my young life."

Lamai frowned. "Are your parents dead?"

"They are now; they weren't then. They didn't like to bother with us, you see." Harrison raked a hand through his hair. A lock fell across his brow. Before she could stop herself, Lamai reached up and swept it back. "Tending us was an impediment to their own diversions. We were left in the care of servants more often than not."

"But you must have told, yes? No father would countenance the mistreatment of his son."

Through the shadows, she sensed, rather than saw, his grim smile. "Oh, I told. Father patted me on the back, said I'd been made a man at twelve, three years sooner than he'd managed the feat."

His words, cold and flat, made her stomach churn. "I'm so sorry, Harrison. No child should have to go through such an experience."

He laughed, humorless. "*An* experience? Oh, my darling girl, it was dozens of them. A hundred, scattered across three long years. I was supposed to go to school. Eton. I refused to go, because Miss Meyler had set her eye on my brother, Dickon. He was only ten, for God's sake. I threw tantrums like an infant until my parents capitulated and got me a tutor instead. I was fourteen when Miss Meyler was finally dismissed."

There was more to the story, Lamai could tell by his haunted expression, but she didn't dare ask. Speaking of the terrible things he'd endured at the hands of a trusted caretaker was plainly a trial, and not one she'd prolong with idle curiosity. Besides, she wasn't sure she could stomach any more.

She gripped his sleeve with a white-knuckled fist. It wasn't fair, clinging to him for support right now, but Lamai was uncommonly distressed at the revelation of his past hurts. Tears once more burned Lamai's eyes, but no longer for herself. She'd all but forgotten Harrison's rejection. But he hadn't.

"The reason I can't … I have trouble …" He brushed a knuckle across her jaw. "I have desires, like any man, but have only rarely been able to bring myself to act on them. I would not wish to burden you with my weakness. You deserve a whole man, Lamai."

Swiping a tear from her cheek, she shook her head. There would be time to consider that later. "Never mind, *farang*. I am most concerned with the state I found you in."

Harrison went to the window and opened the glass and threw back the shutter, admitting a gust of damp night air. Within seconds, he swatted mosquitoes from his neck and hand. "I've spent my life trying to escape what happened." Scratching the fresh bite on his hand, he turned his wrist up. His fingers traced the scars there. Lamai understood a little better now why they existed. "I haven't always dealt well with my suffering."

Lamai wanted to go to him, offer the wordless support of her touch, but she intuited that lending her ear was all he needed just now—indeed, was all he could tolerate. With the memories of improper physical contact playing through his mind's eye, he might not welcome even the most benign touch.

"A year ago, I fell into one of my blue periods," he continued, his gaze scanning the near-empty *soi* in front of the house. "On *Brizo's Woe*, I was so much better. Days full of hard work and more fresh air and sunshine than I knew what to do with … There wasn't time to feel sorry for myself. I thought, I really believed, that I had finally outrun my demons."

"But now you find yourself in a house where similar hurts take place."

His silence answered her conclusion. After a long moment he turned around. A muscle ticked in his jaw. "I cannot stand by and allow the mistreatment of those women. I have to do something."

Ducking her head, Lamai experienced a bitter wave of shame. "I hate what he does," she said, her voice small. "But I have been scared for myself. You are braver than I."

A few quick steps and he was once more before her, this time in the position of comforter. "The power has all been in Gaspar's hands, Lamai. Surviving was the best thing you could do. Believe me, I know what it is to simply endure. Waking up, facing another day … these are not insubstantial achievements."

Lamai's chin trembled. Harrison took her hands in both of his. "You aren't powerless now, and neither am I. Together, we can save those women. Will you help me, Lamai?"

His steady determination helped Lamai find her own mettle. "As if there is any question."

Chapter Nine

Harrison's initial impulse was to gather up the slave women during the night and abscond with them to safety but Lamai, infinitely more familiar with Siamese slavery customs and laws than he, convinced him not to act rashly.

Two days after uncovering the ugly truth of life in Gaspar's house, Harrison attempted a straightforward approach to liberating the women. At a foundry on the outskirts of Bangkok, Lamai had just helped Gaspar negotiate the purchase of a quantity of tin. After Harrison spoke to the foreman, arranging delivery to the warehouse, he joined Gaspar and Lamai in the *yaeng* on Goui's back.

"*Pai dai,*" Panit called, giving the old girl the command to begin the homeward trek.

Once the foundry was nothing but a column of sooty smoke behind them, Gaspar clapped his hands. "What a steal!" the merchant exulted.

"Will you send the tin to Europe, sir?" Harrison asked from the rear bench.

The older man carved an arc with his patrician nose. "No profit to be made there, after the cost of shipping. Other exports are more lucrative. I'll sell the tin inside the city for twice as much as the Siamese merchants, and make a killing."

Frowning, Harrison dabbed his temple with his omnipresent handkerchief. Abstractedly, he noted that he was sweating less than he had been. "Who would pay so much, when the same goods can be had for less?"

Gaspar leaned back in his seat, knees spread wide. Beside him, Lamai was forced to press herself against the arm of the front seat. "My countrymen, for one," the Portuguese man proclaimed. "We're a tight-knit little community, you know. There are so few of us, we have to band together."

Harrison raised an eyebrow at that claim, knowing full well Gaspar D'Cruz was as cutthroat as a pirate. He didn't quite strike Harrison as the sort to participate in a village picnic on the green.

Lamai turned her head to the side and scratched her upper lip, but Harrison would have sworn she was actually suppressing a laugh at her benefactor's claim.

Harrison turned in the same direction, ostensibly to observe the ramshackle dwellings along their route. Dogs, dusty mongrels of every sort, roamed the streets freely. A few yipped at Goui or played with children, but most lazed in doorways or begged scraps from the locals. Panit had explained to Harrison that kindness to dogs was a quick way for a Buddhist to earn good karma; and so, while the roving packs of strays looked intimidating, they were generally well-fed and harmless.

In his peripheral vision, he saw Lamai turn toward him, ever so slightly. Her eyes slid in his direction. Gaspar was in a good humor, and a captive audience for the next half hour. It was time.

"Senhor D'Cruz," Harrison started, turning to face front once more. "I wonder if I might ask you a question, sir."

The merchant raised a hand like a magnanimous monarch.

"Your nation—as well as mine—has outlawed the practice of slavery." Gaspar's shoulders stiffened, but Harrison forged onward, careful to maintain a pleasant, nonjudgmental tone. "I wonder, senhor, how do you justify keeping them in your home?"

Hooking his knee onto the bench, Gaspar turned about to pin Harrison with a hard expression. His lips formed a smile, but

Harrison would have bet his last shilling the fellow regretted not throwing Harrison back into the Gulf of Siam.

"Why, I'm not in my nation, am I?" Gaspar returned, his tone as pleasant as Harrison's had been, while his sharp, dark eyes flashed warning. "Slavery is legal here, and so I am perfectly within my rights to own them."

Lamai, meanwhile, was assiduously deaf to the conversation. Her attention remained trained on the world passing by beyond the swaying fringe of the *yaeng's* curtained enclosure. She had jumped at the opportunity to finally strike back against the man who had been her keeper-tormenter for too many years, but Harrison—taking his turn at being the voice of reason—had convinced her to leave the talking to him. At least to begin with. Gaspar was dangerous. Harrison couldn't countenance Lamai waving the proverbial red flag and drawing Gaspar's wrath.

Since their kiss the other night, Harrison had to admit that his desire for Lamai had ratcheted up several notches. If she was any other woman, he might go ahead and indulge his physical lusts. It had been a few years since last he'd been with anyone. The fallout from sex—his subsequent loathing of himself and, to a lesser degree, his partner—precluded any chance of pursuing that with Lamai. He cared for her. Much better endure this unfulfilled longing than hurt her, as he inevitably would.

But if he couldn't give her the sensual bliss she deserved, at least he could give her his protection.

Meeting the other man's hard gaze, Harrison went on, "Be that as it may, sir, I wonder that you do not feel a moral imperative to refrain from—"

"Senhor Dyer, if you don't approve of my household, you're welcome to go elsewhere. In fact, it would behoove you to return to England at the earliest opportunity, since the culture here in Siam fails to meet your standards. I know of a ship that sails for

Lisbon a little more than two weeks from now. I suggest you secure a berth on it at once."

Would that he could. Harrison would prefer nothing better than to whisk himself away to the other side of the world, to forget he'd ever been inside Gaspar's house and seen the abuse taking place within. The other night he'd been desperate to go, to run away, as he'd been doing in one way or another his entire life.

Since talking to Lamai, though, and divulging so many secrets he'd never told to another soul after his father and Charles, Harrison's own experiences had been very much on his mind. Besides the specific instances of Miss Meyler's mistreatment of him, Harrison remembered the feeling of helplessness he'd lived with for years. For so long, he'd hungered for someone to recognize what was happening to him. To believe him. To help him. Now that he was in the position of witnessing the mistreatment of other people, he would never walk away.

He was still disappointed he'd not realized sooner what was happening. Harrison had seen those three dressed as other menials, but not once had he actually observed them at work. No scrubbing, dusting, polishing, cooking, laundry … They were servants in the household, no question about it, but why hadn't he thought to discover the nature of their servitude?

Over the last two days, he'd told himself it was because Gaspar had been away for most of Harrison's time in Bangkok. Until the other night, he hadn't actually witnessed their misuse. And the girls never spoke to Harrison. The Burmese duo, Mi and Nan, kept to themselves. And Kulap was such a sullen, quarrelsome thing, it was unpleasant to be near her. But their hair, their lack of a place in the household staff—damnation, even their reclusiveness and ill tempers. He should have known. Of all people, he should have known.

Goui stepped across a familiar bridge. Panit called out a greeting to the *mahout* of another elephant they passed. They were almost home. Inwardly bracing himself while maintaining his cool bearing, Harrison laid his cards on the table.

"*Senhor*, I would appreciate seeing the papers of your slaves at the earliest opportunity. I am interested in purchasing one from you."

If Gaspar was at all surprised by Harrison's request, he hid it well. Indeed, he snorted derisively. "I don't suppose you mean one of the scullery maids." He slid a cunning look at Harrison. "If you buy one of my girls, you won't be able to afford passage home."

Harrison smiled. "I know."

Gaspar's eyes narrowed and his steel-stubbled jaw ticked back and forth, calculating. "They aren't for sale, so there's no reason to dig out their papers. Besides, what possible use could an abolitionist such as yourself have for a slave?" The man winked.

In his lap, Harrison's hands curled into fists. "Sir, I'd ask you to reconsider—"

"I won't, *senhor*." Gaspar gave Harrison his back.

"*Yood*," Panit called when they reached the house, though Goui knew her home and was already sighing in relief before her *mahout* gave the word to halt.

Gaspar disembarked and strode into the house without a word, slamming the door behind him.

Harrison stepped down more slowly and reached back to offer Lamai a hand.

"That did not go well." She opened her parasol, a pretty confection of purple silk painted with white flowers. The dark bamboo handle and spokes were a striking contrast to the canopy. Harrison couldn't help but think the leaders of London ladies' fashion would give a tooth for such an accessory. It provided a lovely backdrop for Lamai's golden complexion and dark, dark hair. Although …

He gripped the parasol handle and pulled it to the side. The sun struck Lamai's hair, done up in a loose bun. "There's some red in your hair," he proclaimed in wonder. Reaching out, he passed his other hand over her locks, marveling at the play of light across each strand. "Look at that. Ebony dipped in auburn."

Lamai moved the parasol back into place and wrinkled her nose, clearly unimpressed with his assessment. "You are easily distracted."

"It could have been worse," Harrison said, returning to the topic at hand. Offering his arm, he escorted Lamai to the house. "We knew this was a long shot."

"*Mmmm*," went Lamai, that sound Harrison so enjoyed. "You might not have been the right person to ask Gaspar, but I think we're on the right track. The law says a master must show a slave his paper upon request."

Panit called a farewell; Harrison and Lamai raised their hands to him at the same time.

"The girls should ask, you mean?" Harrison swiped a hand through his hair. It was getting long; he needed a trim. "But if he treats his bed slaves illegally, as you say—refuses to release them when he's had done with them—what's going to make him respond fairly to those women?"

Lamai's mouth curled up in a sly smile. A pulse of longing thudded through Harrison. "Leave that to me, *farang*. I have an idea."

• • •

It was several weeks before Lamai was able to implement her plan, but she put that time to good use. Kulap, Lamai felt, would require special handling, on account of her youth and ... exuberant ... nature. There was no guarantee she'd not run straight to Gaspar with the plan, so Lamai excluded her for now, instead meeting in secret with the Burmese girls.

She'd feared each girl would refuse to leave without the other, but it turned out that while Nan and Mi both had been captured in battle, they hailed from two different villages and had only been brought together by captivity. When they heard the plan, Mi declined at once. "Khun Gaspar rarely takes me," she explained. "I want to go home, but I don't know if I've a home to return to. The Thai army burned my village," she shot bitterly. "Mercenaries raped the women and slaughtered our cattle. At least here I have food, clothes, and a roof over my head. I can't say the same for my brothers and sisters—if they yet live."

"I'll do it." Nan lifted her chin and squared her shoulders. Her slender, shorter stature revealed her mountain tribe heritage, but Nan stood as straight and fierce as a warrior. "I'm not afraid."

Harrison, meanwhile, demonstrated his own sort of courage, which Lamai found most admirable. Despite his impatience to quickly do something about the women, he took Lamai's advice and carried on working at Khun Gaspar's warehouse as usual. When the time for the Lisbon-bound ship to depart came and went, Gaspar took to regarding him shrewdly. Harrison ignored his employer's gimlet eye, and went on managing the warehouse more than competently. He negotiated better prices for transporting goods than the previous manager, and even struck deals to sell wares to more merchants in Bangkok, instead of shipping elsewhere. With Harrison making him so much money, Gaspar had no room to complain about the Englishman's prolonged sojourn in Mueang Thai. Lamai only wished her friend could take pride in his work. She knew it rankled him to increase Gaspar's fortune, but he played his part flawlessly, keeping a steady eye on their ultimate goal.

Lamai very much enjoyed having a co-conspirator. The secret glances she and Harrison exchanged behind Gaspar's back were—to her mind—fraught with import. Lamai was no fool. Harrison had told her plainly that nothing could come of the attraction between them. Who could fault his reluctance, given all he'd been through? And yet, she savored each and every meeting of their eyes.

On the appointed day, Lamai was confident their little confederacy was as prepared to enact their plan as possible, yet she was assailed by nerves. The girls were on display, but only in an ornamental capacity. With a high-ranking official from the ministry of commerce, Sarathoon, in his home, Gaspar daren't risk offending with his usual fleshly brand of hospitality.

Lamai was present to translate throughout the reception and supper. Harrison was there, too; Gaspar proudly boasted of his pet Englishman's skill as if he were a prize elephant. "Much to my regret, Khun Harrison will soon leave my service to return to his own country," Gaspar bemoaned. "I don't know what I shall do without him."

After a meal featuring fish simmered in ginger and lemongrass, the party retired to the salon. When Kulap and Mi entered, it was to entertain with music, not their bodies. They wore ornate golden headdresses and matching costumes of pink and gold silk. Their splendor put the simple band of orchid blooms in Lamai's hair to shame. Kulap sang an old love song in her clear, young voice, dancing with sinuous movements of her lithe arms, while Mi accompanied her on a bamboo flute.

Sarathoon, a stout older gentleman with kind eyes and a ready smile, tapped his hand on his knee and swayed his head along with the song. Leaning close, he murmured to Lamai. "Khun Sarathoon says this is one of his favorite songs," she reported to Gaspar. "His mother sang it to him."

From this tilt of his head, Lamai knew Harrison had heard her. A troubled look crossed his features, but she didn't have time to wonder at it.

Gaspar bowed from his seat, hand pressed to his chest, in acknowledgment of the compliment. "Lamai, call for tea."

She smoothly rose from the floor cushion upon which she had been kneeling and smoothed her palms over the nubby orange silk of her sarong. She felt Harrison's eyes track her path across the room. She longed to look at him in return—for reassurance, as well as for the simple pleasure of looking at the handsome man—but the moment required discretion.

In a vestibule just off the dining room, Nan was making minute adjustments to the assortment of sweets on the tea tray. Her wide eyes flew to Lamai; both her mouth and brow puckered.

"Don't tell me you're afraid now."

"A little," Nan confessed, nudging a ball of sticky rice across a puddle of sweetened coconut milk. She wiped her finger on a napkin, then fidgeted with her headdress—which matched those worn by the other girls. This much Lamai would say for Gaspar: He knew how to cater to the tastes of his guests. "My Thai isn't so good."

"Everything will be fine," Lamai assured the young woman. "Your Thai is better than Gaspar's. You aren't speaking for his benefit, anyway; not really. Just be your most polite and graceful self, and say exactly what we practiced. I'll be there to help you, too." Nan nodded, but her face remained solemn. "Courage," Lamai whispered, giving the girl's shoulder a squeeze. Then she returned to the salon to resume her place on the floor.

A moment or two later, Nan entered. The laden tray looked enormous in her thin arms, but the steadiness with which she carried it belied her strength. Kneeling to lower the tray onto a low table, the Burmese girl poured hot tea into small, handleless cups, which she served to the men with a deep bow. Her powdered face was paler than could be accounted for by cosmetics. Lamai sent up a silent prayer for the girl to be as strong in spirit as she was in body.

Next, Nan carried the platter of sweets to each man, kneeling while Sarathoon, and then Harrison, made their selections.

Finally, she knelt at Gaspar's feet. Their master chose a slice of candied durian fruit. Nan remained in her position.

"That's all, girl," Gaspar barked. "Be on your way." To Sarathoon, he joked, "These Burmese women are good-tempered and nice to look at, but not very bright." Lamai gritted her teeth while translating that one.

"Khun Gaspar," Nan said, "I request that you show me my paper." To her credit, her voice trembled only a little, every word spoken correctly.

"Oooohh," went Sarathoon, as if the request were part of the evening's entertainment, while Gaspar darted a confused look at Lamai.

Upon hearing her translation, Gaspar pasted on a tight smile. "If you'd be so kind, Lamai," he said through thinned lips, "please inform Nan that this will be … handled … tomorrow. Now is not the appropriate time. I have a guest." Rolling his wrist, he gestured to Kulap for another song.

The refusal had been anticipated, but Lamai detected an implicit threat in Gaspar's answer. Harrison must have, too, for he flowed to his feet and sauntered over to take the sweets platter out of Nan's hands. He acted as though he couldn't decide which treat to choose next, but the tense lines of his body told Lamai dessert was not his primary concern.

Moistening her lips, Nan spoke again, assertive even as she kept her eyes downcast. "Forgive me, Khun Gaspar," her voice was stronger this time, "but His Majesty's law requires that a humble slave such as myself must be shown her paper when it is asked."

"This is true," Sarathoon interjected with a nod. "In his infinite wisdom, our glorious king has decreed the bondage papers of slaves must be made available upon request." The fellow flicked his tongue across the top row of his crooked teeth. "I, too, am interested in the just and proper treatment of all—even the lowliest slave. By all means, Khun Gaspar, get the paper. I'll be happy to listen to another song or two while you are away."

Hearing the affirmation of the law from a government official, Gaspar had no choice but to make good on Nan's request. Lamai did not miss the dark glower Gaspar leveled on Harrison when he rose from his seat.

Sarathoon was very interested in Harrison, and Lamai translated back and forth a bit in the parts where Harrison's Thai was weak as the old man asked about the younger fellow's occupation and upbringing. When he learned that the Englishman had gone to university in Oxford, Sarathoon clapped his hands. "Oh, Oxford! How I longed to go to school there, but my father was an envoy to France, so I'm a Sorbonne man."

Harrison's countenance brightened. *"Parlez-vous toujours français, monsieur?"*

Sarathoon let out a booming laugh. *"Mais oui!"* And just that quickly, the two men were conversing with no need for Lamai to act as medium. Harrison moved closer to Sarathoon and offered the platter of delicacies. The older man gesticulated wildly with a cashew biscuit gripped in his hand.

While the men were occupied, Nan cast a furtive glance over her shoulder at Lamai. Lamai wished she could give the girl a hug, but she couldn't risk letting on that she was in any sort of cahoots with Nan. They'd taken a calculated risk in allowing Gaspar to believe Harrison was responsible for prodding Nan to action. If he suspected Lamai was also involved, there was no saying how he'd retaliate. They must tread carefully.

At the sound of her master's approach, Nan snapped her head around, neck bent, her kneeling posture one of perfect obsequiousness.

"Here you are." Gaspar placed the paper into Nan's hands. The girl, undoubtedly illiterate, nonetheless scrutinized each line. Then she came to Lamai, crawling so as to keep her head lower than Gaspar's and Sarathoon's. Clearly, she had taken to heart Lamai's advice to behave with perfect manners.

"How much does it say, Khun Lamai?" she whispered.

Lamai took the sheet and examined each entry. "It says that your value is one hundred baht. You have also incurred expenses beyond your upkeep totaling another one hundred sixty-five baht." Listed were costly fabrics and grooming implements, items Gaspar insisted the girls have so they would meet his standards of beauty. He dared charge them for the implements of their own captivity. Her gorge rose in her throat; she swallowed hard.

Reaching into the waistband of her sarong, Nan produced a little purse. When she pulled out a wad of bills and coins, Gaspar's eyes widened. The Burmese girl held the money out on her hand. "Is this enough?"

Across the room, Kulap and Mi had fallen silent. They, too, watched the unfolding scene with avid attention. Lamai sorted through the currency, straightening out bills and stacking coins. She put two hundred sixty-five baht in Nan's hand, and folded her own fingers around the girl's. "This is enough," she said.

Crawling once more, Nan approached Gaspar. "Master, here is my price. I wish to purchase my paper."

Gaspar blanched. By rote, he looked to Lamai for translation, but he already understood what was happening.

"Marvelous!" exclaimed Sarathoon. "You pay your slaves in money, instead of crediting their papers? Ingenious."

Harrison clapped his employer on the back. "From what I've seen, Khun Gaspar treats his servants unlike anyone else."

Sarathoon came to his feet and patted his paunchy belly, then rubbed a circle across the embroidered cotton jacket. "I will tell the minister of commerce about your novel approach. Very western, but I see it works well here. Credit must be given to you, young lady, for being so diligent in saving. And look," he said, nodding towards Lamai, "there's some left over for starting your new life."

Nan, moving as if in a daze, bent to collect the rest of the money at Lamai's knee. "Did that really work?" she asked in a barely audible whisper. Lamai patted her hand.

Nan tucked the money back into her pocket. Rising, she brought her steepled hands to her forehead and bowed deeply, giving Gaspar honor he didn't deserve.

"Don't forget this." Harrison plucked Nan's paper from the floor beside Lamai. He handed it to Gaspar, who strode to a small desk across the room. He dashed a note of sale across the bottom, then gave the paper to Nan. It trembled in her hands. Tears shimmered in her eyes, even as she laughed.

Lamai's heart welled. They'd done it. Nan was free. When she raised her eyes to Harrison, she saw that he, too, was moved. She would throw herself into his arms and kiss him from joy, if only he wouldn't abhor it. How wonderful it would be to celebrate their mutual victory with a bit of mutual pleasure. He caught her eye and winked. Cheeks warming, Lamai ducked her face. She dreamed of kissing him, but even a tame wink from the man managed to fluster her composure.

Breaking with protocol, Mi rushed across the room to congratulate Nan. Kulap loitered behind, her full lips pouting and her brow furrowed.

Above the happy chatter of the Burmese women, Sarathoon said to Gaspar, "What a delightful evening! The repast was delicious, and I most enjoyed making the acquaintance of Khun Harrison. Lucky for you, Khun Gaspar, that your protégé has decided to remain here a while longer." To Harrison, he said, "I look forward to seeing you often, sir."

"As do I, Khun Sarathoon." Harrison's guileless smile betrayed no hint of the cunning victory he'd scored over Gaspar. Lamai bit the inside of her cheek to stop herself from snickering.

"And then, to witness the emancipation of this lovely lady," Sarathoon further enthused. He bowed to Nan, then took her hand in both of his and patted it kindly. "A freedwoman with as much thrift and sense as you will make a fine wife. Any man would be fortunate to have you help manage his affairs."

After another few rounds of thanks and *wai*, Sarathoon finally took his leave.

As soon as the door had closed behind their guest, Gaspar rounded on the remaining occupants of the salon. "You two, out." With a flick of his blunt index finger, he dismissed Mi and Kulap. The slaves wasted no time in scurrying off.

"As for you," he snarled at Nan, "you have one hour to gather your things and go. Never return here, do you understand me?"

Nan's head bobbed. "Yes, mas—Khun Gaspar." Then she, too, was gone.

It was the middle of the night. Where would Nan go? Lamai's lips parted, but Harrison, catching her eye, gave a quick jerk of his head, warning her from speaking. She shifted restlessly on her knees. Her feet tingled from holding this position so long.

Gaspar paced the salon, a jungle cat on the prowl. His dark eyes flashed; his lip curled in a sneer. "Lamai, translate," he snapped. "I want him to understand every word." Stopping in front of Harrison, Gaspar shoved an angry finger in the Englishman's face. Lamai winced at the rude gesture. "Whatever little game this was, it's over now. I suppose you think you're clever, giving that girl money to buy her paper, and orchestrating events so a government official witnessed it." Miniscule droplets of spittle flew from Gaspar's mouth. His face was ruddy.

Harrison stood steady as a pillar, his eyes as serene as Buddha's, meeting Gaspar's rage with the calm confidence of a man who was in the right. The warmth in Lamai's chest grew as she observed his quiet strength.

"You've hurt no one but yourself," Gaspar went on, flinging his hand into the air. "Your sneaky trick has delayed your departure for months, but I can buy another girl as soon as I like. Tomorrow.

So what have you done, eh? What has your abolitionist zeal accomplished?"

Harrison's mouth kicked up on the side in the half-smile Lamai found so attractive. "I simply held the door open for a lady, senhor. As a gentleman, I could do no less."

Gaspar's face turned puce. A vein throbbed in his temple. "Because I, too, am a gentleman," he said in a strangled tone, "I shall forgive your impudence this time, but there won't be a next time. Do not test me."

Harrison nodded. "I understand, sir."

Lamai caught the twinkle in his eye and knew there was one in hers, as well. She couldn't wait for next time.

Chapter Ten

Before dawn, Lamai slipped downstairs. The house was dark and quiet except for the *tick tick tick* of the clock in the salon. Patting her pocket, she made sure the money was there before reaching for the back door handle.

"Where are you going?" hissed a voice in the dark.

Lamai clapped a hand over her own mouth to smother a yelp and spun around. Harrison padded down the back staircase. He wore buff breeches and an ivory tunic. Though he claimed to prefer the loose Thai *panung* for ordinary wear, he complained that it took him "forever" to fashion the garment into breeches. This morning, he must have chosen haste over personal comfort. His hair was a rumpled mess, too, all shaggy hanks that fell across his forehead and tangled behind his left ear.

Her fingers itched to restore order to his head; she gripped the heavy brass handle, instead.

"I'm going to find Nan."

Harrison absently scratched his left arm through the sleeve. "I was about to do the same."

At this, Lamai raised a skeptical brow. "Oh really? Where did you plan to look?"

He made a little *go, go* gesture with his hands. Lamai opened the door. Harrison followed her onto the back stoop.

"I thought I'd try the nearest *wat*. Monks took me in; maybe they'd shelter Nan, too."

"That's … exactly what I was going to do," Lamai grudgingly admitted. "But listen, *farang*, you need to leave this to me. I'll make sure Nan is safe." His brow lowered and his mouth screwed up in a pucker. "I promise," she insisted, forestalling his argument.

Releasing a sigh, he raked a hand through his hair, which only caused the tangled part to jut out at an exciting angle. Rising on her toes, Lamai smoothed the wayward strands with her palm, then tucked the hair behind his ear.

"There."

Their eyes met and gazes held. Even in the iron twilight of night's end, Lamai felt a golden light of awareness pass between them. Harrison's hand came to hers. His thumb tucked against her palm; she wrapped her fingers around it. Bringing their joined hands to his mouth, he kissed the back of her hand. His lips were warm; the tip of his nose was cool. Quick sparks darted up her arm, infiltrated her blood faster than a strong cup of tea.

She exhaled a little sigh when he released her hand.

Stepping back, Harrison reached into his pocket. "When you find Nan, will you give her this, please?" His extended hand held several folded bills.

Lamai nodded, touched by his generosity, yet she felt a twinge of regret. If only things could be different for them. If only Harrison hadn't been hurt beyond bearing when he was but a child.

The distant sound of a gong recalled her to her task. "I have to go." Snatching the money from his hand, she slipped on her dew-damp shoes and trotted across the lawn to the kitchen, forbidding herself to look back.

Cook screeched when Lamai bounded in with her shoes still on. Lamai danced in place, as if lifting her feet off the floor could cut the offense in half. "I want to make merit."

Looking nonplussed, Cook nevertheless heaped rice, vegetables, and two prawns into a bowl. With a hasty word of thanks, Lamai took the offering and dashed back outside and through the back gate, jogging to meet the monks collecting alms out on the *soi*. There was no need to go to the *wat* when representatives of the *wat* came to her.

Four monks and a layman walked down the center of the road, stopping to accept offerings and confer blessings upon almsgivers. As the group drew close, Lamai stepped forward and knelt. Because monks are forbidden contact with women, the layman took the bowl of food and gingerly tipped its contents into the urn carried by one of the monks before returning it to Lamai. That holy man stopped a respectable distance from Lamai and blessed her with the assurance that her generosity would do her well in this life and the next.

"Excuse me, Luang *phee*," she called when he began to move on. "Do you know if a young woman came to you last night seeking sanctuary? A Burmese woman?"

The monk conferred with his brothers before answering. "We sheltered no guests last night, child."

Lamai's heart sank, but she couldn't give up.

Back home, she placed the dirty bowl inside the kitchen door, then darted over to the stable. Panit was filling the water trough. "Will you get my girl ready, please? I'll take her for her morning walk."

Panit frowned, his weathered face creasing sharply. "Today is lessons. I was going to work on her balance." He nodded to where he had a set a long plank on the ground. This would slowly be elevated over the course of several months, building the young elephant's confidence in her ability to navigate narrow, precarious paths.

"Please!" Lamai clasped her hands together.

"All right, all right." Panit waved dismissively. "I'll fetch her."

While she stood anxiously biting her thumbnail, Harrison appeared at her side. "Did you find her?"

Lamai shook her head. "I'm going to check some of the other *wats*. Gaspar will miss me at breakfast. Please tell him I took Wan Pen for her outing."

"I will."

"We shouldn't have let her just go off last night," she burst. She was plagued by the fear that they had manipulated Gaspar into granting Nan her freedom, only for her to be snatched off the street by another malefactor. Lamai wouldn't rest easy until she knew that the young woman was safe.

Harrison touched her lower back. "Given the situation, we did the best we could. I share your concerns, but I have faith."

Lamai cut a glance sideways. "In your god?"

"In you."

"Oh." It was a whisper, a breath.

The stable door creaked as it swung wide. Wan Pen stepped into the paddock, nodding and flapping her ears in greeting. Goui followed, with Tilda the goat bringing up the rear at a dainty trot.

"I'll be back as soon as I can," Lamai told Harrison. "Gaspar expects me to go to the market with him in a few hours. Assure him I'll be here."

"Very well." A shadow crossed Harrison's face. "Will he be suspicious that it's you taking Wan Pen out, not Panit?"

"Poor Goui!" Panit exclaimed. "She was sick all night. Ate a bad mango, I think. Better now, but I'll be all morning cleaning that stall."

"A bad mango?" Harrison's Thai was improving every day, Lamai noted. "Khun Gaspar will want to know his elephant is on the mend."

"Exactly right." Panit glanced over his shoulder as he handed Lamai up onto the kneeling Wan Pen. "We must be good servants, and tell him everything."

The *mahout* jogged to open the gate. Lamai glanced at Harrison. "A bad mango." His mouth twitched. "I hope he believes it."

"He won't," Lamai said as she passed. "Better make it two."

• • •

The gate closed behind her, and Lamai guided Wan Pen out onto the *soi*. The young elephant was still nervous of jostling crowds and loud noises, but regular outings into the city were helping her grow accustomed to the busy streets.

Wan Pen snorted; a plaintive bleat replied. Lamai twisted around to spot a little tan nanny goat following her large friend. "Naughty beast! Go home." She pointed back in the direction of the house, but Tilda remained steadfast.

Grumbling to herself, Lamai returned her attention to the front. She hoped no harm would come to Harrison's pet, but she had no time to spare returning Tilda to the stable. The animal would have to come along.

At the corner, a food vendor hailed Lamai. "How much for the goat?"

"Sorry, not for sale," Lamai replied. Over her shoulder she muttered, "But it would serve you right to turn into curry. *Som nam naa.*"

Since Nan wasn't at the nearest *wat*, Lamai trekked several *sois* over to an older, smaller temple tucked in a quiet residential area. She waited outside while a novice ran in to ask about a Burmese refugee. He returned moments later, shaking his head.

Thanking him, she expanded her search wider. Nan was not at the next *wat*. Nor the next. By now, the sun was well above the horizon. A bead of sweat trickled down Lamai's jaw, though the rising heat wasn't entirely to blame.

At the bustling market in front of one of the city's largest *wats*, Lamai took a deep breath. This was it. She was out of time. If Nan wasn't here, she would have to go home.

Guiding Wan Pen around the edge of the busy grid of stalls and shoppers, she fended off several more offers for the goat, and two for the elephant. Harried and cross, she approached the *wat* proper. "*Yood*," she called. Wan Pen obediently halted.

Lamai dismounted but hesitated, uncertain about leaving the animals alone outside the gate while she went inside. Wan Pen would probably be safe. As tempting a target an elephant made, it would be mighty difficult for a thief to make off with an enormous and unwilling victim on short notice. Tilda, on the other hand, had already attracted notice. Snatching one little nanny goat would be nothing.

Wan Pen decided the matter. Seeming to sense Lamai's anxiety—or perhaps feeling some of her own—the elephant ducked her head and waggled her trunk between her front legs. Tilda obediently came forward to stand beneath Wan Pen's belly, safe in the enclosure of four stout legs and one ton of loyal friendship.

"Stay here." Lamai patted Wan Pen's cheek. "Take care of Tilda. I'll be right back." Leaving her shoes outside the gate, she entered the temple grounds. Avoiding the main temple so as not to disturb worshipers at prayer or meditation, she skirted several buildings until she found a monk scrubbing dishes in a copper tub perched above a little pit of glowing coals.

"Luang *phee*?" she ventured, stepping forward.

The monk frowned sharply. "You shouldn't be here. No women in this area."

"Forgive my intrusion, brother. I'll return to the public paths in just a moment. I'm looking for a friend, a Burmese woman. Are you sheltering any such guest?"

The monk's face softened. "We do have a Burmese visitor," he said, drying his hands on a dish rag. "I'll go find her."

Lamai beamed. "Oh, thank you! I'll wait in front of the temple."

She scurried over to the front gate to check on the animals. Tilda was lying on the ground, feet straight up in the air, and Wan Pen carefully rubbed the goat's belly with a foot as large as a plate. A crowd gathered around, laughing and clapping.

Lamai chuckled at the display. "Show-offs, the both of you." Content they were not about to be abducted, she hurried back to the temple, just as the monk came up another path, a woman trailing in his wake.

Right away, she knew the woman was not Nan. She was too old, her shoulders stooped, and stout, besides. When the pair reached her, the Burmese woman regarded Lamai in befuddlement. "Thank you, Luang, but this isn't my friend." To the woman she said, "Forgive me for bothering you, auntie." Making *wai* to both, Lamai plodded back out the gate and slid into her shoes.

Well, that was that. She didn't have many free hours, but she would try again to look for Nan another day. While she hoped to find the woman safe, another part of her hoped Nan was already far away. Gaspar would not go easy on Nan if he caught her again.

"That's enough, you charlatan," she scolded when she saw a few coins that had been tossed at Wan Pen's feet. "Show's over," she informed the little audience. Scooping up the coins, Lamai deposited them in an offering box beside the *wat* gate.

Wan Pen lowered to her knees; Lamai braced her hands on the beast's shoulder, preparing to boost herself up.

"Lamai!" Glancing over Wan Pen's head, she saw a small slip of a woman scurrying through the nearest row of market stalls. Nan broke free off the crowd and waved, a smile wide on her broad cheeks. "I thought that was Wan Pen, but when I saw the goat, I knew for sure." She scratched Tilda behind the ear. The goat butted her hip playfully. Nan laughed.

"Thank god!" Lamai stepped around the elephant and hugged the smaller woman. "I've been looking all over for you."

"Why?" Laughing, Nan wrinkled her nose.

"I was worried about you. Khun Harrison is, too. We wanted to make sure you are safe before we can consider your freedom secure. Did you pass the night in another *wat*?"

Nan's smile faded. "It was too late to bother the monks. I slept beneath a table here in the market."

Lamai let out a sound of dismay. "Oh, Nan, what will you do now?" Remembering the money in her pocket, she fished it out. "Here. Some of this is from me, but most is from Khun Harrison. You should have enough now to travel north, though I don't know if it will be safe for you to go home."

Skirmishes along the border of Siam and Burma erupted with depressing regularity, and then there were the coordinated campaigns of armies and war elephants led by princes of both nations that struck deep into enemy territory. War was a favorite pastime of the unhappy neighbors; sieges their common language. Captured Burmese soldiers and villagers taken in raids provided a steady stream of slaves—just as Thai prisoners were forced to labor in Burma. It was just the way of things.

Here in Bangkok—the city to which the royal seat had moved after Burma sacked the old capital of Ayutthaya some forty years ago—the fighting was far away and easy to ignore. But Lamai had seen with her own eyes burned homes and ravaged fields outside of Chiang Mai during her recent trip north with Gaspar. The nearer Nan came to her own country, the more danger she would encounter.

"Don't worry about me." Nan held out her hand for Wan Pen to tickle with her trunk. "I must find my family. I had a young man, you know. Chit. We were supposed to marry, almost two years ago now. If my family still lives, if Chit has not found another sweetheart ..." Her voice caught, and Lamai saw hope mingled with despair in the woman's face.

Her heart hurt for the time Nan had lost. It would be difficult—if not impossible—to pick up her life where she left it. "I wish I had done something for you sooner," she lamented.

Nan shrugged. "You were always kind. I'll never forget you. Or Khun Harrison." She lifted her hand still gripping the money. "He sacrificed his chance to go home to give me mine."

The women said their farewells. Lamai climbed onto Wan Pen, called the command to rise, and waved one last time at Nan. She would never see the courageous young woman again. Regret slipped a finger down her spine, but she was happy Nan would no longer be subjected to Gaspar's cruelty.

She, on the other hand, had to return to her benefactor-tormentor at once. Clucking her tongue, she set Wan Pen on the course to carry her back to the devil's lair.

• • •

Just over an hour later, a sedan chair carrying Gaspar, Lamai walking behind, stopped at the very market where she had just parted from Nan. Lamai's heart flew into a frenzy.

Gaspar liked to visit the markets several times a month to scout new merchandise. Lamai had hurried back from her Nan-hunt so she wouldn't miss their appointment for this outing. What she had not known was which market he meant to visit.

Hopefully, Nan was long gone, but Lamai's stomach cramped as she darted glances up and down the rows of stalls, as fearful of spotting the Burmese woman now as she had been saddened by the prospect of never seeing her again only moments ago.

The crowd of shoppers had thinned; most did their shopping in the early morning or in the evening to avoid the worst of the heat, but Gaspar preferred coming at these slower hours. More time to examine wares and strike bargains with vendors, he'd once explained. The local fishmongers and grocers were generally shuttered by now, leaving behind craftsmen from near and far and vendors in dry goods, such as spices, that could withstand the rigors of travel. Much as Lamai hated to agree with the merchant, his reasoning in this particular was sound.

Stepping out of the hired conveyance, Gaspar arched his back. Besides the obviousness of his skin and height, his clothing marked him for *farang*. No *panung* or breezy tunic today; always looking to awe the peasants he dealt with, he wore breeches, waistcoat, coat, and cravat. No simple cobbler or smith would recognize that his clothes were all looser in cut and lighter in fabric than would pass muster in fashionable Portuguese circles. All they saw was a tall, white man with an entourage of servants and money to spend.

"Let's see … where shall we begin?" It was a rhetorical question, so Lamai didn't respond. She fell in beside Gaspar as he sauntered through the stalls, occasionally stopping to pick up a piece of carved jade or sniff a box of pipe tobacco.

While he browsed, Lamai kept her own eyes peeled for any sign of Nan. A boy dawdling around a florist stall caught her eye. He looked to be about six, with a gap in his milk-tooth smile. In his hand he clasped a little doll crafted from a banana leaf. This he extended to passersby. He didn't seem to be advertising such dolls for sale; rather, he was involving the whole market in a game of make-believe.

"This is Areepong," the boy announced, shoving his green friend into a man's path. "He is a very great teacher."

The man made *wai*. "Blessings to you, master," the fellow said as he rose from his bow.

Lamai laughed. The little scamp glanced over; his eyes went round. "Mama, look!" he cried. "It's the ugly lady with the funny elephant and goat. Where's your elephant, auntie?" he called to Lamai. "She was so silly." Clasping his free hand to his belly, he chuckled, shaking his head.

Several heads turned to stare at Lamai. Horrified by the attention—which might, in turn, contort into Gaspar finding out she had found and aided Nan—Lamai tilted her parasol to shield her face from the gawkers and scurried after Gaspar.

Lucky for her, he did not notice the brief commotion. The Portuguese man had stopped to examine a display of carved wooden bowls and utensils. They were simple goods, cruder than what Gaspar already owned, but he turned a spoon in his hands, holding it to the light and tilting it this way and that, as if it were finely smithed silver. She didn't understand his interest.

He slanted a look down at Lamai. "Ask this gentleman about the wood used in his carvings. I wish to know where he acquires his lumber."

"This is mangosteen wood," she reported after completing her inquiries. "His family's orchard is old, and the trees no longer bear fruit."

Gaspar smiled shrewdly. "Tell him I wish to buy all his lumber. If it hasn't all been harvested yet, I'll even send men to fell the trees."

Upon hearing this, the carver was eager to strike a bargain. Soon, a price was agreed upon. With much bowing and thanks from the Thai man, they took their leave and moved on to other vendors.

A similar scene unfolded at the stall of a woman who embroidered bright floral designs on table and bed linens. When Lamai communicated Gaspar's wish to purchase five hundred tablecloths—far more than she had available—she burst out crying. "*Kob khun ka,*" she repeated over and over. "Thank you, *phee*, thank you. My daughters will help—they sew, too—and we will have your order ready for you in no time at all," she promised through happy tears. "Bless you, *phee*."

Gaspar smiled warmly like an indulgent uncle. "My pleasure, *phar*. Tell your daughters to do their very best work, as it will grace the homes of the grandest ladies in Europe."

The dear woman, staggered by this statement, fell to her knees and bowed her head, once more letting forth a profusion of thanks.

Gaspar's order would employ the woman's family for months, and keep them fed for a year. It was an incredible windfall. Lamai felt the woman's joy almost as if it were her own. At times like this, it was easy to see the Portuguese merchant as she had all those years ago: as her handsome protector, a generous benefactor who shared his abundance with those lucky few in whom he saw potential—be it a man with fine lumber or a scarred girl with a knack for languages.

But that was just one side of Gaspar. There were others—the ruthless, paranoid businessman; the master who was unkind to his young female slaves. All people were capable of good and evil. The Noble Eightfold Path revealed by Buddha addresses this fundamental truth, illuminating the way from suffering to liberation through mindfulness of thought, speech, and action. With all her heart, Lamai believed that each person was on his or her own journey along that path—even if they did not realize it. It was possible to cease actions that hurt others. Even Gaspar was capable of changing. His capacity to bring happiness to others proved it.

"I think we've made enough of a dent in my purse for one morning, don't you?" Lifting his prominent nose into the air, Gaspar sniffed. "Szechuan pepper! Do you smell it? This is the market where that delightful Chinese couple cooks, isn't it? Now, where is their stall … ?"

Laughing at his eager appetite, Lamai hurried to keep up as he followed his nose—and came face to face with Nan. The Burmese woman was a short distance away, her arms loaded with what looked like provisions she'd purchased for her journey. She was two stalls down, directly in their path. And she had not seen them.

At once, Lamai's blood chilled. Gaspar might be capable of changing in another lifetime, but in this one he mistreated the women in his care. "Khun Gaspar!" she yelped. "Oh, Khun Gaspar, look at these … eggs," she finished, latching onto the first item she saw.

The ruse worked. Gaspar spun around before seeing the slave who had wriggled from his grasp. Calling out the Portuguese man's name had alerted Nan. The small woman's face was ashen.

"Eggs? Why the hell are you bothering me about eggs?" Gaspar demanded.

"Just look at them." Lamai plucked one from a basket and shoved it under his nose. "What pretty speckling on the shell! Wouldn't you like to buy these? You'd fetch a good price for them up north."

Her antics were irritating Gaspar, but Nan had recovered her senses and scurried down another row.

Scowling, Gaspar swatted her hand. "Get that out of my face! Since when do I deal in eggs? They'd never survive a trip of any distance. Of all the harebrained ideas—"

Gaspar's voice caught when a young woman stepped from behind a partition. "*Sa wad dee ka,*" she greeted them. "May I help you?" The girl was pretty and young.

The *farang* at Lamai's side straightened. "*Sa wad dee khap,*" he returned. "What is your name, *phar?*"

The girl's face brightened at the foreigner's use of Thai, and at his humble, respectful tone. Lamai's skin crawled.

Another woman, older, joined the younger one behind the counter. "Is that her mother?" he asked Lamai. When he received confirmation, his whole body seemed to thrum with anticipation. "I want her," he said, quite unnecessarily. "I want to buy her. Make the deal, Lamai."

Her cheeks burned. He'd found Kulap just like this, working in the market. One moment she was helping her mother sell cabbages; the next she belonged to a *farang* who would go on to use her body himself, and allow others to use it, as well. Lamai could not forget that she was the one who had brokered the deal. True, she'd secured an exorbitant price for Kulap's parents, but was a woman's dignity worth any amount of money? Of course not. She'd known, even then, what Kulap's fate would be, but Lamai had been too scared to defy Gaspar. Frightened he would take his revenge by giving Lamai herself to one of his friends, as he had begun to threaten. Participating in the purchase of Kulap was a shame Lamai would carry forever.

"Perhaps, Khun Gaspar, the girl's parents would not wish to sell. She is, after all, of marrying age. It could be they have in mind—"

"Do it," he snapped. "I can more than compensate whatever the loss of their daughter or a potential son-in-law might be."

The girl's mother's anxiously observed the Portuguese exchange between Lamai and Gaspar. "Do these eggs not please your master?" she asked. "I have duck eggs, too, much better than these chicken eggs."

Lamai lifted her hand in a reassuring gesture. "No, auntie, your eggs are just fine. The *farang* wishes to buy your daughter."

"Oh!" said the mother. The girl's eyes widened. She covered her face with a cloth; her shoulders jostled, though from giggles or fear Lamai couldn't determine.

"We hadn't thought to sell her," the mother said in a classic opening parley for negotiations. "She's a hard worker." ... *so it'll cost you a lot to take her,* was the unspoken conclusion.

"Oh, well," Lamai said. "She's not for sale," she informed Gaspar, touching his elbow to lead him away.

"B-but ..." he sputtered.

"Wait!" squawked the matron. "How much will he give me?"

"Ah-ha!" Gaspar threw up a finger, triumphant. "She said *how much*. I know that one." Digging in his pocket, he produced a billfold, peeled off two notes, and dropped them on the table. One hundred baht, a typical price for a slave.

"Don't take it," Lamai warned the mother. She used an especially sing-song tone of voice, knowing Gaspar would have difficulty understanding what she said.

The girl peeked over the edge of the cloth to eye the currency on offer in exchange for her freedom. If Gaspar was not who he was, agreeing to be sold into a period of servitude would be standard procedure for a poor girl. The money would help her family, and in time she would be free. But Gaspar was not an ordinary master. He didn't follow the rules.

"Will he give me more?" the mother asked Lamai.

Whether he understood or just intuited the question, Gaspar put down double the amount. The mother chewed her bottom lip. "We could build a new coop. Keep more hens," she told her daughter. "Earn more money, you know, so I could redeem you sooner. It wouldn't be forever."

"What did she say?" Gaspar hissed.

"She says it's still not enough," The lie flew from Lamai's lips without hesitation. "Khun Gaspar, I think you should let this one go. Look, the girl has spots. You don't want a spotty girl."

Before, with Kulap, Lamai had been cowardly. But now she wasn't alone. Harrison was in this with her. Even if Gaspar was angry, keeping this girl out of harm's way was the right thing to do. Feeling Harrison's support, even though he was not with her, gave her the final boost of courage.

"Little sister," Lamai said to the girl, "you don't want to go with this man. He does bad things to girls. He uses them, do you understand me?" Flipping her gaze to the mother she said, "And he lets other men use them, too. Your daughter would not be an honorable servant, but a whore."

The girl let out a cry of dismay and ran behind the partition. The mother retained her composure. With a tight smile, she pushed the money back across the counter and shook her head. Then she, too, retreated behind the screen.

"What the hell happened?" Gaspar rounded on Lamai, white showing around his mouth. "She was going to take the money—I know she was. What did you say?"

Feeling lightheaded from her own boldness, Lamai struggled to present a convincingly apologetic expression. "I'm sorry, Khun

Gaspar, but the girl would not agree. As I feared, she has a beau and is eager to marry, instead."

Gaspar sputtered.

Lamai smiled. "Now, sir, let's see about that Szechuan pepper, shall we?"

Chapter Eleven

The ancient city of Ayutthaya, the former capital of Siam, had been a hub of culture and commerce until 1767, when a Burmese army pillaged and burned the great metropolis. Reduced to smoldering rubble, Ayutthaya seemed to have been dealt a death blow, but the old town refused to die. In the city's Portuguese quarter, established in the 1500s as a religious, commercial, and military presence in the kingdom, a tenacious group of Europeans had remained, with more immigrants returning to Ayutthaya over the last two decades.

It was to this Portuguese settlement that Harrison now ventured, at the behest, and in the company of, his employer. Lamai was with them, too. Gaspar never ventured far without his trusty translator in any event, but ever since Nan's emancipation a month ago, Gaspar grew agitated whenever Lamai was out of his sight for more than an hour or two. Despite the merchant's ire falling squarely on Harrison—and fall hard it had—the man clearly suspected Lamai's involvement, as well.

As a result, Harrison had found precious few opportunities to be alone with Lamai. Gaspar had retaliated against Harrison by switching his method of payment from cash to letters of credit that drew from Gaspar's own bank account. It was a seemingly innocuous shift, but clearly intended to prevent Harrison from providing money to fund another slave. With limited time to plot and no resources to draw upon, their little conspiracy was at a standstill.

They traveled by barge up the Chao Phraya for two days. Rich with silt, the river was the color of milky coffee. When the wind was calm, the aroma of fish and damp plant matter filled the air. Not Harrison's favorite smell, but more palatable by far than the toxic fug that was the Thames as it cut through London, redolent not only of fish and rot, but also sewage and the more-than-occasional decaying corpse.

On the morning of the third day, the poleman steered the barge off the main river and into a canal that cut west, into the heart of the Portuguese Quarter. Ayutthaya proper—what remained of it—lay to the north, so Harrison's first impression of the former Siamese capital was a bewildering sense of being abruptly shuttled, yet again, into another world. He had grown accustomed to the tall, gently sway-backed roofs of Siamese architecture, but now he was confronted with the crisp lines and peaked roof of a Catholic church. The cross at its apex was jarring. Until this moment, Harrison had not realized how prevalent the familiar Christian symbol had been in the background of his old life; the sight of it now provided context to its absence. Having not seen a Christian church since *Brizo's Woe* had stopped for supplies in South Africa, Harrison wasn't sure how he felt about the reunion.

South of the church, a combination of white and Thai men and women worked together erecting booths and festooning buildings with ribbons and garlands.

Catching Lamai's eye, he pulled his chin at the bustling activity. "A market?"

Craning her neck to see above the canal's retaining wall, Lamai made a dubious sound. "It doesn't look like a market. Khun Gaspar, do you know what's going on over there?"

Harrison didn't understand how she could speak to Gaspar so casually, knowing what they did about him. As much as possible, Harrison restricted conversation with Gaspar to matters of business, but Lamai chattered and smiled as she always had done. A survival mechanism, he supposed, though he didn't have to like it. It galled Harrison to work in Gaspar's warehouse, to know that his labors further enriched a cruel and callous man. But he did it, didn't he? What choice did he have? Lamai was the same, he supposed. With so much of her time spent at Gaspar's side, he supposed it was best that she remained on good terms with him. For now.

"Harvest festival," Gaspar answered. "The weather here might not be autumnal, but it takes more than a little heat to stop us Portuguese from throwing a party. Affonso's house," he said, pointing to a residence a little farther down and a short distance from the canal. "And there's Affonso!"

Gaspar's friend stood at the top of a short stone staircase, waving when he spotted the barge. "Welcome, my friends," he cried, enthusiastically pumping Gaspar's hand when the merchant disembarked, then pulling the taller man in for a hug. "And to you, Senhor Dyer," he directed to Harrison, offering a firm handshake. His smile slipped when he regarded Lamai. "And you, madam."

Harrison recalled that the last time Affonso had been in Gaspar's house, Lamai had been instructed to impersonate a maid so she could riffle through Affonso's personal belongings. He had no idea if Affonso had seen Lamai during that visit, and neither Gaspar nor Lamai seemed inclined to offer explanations.

Affonso led them to his house, a white, two-story structure with a balcony running the length of the top floor. On the eastern side of the house, the white stucco was black and gray in places. Where a neighboring home had stood in the adjacent lot, only a stone foundation remained.

All around, Harrison saw evidence of the Burmese invasion—a half-collapsed house here, a front walk leading to nothing there. Harrison turned to look to the north. In the distance, the tree-filled horizon was interspersed with the reliquary towers of Buddhist *wats*, slender, inverted cones standing watch over the desolate remains of a once-proud city.

Upon entering Affonso's house, Harrison removed his wide-brimmed hat. Their host exclaimed in surprise, his hand flying to his cheek. "My boy, what in God's name have you done to your head?"

Self-consciously, Harrison brushed his fingertips over his temple and shorn side-scalp. "The locals seem comfortable keeping their hair like this, so I thought I'd give it a try."

Affonso clucked his tongue. "This wretched heat does send white denizens over the brink sometimes. Well, never mind. It'll grow back soon."

Harrison scowled at Affonso's back when that man took Gaspar's arm and led him deeper into the cool of the house. Lamai caught his eye and winked. Several weeks back, Panit had done the honors of shaving Harrison's head, leaving only the traditional cap of hair on top. Harrison had been pleased with the result—which *was* much cooler than walking around with an infernal blanket of hair all over his head—but Kulap and Mi giggled behind their hands whenever they saw him now, and Gaspar's reaction had been of a sort with Affonso's. Only Lamai told Harrison the style suited him.

In the afternoon, after settling into his guest room and changing into fresh clothes, Harrison joined Affonso and Gaspar for billiards. Like the church, the sight of the felt-topped billiards table induced a touch of cultural vertigo. It was an achingly familiar thing, that squat, masculine table, but misplaced, like him. Affonso and Gaspar drank port and smoked cigars while they played, but Harrison refrained from partaking in that fraternal sacrament. He'd best enjoyed port and cigars with his friends, his Honorables. Over the years, they'd laughed and debated and waxed philosophical while communing with the grape and leaf. He wouldn't tarnish those fond memories by doing the same with a man who kept women for the sexual gratification of himself and his friends, such as Affonso here.

"That will do for me," he said, returning the cue to the rack and closing the billiards room door behind him. Harrison felt an oily slick of contamination clinging to his skin from pretending pleasure in the company of those two. This stalemate in the matter of Gaspar's slaves had gone on long enough. He had to liberate Mi and Kulap. Sooner done, the sooner he would never have to look into Gaspar D'Cruz's soulless eyes again.

Mind bent on scheming, he went hunting for Lamai. With Gaspar occupied with his friend, Harrison and Lamai had a rare opportunity to plot the next emancipation. He located her upstairs, on the balcony. She clasped the railing, her face turned in the direction of the harvest festival. The strains of a merry tune sawed out on a violin reached their ears, reedy but enticing. A smile flitted across her mouth and wonder danced in her eyes as she leaned forward to catch every note in her ears. Her loveliness hit him like a cricket ball to the head. She was so damned pretty. He knew she was—had known it since the first time his gaze traced her profile as she knelt before the Jao Ar-wart of Wat Wihan, but damn. *Damn.* Her swept-back hair accentuated those high cheekbones while stray tendrils curled around the shell of her ear and kissed the column of her throat. Her eyes, the elegant shape of teardrops lying on their sides, never failed to mesmerize him with their ability to communicate wordlessly.

Not for the first time, he wished he was a better man. One that wasn't broken.

She turned at his approach, a dreamy smile on her pillow-soft lips. Beneath the shade of the balcony roof, the heat wasn't quite so oppressive, and with the light breeze tugging at the wayward locks of her hair, she looked fresh and younger than her years.

"Do you want to go?" Harrison found himself asking.

Lamai's shoulders lifted in concert with the arches of her black brows. Her smile widened to a grin. "Oh, yes," she declared. "I would love to."

Harrison liked that about her, how she didn't hide herself from him. She always told him what was on her mind, and she didn't prevaricate about her own wants and wishes—so different from the polite society in which he'd been raised, in which ladies were taught to repress their wants and intellects in order to boost the morale of the men around them. To make them feel more manly.

But Harrison, who had been stripped of his fundamental, biological ability to be a "proper" man before he was old enough to shave, felt better about himself having Lamai on his arm as they strolled to the harvest festival than he ever had in England. Right now, at this moment, he was doing exactly what needed to be done to make this woman happy. Right now, at this moment, he was her provider. It wasn't fire, shelter, or food he provided, but the bounce in her step told him he was, just now, exactly the man she needed. On that thought, his shoulders pulled back and his head floated just a bit, pulling his spine straight and tall.

Ayutthaya's Portuguese Quarter continued to jar him with its echoes of familiarity. Strolling the streets of a European village—albeit one with unmistakable Iberian flair—took his mind home to England. Over the course of their roundabout path to the festival, they passed houses with statues of saints in the garden, instead of the spirit houses preferred by Thai Buddhists. Church-of-Englanders wouldn't have such idols in their flower beds, of course, but Harrison had grown up in a neighborhood with several Roman Catholic families; he was, at least, on speaking terms with the the two-foot-tall Virgins and Francises.

And there, in the distance— "Do you hear that?" Lamai's hand fell away as he lifted his arm to point in the direction of a faint *clang, clang, clang* drifting on a cross breeze from the western side of the settlement. "A blacksmith!" He laughed, delighted with the homey noise.

Lamai raised a brow. "We have blacksmiths, you know. There's nothing particularly English or Portuguese about a hammer striking an anvil." Her wry drawl matched that of any London wit—would have slain Sheri, in fact. *Sheri would love Lamai*, he thought with a pang. As would Henry, Brandon, and Norman. Homesickness struck him then. Not for England, but for his friends. *If only I could speak an incantation and bring my friends to me,* he thought. That would be lovely.

"We have festivals," Lamai volunteered, "but religious ones, not seasonal." She slanted a wry smile up at him. "We've but two seasons: hot and hotter. Or rainy and dry, if you prefer—not quite the same as yours, I think."

"No," Harrison agreed good-naturedly, "we've three: cold and rainy; warm and rainy; and Christmas."

Lamai threw her head back and laughed. They passed burned-out buildings that used to be shops, and then businesses that still operated: the butcher, the baker, and the candlestick maker. Only the chandler wasn't a chandler at all, but a milliner. It didn't fit the rhyme, so Harrison held fast to the other profession.

He wasn't sure when it happened, but at some point, Lamai slipped her hand into his. He only noticed when the breeze crept through the gaps in their swinging hands, stealing a little of their combined warmth.

She must have felt it, too. "Is this all right?" she asked, lifting their limbs. Her voice was carefully neutral, but anxiety played around her eyes. "Does this … bother you?"

"It's nice," he assured her. "I like holding your hand."

They remained joined that way as they reached the center of the settlement where the festival was underway. They walked a circuit around the square to get an overview of the festivities. The afternoon seemed devoted to families, with a juggler performing to a group of rapt children and a table littered with the yellow-crumb carnage of what looked to have been a cake eating contest. Birds of several varieties swarmed the table to pick the leavings like vultures swooping upon the abandoned carcass of some predator's kill. In one shady corner, a fair-haired priest had joined a group of children of various ethnicities around a large, shallow tub where they all bobbed for—not apples, but some Thai variation on the theme—to the laughter and applause of adult onlookers.

His breath hitched as Harrison led Lamai into the fray, and their presence was met with the curious glances of strangers. He held it as they passed a fortune-telling booth where an old Thai woman with a white tuft and toothless smile was dressed in an approximation of a Gypsy seer, such as Harrison had witnessed at many a country fair, a well-worn tarot deck spread on the table before her, the edges of each card tattered, the paper yellowed. The crone eyed Harrison and Lamai speculatively; he inched closer to Lamai and gripped her hand tighter. He held his breath as they passed a booth where a white woman serving up crisp baby potatoes in paper cones glanced at them and frowned. He held his breath, almost lightheaded now, until he saw the crying child.

Beside a tent, a little girl—Thai, by the looks of her, but with long hair in braids—sat on the ground, the skirt of her dress rucked up to show a skinned knee. Her other leg, sturdy and stout, stuck straight out, her booted foot resting on the knee of her mother, who crouched before the child, comforting and kissing the injury better. And next to the mother was the father. A white man. One hand rested on the mother's lower back, while his other rubbed the girl's arm in a soothing gesture.

Releasing his breath and drawing fresh air, Harrison began looking around—really *looking*—and saw that one family was no anomaly. Everywhere he glanced, Portuguese and Thai people mingled together; not just as friends, but as families. He been worried about the reception he and Lamai would have—a white man holding a Thai woman's hand—not because he cared what anyone thought, but because he would hate for any unkindness to be directed at Lamai. But he'd been worried about nothing. The Portuguese had been in Siam for hundreds of years. Naturally, some Europeans intermarried with the Thai population. The result was this community where Portuguese and Thai traditions mingled freely, and couples looked just like Harrison and Lamai. *Not that we're a couple,* he hurried to correct himself. The curiosity he and Lamai attracted was nothing more than the interest small towns always showed in strangers.

After that, Harrison relaxed and began to enjoy himself. He and Lamai shared fried potatoes, the brown paper cone absorbing oil just like the paper wrapped around hot battered fish at home. Grease stains, he mused—what a thing to get nostalgic about.

He sucked the pad of his thumb, savoring the salt transferred from the crisp potato skins. "At home," he said, unable to resist the compulsion to verbalize his feelings, "it's traditional for a young man to squire his sweetheart around a fair. Try to impress her by winning a race or contests of strength."

Lamai's head tilted as she smiled up at him. "How many girls wanted to be your sweetheart at the fair? All the girls in town, I'd wager."

Mouth pulled to the side, he turned to watch a group of strapping youths assemble for a footrace, bending to touch toes or swinging their arms, limbering up young muscles. Sure enough, young women lined the course, some wearing bonnets, some in Thai-style straw hats, some holding parasols. The universal language of young courtship.

"I never walked the village green with a girl on my arm. My youth was too … complicated … for that, I guess you might say."

Complicated didn't begin to touch it. He'd felt utterly isolated by the circumstances of his life at home. By the time he was thirteen, Harrison recognized he had knowledge no one his age should have. Thanks to Miss Meyler, his innocence was long gone. Striving to win a girl's admiration by throwing a rock farther than the other lads seemed hopelessly naive. Pointless.

And yet, he'd wanted to, desperately. There *had* been a girl, Rebecca, with golden curls and big blue eyes and a dimple when she smiled. Harrison had longed for her to notice him, but had been terrified that she might. How could he talk to such a sweet young creature, when Miss Meyler lurked like a spider in her web, waiting to destroy him a little more at the earliest chance? He'd turned his back on Rebecca and every girl that caught his eye thereafter. There wasn't a place in the archery contests for someone like him.

Lamai wrinkled her nose. "It's not complicated anymore, is it?"

Harrison blinked. Sputtered a laugh. "Not complicated? My dear girl, I'm stranded on the wrong side of the world, living with an inveterate evil-doer but dependent upon same for my livelihood, embroiled in a plot against that man to free his captives, and ..." Amusement, exasperation ... something like that went through Lamai's eyes, and Harrison's heart shifted in his chest.

All of that was true—all those problems existed. But Miss Meyler couldn't hurt him anymore. And he'd come to the harvest festival with a pretty girl. He'd held her hand and bought crisp potatoes, and there was a footrace about to start.

He thrust said crisp potatoes into her hands. "Hold this." He winked. "I'll be right back."

Turning on a heel, he passed through the row of spectators and strode across the square to join the adolescents taking their places for the race. The priest—the front of his cassock wet from fruit bobbing—stood to one side, directing boys here and there and gently nudging a wandering toddler back to the safety of the sidelines.

"I'd like to enter," Harrison informed the clergyman. His announcement drew a startled look from the priest, and snickers from several of the nearest youths. The priest's mouth opened and shut wordlessly. Then, resigned, he shrugged and pointed for Harrison to get in line.

"Don't try to keep up with me, old man," said a Thai boy. Harrison turned to regard the speaker of this slander, a lad of fifteen or sixteen, lean and rangy, already taller than most of his countrymen, though shorter than Harrison by a good five inches. A hint of green ringed his brown irises. A child of mixed blood, Harrison surmised, like many others present. Like Lamai. "You're going to embarrass yourself, if you don't break a hip."

Harrison showed his teeth. "We'll see about that, pup. If I do, perhaps you'll be good enough to carry me home—after you collect the prize, of course."

Rolling his eyes, the lad turned away, just as the priest called for the runners to take their marks. Harrison spotted Lamai nudging her way to the front of the assembled spectators. She waved, laughing while the others cheered. Harrison grinned back and wished her laugh wasn't swallowed by the crowd. He loved the sound of her laugh.

At the gunshot, the runners sprang forward. Harrison, larger, heavier, and *older*, God help him, than every other competitor, wasn't as quick off the mark as some of the others. His long legs soon carried him out of the middle of the pack, into the group of five or so who'd pulled away from the rest. The course was simply the dusty road that led from the town square, past some shelled and burned buildings, to a tall gum tree that had grown up in the midst of the abandoned structures.

The adolescent who'd disparaged Harrison's age was in the lead. He glanced over his shoulder as he rounded the tree; his eyes widened when he spotted Harrison among his closest rivals.

As Harrison went around the bend himself, he willed his burning thighs to hold out just long enough that he wouldn't, as the damned cocky youth predicted, embarrass himself. Mercifully, years of boxing and riding—not to mention his months at sea—had given him a body well used to hard exertion. Pumping his arms harder, he passed one boy, then another and another until—with only fifty yards remaining—he pulled even with the mouthy leader.

"I'm not going to lose to an old *farang*," the boy snarled, arms blurring as he put on an impressive burst of speed. "Good try, grandfather."

Grandfather?! That did it. Lungs screaming and sweat pouring down his body, Harrison lowered his head and dug deep for his own last reserves, pushing himself to once more close the gap between himself and his nemesis. The finish line loomed closer, marked by a blue ribbon held between the priest and another man. Harrison's heart pounded, near to bursting, while the insolent whippersnapper would undoubtedly survive this race without inducing a cardiac crisis. He couldn't do it. He couldn't hold on. He—

There was Lamai, yelling wildly, jumping up and down, pumping her fists in the air to cheer him on. And there, *oh thank Christ,* there was the bobbing tub. Right where it had been before, off to the side and out of the way, unless someone went to the effort of making it *in* the way.

Harrison moved to the right, crowding the other runner, forcing the youth closer to the wall to avoid colliding with Harrison.

"Move, you crazy *farang!*" the lad screeched, but too late. The tub was right in front of him. Harrison expected the boy to either drop back and circle behind Harrison or shove him—a move that would result in both of them going down and losing the race.

But the youth had something else in mind. Mouth screwed in determination, he flung one leg out and launched himself into the air to leap over the tub—

And landed in it, his forward foot flying out from beneath him the instant it touched down.

Harrison crossed the finish line just as the lad fell back into the tub with a *splash.*

He was still standing there, hands braced on his bent knees, huffing and wheezing like the elderly fool the boy had called him, when Lamai broke free of the crowd and, laughing, still laughing, threw herself at him. Harrison caught her around the waist and spun a circle, Lamai's arms around his neck temporarily taking away the pain of his foolish endeavor.

"You won, you won!"

"Did I impress you?" he teased but not entirely, setting her on her feet and stepping back so as not to drip too much sweat on her.

"Ever so much," she teased in return, batting her eyes like a proper coquette. But maybe there was something sincere there, too.

The priest shook Harrison's hand, though his scowl made clear he didn't find Harrison's win entirely clean. *Well, and what if it wasn't?* Blood and spirits high, Harrison hadn't much sympathy for the felled braggart. The cause of wooing permitted no honor among the male of the species. Harrison might have done little wooing in his time, but this he knew.

And when the priest handed Harrison his prize—a live white duck in a wicker cage—and Harrison, in turn, presented it to Lamai with a gallant bow, she looked *wooed.* Oh yes, she did.

To the noise of the crowd had now been added the intermittent quacks of the feathered trophy held between them, but Harrison heard none of it. He just kept staring at Lamai as if he'd never been attracted to a woman before, and she stared right back at him, color high in her cheeks and eyes full of mirth and wonder.

Harrison's blood had scarcely slowed from the race; it just kept pounding and pounding, though now it seemed inclined to fuel his fifth limb, right here in the middle of all these decent families and their wholesome festival.

Then the braggart appeared, dripping wet, flanked by another youth. The boy glared balefully at Harrison. The friend at his side made a show of cracking his knuckles in a manner probably meant to menace, but Harrison only sighed. Maybe he *was* getting old, because the thought of having to teach those boys another lesson—this one with fisticuffs—just made him tired. Mentally, at any rate. Physically, he'd never felt so energized.

"Come on," he said, grabbing Lamai's hand and towing her out of the crowd. Let the children think they'd scared him off. He was more than content to leave the rest of the contests and prizes and wooing to the younger set—he'd won his victory.

Leaving the raucous celebration behind them, the pair ghosted through half-abandoned streets and forgotten alleyways. The duck's honks clapped off bare stone walls.

"Hush, you," Harrison scolded. "You'll bring those bully-boys down on us."

Lamai hoisted the basket to examine her gift. "A white duck—any white animal—is good luck, you know. Thank you for giving it to me."

Harrison slanted a smile down at her. "Not a very romantic prize. At home, boys win flowers to present to their sweethearts. Or mothers, if they're so unfortunate."

"*At home,*" Lamai drawled, imitating Harrison's baritone.

He nudged her with his shoulder; she laughed.

Harrison pulled her around a crumbling wall into the corner of what was once some Portuguese trader's front parlor, but was now only pile of stone slowly being overtaken by creeping vines and orchids growing from chinks in the mortar.

"What kind of prize is a duck, anyway?" He took the cage from Lamai's hand and set it down. At feeling the grass that poked through the basket's open weave between its webby toes, the animal shook its white tail and settled down.

"A very good one!" Lamai insisted. "You can keep it for luck, or eat it—"

"You *may not* eat my duck," Harrison interjected with mock sternness, waggling a finger in her face.

Laughing, Lamai grabbed onto his finger. "Don't do that! I've told you, it's rude to point." She pulled his hand down. Harrison tugged free of her grip, slipped his arm around her waist, pulled her close, and kissed her.

She inhaled in surprise, then exhaled a soft moan into his mouth. Harrison brought his other hand between her shoulders, cupping the back of her neck as he tilted his head and parted his lips.

Lamai's mouth opened, her lips a lush portal to paradise. He swept his tongue inside and, ye gods, she was so, so sweet. All warm, velvet heat and molten promises. And he lapped them up, exploring her mouth and lips with his own.

She clutched at his sweat-damp shirt, not seeming to mind the messiness of him. Little mews and gasps escaped her throat as he took and took with his kiss—but then she gave so freely, and took from him in return. Lamai's tongue slipped along his, venturing boldly into Harrison's mouth in the thrust-and-parry of mutual seduction.

Tearing away from her lips, now red and swollen from his onslaught, he kissed her jaw and swirled the tip of his tongue around the shell of her ear before suckling her tender earlobe between his lips and nibbling lightly.

Lamai cried out; her hips involuntarily canted against his. Harrison groaned, earthy and deep. His groin was tight, heavy; his cock twitched and, like it was somehow connected to his spine, sent a jolt through his whole body. He palmed the curve of her waist and hips, slid a hand around to cup a firm buttock. "God, Lamai," he rasped, nudging her chin up with his nose to gain access to her throat. He ran the flat of his tongue down that slender column.

One hand squeezing her backside, he brought the other to her breast and lightly flicked his thumb across her taut nipple. Lamai's fingers were at the back of his head now, holding him close, scrabbling to clasp hair that wasn't there anymore. He squeezed her breast, too, lightly, loving the weight of that soft fullness in his palm. Returning to her mouth, he kissed her hungrily, his body desperate to consume, to claim.

Lamai pulled away. "Stop," she gasped. "Please."

He stopped. Everything. All at once. He was a vibrating nerve of lust, but having never been allowed to say *stop* in those awful years, he took the word entirely seriously.

"I'm sorry," he panted. "I shouldn't have—"

Lamai brought a finger to his lips. "I want to, Harrison, I want to so much. That's the trouble, don't you see?" Tears swam in her eyes, confused and desperate and God, she was as needy as he, wasn't she? She gulped, drawing his eyes to her lovely throat and the points of her nipples pressing against the linen of her blouse. "Being with you like this is too difficult for me. We have to stop now, since … since you can't …"

She lowered her eyes then and leaned her head back against the old stone behind her.

Harrison's heart twisted. His gut twisted. Everything inside him twisted. Or maybe it was *un*twisting, sorting itself out into some sort of proper order for the first time in his life because, God as his witness, he wanted to make love to Lamai. He wanted to part her thighs with his body and sink into her heat, joyously pounding until she was senseless with pleasure. And his desire felt good and right. For the first time in his life.

Maybe I can do this. Maybe I can be with her, and it will be fine. Maybe we— He lifted a hand to cup her cheek; his fingers were trembling. His heart drummed, blood thick with desire, but there was a thread of the old fear, too, weaker now, but primal and undeniable. He hesitated.

This wasn't the time to confront his fear. Nor the place. But that didn't mean he couldn't do *something*.

He kissed her gently. "Please let me pleasure you," he whispered against her mouth. "Even if I can't give you everything, I want to touch you and make you feel better. Good. I'll help you feel so good, I swear, if you'll only let me ..."

She whimpered helplessly and, nodding, melted into his arms.

He groaned in relief and deepened the kiss once more. Bending his knees, he hooked an arm around hers and lowered them both to the ground, settling her onto her back. His thigh nudged between her knees, parting them. Through the thin material of her skirt, he bore his weight against her mound where he knew she needed it most, rocking into that sweet ache while his cock—how could he be this hard without spilling?—thrust against her hip.

Lamai's back arched off the ground on a moan. Harrison rode the wave of her motion like driftwood on the swell, her body dictating his movement. He clutched cool grass in heated fingers, then slid his palm to her front. He tugged her tunic free of her skirt and slipped inside. The silk skin of her belly was incredible, soft and warm and the only thing he ever wanted to touch so long as they both should live.

She shifted restlessly, her hands on his back, nails nipping his skin through the linen of his shirt. Such a sweet little bite. Propping up on his elbows, he worked her blouse free and pulled it up, baring her breasts—blessedly not covered by stays or corsets or any such infernal barrier.

Her nipples were pert, pink-brown berries atop the golden ivory swells of her breasts. Lowering his mouth to one, he brought it between his lips, flicking his tongue over the tip and nibbling lightly, so lightly, before pulling it deep into the heat of his mouth, a firm little button for his tongue to tease.

"Harrison, *Harrison*," she cried, followed by a string of Thai he didn't comprehend but understood deep in his marrow.

"Oh, yes, sweetheart," he murmured, nuzzling her breast with his nose, then moving to the other as he shifted his weight off her lower body. "Tell me what you like, so I can make it so good for you."

"This," she gasped, her head tipping back, eyes rolling to show white.

Tongue lapping lazily at her other nipple, he smiled. "How about this?" Reaching down, he pulled her skirt up, his hand tracing the sleek line of calf and knee and thigh. He should have gone slowly, but he didn't, he couldn't. He brought his hand right between her legs to the center of her, to the silken hair guarding the place where she was so, so wet and hot.

A groan ripped through his chest when his fingers parted her and found her entrance, as good as—better than—seating his cock had ever been with another.

She trembled, shaking with incipient climax. Harrison slid a finger deep inside, while his thumb moved to appease the hard little tyrant of female pleasure, pressing just above that nubbin while his hand rocked, driving one, now two, fingers into her welcoming heat.

"Tell me, Lamai, do you like this?" he asked, his own hips grinding helplessly against her side, his aching cock fruitlessly seeking entrance.

"Yes," she sobbed. "Yes. Please, more." She pulled his mouth to hers and kissed him desperately, the muscles of her thighs clasping tight around his wrist, locking him in place, keeping him with her to ride the waves of her passion as she crested higher and higher and then broke, tumbling in his arms as the waves turned inward, her sheath grasping and sucking at his fingers in delicious contractions.

He drank her cries and added his own, somehow managing not to spill in his breeches, but he did experience a release. As Lamai reached the peak of her gorgeous orgasm, Harrison's heart burst from the fetters that had held it for so long and flew free.

Chapter Twelve

In the after, Lamai drifted back into herself. She became aware of the damp earth beneath her and the warm man above her. Her limbs, heavy with languor, ached pleasantly when she stretched them; the memory of pleasure echoed through her inner flesh, like the imprint of the sun on the back of closed eyelids. Harrison was stroking her face, the scarred half. The perception on the surface was dead, but she could sense his touch in deeper tissue, the sensation muted. She felt the featherweight of his fingertips, the rise and fall as he traced the twisted ridges of flesh, then skated across smooth, shiny patches.

He was kissing her, too—sweet, lazy nothings along her left jaw, temple, the corner of her eye. But it was the hand on the right that held her rapt. When his touch shifted to her brow, her eyes fluttered open.

His scalp, where Panit had shaved off most of his long hair, was a bluish white with an overlay of pink, the naked skin angry at facing the sun. His tuft, nut brown, flopped over his brow to dangle above her face.

"Why doesn't it bother you?" she surprised herself by asking.

"Why doesn't what bother me, sweetheart?"

Her heart smiled when he called her that. *Sweetheart*. Like they were a young couple courting at those country fairs of his youth, instead of a couple of battered veterans of the strife life had put in their paths.

"My face."

His brows, heavy and serious in the best of times, drew together. "Why should it?" His tone was almost defensive.

She playfully swatted his shoulder. "Because I'm ugly, silly."

Now his brows pulled together so hard, they almost touched, almost made an angry V above the clean line of his nose. It would have been comical, were his demeanor not so thunderous.

"You are *not* ugly." He didn't yell, didn't raise his voice, which made Lamai glad. Yelling was inexpressibly rude in her culture, but that never stopped Gaspar from shouting when his temper flared. "You're the most beautiful woman I've ever seen, Lamai." When she snorted, rolled her eyes, he gripped her chin, forcing her to meet his earnest gaze. "You're the most beautiful woman I've ever seen," he murmured, solemn now. "This"—he cupped the right side of her face, cradling it like a delicate treasure— "is just a mask. Like at a masquerade. Do you have those here?" Before she could answer he went on, "Your beauty can't be undone by something you wear."

A touching thought, but— "I can't take off my skin, *farang*."

He grunted, a masculine noise of disapproval. "Don't call yourself ugly." He snugged down beside her, pulling her head onto his shoulder and draping his other arm across her stomach.

Lamai smiled against his neck. *Ugly* was just a word, like *fat*, or *bald*, or *skinny*, or *pretty*. There was no moral or emotional weight attached to these words. Not to Lamai, anyway, and not to most Thai people. She was only bothered when her ugliness was employed as an object lesson in karmic retribution. But Harrison clearly felt otherwise about the word itself. A cultural difference, she supposed. How sad, if true. What must life be like for English people, if they were emotionally invested in their looks? Vanity must always lead to suffering, as time wrought changes on every person's face and body.

Since it meant so much to Harrison, though, she would refrain from calling herself ugly. If he wanted to think her beautiful in spite of the evidence on her face, well, she wouldn't try too hard to disabuse him. She hated to admit it, but his claim that she was beautiful was the smallest bit thrilling.

"How did it happen?" His question was murmured, so quiet she almost didn't catch it. He lifted his head. "If ... you don't mind telling me, that is."

Lamai shifted off his shoulder, propped a hand beneath her head. She sniffed. Four feet away, in its cage, the prize white duck had tucked its beak beneath a wing. The festival was still in full swing. As the afternoon deepened, more musicians had joined the violinist. There was a drum, and some sort of horn. People would dance. All those Thai women married to Portuguese men—more rarely a white woman married to a Thai man, as far fewer unmarried *farang* women came to this kingdom. All those half-*farang* children. They would dance the way their Portuguese husbands and fathers had taught them, but they would dance their mothers' way, too. She wondered if Harrison danced.

"My uncle did this to me." Her eyes were trained on a stain on the stone wall that once protected a family, where a crack wept a streak of rusty brown, like dried blood.

Harrison sucked a quick breath. She felt him go dangerously still. A hand came to rest on the front of her shoulder. "Does he still live?" His voice was ice, almost inhuman.

Closing her eyes, Lamai shook her head. "Put the knife away, *farang*, it's not like that. He did it to protect me."

"That's a swinging great clanker, my dear. If he told you that ... if you *believe* that—"

Lamai propped herself up, elbows behind her on the grass. "Why bother asking, since you know my story so much better than I do?"

After meeting her challenging glare for a moment, he dropped his eyes. "I beg your pardon," he said, chagrined. "Pray continue."

Pushing up to sit cross-legged, Lamai plucked a long blade of grass and twirled it in her fingers. My mother, as you know, was married to an Englishman, Peter Hart." Harrison nodded. "After my father went back to England, my mother and I were alone until I was seven, waiting for him to return or send for us. My mother never gave up hope." She stuck the grass between her teeth and bit down, tasting the green, sweet flavor. "Mama died. I was passed between relatives. Eventually, I went to live with Mama's sister."

The duck lifted its head, blinked a beady black eye, ruffled its feathers. When Lamai looked at Harrison, his gaze was steady on her, paying no mind to the duck or anything else.

"My aunt never approved of my mother's marriage. Said the *farang* was just using her. When he left, well, that just proved it. Aunt claimed my father didn't marry my mother at all, just kept her as a whore, like—"

"Like Gaspar," he said, voice grim.

"But it isn't true," she said in a rush. "I have his ring. Did I tell you that? I have the ring my father gave my mother."

He took her hand, kissed it. "I believe you."

Drawing a breath, Lamai squared her shoulders before continuing. "I was just the half-blood child of a whore. In my aunt's eyes, the daughter of her sister wasn't fit to be anything but a whore, too. I was pretty, so she said I could earn my keep just like my mother. She'd even spoken with a brothel keeper about selling me there."

"How old were you?"

"Thirteen."

Harrison cringed. "Lamai, I'm so sorry. No one should have to—"

"I didn't," she rushed to assure him. "That's what I'm getting to. My uncle, you see, he didn't agree with what his wife had planned for me, so he thought of a way to prevent it: ruin my face. I would still be able to work—normal work—but no man would want me. He told me, and I agreed." She lay back on the flattened grass, her body fitting into the indentation created during their moments of passion. "We went out to the kitchen one evening while my aunt was visiting a friend. I lay down, like this. He scooped coals from the cook fire into a pail, and then he poured them—"

Her breath caught as memory took hold. She felt the heat radiating from the tin pail, saw the orange glow reflected in her uncle's sorrowful eyes just before he tipped it. A shower of sparks.

"But I panicked," she confessed in a small voice. "At the last instant, I turned my head, so they only landed on this side."

"Of course you panicked!" Harrison came to his knees and lunged, covering her with his body as if to shield her. His arms scooped around, held her close and hard. "Jesus Christ, Lamai," he rasped against her ear. "I'm so sorry. What an awful ... I'm so sorry."

She returned his embrace, running a soothing hand up and down his spine, comforting the hurt he felt at her old pain. "I'm not sorry," she whispered. "It worked, didn't it? He made me ugly, and I was never a whore."

The whole, tall frame of him shuddered. Lamai squeezed tighter, not minding how his weight made her a little breathless. It was a new feeling—a good one—to be so cared for. In one way, he couldn't love her with his body, but he had loved her body, had brought her such exquisite bliss. And now he used his body in another way, as her blanket, her comfort, her shield. She was a lucky, lucky woman.

The first mosquito bite roused her from the warm cocoon of their embrace. "It's getting late. We must return to Affonso's."

With a reluctant groan, Harrison clambered to his feet, reached down, and helped her up. The back of Lamai's skirt was damp from the ground. She shook it out and brushed off her backside as her companion plucked leaves of grass from her hair.

"Look down," he said, then examined the back of her head for stray foliage.

Lamai's eyes went to the prize he'd won for her. Since coming to this quiet corner of a shattered town, the captive animal had scarcely complained. Perfectly placid. It made her sad. "We can't keep the duck," she said as she reached down to lift the cage. "Panit will revolt if we bring him yet another animal to tend, or Cook will serve it for breakfast if she gets her hands on it."

They retraced their steps through mossy, crumbling ruins, past the ghostly footprints where homes used to be. He leaned forward to examine the bird Lamai gingerly carried at her side. A troubled look crossed his face. "Do you want to set it free?"

She considered. Imagined opening the cage. The lucky white bird waddling out, testing its wings, stretching them wide and flying into the gold and pink sunset.

Her smile slipped. "No." Regardless of her fancy, the duck was a creature bred to captivity, used to its cage. The fowl would take to a pen, but it would never survive with its wild fellows. Unequipped to fend for itself, freedom would not be a kindness.

In the end, they returned the duck to the priest.

• • •

After miraculously stretched into the next day, too. Harrison had gone to bed more content than he'd ever been, but more troubled, too, after learning how Lamai had come by her scars. To think that she had endured such a thing, that no one had simply whisked her away to safety before drastic measures were resorted to—

He stopped his thoughts before they ran away from him. He recognized what he was doing, attempting to make sense of a past injustice, rewrite the script of time so wrongs could be righted before they ever transpired. It was a futile game he'd played with his own life for years, and it always ended the same way: in despair.

But not this time. This time, he rolled over in bed and deliberately turned his thoughts to the sweetness of her kisses and the silk of her skin and the throaty cries of her abandon. Those were good thoughts, good memories to relive. And so he'd gone to sleep regretting only that Lamai was not in his bed. He woke up missing her, too, with empty arms that longed for the weight of a woman.

He hurried down to breakfast and found her already at the table. She wore a fetching sarong—natural-colored linen with forest green leaves edged in marigold—fashioned into a dress and topped with a yellow wrap that crossed her chest and covered her shoulders. Her hair was caught up in wooden combs at the sides and braided in the back. When she met his eye she smiled, a most becoming flush of color in her cheeks, then promptly ducked her head and hid her smile in her teacup.

Harrison bid his host and his employer a good morning. "Good morning, Miss Hart," he said with a bow. Startled, Lamai gave him a reproving look, cutting her eyes meaningfully at Gaspar. He grinned, just glad to have recaptured her attention.

During the meal, he busied himself wondering how he might contrive to steal her away to expound upon their fledgling intimacy. He considered the tablecloth. *There must be a linen closet around here somewhere ...*

"You two." Gaspar's voice snapped his attention back to the table. "Affonso and I have business to conduct today. You won't be needed. Before we head back home tomorrow, we're going across the river to the Japanese quarter. I'm interested in acquiring some lacquerware. Senhor Dyer, I'll need you to arrange transport of the goods."

"Certainly, senhor." Harrison watched Lamai out of the corner of his eye, but she carefully pointed her attention elsewhere.

A short time later they tumbled out the front door, giggling like naughty young fugitives from the schoolroom.

They ambled down to the river and engaged a fisherman willing to carry them the short distance upstream to the ruined city center of Ayutthaya. On both the eastern and western banks, knots of new construction had sprung up—squalid hamlets in the wasteland that had once been a vibrant city with a population greater than London. At one of these little settlements, a group of people milled around, while a few officials wearing tall, plumed hats and carrying long spears engaged the locals in lively discussion. Their ferryman made to land there, but Lamai urged him to continue.

Harrison turned to watch the scene as they drifted past. His arm came around Lamai's waist and he kissed her cheek. "Why not stop there? Whatever's going on looks civil enough. And there are plenty of people. I warrant we could hire a mule for the day."

Lamai chuffed a laugh. "Believe me, you don't want to get involved. Those guardsmen are sorting something out, from the looks of things. A crime. Thai justice is swift and hard."

"Hmm." Harrison hadn't considered the judicial system of his host country. "For example?"

"Debtors can be made to serve those to whom they owe money. The fingers of counterfeiters are chopped off, while thieves lose a whole hand."

He lifted a brow. "How very Old Testament."

Her mouth cocked to the side. "Death is a less common sentence, of course, but given when it's warranted. If there's been a murder, the offender must be arrested in a timely fashion, or the guardsmen face punishment." She nodded back towards the official matter unfolding on the riverbank. "They might be enlisting the people to help flush out a culprit to save their own skins. But if it is a case of murder, the people won't be so willing to help."

"Oh?"

Sitting up straighter, legs crossed at the ankle, Lamai became animated with mirth. "You see, if murder is done, the killer will be put to death, of course, but the neighbors will be punished, too, fined for not preventing the crime from taking place."

"No!" Harrison tried—and failed—to imagine such a system in England. Magistrates might get away with such a thing out in the countryside, where neighbors all knew one another's business, but it was impossible to think such a system would work in the larger towns and cities. "I suppose fear of punishment is as good a motivation as any to prompt citizens to police themselves."

"*Mmmmm*," Lamai hummed. "That's the optimistic view, but more often than not, what happens is that neighborhoods band together to hide the body and lie to the police."

"What a demented community exercise. I like it."

Chuckling, she rested her head on his shoulder. Harrison kissed her brow. He couldn't believe their good fortune—a whole day to spend together as they pleased. Somewhere in the ruins of the old capital, he was going to find a place to lie down with her again. And this time …

His mind was still on *this time* when they climbed to shore and found a *mahout* untying his elephant from the load of lumber the animal had dragged from a nearby logging site. In answer to Lamai's inquiries, the *mahout* scurried to a pavilion where a handful of men and their pachyderm charges took a break from their labors. He returned with two other men, all of them lugging passenger equipage. Soon, the elephant was fitted with a *yaeng*— this one little more than a wooden bench lashed to the animal's back, as opposed to the fine, covered carriage Gaspar owned.

But the simple conveyance was sufficient to see them into the city, and the *mahout* was eager to earn a few extra coins. As they struck out west from the river, the ruined towers Harrison had previously glimpsed grew larger. When they passed one, he craned his neck to examine the intricate designs worked in brick. The column must have originally been overlaid with stucco or tile, but all ornamentation was long gone, leaving behind the stark beauty of the architecture.

"Your turn."

"Hmm?" He frowned at Lamai. "My turn for what?"

Their hands were joined in her lap. She flipped his arm, traced a finger over the scars. "I understand why you did this. But I wish to understand the why behind the why. What caused such pain?"

His heart leaped into his throat. There was a faint buzzing in his ears. "I did tell you …"

"Some of it, yes. And it was terrible. But not the whole of it, I think."

No longer did Harrison see the long, straight avenues radiating out from the river. His vision was instead filled with a time long gone, memories that had driven him to the brink of self-destruction over and over again. He would never inflict such tawdriness, such horror, on Lamai. Already, he had shared more with her than anyone else since those times he'd attempted in vain to solicit help from his family.

At Lamai's instruction, the *mahout* stopped the elephant and they climbed down. They explored a complex of shattered buildings. Little remained but rectangular foundations with a bit of wall or a few stairs here and there. Centuries of splendor, reduced to rubble.

In front of him, her slim hips swayed side to side, her sweetly curved backside beckoning. His body stirred. He bit back a frustrated growl.

Couldn't it be enough for Harrison to know and protect Lamai? To pleasure her, and maybe—finally—find his own pleasure, too?

Why did she insist on prodding old wounds? Why wouldn't she just let him love her?

She stepped down into a corridor, open at the top but the walls more intact than anything else they'd seen. When he followed her down and rounded the corner, the air rushed from his lungs in a wheeze. Before him was a long line of stone seated Buddha statues, some fifty of them, and every last one desecrated. The heads had been knocked from many. Others were missing hands. In a few egregiously malicious cases of vandalism, the eyes had been chiseled out.

Reflecting on the Buddhist sanctuaries he had visited in Siam—each one a serene place of peace and beauty—he could not understand this senseless destruction.

"Who would do such a thing?" Lamai stood before a particular statue. The white stone robes, hands, and face were blackened with soot. Someone had heaped tinder in the Buddha's lap and set it aflame. She turned her solemn face to him. "Why?" he asked. "The Burmese are Buddhist, as well; why would they do this? I don't understand."

Turning away, she strolled on down the corridor of shame. "If you are looking for answers, *farang*, I don't have them for you. Cruelty is a disaster, the same as a flood. All we can do is survive and recover. And help others get through it, too."

"Like those people back there, helping each other evade the police?"

She gave a wry smile. "Something like that."

Leaving the corridor behind, they wandered through more destruction, climbing over piles of rubble in the path when they couldn't step around them. Harrison marveled at how quickly nature was retaking its own. Vines and weeds, mosses and trees, were finishing what the Burmese army had begun decades before. Plant life insinuated itself into every chink and crack to further the destruction of the old Siamese empire.

She led him into a little clearing surrounded by trees. He saw the lines in the earth that marked the hand of man, but the area had the feeling of a natural grotto, enclosed as it was by the encroaching forest.

A fig tree grew on an elevated portion of earth, its roots cascading over the side like a waterfall carved in wood. Near the base, on the lower level where they stood, a large face of Buddha was captured in the trees' roots.

Turning in a circle, Harrison searched for the statue's base, but couldn't find it. The face was nearly two feet tall. The sandstone carving must have been extremely heavy. How on earth had it gotten here?

"Where ...?" He turned again. It didn't make sense. The head hadn't sprung up from the ground.

It didn't make sense.

Lamai's words finally sunk in. Harrison fell to his knees. All these years, he'd been trying to make sense of what happened to him, to make Miss Meyler's abuse and his family's indifference fit into the narrative of a just universe. His inability to do so had caused him endless anguish.

"Suffering beyond the suffering." Lamai's hand alit on his shoulder briefly, then she, too, knelt in the soft earth before the disembodied Buddha.

Harrison's eyes closed. His hands clasped together on his lap in a bloodless fist. "When Miss Meyler—Eliza—turned her attention from me to my younger siblings, I stopped being the boy she cornered and toyed with like cat and mouse. I pursued her. I refused to go to school, pitched monumental fits until my parents relented and allowed me to stay home with a tutor instead of going to Eton. Told Miss Meyler I couldn't bear to be parted from her." That memory, the taste of that lie, brought acid to his throat. He swallowed. "I sneaked out of my room and went to her bed almost every night."

"All of that, to distract her from your brother and sister?"

He nodded. Eyes still squeezed shut, he spoke into the dark void. Lamai's presence reminded him he was far from harm's reach, and the strange Buddha in the roots gave him a mental image to focus on so he did not visualize too many unpleasant memories.

"I tol—" His throat burned. He cleared it; began again. "I told you both my father and elder brother were unsympathetic to my plight."

"Yes."

"And I did not want to trouble my mother with what was happening, but I knew there was one surefire way to get rid of Eliza. If she became pregnant, my mother would have to dismiss her. So I forced myself to bed her until that happened."

"And was she dismissed?" Lamai was closer. He felt her warmth against his hand, though she did not touch him. It was an offer, Harrison recognized. He accepted it. Slipped his fingers through hers.

"Yes. She was put off without references. Unable to get another post as governess. A few months later, she and her unborn child died in a factory fire up in Manchester." Flinching inwardly, his eyes sprang open and met the steady, accepting gaze of Buddha. "I didn't mean to kill her," he whispered. "I just wanted it to end."

From the corner of his eye, he saw Lamai nod. "You were drowning and found your way out of the flood. You saved yourself."

A generous interpretation of events. Harrison's mother never forgave him for his "affair" with the governess, even as his father winked and nudged. They died believing their son had been a willing participant. To this day, his elder brother, Charles, still sneered at him for "seducing" and "ruining" a "decent woman." As if a boy of twelve, thirteen, fourteen could ever be said to seduce an adult.

Hence Harrison's schism from his elder brother. The younger two had learned of Harrison's sin from Charles. Hence their schism from Harrison.

"This is why intimacy is too difficult for you." Lamai's quiet voice brought him back from the painful rift with his family.

"That's right." There was so much hanging unsaid in the air between them—how he feared and despised Eliza Meyler; his utter shame at taking pleasure in the act, even as he loathed it.

That twisted combination of repulsion and release had gutted him, left him unable to perform that most basic physical act with another person without experiencing guilt and shame all over again. He'd taken lovers only when desperation compelled him. When he discovered that sex with women stirred up that toxic brew of emotion, he tried being with men, instead, but those encounters, too, left him bereft.

Lamai cradled his hand to her chest, clasped it tight between her own. "The flood waters receded a long time ago. It's all right to come down from the high place and rebuild your house now."

She kissed his knuckle, brought their hands to her lap, and returned her gaze forward.

A flood. A simple metaphor. It could be anything, really—a storm, or a blizzard, or a typhoon at sea. He hadn't tried to rationalize the tempest that sank *Brizo's Woe*, because there was no rational explanation for it. Perhaps this was the same. Or perhaps accepting it as such would, at least, help him find peace. Suffering beyond suffering, she'd called it. The idea of stopping the torment he inflicted upon himself for what he'd been through was … big. Daunting. But appealing.

Harrison sat with that for a while, rolled it around in his head and tasted the possibilities on his tongue. While he considered his own suffering and his part in it, Lamai was just … there. Not offering platitudes or claiming divine will or anything of the sort. She was simply present with him, holding his hand. Accepting him. Loving him. This moment was the most profound gift he'd ever been given.

"You know," she said, breaking the silence at last, "it was beneath such a Bodhi tree that Siddhartha Gautama attained enlightenment and became the Buddha."

"Hmm." Harrison nudged her shoulder. "Just like this one?"

She nudged him back. "Just like this."

Chapter Thirteen

Harrison had an idea. Though he and Lamai had not orchestrated another plan for getting Mi and Kulap out of Gaspar's house, the trip to Ayutthaya had provided the inspiration for the scheme percolating in his head.

As usual, the problem was money. Mi was eager to return to her family in Burma, but insisted she wouldn't do so without the means of helping rebuild the home they'd lost to marauding enemy soldiers. It wasn't an unreasonable position; God knew the woman deserved compensation for her years of work for the Portuguese merchant—whatever form that labor had taken. To Harrison's mind, soldiers had no right taking civilians prisoner and pressing them into labor. It was common practice in this part of the world, however, and Harrison knew he'd be wasting his breath complaining about it. To the extent that being taken against one's will could ever be acceptable, the greatest offender against Mi was Gaspar, who had assumed responsibility for her. Instead of treating her well and fairly, he had egregiously abused his position of authority. It was Gaspar who owed Mi compensation, but she would never see a baht out of him. If Mi was to build a new life for herself and her family, it was up to Harrison to give her the nest egg she needed.

He brooded on the problem throughout the day. When the shipment of lacquerware from the Japanese merchant in Ayutthaya arrived, Harrison brought the man's agent to the office for a drink of contraband sherry while they settled their business. After both men signed delivery receipts for the records of each enterprise, Harrison went to the corner safe for the balance of money owed.

Licking his finger, he flipped through a stack of notes, quickly peeling off what he needed. He moved to return the remainder of the cash to the safe. He paused, staring at the wad of currency in his right hand. Enough for a Burmese peasant family to build a house—enough for them to live comfortably for years.

And why not? Righteous indignation burned through Harrison's veins. His hand tightened on the money. What Gaspar had done to Mi was an atrocity. People like Gaspar D'Cruz and Miss Eliza Meyler deserved punishment. They deserved—

No. No. Whipping himself into a vengeful fury wouldn't do Mi or Kulap—or himself—any good. The tension drained from his fingers; he left the money on the shelf and closed the safe, then returned to his Japanese guest, giving that good man the money he was owed.

Gaspar was unscrupulous, but Harrison was not. And though his ideas for liberating Gaspar's slaves might be underhanded, they were morally sound. Not so stealing money from the man's business. If Harrison couldn't liberate two women from forced prostitution with his integrity intact, then he had no place acting. Besides the risk to himself, there was always the possibility that blame might fall on Lamai. Protecting her had become his highest priority. When all of this was done, when Mi and Kulap were free, Harrison would take Lamai away from the Portuguese merchant's foul influence. Gaspar wasn't the only man in Bangkok who would prize a translator like Lamai, and Harrison could find work with another merchant. The two of them … they would be fine. But first, Harrison had to navigate them through this.

In the afternoon, when the warehouse laborers broke from the heat for a few hours before returning in the early evening, Harrison paid a call at the home of Sarathoon, the French-speaking commerce official. Meaning only to leave a note asking for an appointment at the gentleman's earliest convenience, Harrison was surprised when the servant who answered the door invited Harrison to follow him through the house to an inner courtyard.

In a secret oasis surrounded by tall walls, but open on the sides to catch the breeze, Harrison found Sarathoon reclining on a couch, reading a book. A large banana tree and a stand of bamboo provided additional shade, and a burbling fountain contributed the illusion of coolness, if no actual relief.

The older Thai man's eyes lit when he saw his guest. "Khun Harrison!" he exclaimed, rolling onto his side and pushing himself up to greet the Englishman with the proper *wai*. He gestured for Harrison to sit on the couch, then called for a servant to bring refreshments.

"So, what brings you here, my young English friend?" Sarathoon asked, speaking French. "Nothing serious, I hope! I have a new volume of Voltaire." Picking up his book, he waggled it in a strong, brown hand. "Have you ever seen one of his plays performed? Delightful! I do miss French theater from my years in Paris."

"I'm afraid I've never had the pleasure," Harrison answered, "but I read him extensively at university." Unable to resist his new friend's good cheer, he found himself often laughing while swapping favorite lines of the Frenchman's satirical pieces. After running through the highlights of that intellectual giant, Harrison took a sip of cool fruit juice. "There was a reason I visited today, besides the pleasure of discussing French philosophy."

Sarathoon tilted his head. "What troubles you, my friend? Your smile vanished faster than an opera girl's virtue." That earned a chuckle. Sarathoon, on the other hand, roared with laughter at his own jest. "I've been holding onto that one for so long! None of my fellows at the ministry of commerce appreciates an opera joke."

While Sarathoon dabbed his eyes, Harrison explained that he needed hard currency, but Gaspar paid him in letters of credit. He pulled them out of the pocket of his coat.

Sarathoon took the letters and fingered through them. "These are good anywhere in Bangkok. Whatever you need, you can buy it right here in the city. No problem."

Harrison acknowledged the statement with a nod. "True, but I have a … particular need for currency." The letters of credit wouldn't do Mi any good outside the city, much less in the mountains of Burma. Thai coinage, however, was good throughout the kingdom of Siam, and freely exchanged along the borders of its neighbors.

Leaning back, Sarathoon leveled an assessing gaze on the younger man. From a pouch on the refreshment tray, he pulled out a small clay pipe. After Harrison declined the offer of a smoke, Sarathoon stuffed the bowl with shredded tobacco, lit it and puffed several times, filling the air with a rich, fruity aroma. Then he waggled the stem at Harrison, bluish-white smoke streaming from his mouth. "Gaspar D'Cruz pays his taxes on time, and he gives tribute to the king several times a year. His name is known at court, even though he's not yet risen to His Majesty's circle of acquaintance."

Innocuous on the surface, Harrison heard the implicit warning in these remarks. Gaspar wasn't as powerful as he wished to be, but he wasn't without influence—and the power he did have granted him a good bit of latitude. From Lamai, Harrison already knew the misdeeds of *farang* merchants like Gaspar were frequently overlooked by Thai officials. And from his own experience, he knew Gaspar was both petty and dangerous.

Choosing his words carefully, Harrison proceeded with caution. "The king, I have heard it said, is gracious and wise."

"*Mmmmm*," Sarathoon agreed. "This is true."

"He values honesty and fair dealing among all who are subject to his laws, free men and slaves alike."

"He is as just as he is wise."

"Not all men respect these virtues, but I am glad this kingdom is led by a man who does."

Sarathoon resumed puffing on his pipe. After a moment, he tapped out the ash and stood. "I'll buy your letters of credit. It's nothing to me if my cook does the shopping with my notes or Gaspar's."

He led Harrison to his study, where the exchange of money for notes was made, then the two men parted cordially. Harrison promised to visit again soon.

After the evening hours of work at the warehouse were completed, Harrison hurried home. Now that he had money in hand, he was eager to finalize the plan to see Mi on her way to freedom, for which he would need the assistance of his favorite co-conspirator.

He did not have an opportunity to meet with Lamai before supper. During the meal, he noted with concern dark circles beneath her eyes. Her face looked drawn, and she picked at her food, eating little. She met his glance a few times and slid a secret smile his way, but something was wrong.

After supper, instead of joining the men in the salon, she excused herself and bid them a good night. Harrison watched her ascend the stairs, frustration gnawing on his ribs. He wanted to take her in his arms and ask what the trouble was and make everything better for her. While Harrison had spent the day at the warehouse, excepting the hour or so at Sarathoon's, Lamai had been cooped up with Gaspar, penning letters on his behalf. Had something untoward happened?

He was sorely tempted to dart up the stairs after her, but it was imperative he not give Gaspar any reason to scrutinize him and Lamai more closely than he already did.

Gritting his teeth, he stalked after Gaspar into the salon. Without Lamai to act as a buffer between the men, the atmosphere was tense.

"Port, Dyer?"

"No, thank you." Harrison took a deck of playing cards from a drawer and began laying out a game of solitaire.

"Everything go well with the lacquerware transaction?"

"Perfectly."

"Hmm."

Harrison felt Gaspar watching him, but he kept his own gaze focused on the cards. After several tense moments, Gaspar took up a book. The muscles between Harrison's shoulder blades eased.

The merchant rang for tea and sweets, as he did every night. But when the servant delivered the tray, he had an additional instruction: "Send Mi here."

At once, Harrison bristled. His eyes snapped to the doorway when the Burmese girl appeared. She spared a single, panicked glance for him before she knelt in front of Gaspar.

Kulap was Gaspar's favorite. Why had he called for Mi tonight? He must realize Harrison was planning something, or perhaps Mi herself had let something slip to Kulap. The younger bed slave was temperamental, jealous. Mightn't she have run to Gaspar to tattle on Mi in a fit of pique, or to curry favor?

"Rub my feet."

Gaspar thrust his toes into the girl's lap. Harrison wrinkled his nose. Though the servants kept the house clean, going barefoot inevitably led to grimy soles. If Gaspar wished a foot massage, the considerate thing would be to bathe them first. But he did not concern himself with what his slave might find distasteful. She was his to use as he pleased. Mi bent her head to the task, kneading the soiled toes and heels with her thumbs.

Unsavory as Harrison found the order, at least Mi hadn't been sent to Gaspar's bed. The master leaned his head back and sighed contentedly. All was right in his world. Harrison's stomach lurched.

Mi chanced a glance at Harrison. Her eyes—narrower than Lamai's and so dark as to be nearly black—brimmed with worry.

He gave her what he hoped was a reassuring smile. *We'll get you out of this, Mi. Just hold on a little longer.*

For the sake of appearances, Harrison continued flipping cards and occasionally shuffling them. He'd no interest in the game, but he couldn't bring himself to leave Mi alone with Gaspar, either. Hopefully, Gaspar would soon tire and go to bed, and then Harrison could check on Lamai—

"That will do." The older man pulled his feet off Mi's lap and stood, stretching and yawning.

Gathering up the cards, Harrison prepared to make for his own chamber.

"Mi, get Kulap," Gaspar directed. "Both of you come to my room." He lifted two fingers to make sure the girl understood.

Harrison's stomach dropped. "Senhor," he blurted. Words of protest formed on his tongue.

Gaspar lifted a brow. "Well?"

In the doorway, Mi looked over her shoulder and shook her head ever so slightly.

She was right; he couldn't step in yet. He had to bite his tongue and bide his time until he and Lamai had a solid plan in place.

He forced his lips into a smile. "I just wanted to wish you a good night, sir."

$$\bullet\ \bullet\ \bullet$$

Curled up on her side, Lamai squeezed her eyes against the pounding inside her skull. If she could get to sleep, the pain would probably pass during the night, but slumber was elusive when her very eyeball pulsed in its socket.

There was a scratching on the door, then the sound of it opening on well-oiled hinges and quietly closing again. *Harrison.* No one else would come to her like this.

Bare feet shuffled on the wood floor, then scuffed softly over the pile of the rug. "Lamai?" he whispered into the darkness.

"Here." She propped up on an elbow, reaching out with her other hand to capture his extended arm. With a tug, she brought him down onto her low bed. Their arms entwined; Lamai savored the sweet embrace. She'd missed him all day.

"What's wrong?" he murmured into her ear. "I could tell you weren't feeling quite the thing earlier."

"My head." Lifting his hand, she brought his palm to her right temple. "Here."

"Is … Is it caused by your injury? Do you need a doctor?"

An obvious conclusion to draw, but no. Lamai's cheeks burned; she was glad of the concealing darkness. "My head often aches like this before my … each—each month," she stammered. She wondered that her face didn't glow red.

"Oh." Kissing her brow, Harrison sifted his fingers through her hair. "That's all right, then." He rubbed firm circles on her scalp; his thumb pressed into her temple with just the right amount of pressure. His other arm came behind her neck tipping her chin up. "Not that I want you to hurt, you understand. I'm just glad to know you aren't sick with disease or troubled by your scars or …" She heard his breath catch. She flattened her palm on his chest, her fingers skimming upward to his neck. His skin there was warm and tender like a new puppy. Naked. She felt the action of his throat when he swallowed; detected the vibration of breath in his windpipe; skated her little finger over his pulse. So much life in one defenseless spot. And he exposed it to her freely.

"I was worried," he concluded.

Turning to give him better access to the right side of her head, she smiled against his chest. The burgundy jacket and blue sash he'd worn earlier were gone; he wore only his *panung* and shirt. Nuzzling the open vee neckline, she breathed his scent into her lungs. His skin bore the herbaceous aroma of his washstand soap, but she detected, too, the sweat of the day's labors, and another scent that was just Harrison—male and utterly appealing.

His fingers continued to work their magic across her scalp, down her jaw, and into the muscles of her neck. Lamai groaned as the pain began to ease. *Bliss.*

As one ache receded, though, another rose in its place. She shifted against him, aware of his broad chest and the hard thigh hooked across her legs. Lamai lifted her head to kiss the side of his throat. Tentatively, her tongue touched him there, tasting the faint salt; his heartbeat thumped hard.

Reaching a hand to his nape, she brought his mouth to hers. A quiet sigh escaped her as their lips met. Something in her unfurled, eased by the caress of his lips and tongue as her pain had been by his fingers.

Cupping her shoulder in a big hand, he lifted his head. "We don't have to do anything like, like this. That's not why I came to you. I was concerned you were ill, and I wanted to discuss—"

Slipping her hand up the back of his shirt, she skimmed the flat of her palm up his spine, then raked down lightly with her fingernails. Harrison let out a sharp hiss. His penis stirred to life against the hollow of her belly, lengthening and hardening as she scratched his back again.

"You took the pain away," she murmured, throwing off the light counterpane so she could sit upright on her knees. The ends of her loose hair tickled the small of her back.

Harrison's hand came to her waist, paused, then quickly explored upward to cup a breast. "You aren't wearing any clothes!"

She chuckled softly at his scandalized tone. "Do you wear clothes to bed, *farang*? For me, it's too hot."

A faint beam of moonlight through the shutters caught the white of his wolfish grin. His fingertip traced a lazy circle around her nipple, then pinched. Lamai shivered; the flesh between her legs throbbed. "I'll never breathe a word of complaint, I vow." He lifted his arms so she could pull off his shirt, then he made quick work shucking his *panung*.

If only she had light to see by—motes of moonlight were insufficient to satisfy her curiosity. Rallying her ingenuity, she explored him with other senses. Her fingers combed through the hair dusting his upper chest; she gathered palmfuls of firm muscle in the place corresponding to her breasts. The pads of her thumbs found his small male nipples and danced over them with light flicks of her nails. He inhaled, sharp and quick. Lamai hummed in answer.

Pushing him onto his back, she bent forward, her knees tucked neatly beside his hip, and brought her mouth to the hollow of his throat. Not precisely kissing, she dragged her mouth down his sternum, experiencing the springiness of his hair on her lips, pausing to test the smell and taste. Lower, she traced the space between each rib and rained kisses over the flat plane of his belly. Harrison's navel was a tiny bowl rimmed with more hair, like a man's mouth in miniature, outlined with mustache and beard. The image made her smile, turning her kiss there into a nip of teeth.

Throughout her exploration, she was exquisitely aware of the rod between his legs. It bobbed when her breast brushed it, velvet skin on velvet skin. As she worked her way down his abdomen, she brought a hand around his stiffness, squeezed, then ran her fingers up the thick vein along the ridge to bring her palm skimming over the rounded tip.

He let out a strangled groan. "Damnation, woman." His hands knotted in her hair, spilling her tresses across his thighs. Lamai liked the little spark of tension where he held her tight. It urged her on, giving her the courage to lower her face to his groin.

At first, she meant only to repeat the experiment she'd performed on his torso, to learn all she could with touch and smell and taste. But when she buried her nose in the thick curls at the base of his shaft and touched him with her tongue, his stomach flexed, the hands in her hair suddenly too tight, the cords in his arms taut like bowstrings.

She recoiled, realizing what she'd done. "Oh, Harrison," she gasped, "forgive me."

"For … give … what?" His voice was strained, his hips making little jerking motions.

"I shouldn't have touched you there. You didn't want to …" She brought her hands to her cheeks, mortified that she'd done something to distress him the way that dreadful woman in his past had done. "But you were bare and I got carried away."

A laugh-growl rumbled in his chest. Harrison's arms came around her waist and he flipped her onto her back, reversing their positions. His mouth crashed down on hers, tongue driving deep.

"Hush," he rasped when he tore his lips away. A hand came between her legs, parting, petting, finding her slick. "This isn't like any of those other times. I don't just want this," he said, swirling a finger around her opening and then plunging it deep, "I want *you*. I need you so goddamn much, Lamai." He brought his finger to his mouth and tasted, groaned as if he'd never sampled anything more delectable.

Lamai was deeply shocked—but thrilled, all the same. His enjoyment of her body was intensely arousing. As good as the actual, wicked things he did to her.

"I love you, Lamai."

His words undid her, then remade her all at once. She clasped his face and kissed him fiercely, golden light blazing through her chest. "I love you, my heart. My only heart." When had she known she loved him? Certainly not at first—the scraggly, half-starved *farang* had been a profound annoyance. But loving him was nothing she had to think about, it was as natural, as normal as her own breath. Already, he was an inextricable part of herself. When had that happened?

He touched the tight bud at the top of her folds. Lamai lifted her hips in invitation. "If you want … If you're ready …"

She felt him smile against the crook of her shoulder. "I feel like I've been waiting forever." He bit her playfully, then settled his body in the cradle of her thighs. Somehow, her legs knew to bend at the knee, hitch around his hips.

He drew the tip of his penis up and down the length of her slit, coating himself in her wet. Lamai's inner muscles twitched, eager, wanting. She made a needy whimper.

"*Shhh shhh shhh.* Almost, sweetheart."

One small nudge seated the head just inside her entrance. He brought a hand to her hip, lifted her backside. The press of his knees shifted the bed. Lamai clutched at his neck, his back as he eased forward, his taut buttocks maintaining a steady degree of pressure as he filled her. Then he withdrew slightly, only to recommence his forward progress. His girth stretched her from within. At first, the discomfort of the unfamiliar intrusion was all she felt, going on and on. Aware they were not alone in the house, she pressed her face into Harrison's chest to muffle her moan.

"I'm sorry," he said, taking it in his turn to apologize. "So sorry, sweetheart." His arm hooked around her head and he kissed her temple, her cheek. "That's the worst of it done. It won't ever hurt like this again, I swear. Lamai?" She lifted her face. Even in the crepuscule gloom of her chamber, she felt the intensity of his stare. "I love you."

The glow inside her shimmered and spread. Her muscles ached, but what was a little soreness to the overwhelming joy coursing through her veins? "Love you, Harrison. Love you." She offered her mouth and he kissed her with heartbreaking sweetness. His hips began to move, rocking gently. Surging upward, he angled to meet her sensitive bud with every stroke.

Lamai's lips parted on a gasp. There was no more pain, only pleasure like he'd brought her before. Gradually he increased the tempo of his thrusts, moving faster, pulling out farther and driving deeper. Lamai bit her lip to stop herself from crying out. Harrison, panting, must have sensed her predicament—or maybe he wanted to cry out, too—for he sealed his mouth to hers, feeding her his groans so they rumbled through her throat, and drinking her cries in return.

Tension built at the place of their joining, spiraling up her spine and through her limbs, every muscle focused on that all-consuming ecstasy. Her hips canted in time with his now, rising to meet his thrusts with her body's greedy demands.

Propping onto an elbow, Harrison grasped her arm, pried her hand from around his neck, and laced their fingers together. Palm to palm, he clutched their hands against his chest, to the galloping of his heart.

"Lamai." Her name was a harsh whisper in a dry throat, a thirsty man's desperate plea. "Love." He lost all rhythm, pounded mindlessly, relentlessly.

The coiling pressure seeded between her legs wound tighter and tighter—impossibly tight—until it turned inside out and spilled in the other direction, bowing her back off the bed as wave upon wave of pleasure crashed over her. She could only surrender to the cataclysmic pleasure, let it have its way with her. This was what it was to drown, to die, helpless against an unstoppable force. She gladly perished.

Vaguely, she was aware of his hand crushing hers in a viselike grip as his hips locked flush with her pulsing core. His shaft spasmed within her sheath, spilling his release against her womb.

He collapsed beside her and gathered her into his arms, her back to his chest. Lamai's head, splitting not long ago, now buzzed with the aftereffects of lovemaking. She twisted around, brought her palm to his stubbled jaw.

"I love you, Harrison Dyer. I'm glad we made love, and I'll keep being glad, even if you're not."

He touched his forehead to hers. "I crossed to the world to find you, Miss Lamai Hart. I'll never be anything but thankful for what we've done—and I'm never letting you go."

• • •

Several hours later, Harrison let her go.

Regretfully.

Sorrowfully.

With every fiber of his being clamoring to stay exactly where he was and hold her and love her all through the night. In years gone by, this moment of parting could never come soon enough, the brief euphoria of release undone by dark memories and bitter remorse.

Not this time. With Lamai, he wanted only to take comfort in her sweetness, and make her collapse in ecstasy again. With the lights on.

For a man who'd lost his faith decades ago, the wonder of loving Lamai—and being loved by her—was nothing short of a miracle. To the depths of his charred and withered soul, Harrison had believed he would never have something so special, so extraordinary. So normal. So blessedly normal.

But Gaspar loomed large in Harrison's mind, the monster down the hall that needed slaying before he and Lamai and the slave girls and everyone in the kingdom could find the happy end of their story.

"Remember Ayutthaya?" he said in the night-quiet voice of lovers' stolen moments. Deftly, he folded and twisted his *panung*, his hands familiar enough with the task now to perform it in the dark.

"Are you thinking of Mi?"

"Hmm. Do you think it would work?"

She was silent for a few minutes. Harrison stood beside the bed now, shifting his weight from foot to foot, toes wriggling on the soft nap of her Persian rug.

"It might work." Her voice was clear, though her features indistinct. "You'll have to get rid of her account paper."

"Do you know where he keeps it?"

"In his desk. I'll get you the key and lead him out of the house."

He bent to kiss her, this marvelous woman who enticed his body and astonished him with her intelligence and sheer gumption. "And I'll take it from there, sweetheart."

Chapter Fourteen

Waiting was a nerve-wracking enterprise, but Harrison realized it would be best to allow Gaspar to present them with an opportunity to set their plan into action, rather than attempt to create some harebrained diversion.

In the week following the night that, in Harrison's mind, consolidated him and Lamai into a single, irrevocable fact, they had quietly worked behind the scenes to ensure Mi's escape would go off without a hitch.

Well, Lamai had quietly worked, Harrison corrected as he entered the breakfast room for the seventh time since that wondrous night. While he'd gone through the motions of toiling daily in the dockside hub of Gaspar's mercantile empire, Lamai had spoken to members of the household: Panit, Cook, the other servants. When Panit heard the scheme, Lamai reported, he'd laughed until his sides ached and tears streamed down his cheeks—which Tilda had greedily lapped from the *mahout's* face.

When he sat down at the table to break his fast on rice and some steamed sea creature he'd rather not examine too closely, Harrison quickly realized their day had come.

"... damnable bother. Don't care what my drapes look like," Gaspar was grousing to Lamai. "Why don't you just choose for me?"

"*Mmmmm,*" she hummed, that verbal quirk that could mean anything or nothing, and which had come to feel like salve to Harrison's ears. "Senhor Branco doesn't trust Siamese servants, if you recall—especially women, for some reason—so you'll have to write a letter for me to present. One of the maids says you need new shirts, as well. Shall I go to the tailor and order some while I'm out?" She inclined her head, as if studying her benefactor's midsection. "I'll tell him to add three inches in the middle."

Gaspar choked on a bite of sticky roll. Gooey blobs of pastry fell from his mouth and landed in his neatly trimmed beard. A sliver of almond adhered to his lower lip *"Merde, menina!"* He swiped a napkin over his chin. "I'd be swimming in linen. My measurements haven't changed."

Lamai tilted a brow that penned reams of skepticism. "You haven't been measured in nearly a year." She spooned a bite of rice-and-sea-something into her mouth.

The merchant glowered darkly at his honeyed roll, then pushed his plate away with a sound of disgust. "Fine, I'll go."

"Mmmmmm."

Harrison marveled at the way Lamai neatly manipulated Gaspar right where she wanted him. *Clever minx.* He would be wise to take heed, as he foresaw her handling him just as easily in the future. He and Lamai, discussing *their* drapes or *his* shirts … it was a beautiful thought. That was his dream, he realized. Forget horse farms or sailing the high seas—Harrison only wanted Lamai to tease him into taking her shopping for the rest of his life.

A sobering thought intruded: It was quite one thing for a woman to have her say in minor domestic matters like upholstery and apparel; larger issues like the mistreatment of slaves and herself were beyond the purview of Lamai's deft influence.

That's why she has me. Alone, neither of them could combat the rich and influential merchant. It took the two of them together to do the thing.

"Perhaps we should bring Kulap," Lamai suggested, scraping up the last of her rice. "After all, it is she who sees your drapes most often. She probably has opinions."

"I don't care to hear her opinions."

"*Mmmmm,*" Lamai went again, casting another innocuous glance at Gaspar's belly.

The man's face reddened; his nostrils flared. "Bring her, then." He tossed his napkin over the remains of his sweet roll. "Tell her to wear something pretty, and I'll buy her a new trinket."

"I'll fetch her right now." Lamai hopped up. Swiveling, her hand clipped Gaspar's cup of coffee, splashing a steaming, dark stain onto his coat.

"Oh!" she gasped just as Gaspar roared incoherently. "A thousand pardons, Khun Gaspar!" she cried. "Quick, get out of this before it seeps through to your shirt." Nimbly, her fingers worked the several buttons on his morning coat. She whipped it off his shoulders and pushed him out for a fresh one before Harrison had time to close his gaping mouth.

After he stalked from the room, Harrison's jaw closed with a click of teeth. He lifted his hands and clapped slowly. "Bravo, madam," he said sotto voce. "What's the Bangkok equivalent of Drury Lane? You belong on the stage."

Lamai's eyes twinkled mischief. With her hair in twin braids that had been looped and twisted into a bun, she looked like a Siamese milkmaid with a mind to filch the cream. "Vanity is his shortcoming. He's almost fifty, but he's desperate for Kulap to be smitten with him. Haven't you noticed how he gives her gifts?"

She thrust her hand into one coat pocket, then the other. With an underhand toss, she lobbed something metallic across the table. Harrison caught a ring that held five keys. He dropped them into his own pocket.

"He buys things for all the girls," he pointed out, recalling the fight he'd witnessed between Kulap and one of the Burmese women over some bauble or other.

"He outfits his bed girls nicely to impress his visitors," she clarified, "but Kulap is his favorite. She gets sweets and other little gifts the others never do. Like he's courting her." She pulled a face. Harrison shared her distaste.

The muffled sound of a banging door traveled through the ceiling. The reminder of Gaspar's imminent reappearance sent Harrison to his feet. Rounding the table, he grabbed Lamai around the waist and kissed her soundly. When he lifted his head, the glaze on her eyes and color in her cheeks gave him a heady dose of male satisfaction.

"Best get Kulap now." He patted her bottom.

"Be careful today," she whispered, grasping his hand and bringing it to her lips.

"You, too." He smoothed the worry lines between her brows with his thumb and kissed her once more. "I love you. Everything will be fine. You'll see."

"I love you, too." She smiled and was gone, her sarong swishing around her ankles.

While Panit readied Goui to transport Gaspar, Lamai, and Kulap on their errands, Harrison engaged the merchant in a conversation about business, meetings he had scheduled with various traders, invoices on which Gaspar's signature was required. Everything dry and bland and normal as he waved them off and sauntered back into the house.

He waited several minutes. Comfortable the coast was sufficiently clear, he exited the house again and strode across the lawn to the kitchen. "Where's Mi?" he asked Cook.

The woman, already at work on supper, pointed her wooden spoon at a drab curtain hanging across a doorway at the rear of the room. "Is it time?" she asked in Thai.

Harrison nodded. "Are you sure you're willing, *phar*? If you won't help, now's the time to say."

The lady cackled, showing gaps in her mouth. "It's about time someone stood up to the *farangs*." She shot him an apologetic look. "Not you, Khun Harrison." Reaching up, she rumpled his tuft. "You're practically Thai. You make me proud."

Impulsively, he bent down to kiss her weathered cheek. "Thank you, auntie."

Tossing the curtain partition aside, he found Mi sitting on the packed-earth floor of the back room, shelling peas into a bowl. Her fingers stilled on a slim green pod.

"Ready, Mi?"

For a long moment, she only stared at him with solemn eyes. Then a grin split her face. "Yes!" She clambered to her feet and brushed her backside. Depositing her incomplete work beside Cook, she bade the older woman a quick farewell. She scurried ahead of Harrison into the house and up the stairs to fetch her bags.

Meanwhile, Harrison entered Gaspar's study. On the third try, he found the correct key to unlock the side drawer. He slid it open and flipped through documents. Harrison recognized Lamai's hand on some of those scripted in Siamese.

"Where is it?" Mi demanded. She had a bedroll strapped to her back and a small canvas bag slung across her body.

"I'm looking. Are the rest of your things packed? I'll fetch them down for you."

She shook her head. "I want nothing from this place." There was venom in her voice, and hurts long denied.

He gave her a sympathetic smile, then glanced back at the files. "Ah-ha!" He pulled out two documents. Each page showed Siamese script on the left, and Roman lettering on the right. He recognized the Portuguese words for *account* and *servitude*. Spreading them out on the desk, Harrison glanced between them. "*Erm*, I don't suppose you know which one is yours?"

Mi, worrying her bottom lip between her teeth, came to stand beside him. The top of her head only reached the middle of his bicep. "I can't read," she confessed. Then: "There!" she cried exultantly, jabbing her finger at the bottom of the Siamese portion of a page. "Mi. My name." She grinned at him, triumphant.

Returning her smile, Harrison handed her the paper.

The young woman drew a breath, then slowly, carefully, ripped the paper that named her a slave into long strips. Each of these she tore into small squares, which she piled onto the desk. Then, to Harrison's surprise, she began eating them.

Raising a hand, he opened his mouth to protest. *Ink isn't wholesome.* But he dropped his hand and let her have her way. Bondage wasn't wholesome. Forced prostitution wasn't wholesome.

"There," she said after gulping down the last of it. "Tomorrow or the next day, my paper will be shit."

"It always was," Harrison returned, admiration swelling in his chest. Mi and Nan had both shown such fortitude through their trials. They deserved nothing but happiness for the remainder of their days. Speaking of which—

He handed her three-quarters of the money he'd received from Sarathoon in exchange for Gaspar's letters of credit. Having arrived in this country with empty pockets, he couldn't put himself back in the position of being entirely at the mercy of charitable (or not so charitable) strangers.

"Do you wish my escort anywhere?" he asked as he opened the front door. "I'll see you to the docks or—"

"Thank you, Khun Harrison, but no." Mi's eyes were restless on the *soi* beyond the front drive, eager to melt into the passing traffic and move into her future. She wasn't looking at him anymore. He was already part of her painful past.

He understood the sentiment.

"Good luck to you, Mi."

After she passed through the front gate, Harrison turned to find a knot of servants in the front hall. "Everyone prepared?" Nods all around. Harrison gave them a sharp nod in return. "Excellent.

Dispose of everything in Mi's room, then go on about your usual duties. You know what to do when the time comes."

Back in Gaspar's study, Harrison glanced at a clock. Lamai's ruse would keep Gaspar out of the house for a couple hours yet, but Harrison needed to be seen at the warehouse. If he hurried, he could direct the loading of a junk before the workmen took their afternoon break.

Kulap's contract lay on the desk, and the drawer was still open. Harrison returned the paper for the last slave—*One to go!*—to its place. Stuffing that document in resulted in several more being knocked askew. Harrison tried to straighten them in the drawer, but made a hash of it. Cursing under his breath, he pulled the stack out to tap them back into order.

The documents were in Portuguese, he noted idly. No surprise there, but—

"Why, you bastard," he ground out between his teeth as he read the contents of a shipping contract. "You ... whoreson hedgepig." His vision narrowed to pinpoints, until all he could see was the abominable text scrawled in Gaspar's hand. "You cowardly maggot pie gore-bellied weasel ..."

Gutter talk flowed from his mouth like steam from a dragon's nostrils, but Harrison didn't notice the filth tripping from his tongue.

Finding fresh foolscap, he bent to the task of copying the damning pages, then returned the originals to their places. Slamming closed the drawer, he locked it and strode out, papers clenched in his fist.

• • •

By the time they returned home at midafternoon, Gaspar was cross, Kulap was crying, and even poor Goui's ears were wilted.

Lamai, on the other hand, was delighted, having successfully dragged out the outing hours longer than it should have taken.

At the Portuguese draper's, she'd made a fuss over Kulap, sitting her down at a table to examine samples of fabric, asking questions pertaining to the origins of each weave, and translating the shopkeeper's increasingly terse answers to the bewildered slave. Gaspar nearly ground his molars to dust as Lamai and Kulap bent their heads to the task of selecting one out of the dozens of bolts Lamai ordered down for the girl's consideration.

Her efforts at the tailor were less effective, as the Thai man whisked Gaspar into another area for the fitting. While he was gone, she turned her energies on Kulap. "Look at this fine hat," she said to the girl. "Khun Gaspar would look very smart in it, don't you think?"

Kulap lifted one shoulder. "When do I get my treat?"

"Soon!" Lamai assured her. "I think Khun Gaspar would be pleased if you took an interest in his wardrobe. After all, he wanted you to select his curtains, which is a great honor. Keep being agreeable, and he might even buy you the ivory bracelet you've had your eye on."

Kulap sighed and looked out the window. Lamai's bait served its purpose, though, as the adolescent did make an attempt at selling her master on the hat. When he brushed off her suggestion, Kulap tried another, then perched a third atop his head at a jaunty angle. Gaspar slapped her hands away and pointed her outside, then refused to take her shopping for herself as punishment for embarrassing him.

The girl sulked the whole way home, tears spilling over her flawless cheeks. Gaspar grumbled about the universal foolishness of women, and Lamai smiled to herself. Harrison had had plenty of time to get Mi out of the house and dispose of her contract of bondage.

Indeed, when they trooped into the house, everything was quiet and normal. Gaspar stalked into his study. There was a sound, as of a locked drawer being ineffectually tugged, and then a curse. "Where the hell are my keys?" Gaspar roared.

Lamai hurried into the study and made a show of looking under the desk and on the shelves. "Not here," she reported. "Maybe they fell out of your pocket this morning. Kulap," she called. When the girl appeared, she said, "Please look for Khun Gaspar's keys in his room."

She took herself into the breakfast room while Kulap went upstairs, and repeated her search mummery. After some minutes, Kulap returned. "I found them, master." She bowed, presenting the keys on her outstretched palm. "They were in the pocket of a dirty coat." Kulap's demeanor was so meek, Lamai felt a twinge of guilt for getting her into trouble with Gaspar. Then she realized how demented it was to regret causing a rift between a girl and her abuser, and felt cross at herself, instead.

"Oh, you must have forgotten to grab them when you changed your coat," Lamai said, clucking her tongue. Gaspar gave her a sour look, then went into his study, slamming the door behind him.

Harrison arrived an hour later, ledgers stuffed beneath his arm and a harried expression on his face. Lamai raised her brows in silent question. His mouth was set in a grim line; he gave no hint about Mi's departure. He knocked on the study door, then spent the hours until supper holed up with Gaspar, hammering out some inventory issues.

Everything continued normal through the evening meal. Except, Lamai could not help but notice the lines etched around Harrison's eyes and mouth. A spurt of anxiety shot through her stomach. Maybe he was just nervous. She caught his eye, smiled reassuringly. In return, he lifted one corner of his mouth halfheartedly.

Almost immediately upon entering the salon after their meal, Gaspar threw himself into his chair. "Fetch Mi," he barked to no one in particular. "My feet hurt."

Lamai and Harrison exchanged a look.

She pressed her palms against nerves fluttering in her belly. "Who, Khun Gaspar?" she asked, her voice even.

"Mi," he repeated.

"I'm afraid I don't know who you mean," she answered mildly.

Gaspar gawped. "Mi, you stupid girl. Burmese Mi."

Lamai shrugged, eyes wide.

"Is that someone I should send for, sir?" Harrison contributed. "A foot masseuse?" He turned to Lamai. "Is that a specialized profession in Siam?"

The merchant's mouth worked silently. "What the hell is wrong with you two?" he spat at last.

Harrison frowned. "Are you quite alright, *senhor*? You look a trifle jaundiced."

Gaspar shot to his feet and stomped into the hallway. "You there." He snatched a footman by the arm. "Go get Mi."

The man wrinkled his nose, confusion writ across his face.

Gaspar tried a maid who poked her head around the corner at the sound of the ruckus. "Mi. Where is she?"

"Who, master?"

The man's hands worked into blockish fists at his sides. "Get. Kulap." The maid bowed, then scurried away. Gaspar rounded on Lamai and Harrison, but said nothing. When the young bed slave appeared, he directed her to fetch the other girl. Kulap bowed and withdrew, and Gaspar *harrumphed*. *There*, he seemed to say. *Someone in this house hasn't taken leave of her senses.*

Kulap pattered back into the salon. "She's gone, Khun Gaspar. Her room is bare."

"*Whaaat?*" he roared. Shoving Kulap roughly aside, Gaspar took himself to the slave girls' quarters. Lamai heard him thumping around upstairs. With Kulap crouched on the floor, rubbing her arm where Gaspar had struck her, Lamai didn't dare so much as look in Harrison's direction.

Gaspar's bellow of rage echoed through the house. Even Lamai, more used to the *farang's* loud tempers, flinched. Kulap covered her head, as if the walls were tumbling down.

"Panit," Gaspar yelled, his voice coming closer. "You, go to the stable and tell Panit to come here. Get Cook, too."

In short order, the *mahout* and cook stood in the salon. "What do you know about Mi running away?" Gaspar demanded of Panit. "Did you help her?"

"Khun Gaspar, I was with you all day!" Panit protested. "How could I have helped this … what did you say she's called?"

A vein throbbed in Gaspar's temple as Lamai translated Panit's words. He leveled his glare on the cook. "You?"

The cook looked at Lamai. "I have a daughter. Tell the fiend that I have a daughter. What he does to those girls is a disgrace. He should be stuck full of spears and set on fire."

Lamai blinked. "She says she's never heard of this Mi person, either, Khun Gaspar."

The merchant quivered like an overplucked harp string. "I want the police. Get me the guards," he ordered Panit. To Lamai and Harrison, he said, "We'll see how funny your little prank is when you're charged with aiding the escape of a slave." He smirked. "You didn't think I'd summon the law, did you?"

Actually, they'd counted on it.

She and Harrison remained in the salon under Gaspar's gimlet eye until Panit returned with four police officers. Three of them milled around the room examining the foreign merchant's riches while the captain, Jettrin, patiently took Gaspar's report.

From the corner of her eye, Lamai saw one of the guardsmen turn a blown glass paperweight in his hands. It disappeared into his pocket. *Let them strip the house.* A man who kept women as bed pets, and who had used threats and promises to coerce Lamai into doing his bidding for so many years didn't deserve blown glass paperweights, or anything else.

Captain Jettrin wrote down the last of Lamai's translation of Gaspar's complaint. "*Phar*, what do you know about this?" the officer asked her.

"No one knows this Mi person he keeps talking about." She shook her head sadly.

"What are you saying?" Gaspar demanded. "Speak in Portuguese."

Lamai cringed as if embarrassed by her benefactor's outburst. "I don't mean to imply Khun Gaspar is lying, *phee*," she hastened to assure Jettrin. "We were out for a long time today, Khun Gaspar and I. Maybe the heat touched his head. You know how delicate *farangs* are."

The captain grunted. His eyes moved from Lamai to Gaspar to Harrison, who stood near the wall, hands clasped at his back, doing his best to stay out of the fray. "Who is that?"

She gestured him over. Harrison made appropriate *wai* to the captain as Lamai introduced him. "I'm honored to meet you," Harrison said in Thai.

Jettrin's bushy brows lifted to his shaved scalp. "A *farang* who speaks Thai! Not many like you around, *phee*. What can you tell me about the runaway slave?"

Hands spread in a gesture of helplessness, Harrison seemed at a loss for words. "There is no runaway slave, *phee*. I'm worried about my employer. Usually his wits are as sharp as yours or mine. Can you recommend a good doctor?"

The gazes of the three of them slid to Gaspar, whose face was mottled purple. His cheeks were puffed, his eyes bulging. He looked on the verge of apoplexy. "Tell them to search the room!"

Lamai conveyed this instruction to the captain, who dispatched two of his men to that task. They returned moments later, shaking their heads.

"I want a manhunt." In a state of high agitation, Gaspar paced in a tight circle. "Tell them to get out there and look for Mi," he shouted, flinging his hands about.

After Lamai communicated this to the captain—an apologetic tone in her voice—the officer shook his head.

Gaspar fumed, then struck his fist into his opposite palm, eyes clearing. "*O papel!*" he burst. Arms pumping, he trotted down the hall.

"Where's he going?" the captain wanted to know.

"He said, 'The paper,'" Lamai explained.

Nodding, the captain snapped shut his little book. "If there's a paper, but no slave to go with it, that will clarify matters." He followed Gaspar down the corridor, with the herd of curious policemen and servants on his heels.

Craning her neck to see past the onlookers crowding the study door, Lamai saw Gaspar tear a paper from the drawer with a crow of victory. Scanning it quickly, he tossed it aside and dove back into the drawer.

The police captain took up the discarded paper. "This is a contract of service," he said. Reading it over, he expounded, "One Thai national, female, fifteen years of age." He whistled. "Paid a fortune for her, too."

"A girl named Kulap," Harrison volunteered. "She is here."

The captain glanced up from the paper. "Show me."

A maid was dispatched and Kulap was escorted into the melee. "Is this your paper?"

The girl, trembling, glanced at the account sheet. Her head jerked up and down.

Lamai held her breath, fearful the captain would ask Kulap about Mi. At a word from the adolescent, their conspiracy could unravel.

But the captain didn't ask. By law, slaves were prohibited from giving testimony. Flicking two fingers, the officer dismissed Kulap. The girl bowed and made a hasty retreat.

Sighing, Jettrin set Kulap's paper on Gaspar's desk. "Please tell Khun Gaspar that unless he can provide us with evidence of a missing slave, there's nothing we can do."

"*Kob khun khap,*" Harrison intoned politely. "Thank you for your assistance, Khun Jettrin. I apologize for the inconvenience of a false alarm."

The police trooped out. Lamai hoped they'd helped themselves to a few more sundries.

The front door closed behind them; a tense silence filled the house as the gawping servants made themselves scarce.

Gaspar stood behind his desk, fisted knuckles pressed to the surface. His hunched shoulders heaved up and down. At last, he lifted his head to level a look of sheer loathing on Harrison, who stood on the other side of the desk, arms crossed.

"I brought you into my home." Gaspar's voice was low, hoarse. "I saved your life, you English dog. I gave you work. I paid you generously. And this is the thanks I receive?"

"It was the honest people who fished me out of the sea who saved my life," Harrison said, "and the good monks who restored me to health. You gave me a place to stay, yes, and work, too—and for that I am grateful. But my gratitude does not extend to overlooking vile acts perpetrated against powerless innocents."

Lamai's heart was filled with pride as she watched her love face down the man who had been both her mentor and tormentor. She wanted to caper and cheer and kiss Harrison's lips, now set in a stern line against their nemesis.

Gaspar's breath heaved through his nostrils, hot and loud. "You stole my slave," he shouted, his fist crashing against the desk. "My legal property."

Planting his hands on the desktop, Harrison leaned forward, bringing his nose to within six inches of the other man's. "What slave?"

Gaspar roared wordlessly. Harrison straightened. "Come, Lamai," he said, extending his hand. "Let's go."

A jolt of apprehension shook her; she tugged Harrison's proffered hand to catch his eye. *Kulap*, she mouthed. They hadn't yet settled on a plan to liberate the youngest bed slave, but Lamai was uneasy abandoning the girl. They should just take her, damn the consequences.

Harrison grimaced, regret in his eyes. He tucked her against his side and placed a hand on her back. "Later," he whispered almost imperceptibly, leading her to the door.

Behind them, Gaspar shouted for Lamai to stop and come back *this instant*. "You have nothing without me, girl. If you leave, you'll never see your father again. Are you willing to take that risk? To your mother's family, you're just a half-blood orphan with a ruined face that nobody wanted."

Harrison stopped. She felt him bristling all over, ready to jump to her defense.

Lamai was tempted to turn and fling words herself. Years of pent-up resentment and fear bubbled in her throat. But giving in to her anger would make her no better than Gaspar. Releasing a torrent of those terrible emotions would only flay her own heart, cause her more hurt. She brought to mind the serene face of Buddha in the Bodhi tree, and let her anger go. She squeezed Harrison's hand. "He isn't worth our suffering, love. Never mind."

Together, they left Gaspar's house. Lamai, too, was finally free.

Chapter Fifteen

After a mad dash to the warehouse, where Harrison retrieved a sheaf of documents from the corner safe, he led Lamai south through the streets. The closer they got to the king's palace, the grander and more ostentatious the houses became.

"Where are we going?" Lamai asked. With the excitement of their daring deception behind them, Lamai was dead on her feet, stumbling along at Harrison's side. "If it's much farther, we should hire a boat." Though it was the small hours of morning, there was always traffic on the river. The side canals were less traveled at this time, but neither were they desolate.

"Almost there," Harrison assured her, putting his arm around her waist for support. "Remember Khun Sarathoon?"

"From the commerce ministry?"

"Yes. He's expecting us."

This news was surprising, to say the least. Lamai could see why the man would appeal to Harrison—with his experience in Europe and fluent command of French, the genial, middle-aged bureaucrat was able to talk to Harrison about topics of which Lamai was ignorant. Yet the news troubled her, too.

"How much does he know?"

"Some, but not all."

"Are you sure you can trust him, Harrison?"

He halted, scrubbed a hand through his short hair, and kneaded the muscles of his neck. "Not entirely," he admitted, "but we need him."

That feeling reared up again. *You don't need him—you have me.* She was jealous, she realized. Jealous that Harrison was inviting someone else into his confidence when it had been just the two of them for months. Suddenly she wasn't enough?

It was an unworthy thought. She chastised herself. They had nowhere else to go, after all. She trusted Harrison, and if Harrison trusted Sarathoon, then Lamai should, too.

Stretching up on her toes, she kissed the underside of his jaw. "Almost there, you said?"

She sensed his grateful, tired smile as they resumed their flight through the dark streets of Bangkok.

Sarathoon's house lay beyond a huge iron gate. A large hanging lantern on the front portico cast enough light for Lamai to discern what she vaguely recognized as a French design in the metalwork.

Their host greeted them in a lavish entry hall, his kind eyes squinting as he smiled his crooked-toothed smile.

He led them to a sitting room floored with broad marble tiles. Sarathoon invited them to sit, and Lamai sank gratefully to the floor, allowing the cool stone to absorb some of the heat from her flushed skin.

Harrison took a cushion beside her while their host sat on a low chair, legs sprawled before him. "So," Sarathoon said, producing a pipe from his pocket. "I got your letter, Khun Harrison. Very bad business." Shaking his head, he lit his pipe, puffed, and offered it to Harrison. The Englishman declined. "Forgive me, Khun Lamai." Sarathoon inclined his head. "I shouldn't speak of this unpleasantness in front of you. My wife has had a room prepared for you."

"Lamai knows everything that went on in Gaspar's house," Harrison interjected. He paused, then said something in French.

The hair rose on Lamai's nape. What didn't he want her to understand?

Sarathoon chuckled. He waggled his pipe in her direction. "She's a beautiful girl, Khun Harrison. I wouldn't want to let her out of my sight, either."

Heat that had nothing to do with the warm, sticky night crept up her neck. Was that what Harrison had said? Maybe she should go to bed; her thoughts were so disordered, she was finding knavery in every innocuous remark.

The older gentleman rang a little bell on a nearby table; a servant carried in a carafe of water. Lamai gratefully drank and accepted a second glass.

"I made inquiries this afternoon," Sarathoon said, settling back with his pipe and beverage. "A ship bound for Bombay leaves one week from tomorrow. You should be on it, Khun Harrison. You're welcome in my home, but I won't be able to protect you out there —" he jerked his chin at the window "– and you don't want to hide here forever."

Leave? Lamai's wide eyes flew to Harrison. A troubled expression furrowed his brow.

"What I told you about the girls … one remains in Gaspar's power. Kulap. I have to free her, as well."

Sarathoon's kind face creased in a sympathetic smile. "You did well, my friend. You helped two women escape hardship. Now it is time to think of your own safety. Take the ship to Bombay. From there, you'll have your pick of East India ships sailing for London."

"But Kulap—"

"I'll see her removed from that man's house." The older man tapped his chest with the hand holding his pipe. "You have my word."

Harrison's eyes—those light, golden-brown eyes she loved so well—found hers. She wished she felt free to put her arms around him, or even hold his hand, but it would be unseemly to do such a thing in company.

"Will you give us a moment, Sarathoon?" Harrison asked, his eyes never leaving Lamai.

"Certainly." The man grunted as he hoisted himself upright. "Just ring the bell there when it's safe for me to come back in. Don't ring too soon!" He chuckled on his way out of the room.

The instant they were alone, Lamai reached for Harrison. He took her hands and kissed them. "A ship home," she said, struggling to keep her tone cheerful. "Exciting news. How do you feel about it?"

Harrison shook his head. "All that matters to me is how you feel about it." He rose from his sitting position to one knee, his other leg propped out at a right angle. What an awkward posture. Lamai blinked up at him.

"I think," he said, sounding a bit flustered, "usually you'd be seated on a chair, or perhaps standing …"

"Usually when?" Lamai peered closely. Moisture beaded on his upper lip, and his brow looked suspiciously damp. "Are you fevered? You're behaving peculiarly and have the sweats." She reached to test the temperature of his head. Harrison snatched her hand.

"Never mind," he muttered, flopping onto his backside and crossing his legs. "Lamai, you know that I love you."

She did, but she never tired of hearing it. She brought a hand to his cheek. "As I love you, my heart."

"I want to be with you. For the rest of my life. Will you come to England with me, Lamai? We'll find your father and—and marry me, I meant to say." He tapped himself on the temple with a fist. "Should have said that straightaway. God, I'm making a hash of this. Just …" Air whooshed through his parted lips. Grasping her waist, he pulled her into the cradle of his lap and kissed her.

Lamai's arms came around his neck as he slanted his mouth over hers. Desire flared through her blood and settled in her bones, in the very marrow of her being. His tongue was wicked and teasing while his lips were everything gentle and kind. He was all of that— her lover and friend, the keeper of her heart and the ruler of her passion. His hand skimmed up her side to the swell of her breast.

"Will you marry me, Lamai? Will you be my wife and let me be your husband?"

Let me be your husband … There was something so unbearably sweet and uncertain in his words. This beautiful man who had been a damaged boy and a wounded adult, who had found his way through hell to be capable of fully expressing his love, and he wondered if she would *let him* be her husband? Lamai should be on her knees, begging him to allow her to be his wife.

Oh! That's what the knee was for. A supplication.

She was glad now that he hadn't stayed on his knee. Harrison Dyer should kneel before no one.

"I would be honored to have you for my husband." She fought back a mist of tears as she smiled, holding his beloved face, rubbing her thumbs over his rough stubble. "You are dearer to me than anything or anyone in the world, my *farang*. I will come to England with you and be your wife, and I'll never give you reason to be sorry."

His eyes shone when he crushed her to his chest. Lamai pretended she didn't notice the hand swiping at his face.

Some time later—not too long, but long enough to leave her breathless—Harrison rang the little bell. They met Sarathoon standing together, Harrison's arm around her waist, their hands joined. Their host eyed them speculatively. "What is this happy glow that shines so brightly from you both, my young friends?"

But an answer was not necessary, as he continued forward to shake Harrison's hand and kiss Lamai's cheek. "Passage to Bombay for two, then?"

After another round of congratulations, Harrison escorted Lamai to the door of her guest room. Despite the hour, a female servant waited within with a tub of hot water. Lamai was suddenly beyond exhausted by the events of the day. She swayed on her feet. Harrison steadied her and kissed her brow.

"Good night, sweetheart," he murmured, bringing the kiss to her mouth. "I won't disrespect our host by impugning your honor beneath his roof, but rest assured I'm aching to do just that."

Giggling and overflowing with the golden light of her happiness, Lamai slipped inside her room. In a week, she and Harrison would be sailing to their new life. All they had to do was enjoy Sarathoon's hospitality and bide their time for seven days.

As she burrowed into the soft bed, she heard, faintly, the rumble of male voices. Harrison and Sarathoon, a baritone and tenor in a duet of conversation, talking deep into the night. Lamai drifted to sleep to the lullaby of those voices. She was loved and she was safe. All she had to do was wait.

After years of suffering and months of effort, nothing could be simpler.

· · ·

Lamai slept far later than usual. The sun was fully above the horizon and the heat of the day already intensifying when she encountered her betrothed in the front hall. Harrison's eyes were set in dark hollows and red-rimmed, as if he'd not slept a wink. He wore a clean *panung*, but the same shirt and coat as yesterday. They'd departed from Gaspar's with only the clothes on their backs, and while Lamai had been provided with fresh sarongs and tops, it was unlikely anyone in the house had proportions sufficient to fit the tall Englishman's lean torso and long arms.

"Good morning. Have you already eaten?" She stepped into his offered one-armed embrace, touched her head and palm to his chest, and breathed. His shirt might not be fresh, but beneath the soft material his skin smelled of soap.

"Hullo, sweetheart." His fingers toyed with her braid; his smooth-shaven chin skimmed her cheekbone as he tucked a kiss against her temple. "I was afraid I'd miss you this morning."

Her index finger traced a curlicue on his chest. "I missed you last night," she whispered. Her other arm slipped around his middle. Shyly, she dipped her fingertips into his waistband at the small of his back, the channel between his firm muscles creating an avenue for her inexpert advances.

A chuckle rumbled through his chest. "I missed you, too, minx, but that's not what I meant."

Brow puckered, Lamai lifted her head just as a harried Sarathoon bustled into the hall, a servant bearing luggage in his wake. "Good day, Khun Lamai." The gentleman's voice was chipper as ever, but he, too, wore the effects of a sleep-deprived night. The folds beneath his eyes were puffy, the skin at his jaw slack. "Give your fellow a kiss. Don't mind me! I am not even here; I am a ghost. Young lovers must have their sweet goodbyes."

Alarm pulled her back. "Goodbye?" she echoed.

One hand planted on his hip, Harrison scratched the side of his nose with the other. That hand gestured, fingers opening and closing, trying to grasp something. "I, um, I have to go away for a few days. We do. Sarathoon and I."

Lamai swiveled to look at the finely dressed official. True to his word, Sarathoon ignored them entirely, instead digging through one of his bags and clipping off instructions to his servant.

"Where are you going?" she asked, turning back to Harrison.

"Ayutthaya."

"Why …?" Blinking shut her eyes, she pressed a finger to her forehead. "We're supposed to sail in one week."

"We will," Harrison rushed to assure her, taking her hand in both of his. "This won't take long. Four days."

She gaped at him, incredulous. Traveling to Ayutthaya took all of one day and part of the next. Allotting four days to get there and come back again left barely any time to conduct his mystery business. What task could possibly have necessitated this sudden departure?

When she asked just that, he shifted his weight from one bare foot to the other. His toes, the big ones topped with a scant few strands of brown hair, were bluish beneath the nails. His fingers, too, were cold.

"What's going on here?" she demanded. "Tell me. Please!"

His eyes, translucent and tawny in the morning light like the brandy Gaspar sometimes drank, flashed frustration. His lips pursed, then pulled to the side. Leaning close, he said in a low voice, "Yesterday I found information—"

"*Bwap!*" Sarathoon yelped. Startled, Harrison jerked upright. "No talking about it, Khun Harrison—you heard the minister. A stray word in the wrong ear could ruin everything. Do you want that on your conscience?"

Instantly, as if in reflex, Harrison clamped an arm across his own body, shoulders hunching slightly. "No." Just that one, simple word, but there was torment in it, as well as determination. Like the smell of his clean skin behind the tang of street grime on his shirt.

"Time to go." Sarathoon took Harrison's elbow. "We're going to miss the barge if we don't hurry."

"Minister?" Lamai pawed at his hand. "Harrison, I don't understand. Please, tell me what's wrong."

"I'm sorry," he moaned. "I can't. I just ..." Grasping her jaw, he kissed her, hard and brief. "Four days, sweetheart. That's all."

"No." Panic welled in her throat. Sarathoon tugged him to the door. "No, Harrison, wait—let me come with you."

"Just stay here, Lamai," he said over his shoulder. "I'm coming back for you. Be here before you know it."

His fingers slipped from her grasp; she staggered back. *I'm coming back for you.* Just like her father.

Chapter Sixteen

For four days, Lamai prowled inside her own mind like a caged animal. She'd have prowled Sarathoon's house, too, but his wife—an elegant lady of middle years swathed in silks and possessed of perfect, subdued manners—found Lamai's restlessness unsettling and begged her to *please, child, be still.*

The lady of the house passed her days crafting exquisite works of silk embroidery while her maids blew haunting melodies on bamboo mouth organs, or plucked them on the strings of a lute. Quiet voices, titters muffled behind a hand. Recalling how Harrison always beamed at Lamai's laugh—her real one, loud and free—made her feel even more constrained by her lovely hostess and her perfect, mild life. How did Sarathoon, always so free to jest and laugh, get along with such a timid creature?

Nevertheless, despite her vexation, she tolerated the padded confinement, counting the hours until Harrison would be back.

By suppertime on the fourth day, Lamai was forced to concede he was unlikely to return as scheduled. The barge on which Harrison and Sarathoon traveled may have been overset by river pirates. Or fever may have swept through the boat. He might be sick in Ayutthaya, all alone with no one to tend him. Some illnesses worked fast, killing the victim only hours after the appearance of a rash. He might be dead already, she thought, fear springing from brain to gut, quashing her appetite.

She tossed that night, flopping around the bed like a stranded fish on the riverbank, vainly seeking out the comfort of a cool spot. Wrestling with her worst thoughts, Lamai tried to convince herself all was well. Harrison was coming back. *Of course* he was. If bad luck had befallen him, she would have heard about it. Ayutthaya was just up the river, not on the other side of the world. Therefore, since she had not received bad news, everything must be fine. It only stood to reason, then, that she should carry on in the expectation of departing on the ship bound for Bombay in three days. *So soon.* Anxiety had her curled in a ball. What if he was late? What if they missed the ship?

Tossing back the covers, she gave up sleep as a lost cause. Nude, she paced the length of her guest chamber, back and forth. The movement of air over her skin caused her nipples to pebble. She brushed a finger across the turgid flesh, pinched it lightly as Harrison had. Her womb clenched in response. Lamai knew enough from hearing the bed slaves talk to know she could bring herself off, pry from her own body the release Harrison had given her. But those sensations were for sharing and enjoying with her beloved.

She raked her hands over her scalp. Lifted her braid and coiled it, clasped the bun to the back of her head, let it fall again. What was she going to do? What *could* she do? Of a certain, she couldn't go out searching for Harrison, no matter what her nerves said. Crossing to the window, she threw back the shutter and leaned on the sill, leaning her bare torso into the damp night air.

"We're going to England," she told herself. "We're leaving in three days."

What did people do before a trip? Pack, of course. Had Lamai packed? Not at all. There. Preparing for the journey was how she would spend the next two days. Wouldn't Harrison be proud to return and find she'd taken care of everything? She'd told him he would never be sorry he chose her. More than that, she wanted him to be glad. She wanted, every day, to give him the happiness he'd gone without for so long. For every year Miss Eliza Meyler had stolen from Harrison, Lamai would give him five good ones. Ten. For every day he had tormented himself with guilt for that dreadful woman's death, every day he had forbidden himself love and pleasure, Lamai would give him a month of joy.

Everything they owned in the world was still at Gaspar's house. Lamai didn't need anything but some clothes and a few necessities, which, if she was honest, she could easily reacquire with some shopping. But her father's ring was there. She couldn't leave without it, the proof of her claim. When they found her father in England, she would show it to him and say—there, instead of in Bangkok as she'd always pictured it before—"Here I am, Father, your own dutiful daughter." Only, when she met him, she wouldn't be alone. She would have her husband at her side. Her English husband. Before meeting Harrison, she never dreamed she'd marry an Englishman; but she was, and wouldn't her father be pleased?

And poor Harrison, she thought, with only one properly fitting shirt to his name. There wouldn't be time to buy new, as anything that hung correctly on his large *farang* frame had to be custom tailored.

There was a quickening in the sky, a shifting at the hem of day as the indigo dome was suddenly stitched to the earth with a paler thread.

Decision likewise threaded up her spine.

She would go to Gaspar's. It was a risky proposition, but not a great one, as business usually took him out of the house in the mornings. She would sneak in the back, through the stable yard and kitchen garden. Should Gaspar be home, she would not so much as enter the house. Panit or Cook or one of the other servants could go inside and fetch a few things without rousing suspicion. If he wasn't there, she would go herself and make quick work of gathering what she needed.

Either way, Gaspar D'Cruz would never see her, never know she'd been there.

The eastern sky continued its daily metamorphosis, the mundane magic of being one thing, and then being something else. In the kitchen behind the house, Lamai heard the clanking of pots. Servants were already up. Lamai imagined telling her hostess what she intended, and perfectly visualized the conniption the poor woman would have at her guest's impropriety. If Lamai was going, she should do it now, before that confrontation became unavoidable.

Quickly, she dressed, transforming a sarong into breeches. It wasn't as voluminous as a *panung* so the resulting trousers were shorter and tighter than she preferred, but Lamai liked having her legs free. Just in case. She tossed on a tunic. In the back hall, she swiped a hat from a hook that also held a lady's gardening apron. Easing open the back door and quietly closing it behind her, she exited into Sarathoon's garden. Floral aromas hung heavy in the dew-wet air, accompanied by the fragrant steam of jasmine rice drifting from the kitchen.

She glanced at her bare feet. "Hell," she huffed, a delightful English word. Lamai's shoes were in the entry hall, beside the front door, and she didn't want to tromp all the way back through the house to retrieve them.

"I'm just borrowing, not stealing," she murmured as she placed her feet in a pair of sandals. They were too short and pinched her toes, but at least her soles were protected. There was a large side gate here, just like at Gaspar's, for the coming and going of Sarathoon's elephants, through which she let herself out. At the mouth of the alley between neighboring properties, Lamai took careful note of her surroundings. It had been dark when she arrived, and she'd relied on Harrison to know the way.

Once she was near the river, navigating her way to Gaspar's was no problem. Not wanting to get there too early and risk finding him still at home, she stopped at her old neighborhood *wat* to pray. Touching her head to the floor in front of Buddha three times, Lamai sent good wishes out to Harrison, wherever he might be.

Come home, my heart. Just come home.

When she entered Gaspar's property by the back gate, it was midmorning, the merchant's favored time of day to stroll the marketplaces or take meetings. She ghosted across the quiet back garden, clambered over the paddock fence, and went into the stable.

Right away, she noted Goui's empty stall. *He's not here.* Tension drained from her chest. Wan Pen was here, however, and the young elephant's head came around at the sound of Lamai's entrance. She sounded a high-pitched squeal and came to the door of her stall, ears flapping expectantly.

"How are you, my favorite girl?" Lamai petted Wan Pen's trunk and showered her with kisses. "Are you all alone? Where's your nanny, huh? Where's Goui? Poor baby!" The tip of the elephant's trunk wetly nosed across Lamai's face. Laughing, Lamai closed her eyes and let the little girl have her fun. "Such sweet kisses! Thank you so much."

"Baaaa." A hard, goaty head thunked into Lamai's hip.

Wiping her face, she glanced down at Tilda. "Hello to you, too." She stroked the animal's ear. Tilda snuffled her palm. "I don't have anything for you beggars." The fruit basket was in its customary place, so Lamai fetched out a treat for each of them. "I'm glad you have each other," she said as Wan Pen made short work of a hand of bananas and Tilda crunched on cabbage. She would miss them when she and Harrison were gone, miss the good, trusting hearts of these loyal creatures.

After bidding Wan Pen and Tilda goodbye, Lamai went to the back door, wrapped her hand around the knob. Her stomach fluttered. Steeling herself, she opened the door.

Silence.

She didn't know what she'd been expecting, she thought, stepping into the familiar back hall. Gaspar wasn't home. No harm would befall her.

First, she went to Harrison's rooms. She glanced around the sitting room and shuffled through the books piled on the table. Nothing stood out as imperative to take, but she scooped up several, anyway, for reading aboard ship.

In the bedroom, she crossed to the armoire and pulled out a stack of shirts. She turned around to set them down on the mattress. "Oh. Hello," she said to the battered trunk at the foot of the bed.

It was the only thing he'd salvaged from the sinking of his ship. Well, that and Tilda. But since the goat wasn't making the voyage, perhaps Lamai should bring the trunk. Though her Buddhist beliefs taught non-attachment, still she hated to think of Harrison losing every earthly possession all over again. Too, she could stash her own things inside for hauling back to Sarathoon's house.

She flipped up the lid. The trunk wasn't empty. She recalled that he'd given a beautiful tea set to Wat Wihan, where he'd recovered from his ordeal at sea. There were some neckcloths, another book or two, a shaving set, and other assorted knickknacks, but plenty of room for his clothes and hers.

The trunk was several feet long; gripping the brass handles, she hefted it up with only a slight strain. She wouldn't be able to carry it through Bangkok, but if she didn't load too much into it, she'd be able to manage long enough to locate and hire a porter. Replacing it on the floor, she put the books and shirts inside, then added some more clothes. From the bottom of the cupboard she fished out his battered leather boots. She smiled when she remembered how ridiculous he'd looked in a *panung* and boots. He'd not worn them since coming to Bangkok and getting outfitted with sensible, easy-to-remove shoes, but he would need them again in England.

That last addition made to the trunk, she closed the lid and lifted. *"Ooof."* Was it the boots that weighed so much? Shuffling down the hall, Lamai went to her bedchamber. Making her selections with an eye toward the weight she would have to carry—possibly all the way to the river—she packed only a few favorite sarongs, two clean tunics, a night rail (sleeping naked at sea was probably frowned upon), and her hairbrush and comb.

After neatly organizing these things in the trunk, she went to her treasure box, and took out her father's ring. The gold, gleaming in the sunlight, never dulled or tarnished. Its promise was as bright and new as it had always been. *I'm coming back for you.*

"It's all right, Father," she whispered. "You stay there. I'm coming back for you."

"What are you doing here?"

Lamai gasped and whirled to face the door, clasping the ring in her fist. "Kulap," she breathed. "You scared the life out of me."

The girl's hair was down. Lamai couldn't remember ever seeing it other than arranged in a pretty style. When she stepped into the room, Lamai's eye was drawn to a purple shadow on Kulap's jaw. Gingerly, Lamai touched the bruise. Kulap winced; Lamai hissed.

"He did this to you? He hit you?" As if forcing women into his bed wasn't enough, now the fiend had taken to brutalizing them, as well.

Kulap's chin trembled. "It's your fault," she cried. "You've ruined *everything*!"

Lamai drew back, stunned. "How have I—?"

"Everything was fine before you and that stupid *farang* put ideas into the heads of the Burmese witches and made them run away. That was a mean trick you played with the police, Lamai, very mean. You made Khun Gaspar lose face. You know what a proud man he is, but you made him look a fool. He was so angry …" Tears welling, the girl covered her mouth.

Lamai's heart lurched. "So angry that he hit you?" Kulap looked away.

Sarathoon had promised he'd liberate Kulap, but how could Lamai leave the girl here another moment, vulnerable to Gaspar's punishing hands? Harrison would be happy, too, to know they had finished the task they'd set for themselves of freeing all three of Gaspar's bed slaves.

"Kulap," she said, slipping her father's ring onto her thumb so she could hold the girl's hands. "Come with me. Right now. I can take you to a place where you'll be safe."

The adolescent jerked her hands out of Lamai's grip. "Are you crazy? Do you know how angry Khun Gaspar would be?"

"It doesn't matter," Lamai insisted, "because you'll be *safe*. Khun Harrison and I, we have a friend who can protect you." She grabbed Kulap's wrist. "All will be well."

"*Nooo*," Kulap whined. "He'll be sad without me."

Lamai made a sound of disgust. "Kulap! Listen to yourself. What does it matter if he is sad? After everything he's put you and Nan and Mi through, all the times he's used you, or offered you to his guests? After all he's done to me, as well? He *should* be sad, Kulap, he deserves misery for the rest of his days."

Their hands still clasped, the girl swung their positions around, turning so Lamai's back was to the open door. *If I can just get her out the door, she'll come to her senses.* "Calm down," Lamai said, as Kulap was now leaning back, digging her feet into the floor like a truculent child. "Just come with me for an hour or two, Kulap, and see where you can stay." Kulap would probably love Sarathoon's wife and her luxurious, mannered world. "If you don't like it, you can come back."

"But …" Kulap gave another tug against Lamai's grasp, but weaker. Indecisive.

Though her grip remained firm, Lamai's voice turned gentle. "I know you've had a rough time of it, Kulap. Ever since you arrived here, you've borne the brunt of his attentions. You don't have to live this way anymore. Please let me help you. Come on, Kulap, come with me."

Heavy hands landed on Lamai's shoulders "Stealing my slave, girl?" Gaspar's hot breath washed over her cheek.

Lamai twisted in his grasp. The Portuguese man's eyes were twin coals, hard and burning. "Not enough to take two of them, you had to come for the last one?"

Lamai wriggled, tried to break free, but the big man maintained his bruising hold. Raising her fists, she pounded his chest, his wrists. "Let me go! I'm not a slave."

"What you are is a thief." Lips peeled back in a sneer, he spat his words. "Caught you red-handed. There won't be any lying to the police about it this time, *cadela*."

When she pummeled his chest again, Gaspar caught her by the wrist and jerked her arm up. Her fist in front of his face, he barked a laugh. "After all these years, you still believe that fairy tale about your father?" He shook her wrist, painfully jarring her hand.

Lamai's mouth set in a stubborn line. She wouldn't give him the satisfaction of answering his jibes.

Unperturbed by her silence, Gaspar kept going. "Where do you think this ring came from, eh?"

"My—my father. It's his family ring."

Gaspar snorted. "It's *some* family's ring, but not Peter Hart's. You think a petty officer for some inconsequential trade expedition would have a family sigil? He won it in a game of dice off some sailor, who'd lifted it from the dead body of some swindler, who'd— Well, you understand what I mean."

Lamai felt the blood drain from her face. It wasn't true. It couldn't be. He was *lying*. "Mother," she heard herself saying faintly. "He gave it to Mama. His family."

Gaspar tutted, almost pityingly, were it not for the cruel grip on her wrist that was causing her hand to tingle painfully. "You were Peter Hart's *second* family, my dear. He had a wife and children back in jolly old England. Oh, don't mistake me," he said at her stricken expression, "he quite liked your mother, Waan. Doted on her better than a whore deserved. Enjoyed playing house with her and dandling you on his knee."

A sob rose in her chest. "I don't believe you. You'd say anything to hurt me."

With renewed vigor, she twisted and flailed, finally breaking free and ducking to dart past him. His hand caught on her braid, snapping back her head. Wrapping his fist in the braid, he pulled her hair, hard, forcing her to her knees.

"You're right about that—I would say anything to hurt you. I'm very put out with you at the moment, Lamai, but every word I've said is true. Who took Peter's unwanted brat from the relatives who tried to burn her up? Why, his old friend Gaspar D'Cruz, is who. Who educated you, sheltered you, fed you, and asked for so little in return?" he roared, crouching down to glare balefully. "Well?" He yanked her hair. Lamai cried out. "Who?"

"You," she gasped. "You, Khun Gaspar."

"That's right, me. And in return, you have done me a very nasty turn, my girl. You brought that viper into my house, sowed discord, aided the escape of two slaves, and caused my servants to turn on me. You will pay for what you've done." Glancing up to where Kulap must have still stood behind Lamai, he said, "Get the machete from my room."

The slave girl brushed past. "Kulap, no!" Lamai cried, panic rising in her throat.

Gaspar hauled Lamai to her feet by the hair and marched her down the stairs to his study. Pushing her roughly to the floor, he released her at last. Lamai sprawled, pain blossoming across her head as blood rushed to her abused scalp.

She heard the turn of a key and panicked, but he was opening his desk drawer. Grateful for having had the foresight to wear breeches, Lamai pivoted on her knees and clumsily lunged to the door. Kulap reached it just before Lamai did, brandishing a wicked looking long knife with a thick, curved blade. Lamai's feet stuttered to a halt. Her gaze collided with Kulap's, and for a second, Lamai saw ambivalence in the girl's eyes.

"Come in, Kulap. Close the door and lock it."

Kulap's eyes shuttered, extinguishing that flicker of hope. She turned the key in the lock and placed it in Gaspar's open palm. He pointed to the desk; she set the knife on the polished surface.

Gaspar pawed through his papers. "Ah, here we are. He extracted a paper, yellow with age, and offered it to her. Lamai's fingers curled to her palms. "Go on," he urged, pleasant now, "take a look."

Her stomach sinking, she did. It was a letter written in a hodgepodge of Portuguese and English. *Dear Gaspar, my boon companheiro,* the missive began. Slowly, Lamai worked her way through the note, struggling with the writer's nearly-illegible scrawl and flagrant abuse of two languages. Gradually she began to make sense of it. *Fine times these past few years ... Made enough ... restored to solvency ...* And finally: *Por favor, keep an eye on my esposa siamesa and the kid. They were good pets.* Kid? A little goat? *Oh,* she realized. *A child. Me. I was his pet. Like Tilda.*

And there, at the bottom, *Gratefully your faithful friend, Peter Hart.*

The letter slipped from her fingers. Gaspar glanced up from where he was bent over the desk, hastily jotting down some lines. "Believe me now?"

Lamai swallowed. There had been nothing in the letter about another wife in England, but evidence enough to show her father hadn't really been committed to Waan and their daughter, Lamai. He'd called them his pets. Dumb beasts for whom he felt fond affection, but nothing more.

Gaspar turned the paper he'd been writing and slid it across to her. "Sign this."

Contrado de servidão was written across the top. *Contract of servitude.* "You must be joking!" She shoved the hateful paper away. "I've never been your slave in eight years. Why would I sell myself to you now?"

His lips curved into a thin smile. Lamai sensed Kulap moving behind her, but she didn't take her eyes off of Gaspar. He was the danger.

"Our situation is different now, my dear," he explained. "You have robbed me of two of my slaves. You will reimburse me with your own service."

Her chin rose a notch. "Never."

"You damaged my reputation with Siamese officials." His right eyelid twitched. "You owe me reparation."

"No."

Grasping the handle of the knife, he rounded the desk, stalking, shoulders hunched toward her. Face suddenly red once more, he shouted, "You tried to steal my property. You're a thief. Sign the paper, or I'll take your hand."

Without hesitation, Lamai slammed her arm flat to the desk. "Then take it, you bastard!"

His eye twitched furiously now. He raised the blade high. Cringing, Lamai averted her gaze and braced for impact.

Kulap yelped.

Lamai turned her face just as Gaspar forced the slave's arm onto the desk. "Keep your hand," he sneered. "I'll have hers, instead."

"No!" Lamai's shout was lost in Kulap's scream of fright. She babbled and cried, begging her master to spare her, begging Lamai to save her.

"Sign," Gaspar ordered.

Lamai hesitated.

Down came the knife, and off flew the tip of Kulap's left index finger. Kulap wailed. Blood spurted from the injury. Lamai was stunned into idiocy, blank with shock.

"Sign," Gaspar repeated. "Next time it will be her hand."

"Please," Kulap begged, her voice a guttural moan, tears streaming down her face. Lamai didn't know if she meant to implore her or Gaspar. "Please, please, please."

Gaspar raised the knife. Kulap screamed.

"Stop!" Lamai reached for the paper. "Just stop," she cried. She scrawled her name across the bottom.

At once, Gaspar released Kulap. The girl flung her arms around Lamai, weeping on her shoulder and bleeding all down her back. "There, there," Lamai comforted her. She took the girl's hand and wrapped the severed finger in the tail of Kulap's tunic to staunch the flow. In a mindless daze, Lamai uttered soothing words. As she tended the girl, her eyes moved to the paper bearing her name. How the hell had this happened? What had she done?

With the stroke of a pen, she'd become a slave.

Chapter Seventeen

Four days, he'd told Lamai. He'd known that was an optimistic estimate, but the police official—not the captain who'd come to Gaspar's house, but a top-ranking minister appointed by the king—who had met with him in Sarathoon's library in the dead of night, insisted it would be a quick operation. Up the river and back again. Based on the information Harrison had found in Gaspar's desk (and passed to the proper authorities earlier in the day via Sarathoon; thank God for that gentleman's connections), the minister of police had hastened to obtain a writ of search and seizure for the house and other properties connected to Affonso Sales, a Portuguese national who resided in Ayutthaya. The search had uncovered twenty-five women in chains, huddled together on the straw-strewn floor of a ramshackle barn.

Four days, the minister had assured Harrison. Being a bureaucrat with no practical policing experience of his own, however, the man had underestimated the time needed to complete the mission. Or perhaps he'd stretched the truth, in order to ensure the cooperation of the Englishman who planned to depart Siam's shores in a week's time.

However it happened, Harrison returned to Sarathoon's home in the company of his footsore host in the midafternoon of the sixth day, only a handful of hours before he and Lamai were expected to board ship in preparation for departure at first tide tomorrow.

Exhausted, aching, and bruised in strange places (the bottom of his left foot—why?), nevertheless the anticipation of seeing his fiancée gave Harrison a dose of stamina. "She'll be cross," he fretted to Sarathoon as they passed through the wrought iron front gate topped with a stately *fleur de lis* incongruent with its surroundings. "We're two days late. I promised her four—"

Sarathoon slapped his midsection with the back of his hand. "Stop that! You can't go into marriage tying yourself in knots over pleasing your wife all the time. You're the husband—it's her job to please you, not the other way around."

This perspective from a friend he otherwise admired was disappointing. "Don't you want your own wife to be happy?"

Lamai's shoes—battered canvas slippers with supple leather soles—were on a low shelf just inside the front door of the mansion, neatly lined up alongside a couple pairs of finer footwear. Slipping off his own shoes, Harrison glanced around the ornate entry hall with its blue-gray marble floor and pillars, gilded woodwork, and exquisite Siamese artwork, expecting Lamai to appear at any second to ring a peal over his head. He would just have to win her back to sweetness with melting kisses, then, wouldn't he?

"I give my lady the means to make herself happy," Sarathoon boasted. "Whatever she wants, she has. My duty is to provide; her happiness is her own concern, as mine is mine."

A rather dismal way to go through life, Harrison thought, yet no different from the marriages of many British aristocrats. The *ton* was lousy with husbands and wives who lived parallel existences—close, but never touching. From the many hours of talk afforded by river travel, Harrison had learned that Sarathoon was, in fact, a third cousin of the king. Not a royal, but certainly aristocratic. Perhaps his marriage was like so many others—arranged for social or political reasons, rather than personal inclination.

Such a bloodless partnership was not for Harrison. He was very much personally inclined toward his intended. After he'd soothed her temper with apologies and kisses, if she was amenable and they could source an unoccupied chamber, Harrison had every intention of losing himself in her body. It would have to be quick; they hadn't time enough to linger in their loving. But the preceding days had been trying, and he needed her. The depths of his need surprised him. Even after discovering he could engage in sex acts with Lamai without suffering debilitating aftereffects, he thought he'd merely gained the ability to enjoy what other men enjoyed with their partners. Blessing enough! Hallelujah!

But this need ... this wasn't just physical. Harrison's soul, his heart, his inner Buddha—whatever name one wanted to call it— felt wrong, and had done since he'd left Lamai crying and begging him not to go. The wrongness intensified as the days passed, a sort of sad, itchy yearning that made him feel like the world was slightly off plumb. In other times, he would have withdrawn at the onset of such an unsettling emotion, isolated himself from his friends while the sadness festered and grew into a full-fledged bout of melancholy.

He knew the cause of this particular heartache, and he knew its cure. When Lamai was once more at his side, when he held her in his arms, the world would be right again.

The footman who'd opened the door waited until their shoes were off and Sarathoon had been divested of his hat before softly announcing, "Master, the mistress asks that you call upon her at once."

Sarathoon frowned; Harrison grinned. "Not worried about her ladyship being displeased, I hope?"

The man didn't respond to his teasing. "She never summons me, unless something is wrong."

Harrison's smile slipped. He hadn't been invited, but he fell into step with Sarathoon as the older man hurried through the house, cutting across the inner courtyard to the wing where his wife lived.

They found the lady, whom Harrison had not previously met, seated on a tufted stool before an embroidery frame.

When the men entered, she rose and bowed, prayer-hands at her chest. "*Sa wad dee ka*, husband." She acknowledged Harrison with a graceful bend of her neck. "Greetings to you, as well, *phee*. You are most welcome."

Harrison sketched a brief bow. *"Phar."* His gaze raked the handful of maids keeping their mistress company. Lamai was not among them. A cold fist clenched his gut.

"Why did you summon me, wife?" Sarathoon's tone belied his own impatience.

"You should know, husband, that Khun Lamai is no longer here. She departed two days ago."

Harrison had known it. As soon as the servant said ... when she wasn't with the other women here ...

"Gaspar," he choked out. "He took her."

The lady of the house drew back slightly. "No one entered this house to do mischief, I assure you. The girl disobeyed instructions and left. She was seen by a gardener."

"Her shoes ..." Even though he knew it was true, part of him grasped for a way out. A loophole, no matter how absurd. "Her shoes are in the front hall."

Sarathoon's wife sniffed. "The young lady made herself free with my garden slippers."

Harrison clenched his hands behind his head. "Gaspar D'Cruz has her. He must." There was no other explanation for Lamai's absence. She would have waited for Harrison. She loved him. *She loved him.* She wouldn't have left him. Not like this. Not without a word—

"Wait." Something the lady said hit him in the solar plexus. "Did you say she's been gone for *two days?*" A graceful nod. Harrison moaned, dropped to his haunches, head clasped in his hands.

Two days. Two days. Two days. It kept hammering against his skull. Harrison knew what could befall a person at the mercy of a malefactor in two hours. Two days was an eternity. Memories from his early adolescence, flashes of image and sensation, flipped through his brain. That's what was happening to Lamai.

His lungs heaved as they'd done after that footrace. His head felt oddly disconnected from his body. Good lord, was he fainting? How unmanly.

No. No time for swooning. He didn't even have time to make love to Lamai properly, came the abstracted thought. They had a boat to catch. He lurched to his feet. "Gaspar has her, I tell you. We have to save her. This instant."

Sarathoon steered him all too easily to a chair and pushed him into it. Odd, Harrison observed, his knees were weak.

"No, my friend, we won't go haring off."

Rage. He shrugged the older man's hand from his shoulder. "We must! Every moment we waste is a moment he could be hurting her." His eyes narrowed with sudden suspicion. "Did you know this would happen? Is that why you won't help? Or are you just a coward?"

A gasp of dismay from the ladies. Sarathoon's eyes widened; a touch of color drained from his deep-bronze face. "Such little credit you give me, my young friend." His shoulders drooped, his voice wounded. "Have I not helped you every time you've asked it of me?"

Harrison dropped his face into his hands, thoroughly ashamed of himself. "Forgive me, *phee*," he said, lifting his eyes to the sad ones of the Thai aristocrat. "I spoke rashly." Licking his lips, he sought words to convey the urgency of the matter. "But Gaspar mistreats women. Even if he wasn't involved in abducting and selling unwilling women, he abuses the ones in his own home."

"His bed slaves." Sarathoon nodded.

The women Gaspar kept inside his own home—Kulap, Nan, Mi, and the ones who had come before them—had all been legal acquisitions. Even if he'd skirted the law in his treatment of the women, he'd had the proper documents for each and every one. Not so for the peasant women he and Affonso Sales had been partners in rounding up and selling outside the country. Gaspar's legitimate business activities had provided excellent cover for the unspeakable ones he conducted in the shadows.

Clearing his throat, Harrison forced the fresh memory of those desperate women from his mind. They were safe now; Lamai wasn't. "As if that weren't bad enough—and it is—Gaspar is particularly angry at Lamai for her part in freeing those slaves from his control. If he has her, it won't just be ..." His breath stuttered in his throat. "He won't merely tamper with her. That's why we must go immediately. This very moment."

Sighing, Sarathoon crouched in front of Harrison's chair and patted his hands. "Believe me, Harrison, I understand. And I will help you. But this is Siam, and rich *farangs* like Gaspar D'Cruz must be handled the right way, if you hope to see justice for Khun Lamai."

"What's the right way?" he asked, leery of any course that did not entail immediate action.

"The raid in Ayutthaya and the evidence found there proved your information was good, yes?"

"Yes ..." Where was the older man going with this? There wasn't nearly enough sallying forth with extreme prejudice in this dialogue for Harrison's liking.

"Well," Sarathoon continued, nodding and patting Harrison's hands like a kindly father, "even now, that evidence is being disclosed to the authorities. I should be reporting our findings to my superior at the ministry of commerce right now, in fact. Very soon, there will be a writ of search and seizure issued against Gaspar D'Cruz. At that time, the full force of the Thai government will move against him, as it did against his partner, Affonso Sales. If Khun Lamai is in Gaspar's house—"

"She is, God damn you."

"—then she will be found and brought to safety."

Only when a dull pain throbbed in his jaw did Harrison realize his molars were clenched together to the point of cracking. "How long is *very soon?*"

"Tomorrow morning, I'd imagine. No more than a day or two. You saw how quickly they moved on Affonso."

"A day or two?" Harrison bolted out of the chair and strode for the door. "Unacceptable." If the authorities couldn't get an innocent woman out of harm's way any sooner than a day or longer, then Harrison would damn well do it himself.

"Do you want to see Gaspar go free?" Sarathoon's sharp words halted Harrison. He turned to regard the older man, now pushing to his own feet with some degree of struggle and popping of joints. "Everything must be done properly, Harrison, or the whole case could fall to pieces."

A few steps brought him nose-to-nose with Sarathoon. "How?" he challenged. "We have Affonso's confession. The barn full of women abducted from their villages. The shipping manifest—" Acid rose in his throat. Damn it all, this wasn't even the first stock of women who had been rounded up to be shipped and sold to the highest bidders. *Livestock*, Gaspar had called them euphemistically to conceal his true purpose. *Cattle*.

Sarathoon gave his arms a friendly squeeze. "Everything rides on technicalities, my rash young friend. The Portuguese have the strongest diplomatic and economic ties to the kingdom of any European nation, and the crown is keen to maintain those good relations. That's why *farangs* are given such leeway. The Portuguese embassy is bound to involve itself in a case of this magnitude. Any hint of impropriety on our part will call the legitimacy of the investigation into question."

"... and jeopardize relations with the West," Harrison concluded. He pressed the heels of his hands to his eyes. He couldn't believe the welfare of the love of his life had become a matter of international politics.

Suddenly, more intensely than he had since washing up on this far-flung shore, he longed for his friends, the Honorables. Once, what now felt like a millennium ago, Harrison, Brandon, Henry, Norman, and Sheri—armed with Harrison's brace of pistols and a motley assortment of surgical knives—had rescued a woman abducted by a crazed grave robber. The woman in question was Brandon Dewhurst's love. That was all the rest of them needed to know to answer his call. Then, as now, Harrison had deeply felt the outrage of knowing a person was being held against her will. But Brandon's anguish had been even more compelling, and Harrison had done all within his power to restore his friend's love to him. They all had.

What he wouldn't do to have those fine men with him now. There would be no talk of writs or diplomatic relations, just steely resolve and a scramble for improvised armaments.

But the Honorables were far away—nine months by sea away.

"I'll wait," he moaned, hating himself for saying the words, but unable to find a way around them.

Oh, he didn't give a tinker's damn about Siam's economic relations with Europe. He would burn every trade agreement and dance a jig on the ashes if doing so could secure Lamai's safety. But he couldn't so blithely ignore the women Gaspar and Affonso were responsible for abducting and illegally selling. Lamai wouldn't thank him for putting his gnawing need to have her back above obtaining justice for Nan, Mi, Kulap, and all those women whose names he didn't know. She would want him to wait.

Sarathoon embraced him, placed a paternal kiss on his cheek. "This is the right thing to do, my friend." He slapped Harrison's back twice, then turned to his wife. "Forgive the disruption, my lotus blossom. Please, continue with your day."

They decamped to the study, where Sarathoon quickly penned notes to the ministers of police and commerce, explaining the dire turn in events and begging haste in issuing the writ of search and seizure. Then they settled into the courtyard, where Sarathoon contentedly puffed on his pipe while Harrison metaphorically climbed the walls.

After an hour and a half of pacing, he could take no more.

"I'm going," he announced.

Sarathoon clucked his tongue. "Don't. It won't be much longer now."

But Harrison was already shaking his head, etching the air with an arc of denial. "I can't stand not knowing whether she's in danger, or hurting, or—" He swiped a palm down his face. He hadn't shaved in nearly a week. His whiskers were thick, on their way to reverting him to the scraggly castaway he'd been when he first met Lamai.

"I promise I'll just watch, all right?" he offered. "I'll try to wait for the police. But if she needs me ..."

Sarathoon chuffed smoke through his nostrils. "Very well, my impetuous friend, be off with you. Frankly, I'm surprised you waited this long. Please let me know when Khun Lamai is safe. *Bon courage.*"

• • •

There was no such thing as getting someplace in a hurry in Bangkok. Transportation options were: one's own feet, canal or river boat, plodding, mushy-footed elephants, carts drawn by equally unambitious oxen, or sedan chair. At the moment, jogging through pedestrian-clogged marketplaces and darting across canal bridges, Harrison was in perfect sympathy with the Bard's King Richard III.

"My kingdom for a horse," he wheezed, feeling the full effect of the day's stifling heat. What he wouldn't give for a sure-footed mount to gallop through the streets. He spared a glance for a lone gray cloud drifting nonthreateningly across the sky. The summer deluge was but a distant memory. Siam's dry season was technically cooler than the rainy season, but one would only say so if one possessed a perverse sense of humor. No part of this November day in any way resembled the season known to milder climes as "autumn." A fat drop of stinging sweat fell into his eye. Harrison scrubbed it with a fist and kept going.

At the mouth of the alleyway beside Gaspar's house, a four-foot monitor lizard lazed in the sun. The beast lifted its head at Harrison's approach and hissed, showing its needle-sharp teeth.

"I've got fangs, too, you pego-faced bugger." Baring his teeth, snarling and waving his arms like a madman, Harrison charged. The giant lizard skittered back, then darted beneath the nearest shrub, disappearing in the undergrowth.

Inside the familiar back portion of the property, he crept along the kitchen wall, keeping a wary eye on the house. A second-floor window opened. Harrison ducked behind an upended wash tub. Peeking around, he exhaled relief at the sight of a maid shaking a rug. When the servant had pulled the rug back inside and closed the shutter, Harrison broke for the stable, sprinting across the open lawn.

Planting a hand on the paddock fence, he vaulted over the rail, scarcely slowing his race. The large door stood wide open, as it usually did to permit the elephants to move from interior to exterior as they pleased. He bolted through the opening, plunging into the comparative darkness of the stable, and slammed straight into Panit.

Without visual confirmation, he recognized the *mahout* by the distinct *eau du éléphant* he knocked off the man's skin—an aromatic cloud of dust, heat, straw, and grassy dung. The small, lean fellow rolled with the collision and regained his feet while Harrison was still seeing stars from the impact of the man's stony cranium with his nose.

"*Aaargh,*" he moaned, clapping his hands to his face. "Christ, I think it's broken."

"Khun Harrison! So happy to see you, *phee.*" Panit extended a hand to help the large Englishman to his feet. They went deeper into the stable, where the slant of afternoon light turned dust motes into glittering ornaments suspended in midair.

Swiping his sore nose with the back of his wrist, Harrison came straight to the point. "Is Lamai here?"

"Yes, yes." Tilda and Wan Pen moseyed over. The *mahout* patted Wan Pen's trunk. "Poor girl knows Lamai is inside the house. She's been calling for her to come out and visit, and doesn't understand why she can't."

Can't? That sounded bad. "What's going on in there, Panit?"

"Very bad, *phee*, very bad. Khun Gaspar told Kulap, who told a maid, who—"

"Gossip mill. Understood. What, exactly, did Gaspar say?"

"That Lamai must be broken to obedience."

Broken? The dreadful implications of the word tumbled through his mind. Harrison didn't suppose Gaspar meant to break Lamai with the same gentle methods of teaching and persuasion Panit used to train Wan Pen. Dread coursed down his spine and slithered into his gut.

"He won't let her outside," Panit continued, "because she'll try to run away again."

Damn right, she will. Despite his new fears, Harrison felt a fierce rush of pride. His Lamai was a fighter.

"Oh, why did she come back?" Panit moaned, twisting his hands. His walnut-dark face was etched with such woe. "She'd gotten away, Khun Harrison. What possessed the girl to come back here and steal Kulap?"

Taken aback by that assertion, Harrison's jaw dropped. "She wouldn't. Sarathoon had already promised to help Kulap. What gave you that idea?"

"Mmmmm," Panit hummed, looking at him askance.

Harrison huffed. "Do you know where in the house she's being kept?"

Panit shook his head. "I haven't seen her since day before yesterday. She was already here when I brought Khun Gaspar home, I think. I didn't know she was here. I'd just gotten Goui cooled down, when here was Lamai running out the back door. She didn't make it very far." He crossed his arms across his bare midriff. "All I know is what's come from Kulap, but *she* isn't let outside, either. The master hasn't come out for days." The *mahout* lifted troubled eyes. "You need to take them away, Khun Harrison. You need to take them both."

"That's why I'm here."

The Thai man blew out his cheeks. Nodded. "How can I help?"

Harrison clapped him on the shoulder in wordless thanks. "May I lie low here in the stable? I'm expecting some company ..." Briefly, he filled the other man in on the expected police action. Brimming with enthusiasm, Panit leaned forward to whisper conspiratorially, "This is excellent, Khun Harrison! I'll be lookout and bring them here."

He scuttled off. Through a knothole in the plank wall, Harrison watched him cross the yard to the alley gate. Slinking to the front of the stable, Harrison hung back in the shadow and examined the house. No signs of life. He watched for half an hour. Every instinct screamed to rush inside and find Lamai, but he promised he'd wait for the police. If he could just get a glimpse of her, know that she was safe ...

Motion in the corner of his eye. Panit, crouching in the scarcely-ajar alley gate, waving him over. An oily feeling rolled through Harrison as he stepped into the open and hastily reversed his initial covert approach. This was pressing his luck too much; he would be spotted. If not on this pass then the next. He couldn't foul this up.

A loud clatter in the kitchen. Shouting voices. Harrison dove for the gate as if leaping clear of a mortar strike.

Another graceless landing. Shoving himself to hands and knees, he spit out a clump of packed alley dirt, which was, in fact, primarily comprised of elephant dung. He wished he didn't know that.

"Look, *phee*, the police are here." Panit hooked a hand under Harrison's armpit and helped him up.

Brushing off his palms, Harrison was surprised to see a familiar face leading the group of officers. "Khun Jettrin." He inclined his head to the captain.

The policeman returned the nod. "Khun Harrison. Pleased to see you again, though I wish the circumstances were better." At the Englishman's continued bemusement, he snorted a laugh. "Seasoned guardsmen know when they're being bamboozled by the locals. I wondered, the other night, why not just the servants —" his sharp gaze cut to Panit "– but an educated woman and another *farang*, too, would go to the trouble of covering the escape of a Burmese slave girl."

Panit inched toward the gate, as if to make a break for it at the first sign he might be in trouble for lying to the police.

Harrison's face turned to stone. "I'm afraid you're mistaken, *phee*. There was no—"

Jettrin waved a dismissive hand. "You had good reason, if the rumors I dug up about Gaspar D'Cruz and his female slaves are true."

"They are."

The officer shook his head, made a phlegmy sound of disgust. "Word came from the ministry, not an hour ago. Big arrest of a rich *farang*. We're to watch the house, make sure he doesn't get away before the writ arrives."

A stone landed in Harrison's stomach. "*More* waiting? Jesus Barnaby Christ!" Hands on hips, he swiveled, paced to the dead end of the alley and back again. And did it again. And again.

This waiting was maddening. Lamai needed him. He could sense her on the other side of those stuccoed walls, afraid, and he was here—*right here*—not doing anything about it.

Panit went back into the property and returned a few minutes later with a cup, which he handed to Harrison. "Drink," he instructed. "Cook says you have to keep your strength up."

He felt a pulse of dismay at Panit spreading word of Harrison's presence, but then he remembered the hard words that worthy woman had had for her employer. Cook was on his side. He tipped back the cup, swallowed a mouthful of coconut water. The taste always reminded him of his first days in Siam, when he was alone and destitute and dying. Every step of the way, he'd been welcomed and helped by good-hearted people—Wirat and the other monks of Wat Wihan; the servants who helped him learn Thai; Sarathoon. And Lamai. Lamai most of all. She had granted him the gift of love. The all-encompassing sort, given and received, felt and expressed in the heart and with words and with the body. She'd shown him ways of framing his past so that it no longer consumed his present and cast a shadow across his future. Harrison was more himself now than he had been since he was twelve years old. Lamai had given him that.

"I'll wait," he said again. Disliking the words still, but resolved to follow the course that allowed for the most complete resolution.

Two guardsmen returned to the *soi* to patrol the street, sauntering past Gaspar's house at a leisurely pace, hands slouched across the pommels of the short spear each wore at his left hip. Just a couple of police on their usual rounds.

Panit returned to the stable. He had more freedom of movement than anyone, but Jettrin cautioned that too much unusual activity would arouse suspicion. Cook, eager to contribute to the cause, allowed one guard to observe the house from inside the kitchen.

Harrison, along with Jettrin and the remaining two guards, waited in the alley. After a while, the guardsmen crouched and played a dice game on the ground. The same coins passed back and forth as one man won, then lost the next two games before his luck returned.

The sun went down, and still there was no writ. Harrison's eyes bored into the upper-story windows he could see from his angle on the ground, willing the shutters with their stripes of lamplight cutting through the slats to open, to grant him a vision of Lamai.

They remained firmly closed.

Finally, as full dark settled over Bangkok like a shawl across the shoulders of a thin-blooded crone, he heard the snuffling of an approaching elephant, a *mahout* instructing his charge, "*Leo kwa.*" The animal, outfitted with a smart *yaeng*, turning into Gaspar's entrance.

The writ. Thank God.

"You should meet them," Harrison told Jettrin, giving the captain's shoulder a nudge. "They'll need you and your men to come in, make the arrest. Unless we're taking up positions at the rear …" He cast a sideways glance through the crack between the halves of the back gate.

"That's not the writ," Jettrin said. "It'll come by a courier on foot, not an elephant."

"*WHAT?!?*" That did it. All the strain of the day, all the anxiousness held at bay through long hours of waiting, it all came crashing down at once. "That is it," he hissed. Jabbing a finger in Jettrin's face, knowing it was a gross breach of Siamese etiquette and doing it anyway, he railed against bureaucratic inefficiency and the crime against humanity that was paperwork. "While we're skinking around in a shit-strewn alley, waiting for your sacred writ to pass down from on high, an innocent woman—two innocent women—are in there. *Suffering.* You can go on waiting if you like, but I'm not waiting any longer." The wrathful finger swiveled to the house. "I'm going to get my wife, and if you don't like it, you can …" He concluded the sentiment with a colorful English phrase that denoted a physical impossibility.

Then he stomped through the back gate. Now that it was night, there was little danger of being spotted by the mansion's inmates. Fifteen feet from the back wall, the sound of multiple male voices reached his ears. Though he couldn't make out the words, he discerned the cadence of Gaspar's native Portuguese.

Ah ha! Gaspar had company—the arrival on elephant. He and his guest would be occupied with supper, giving Harrison a window of opportunity to sneak in, get the women, and make their escape.

He dropped to hands and knees and crawled the remainder of the distance, ignoring the jab of splinters in his palms as he crept over the mulched border lining the rear of the house. The dining room shutters, a row of three pairs, were all closed, except for one panel on the far right, which was cracked to encourage air circulation; that room quickly grew stuffy when filled with people, hot food, and burning lights.

Slowly rising, fingertips scaling the wall hand-over-hand, he held his breath as his eyes lifted above the window sill. The air *whooshed* from his lungs.

Empty. The men were not in the dining room.

For their voices to be coming out the back, though, they had to be in the only other public room on the rear of the house, the salon.

Apprehension stole through Harrison's limbs, making them stiff and awkward as he resumed his crawl along the foundation.

They're having a drink, he told himself. *Just an apéritif before supper. It doesn't mean—*

But it did. He felt in his bones that it meant something. Still, it was a shocking blow to see two women in European-style dresses kneeling before three men, Gaspar and two other *farangs* Harrison didn't recognize.

At first, he didn't bother listening to the men; they weren't even looking at the women. Instead, his attention was all for Lamai. A hasty scan of her left profile didn't reveal any evidence of trauma. Though her eyes were demurely downcast, her mouth was pursed in a stubborn pout. Her bare arm and left hand, resting lightly on her thigh, also seemed hale and unharmed. That didn't mean she didn't harbor hurts elsewhere—even ones that mightn't show at all. Still, there she was. Alive and relatively well, gumption intact. His soul sighed in relief as he drank up the sight of her.

"… know about selling locally," Gaspar was saying. His voice was the salesman's drone, with a slight musical intonation that aimed to entice even as he held himself aloof. "Prior herds have gone to Japan and to Arabia. The current pack is meant for Lisbon." The merchant took a long sip of his drink and turned an uninterested, almost sleepy, gaze toward the window. Harrison ducked his head.

"Unjust!" declared one of the guests. "Why send your fair beauties to the mother country, when your compatriots here are clamoring to buy your goods?"

"Clamoring?" Gaspar's voice rang with false incredulity. "I don't know if I'd say that, *senhor*. Certainly, there's been interest expressed here and there, but … well, I just haven't decided. Call it patriotism, if you like, but I feel a strong pull of generosity, a desire to share with our friends at home the bounty we've enjoyed here."

A long pause.

Harrison's forehead rested on the wall. The conversation in the salon—couched as it was in genteel tones and euphemisms—was the foulest he'd ever had the misfortune to overhear. Anger pulsed through his head, stiffened his neck to the point of aching. His only consolation was knowing—as Gaspar did not yet know—that his so-called *herd* of captives had already been discovered, the women moved to safety.

A rustle in the underbrush alerted him to another's approach. It was Jettrin, slithering on his belly, propelling himself forward with elbows and feet. His crawl reminded Harrison of a monitor lizard, low to the ground and undulating. The police captain had abandoned his tall hat. His short spear dragged at his side, plowing up little runnels in the grass.

When he'd pulled to a squat, Harrison eyed him hopefully. "The writ?" he barely breathed.

The captain shook his head once, his expression sympathetic.

Harrison squeezed shut his eyes, crumbling inside, struggling against feelings of betrayal such as he'd felt as a boy, when his family had done nothing to rescue their abused son and brother.

"What price do you mean to have for them?" asked one of the men in the salon. "Surely, it would be more profitable to sell here first. You might not fetch as high a premium as our *irmãos* back home would pay for an exotic import, but you'll save yourself the cost of shipping."

Such bland pragmatism regarding the illegal trade of human beings. Harrison's blood boiled. Jettrin had an ear cocked, an inquisitive crease in his brow. *He doesn't understand,* Harrison realized. *He doesn't know Portuguese.* He envied the man's ignorance, wished he'd never bothered to learn the language, either.

"They're discussing shipping and buying slaves," Harrison explained in a whisper. "But not the usual slaves. Bed slaves. And they didn't sell themselves, they were taken—"

Jettrin cut him off with a sharp gesture. "I know," he hissed. The captain lifted his head, peeked into the room, ducked down again. "Khun Lamai," he whispered, "your betrothed, she's the one in the green?" Harrison nodded. Jettrin tutted softly. "Shame he's got her fettered like a mad bull elephant."

Harrison's eyes flew wide. He bolted up, remembering just in time not to expose his entire face. Blood thundering behind his eardrums, his eyes skittered to Lamai. Her hands, as he'd seen before, were fine. Free. But her ankles … She had shifted her posture, pulling the hem of her leaf-green silk frock high up on her ankles, revealing a thick iron band around each slender limb, and a chain between them.

No, he mouthed, forcing his throat shut to stifle the groan of despair that pushed up from his chest. What had that beast done in his bid to *break her to obedience*?

"... interesting point." Gaspar moved to the women, each step an indolent swing of his leg. He hadn't a care in the world. Harrison had never hated a person more. The impotent rage he'd felt for Eliza Meyler was but a puddle to the ocean of fury that flooded every fiber of Harrison's being. The merchant ran a palm over Kulap's head, patting her like a faithful hound. Harrison looked closely at the younger girl for the first time. She'd lost flesh from her pretty, plump cheeks. Her left hand was swaddled in a bandage.

"I suppose," Gaspar said, dragging a finger down Lamai's neck—her passivity when Gaspar touched her added another layer to Harrison's distress, "I might be induced to sell locally. To a select few gentlemen, that is."

The other men chuckled, as if he'd made a fine jest. "Naturally. I, myself, would be willing to pay a handsome sum." He named an exorbitant figure. Gaspar's hand closed around Lamai's shoulder. His lips curved in a satisfied smile.

"Me, too," said the other. Licking his lips and darting a look at his companion, that one ventured, "I want to sample first, before I agree to buy." He shifted his weight towards Kulap.

The other buyer, too, sent a lecherous look to the women on the floor.

Gaspar's nostrils flared. "Naturally. Discerning gentlemen such as yourself must know they are getting quality goods. Alas, I've only these two here at the moment, and there are three of us. I trust you don't mind sharing?"

The gathering's banal atmosphere dissipated, like dew burning off in the morning sun. No longer were they three businessmen working out the tedious details of a deal, but a trio of predators bent on the kill.

To hell with the ministry of police. This ended now. Harrison snatched Jettrin's arm. "They're about to rape the women."

Jettrin's jaw clenched. He nodded once, as if making a decision. "Let's go."

Harrison was on his feet before the words left the captain's lips. He didn't care whether or not the officer accompanied him. Lamai needed him. Now. Getting to her was the only thing that mattered.

• • •

"I trust you don't mind sharing."

Lamai's stomach was cold, her innards going to water. Her two days of avoiding the fate of a bed slave—thanks to Gaspar's distaste for her falsely-reported menses—were over. Soon after signing the hateful contract, she'd rashly attempted escape. For her sins, she'd been chained, then forced to watch Kulap take a beating in punishment for Lamai's misdeed.

Two days of scheming. Refusing to eat, then stuffing herself so she'd have the strength to fight when the time came. Two days of being locked in her room, seeing no one but Kulap, who delivered her food.

Poor Kulap. The girl who had once preened in her status as the master's favored bed slave now trembled at Lamai's side. A fat tear dripped off the end of her nose.

"I've no quarrel with sharing," said one of the Portuguese buyers, "but I want a go at the ugly one first. The other one looks a little … broken for my taste." His dark eyes gleamed. His chest puffed like a cock as he strutted to Lamai and ran his palm over her unscarred cheek.

Lamai had been on her knees before *farangs* in the past, when Gaspar wanted to punish her or use her as a spy. But he'd always pulled back at the last, never permitting any of his friends to actually use her. He wasn't going to stop them this time.

The other one crossed to Kulap, grabbed her arm, and hauled her to her feet. The girl cried out.

"Kulap!" Lamai gasped.

She'd taken her eye off the man in front of her for but a second, but it was long enough for him to crouch and thrust a hand at her chest. Instinctively, Lamai shoved, knocking him onto his rump. Jumping to her feet, she broke into a sprint—

And went sprawling, knocking an antique Chinese urn to the floor as she fell. The fetters. She'd forgotten the blasted chains on her ankles.

"Bitch!" Gaspar wrenched her up by the wrist. "How dare you strike my guest, you ungrateful little half-blood whore!"

A roar rent the air as Harrison burst into the salon with a policeman, Jettrin, at his side.

The *farang* with Kulap shoved her into Harrison; Harrison caught the girl, but stumbled. Jettrin charged that fellow, hand on his spear. He was too slow in drawing it; the *farang* felled him with a fist to the guard's jaw, then made a lunge for the weapon.

Harrison, meanwhile, scrambled to recover his footing. Setting Kulap aside, he tackled the man before he could grab the spear.

Taking advantage of the pandemonium, Lamai yanked free of Gaspar's grasp. Shuffling as fast as her chain would permit, Lamai grabbed bronze figurine of a *naga*, a mythical river serpent, from a nearby side table. "Harrison," she yelled, and threw the sinuous creature. It tumbled through the air, end-over-end. Her Englishman's hand snapped up, snatched the bronze, and brought it down on his rival's temple with a heavy *thud*.

The man Lamai had pushed over not a minute ago was still on the floor, gaping at the chaos in wide-eyed disbelief. When Harrison landed the blow on his friend, the man yelped and covered his head with his arms.

The police captain groaned. Distracted by the sound, Harrison glanced back at him.

Gaspar made a run for it. Lamai lunged, but the chains did their work. She howled in outrage.

Harrison flowed to his feet, the police captain's spear in his hands. As Gaspar made to dart past, Harrison swung, catching Gaspar across the windpipe with the shaft of the spear. *Thwap.*

Gaspar stumbled, clutching his throat, then fell to his knees, wheezing. In an instant, Kulap fell on him, hands flying, clawing his face with her right hand, and battering him with the bandaged club of her left. Weakly, Gaspar attempted to fend off her blows, but Kulap was a woman possessed, screaming wordlessly, her nails digging bloody stripes in his skin.

Harrison hovered on his toes as if to intervene, but ultimately left Kulap to her revenge. Of them all, the young girl had perhaps suffered the most from Gaspar's cruelty.

Instead he came to Lamai and helped her to her feet, only to lift her off of them in a tight embrace. She clung to his shoulders, pressing her mouth to his neck just as he rained kisses onto her temple and cheek. Emotion welled, threatened to overtake her. Lightheaded with a conflation of terror and relief and joy, she pushed back.

"That was a bloody marvelous throw," he praised, setting her down.

"It was a bloody marvelous catch," she returned with a wobbly smile.

Rubbing his jaw and grumbling about missing the fun, Jettrin staggered to his feet. He took a long look at Kulap and Gaspar, then approached the *farang* still huddled on the floor. "You are under arrest, *phee*. If you attempt to flee, it will go very badly for you. Do you understand?" He gave the man a poke in the rib with his spear for emphasis.

The man screeched and blubbered, clasping his hands before him, promising to do whatever the kind officer asked if he would only please not tell his wife what had transpired here.

When Jettrin heard Lamai's translation of the Portuguese, he shook his head and sighed. "They never want the wife to know. Why don't they think of that before putting their little pink worms where they don't belong?" Taking advantage of the man's clasped hands, he pulled a length of silk cord from a pouch on his belt and quickly bound the miscreant's wrists together.

Kulap's fury had begun to burn itself out. Her face, contorted with rage, now collapsed, crumpling into a mask of grief. A sob tore free of her throat.

Lamai hurried to the girl, took her by the arms, and guided her to the couch. She sat beside Kulap and held her as the girl cried against her shoulder. Rocking gently, Lamai stroked Kulap's hair and made shushing sounds, like a mother soothing her child. She rested her scarred cheek on the top of Kulap's head and met Harrison's pained gaze. He wanted to help, she knew, but this was nothing he could defeat with a well-timed spear to the throat. In time, Kulap would heal, as Harrison had.

Gaspar, bleeding profusely and coughing, rolled side-to-side on his back like an inverted tortoise. Harrison placed a foot on the man's chest, pinning him in place while Jettrin tied the merchant's hands and ankles. Gaspar *might* have made a sound like *puuuuh*, as if all the air he'd managed to collect had been crushed out by something heavy, forcing him to gasp and wheeze all over again, but no one could really say for sure.

Just as Harrison and Jettrin finished securing the third prisoner, one of Jettrin's men burst into the room, triumphantly holding aloft a document bearing a large wax seal. "The writ!" he proclaimed.

An extremely official-looking personage in red robes and a yellow sash entered on the guard's heels, saw the state of the salon, and froze where he stood.

Lamai, Harrison, and Jettrin exchanged a look. The captain straightened and made *wai* to the newcomer. "Minister, sir! You're … here. Yourself."

Gaspar struggled against his bindings until he managed to sit up. "They entered my house without a writ! Savagely set upon me and my guests. See for yourself. I demand to be unbound at once. I'm being held without cause. I'll bring suit against the police! I have friends in the government—"

"The writ arrived five minutes ago," Harrison said. He came to stand beside Lamai, put his hand on her shoulder, and gave it a reassuring squeeze.

"That's right," Lamai said, her arms snugging tighter around Kulap's shoulders. "Khun Jettrin had the writ in hand when he entered the salon five minutes ago."

Jettrin's eyes twinkled. "Of course I did! I would never execute a search and seizure without a writ."

Gaspar squawked. "Why, you charlatans! Every one of you a bold-faced liar. Minister, you must dismiss this rogue from your force. And as for that fellow over there, Harrison Dyer, why, he should be arrested for trespass. And her, Lamai, for attempted theft of my property."

The Minister of Police attended Gaspar's tirade. He raised an imperious brow, turned a sharp eye on Harrison, and then Lamai.

Her breath caught in her throat. With a single word, the government official could free Gaspar and undo everything Lamai and Harrison had done. *Please*, she silently begged the minister. *Please*.

The official looked back to the bound Portuguese man and bowed. "I regret to inform you, you are mistaken, Khun Gaspar. I, along with the writ, arrived five minutes ago. Everything was executed most properly."

• • •

While the police, led by Jettrin, retrieved incriminating documents from Gaspar's desk and searched the house for any additional evidence, Harrison was busy assuring himself of Lamai's well-being.

"I'm fine," she told him for the tenth time. "My ankles just hurt a little." She waggled her feet up and down, working out the cramps from her two days in fetters. Wide, red bands marked her skin where the iron cuffs had chafed. It was just as well Gaspar had already been taken away. If he were still here, Harrison might well dismember the villain.

His palms kept passing over Lamai's face and arms. He brought her hands to his mouth and kissed them, front and back. Then he tipped up her chin and kissed her soft lips, the comfort of it working like a balm on his battered nerves. He wanted to haul her into his lap and hold her tight, but Kulap had fallen asleep with her head on Lamai's thighs. It would be heartless to usurp the girl, though a selfish portion of Harrison wanted to do just that.

"I'm sorry I wasn't here, sweetheart," he said—not for the tenth time, only the fourth or fifth.

Lamai gave him a tired smile. The scars seemed to pull a little harder on her eye and mouth. Her thumb traced the curve of his lip, her eyes following, as if fascinated. "It's not your fault Affonso escaped and had to be hunted down again, *farang*. I'm so proud of you for saving all those women. When I heard Gaspar and those men talking tonight, I realized what he was doing. So, he and Affonso, the business they had to discuss that day in Ayutthaya, while we were at the festival …?"

A shadow crossed her face. "Don't do that," he said. "I've spent far too many years reliving events I can't change. We didn't know—God knows we'd have done something if we had."

She tilted her head, pulled his brow down to touch hers. "Thank you." Her fingers came to his nape, lightly caressing. Longing tugged at his gut.

"We missed the boat," she said, her voice glum. "I'm sorry for that, too. If I hadn't been so foolish, you would be on your way home."

Harrison's heart, still clumsy at this loving business, tipped over in his chest, spilling a great deal of warmth and happiness and, God, such *feeling*.

"Lamai," he moaned. Scooping an arm beneath her legs and around her back, he gently extracted her from Kulap. His turn. The girl snored on. He pulled Lamai onto his lap and crushed her to his chest, laughing and crying and feeling like a deranged man—an utterly blissful idiot. "Sweetheart," he said against her ear, "I *am* home. I've been home for a long time now."

Turning her head, Lamai kissed him, lips parting the moment they touched. Their tongues fondled one another, sliding and teasing and stoking heat. His hand came to her hip, desperate to turn her around to straddle him. He needed to sink into her, to have the primal reassurance that came from joining his body with hers. Lamai moaned, her hand bunching in the shirt at his waist, tugging.

Kulap made a fretful sound, and Lamai pulled away, biting her lip and casting a coquettish look at him from beneath her lashes.

Harrison groaned. How soon could he get her to bed?

Then a thought struck him, and he mentally kicked himself for a fool. There were other reasons they'd planned to go to England, other reasons she had for being sad about missing the ship. "I only cared about going to England to get you away from Gaspar, and to help you find your father. Gaspar's the court's problem now, but your father—"

She touched a finger to his lips. "If he wants me, he'll come, and I'll welcome him. But I'm not letting that part of my past control me anymore. You helped me learn to move on."

He was humbled by her words. How could they be true, when she was the one who'd done so much to teach him?

Maybe he thought, wonderingly, maybe they really had helped and taught each other. Alone, each of them had been entangled by scars from the past, but together … together they were free.

"I love you, my heart," she said, bringing her lips to his brow. "I love who we are together."

Joy poured through him in a torrent, all the happiness he hadn't had for so many years, a river swollen by an inundation of love. "And I love you, Lamai. More than I ever knew it was possible for me to love."

Their mouths came together again and it was rapture, ecstasy, a perfect melding of hearts. This time, her knee hitched over his lap. Her hands came to his shoulders and she pressed against him, rocking into his hardening length. Aware of the slumbering young woman nearby, Harrison stood up. Lamai's legs hugged his waist, her heels snug at the small of his back.

With one hand on her bottom, the other on her back, he went upstairs. Lamai kissed his neck, his jaw. Her black hair tickled his nose and filled his head with the heady scent of woman. His woman.

He couldn't wait long enough even to get to his bed. Hers was nearer. Panting, tugging at the buttons on her back, he carried her into her room.

Someone yelped.

Lamai gasped.

Harrison shouted, "Christ!"

Wheeling around, he found Jettrin standing beside the wall, clutching a book to his chest and looking decidedly *caught out.* Harrison's trunk, the one Sheri had given him, was on the floor, open.

The captain hastily composed himself. Cleared his throat. "Khun Harrison. Khun Lamai. I think we're all done here." He turned to go, the volume of erotic illustrations tucked under his arm.

"Find anything interesting?" Harrison called after him.

"Just a few things I need to examine." Ears flaming, the officer fled, calling out to round up his men.

Alone at last. Harrison fell back on the bed, Lamai's body above him, and a whole world of love at their feet.

• • •

The Hon. Henry De Vere
De Vere and Sons Shipping Company
London, England

Dear Henry,

Through a series of rather mundane events, I have come into possession of a warehouse of goods confiscated by the Siamese government from their previous owner, as well as a house, two elephants, a goat, and a license from the crown to operate as an independent merchant of imports and exports within the kingdom.

I trust the cargo of the ship that carries this letter will meet with your satisfaction. Of particular interest is a selection of fine Japanese lacquerware. There are some Siamese parasols that I'm confident will be snapped up by ladies of fashion. Mind that the spices are kept dry in the London warehouse. The cardamom alone is worth a princely sum. Nothing can recompense for the souls that perished with *Brizo's Woe*, but I believe the value of these goods will, at least, offset the financial calamity of losing that fine ship. I will send another cargo in six months' time. Please be so good as to assemble a cargo of English wares for the return of this ship. The kingdom of Siam is eager to connect with the western world, and those goods our countrymen craft with such distinction—silver, leather, tea services, etc.—will do brisk trade here.

I have entrusted this letter, and this inaugural cargo, into the hands of my particular friend, Sarathoon. I hope you'll forgive my forwardness in offering him a position, but as he is a former official with the Siamese ministry of commerce, I can think of no better ambassador to deliver these goods and advise you in expansion of your concerns in the east. Frankly, he's too good for us. I believe he was won over by his own curiosity to see our little island, rather than any persuasive reasoning on my part. I know you will show him every hospitality and embrace his friendship as I have done.

Finally, a bit of personal news. I have married. Henry, I have married the most beautiful, marvelous woman who ever— Well, I hesitate to inundate you with a deluge of superlatives. Suffice it to say, they all apply. Lamai is to me what your wife is to you. I think that says it all.

Please give my warmest regards to our friends. You all are often in my thoughts.

Be happy and well, Henry. I am. At last, I am.

Yours in friendship,

Harrison

The Hon. Harrison Dyer

De Vere and Sons Shipping Company

Bangkok, Siam

Epilogue

It was that most treasured English rarity: a glorious summer day. Beams of white-gold sunlight showered through boughs of oaks and elms, and highlighted a fat black-and-white cow grazing on tender clover in a picturesque pasture. A gentle breeze swept around the traveling party and raced ahead down the lane, rustling the leaves and lifting the hair on Harrison's nape.

He shivered.

"I remembered the place as a good deal warmer."

His wife turned from her seat behind the elephant's ears, slanted a skeptical brow. "You've spent the last nine months arming me and the children to survive a Siberian expedition. After all that buildup, this mild weather is a bit of a letdown. I don't know what you're complaining about."

He flashed an unapologetic grin. "Perhaps I just want you to feel sorry for me and offer to warm me up."

Lamai rolled her eyes, but a smile tugged the left corner of her mouth. Awareness pulsed between them. Lamai had taken great pains with her appearance today. She wore a prim, high-collared blouse, short gray jacket with white trim, and a matching split skirt. A dainty straw hat perched atop hair that had been curled and coiffed and pinned until not a strand fell out of place. His fingers itched to plunge into the silken mass of inky locks, muss them up, and divest her of that costume.

The direction of his thoughts must have been obvious. "Don't distract me," Lamai lightly chided, returning her attention to driving. But he saw the flush on her cheek.

"*Eww!*" squealed a child.

Harrison's third-born—and only daughter thus far—Angela Waan, age four, scrambled up to stand on the seat beside him. "Tilda is *sick* again, Phoo! She'll get it on my *feet!*" The girl's slim fingers clasped his sleeve for balance.

"Your feet don't even touch the ground," the child's father pointed out. Nevertheless, he wrapped an arm about the dark-haired moppet and settled her onto his lap.

Lying on the floor of the carriage, Tilda looked as green around the gills as it was possible for a goat to look. During their long voyage, the now-aged goat had regained her sea legs with little difficulty, but returning to land had proved a trial for the beast.

"Phoo, are we almost there?" bellowed a boy from the second *yaeng.*

Harrison didn't need to turn to recognize the voice of his second child, Quincy Prem, who seemed to live by the credo that if he had something to say, everyone in a five-mile radius should hear it.

"Hush!" scolded Harrison Sumate. At seven, Harry took his responsibilities as eldest child very seriously. "Phoo *told you* not to shout."

"I hear you, too, Harry," Harrison called over his shoulder. But his words were already lost in the sounds of a fraternal squabble—swatting and squealing and small feet drumming the floor. The baby, Sarathoon Henry, started crying.

Harrison sighed.

Kulap, who had remained with Harrison and Lamai and was a much loved member of the family, jumped into the fray to settle the cranky travelers. "Both of you stop, or Panit will set you down and you'll have to walk the rest of the way."

Lamai, head cocked, asked over her shoulder, "Do you ever wish you were lost at sea again, *farang?*"

"Sometimes," Harrison admitted with a chuckle. "Just for a few hours."

"When we get there," she continued, "do you suppose we can disclaim them? Pretend we've never seen these urchins before in our lives?"

"Mèè, you wouldn't!" Angela protested, scandalized. "You love us better than anything."

Her mother laughed, silvery and bright, a sound that never failed to make Harrison's heart roll like that of an infatuated schoolboy.

He hugged his little girl and kissed the top of her head and breathed her baby scent. "Mèè does love you and your brothers more than anything in the world; you know she likes to tease."

"More than you?"

"I think we're all the same in her heart," he explained, resting his cheek against her shining locks. Angela plucked from the seat a painted wooden rabbit on wheels with a pull string—a treasure recently acquired in London, and rolled the toy up and down Harrison's arm. "In my heart, anyway, you and Harry and Quincy and Sarathoon and Kulap and Mèè, you're all one, great big heap of love. My family." His voice caught, but his daughter didn't notice. Just as well. A little girl didn't need to see her father become misty-eyed every time he considered how damned lucky he was. How impossibly, marvelously lucky.

Cupping her hand to his ear, Angela whispered, "I think Mèè really loves Wan Pen best."

Harrison laughed. "You might be right about that, poppet."

"Is this our turn?" Lamai called.

Harrison squinted, made out a familiar post and finial that marked the head of a drive. "That's it."

"Leo kwa," Lamai told her elephant.

Nerves buffeted Harrison's middle as Wan Pen, and Goui behind her, bore his family down the drive of Elmwood. He hadn't seen his friends in years. So much time had passed … would he recognize them? Would they recognize *him*? He'd exchanged letters with them all through the years but standing there in person … what would they have to say to one another?

The house came into view then. Elmwood, a rambling old place where Brandon and Lorna Dewhurst lived with their children and Lorna's brother, the young Lord Chorley. On the lawn in front of the house—children. So many, *many* children. "Good God, there must be twenty of them."

A few tykes played football with a man who towered over them by a mile. "Norman?" From this distance, his old friend looked just the same. And over there, holding a baby—

Just then, the herd of youngsters spotted the elephants trundling down the drive, and pandemonium erupted. Screeching and whooping like a Mongol horde. Parents were hard-pressed to contain their jubilant offspring until Wan Pen and Goui stopped in front of the house and knelt to deploy their passengers.

Then the mob descended, a veritable stampede of short pants and pigtails and so many little feet in half-boots. Angela clung to Harrison's neck, burying her face against him as the juvenile wave broke around them.

"Oh my god, Aubrey Zouche, get away from that animal's mouth. Come here at once, you scoundrel."

Sheri plucked an impish boy away from Goui, then turned to Harrison with that same old insolent smile. He extended his hand. "Well, Harrison?" They clasped forearms. And just like that, Harrison was home.

Sheri introduced his son to Angela, and the two scampered off just as the rest of the adults cut a path through the throng of offspring to surround Harrison and Lamai.

After the handshake from Sheri, there was one from Henry, who several years back had made him a full partner in his business—now known as De Vere and Dyer and Sons Shipping Company. Then Norman, whose large paw enveloped his. And finally Brandon, their host, clapped his shoulder and shook his hand.

"Welcome home, Harrison." There were faint smile lines around Brandon's eyes now, and the silver that used to frost his temples was now liberally scattered throughout his dark hair; but then, Harrison supposed, taking in the warm faces of his friends, they were all a little more creased and gray than they used to be, but the bonds of friendship were undiminished by time.

"Thank you for having us," he replied, then surprised Brandon—as well as himself—by pulling the other man into a brotherly embrace.

The ladies were there, too: Lorna, Claudia, Arcadia, and Elsa—four remarkable women, each of whom inspired the adoration and devotion of one of Harrison's friends. Hovering on the periphery, smiling eagerly, waiting for the old cronies to make their greetings so they, too, could descend upon him.

Before the feminine avalanche commenced, Harrison put his hand at the small of his wife's back. Glancing down, he caught the anxious tension in her eyes and gave her waist a reassuring squeeze. "Everyone, this is my wife, Lamai Hart Dyer. Sweetheart, these are the Honorables, whom you may have heard me mention from time to time."

One by one, the gentlemen stepped forward to greet Lamai. Sheri, that inveterate charmer, delivered a kiss to the back of her hand, which caused Lamai's cheeks to flood pink. The others comported themselves much more appropriately, bowing nicely and introducing their wives, until Henry's turn, when he wrapped Lamai in his arms. "Thank you for taking care of him for us,"

Harrison heard his friend and business partner murmur. "Thank you for saving him."

Lamai was more flustered than before, but pleased, too, Harrison could see. She regarded Henry shyly from beneath her lashes. Taking a few steps back, she gathered her composure, brought her hands together at her chest, and bowed, making *wai*. "*Sa wad dee ka*. I'm honored to know you all."

Lorna came forward again, peach blossoms blooming beneath the wash of freckles on her still youthful face, her riot of curls gilded by the sun. "You are most welcome at Elmwood, Mrs. Dyer. Please, make yourself at home." She took Lamai's hand. As if a signal had been given, the other ladies drew close around, incorporating Lamai into their circle. On a cloud of muslin and laughter, the ladies led Lamai away to an arrangement of lawn chairs, from which they could enjoy refreshments and a coze whilst keeping an eye on their boisterous children.

Harrison smiled. He known the Honorables and their families would provide a warm welcome and much-needed support. Some years back, they had helped him track Lamai's father to a grave in India, where he'd perished ten years prior…on his way back to Siam.

Peter Hart had had a wife and children in England, after all, but after Mrs. Hart died and the children were grown, it seems he'd decided to return to the family he'd left on the other side of the world. With Harrison's support, Lamai had written to her half-siblings, and two daughters had communicated a desire to make contact. It was primarily for this reason that their family had returned to England, though Harrison had sorely missed his friends these past years, and longed for their companionship. If Lamai's hoped-for relationship with her half-sisters did not flourish, she would need stalwart friends to fall back upon.

Speaking of … Harrison turned a circle, searching out his own four, but they had already melted into the group, making instant friends the way children do. Even Kulap had been relieved of baby Sarathoon; a girl child with honey hair and a sunny disposition—and the unmistakable look of Claudia—held the two-year-old's pudgy hand as he toddled over the grass.

"Your daughter?" Harrison inquired, nodding to the pair.

Henry nodded. "Opal, my eldest. I've five, all told."

Harrison let out a low whistle, then glanced to Brandon. "You?"

"Two."

"Just one for Elsa and me," Norman supplied.

"Then who's responsible for the rest of these infants?" Brow raised, Harrison cast an eye at Sheri.

The other man's ears pinked. Plucking his quizzing glass from his waistcoat, he twirled the handle in his fingers, a nervous tell stretching all the way back to their days at Oxford. "Seven of them are mine. And number eight is on the way."

The other three hooted, as if Sheri and Arcadia's fecundity was a familiar well of humor, but Harrison could only marvel that a man who had once cared for little beyond his own amusement had so wholly transformed into this pillar of familial zeal.

The fresh and glorious morning gave way to a warm and glorious afternoon, in which parents joined children for lawn bowling and cricket. Lamai and Panit took the English children for elephant rides, while Harrison's brood were much more interested in the ponies belonging to Brandon's and Henry's daughters.

Pausing for a drink of lemonade, Harrison's gaze swept the field filled with men and women and children. Brandon joined him at the refreshment table. Harrison pressed a drink into his friend's palm. Both of them watched their families for a few quiet moments.

"There were only five of us," Harrison mused at last. "Back then, in that dank Oxford tavern. Look what we've become."

He wasn't speaking of numbers, though the growth of their core group of friends into this extended family of choice of thirty-odd individuals was most impressive.

"Lucky devils, aren't we?" Brandon said, articulating Harrison's thoughts.

When Harrison looked upon these fine men and their fetching, strong spouses and their impossibly beautiful children, he saw threads of loyalty and love connecting each person with the others, a whole tangled, messy, web of it, in which each of them was lucky to be caught. More than a web, their bonds created a safety net, too, through which no precious child's hurts would slip, unnoticed or unacknowledged.

Lamai clambered down from Wan Pen for the last time that day. Tilda scampered while Panit divested the elephant of her *yaeng*, impatient for her friend to play.

"So," Brandon asked, as the elegant Thai lady in English attire made her way to her husband, "will your sojourn in England be one of short or long duration?"

Siam had been good to Harrison, had given him a place to heal and grow and love. He would never close the door on the possibility of returning there someday but he'd needed to come back to England, to share his whole, mended self with the people who had cared for him when he was broken. For now, he was utterly, finally, home.

"You know," Harrison said as he opened his arms for Lamai to step into them, "I think we'll stay for a while."

Acknowledgments

First and foremost, I must extend my gratitude to Darika Sarunyagate, without whose help this novel would not have been possible. Da, thank you for sharing your country with me, and for all of your research help. Thanks, too, to David, for his gracious hospitality, and also for having the smarts to marry such an incredible woman.

Thanks to Jana Igunma of the British Library for providing invaluable guidance for my research. Elephant Nature Park in Chiang Mai, Thailand gave me incredible hands-on experience with Asian elephants.

Special thanks to Tara Gelsomino, Julie Sturgeon, Jess Verdi, Joanne Soper-Cook, and the whole Crimson Romance crew for the editorial direction and friendship throughout the five books of this series. Thank you for embracing my vision and making my books so much better than they were when I handed them to you.

To all of my friends and family who have supported and encouraged me on my writing journey, you have my heartfelt appreciation. Michelle and Sarah, my special ladies, your friendship has carried me through more times than I could count. The Oasis, you're the best cheering squad a girl could ever hope for. My CR Sisters, thank you for your wit and commiseration. Mom, Dad, Amanda, Dave, Deb, Dylan, Alex, and Mira: I love you. Thank you for loving me back.

Finally, Jason … you are my partner and friend and my love and my pillar of fortitude. I couldn't do this without you. Thank you for believing in me. Also, you're a dork.

Glossary of Thai Terms

*Note: Thai words are correctly spelled in Thai script. There is no standardized Roman spelling of the Thai language, merely phonetic approximations.

BAHT – Thai unit of currency

FARANG – Term used for Europeans and North Americans

JAO AR-WART – Title given to the head monk of a Thai Buddhist monastery

KHUN – A general courtesy title of address that may be used in front of anyone's first name, male or female

KOB KHUN KA (f) or KOB KHUN KHAP (m) – Thank you

LEO KWA – Turn right

LEO SAI – Turn left

LUANG – Title of address given to a Thai Buddhist monk

MAHOUT – Elephant trainer and caretaker

MÈÈ – Mother

MUEANG THAI – A nation in Southeast Asia, formerly called Siam by westerners. Modern-day Thailand

PAI DAI – "Go ahead"

PANUNG – A large, rectangular garment worn on the lower body that can be draped, folded, and tied into a variety of styles

PHAR – Auntie, respectful term used in similar sense of "Miss" or "Madam"

PHEE –Big brother, respectful term used in similar sense of "Sir" or "Mister"

PHOO – Father

SA WAD DEE KA (f) or SA WAD DEE KHAP (m) – Hello

SOI – Road or street

SOM NAM NAA - "Serves you right" or "You got what you deserve"

WAI – A polite greeting consisting of holding hands together "prayer style" and bowing. The height of hands and depth of bow vary depending on the rank of the person one is addressing

YAENG – A passenger seat or carriage on an elephant's back

YOOD – "Stop"

Author's Note

I wonder ...

That magical little phrase has been the impetus behind every one of my stories. Following my own questions has led me to colorful characters and fascinating corners of Regency history, which I have been delighted to share with you.

Love Beyond Measure started this way: *I wonder what the British were up to in Siam during the Regency period?* In early 2015, as I prepared to visit family in Bangkok, this question kept nabbing my curiosity. Surely, I thought, the British Empire was doing *something* that would make an intriguing backdrop for a novel. I decided to find out, and devote part of my trip to on-the-ground research.

Much to my consternation, the answer to my question was *absolutely nothing.* The British governor of Hong Kong, Sir John Bowring, conducted the first official mission to Siam in 1855 to establish diplomatic and trade relations between Britain and Siam, far too late for my hero's ill-fated expedition. This proved to be an opportunity for my narrative, however, when I realized that without so much as an embassy to turn to for help, Harrison could be well and truly stranded in a strange land.

If Harrison was to meet any westerners in 1818 Siam, they would almost certainly be Portuguese. As depicted in the novel, Portugal had a strong economic presence in Siam as early as the fifteenth century, and a greater expat population than any other European nation. Ruins of the Portuguese quarter in Ayutthaya still remain, and the Bangkok National Museum houses a fascinating collection of artifacts recovered from the site. I have taken the artistic license of maintaining a small community there; in truth, the Portuguese quarter was entirely abandoned following the Burmese sack of Ayutthaya. Most of its inhabitants moved downriver to the new royal city of Bangkok. A small community descended from those Ayutthaya-era Portuguese merchants still lives in Thailand.

A note on the usage of *Siam*, *Thai*, etc.: *Siam* is an exonym given by outsiders to the Kingdom of Mueang Thai. Natives of that land have historically referred to themselves and their language as *Thai*, never *Siamese*. I have endeavored to maintain that designation as much as possible, relegating the usage of *Siam* and *Siamese* to non-Thai characters.

On elephants: Asian elephants are smaller than their African counterparts (though still enormous!). They are intelligent, gentle creatures with rich emotional lives. The nanny-baby relationship between Goui and Wan Pen is a common one in elephant herds. Even when a young elephant's mother is present, a nanny elephant steps up to help tend the little one. In Thailand, elephants and people have lived and worked together for many centuries. Unfortunately, depletion of their forest habitat and exploitation by unscrupulous entrepreneurs have landed the Asian elephant on the endangered species list. If you find yourself in Thailand and wish to meet these amazing creatures, please give your business to groups that place the elephants' welfare above tourist entertainment. I highly recommend Elephant Nature Park in Chiang Mai, Thailand, a magnificent rescue and sanctuary.

Stepping so very far away from the familiar grounds of Regency England was quite the challenge. I was fortunate to have the assistance of my Thai sister-in-law, who set me straight on a number of matters. Without her translation of various research materials, this book would undoubtedly have numerous, glaring errors. I am indebted to her for her generous aid. Whatever inaccuracies may remain are entirely my own.

Finally, thank you, dearest reader, for sticking with me throughout this series. I have loved every letter, tweet, comment, and review that you've shared with me. You're all witty and wonderful, and I'd be a lesser writer without your support. Please let me know what you think of *Love Beyond Measure*. As ever, I look forward to hearing from you, and sharing many more adventures with you in the future.

Best wishes,

Elizabeth

Printed in the United States
By Bookmasters